Italian BACHELORS

UNFORGOTTEN LOVERS

ITALIAN BACHELORS
COLLECTION

July 2017

August 2017

September 2017

October 2017

November 2017

December 2017

Italian BACHELORS

LYNN RAYE HARRIS
JANETTE KENNY
ELIZABETH POWER

MILLS & BOON

HarperCollins
PUBLISHERS · Since 1817

Published in Great Britain 2017
By Mills & Boon, an imprint of HarperCollins*Publishers*
1 London Bridge Street, London, SE1 9GF

ITALIAN BACHELORS: UNFORGOTTEN LOVERS © 2017
Harlequin Books S.A.

The Change in Di Navara's Plan © 2013 Lynn Raye Harris
Bound by the Italian's Contract © 2014 Janette Kenny
Visconti's Forgotten Heir © 2013 Elizabeth Power

ISBN: 978-0-263-93134-1

09-1017

Printed and bound in Spain
by CPI, Barcelona

THE CHANGE IN
DI NAVARRA'S PLAN
LYNN RAYE HARRIS

*One more time for my sweet cat, Miss Pitty Pat
(MPP). This is the last book we wrote together
before she succumbed to heart disease. Which,
of course, means I wrote it and she lay on my
feet or legs or lap, depending on her mood.
I miss her like crazy.*

USA Today bestselling author **Lynn Raye Harris**
burst onto the scene when she won a writing contest
held by Mills & Boon. The prize was an editor for a
year – but only six months later, Lynn sold her first
novel. A former finalist for the Romance Writers
of America's Golden Heart Award, Lynn lives in
Alabama with her handsome husband and two
crazy cats. Her stories have been called "exceptional
and emotional," "intense," and "sizzling." You can
visit her at www.lynnrayeharris.com

CHAPTER ONE

"YOU, GET UP."

Holly Craig looked up at the man standing so tall and imposing before her. Her heart skipped a beat at the sheer masculine beauty of his face. He had dark hair, piercing gray eyes and a jaw that had been chiseled out of Carrara marble. His nose was elegant, tapered, and his cheekbones were so pretty that supermodels must surely swoon in envy at the sight.

"Come on, girl, I don't have all day," he said, his tones sophisticated and clipped. And Italian, she realized. He had an accent that wasn't thick. Rather, it was refined and smooth, like fine wine. Or fine perfume.

Holly clutched her case—a secondhand case that wasn't even real leather—to her chest and shifted on the couch. "I—I'm not sure you have the right—"

He snapped his fingers. "You are here to see me, yes?"

Holly swallowed. "You are Mr. Di Navarra?"

He looked irritated. "Indeed."

Holly jumped up, her heart thrumming a quick tempo. Her skin flushed with embarrassment. She should have known this man was the powerful head of Navarra Cosmetics. It wasn't as if she'd never seen a photo of the man who might just hold her entire future in his hands. Everyone knew who Drago di Navarra was.

Everyone except her, it would seem. This meeting was

so important, and already she'd got off on the wrong foot. *Easy, ma belle,* her grandmother would have said. *You can do this.*

Holly stuck her hand out. "Mr. Di Navarra, yes, I'm Holly—"

He waved a hand, cutting her off. "Who you are isn't important." His gaze narrowed, dropped down over her. She'd worn her best suit today, but it was at least five years out of season. Still, it was black and serviceable. And it was all she had. She lifted her chin, confused by the strange meeting thus far, but not yet willing to ruin it by calling him on his rudeness.

"Turn around," he ordered.

Holly's cheeks flamed. But she did it, slowly turning in a circle until she faced him again.

"Yes," he said to an assistant who hovered nearby. "I think this one will do. Let them know we're coming."

"Yes, sir," the woman said, her manner cool and efficient as she turned and strode back toward the office they'd both emerged from.

"Let's go," Drago said. Holly could only stand and watch him stride away from her, bewilderment muddling her head and gluing her feet to the floor.

He seemed to realize she wasn't with him, because he stopped and turned around. He looked impatient rather than angry, though she suspected angry was next on the agenda.

"Are you coming or not?"

Holly had a choice. She could say no, she wasn't coming. She could tell him he was rude and appalling and she'd come here for an appointment, and not to be talked down to, scrutinized and ordered around.

Or she could go, figure out what his strange manner was all about and get her chance to pitch him her ideas. The case in her hands was warm, fragrant with the samples she'd tucked inside. It reminded her of home, of her grand-mother and the many hours they'd spent together dreaming about taking their perfumes to the next level, instead of only blending them for the friends and townspeople who purchased their custom combinations.

She'd come a long way to see this man. She'd spent every bit of savings she had getting here, with only enough for her lodging and the return trip home again. If she lost this opportunity, she lost far more than money. She lost her dream. She lost Gran's dream. She'd have to go home and start over again.

Because Gran was dead and the house would soon be gone. She couldn't afford to keep it any longer. Unless she convinced Drago di Navarra that she had something worth investing in. Something worth taking a chance on.

And she would do whatever it took to get that opportunity.

"Yes," she said firmly. "I'm coming."

Drago could feel her eyes upon him. It was nothing he wasn't accustomed to. Women often stared. It was not something he felt was an inconvenience. No, it was an advantage, especially for a man in the business he was in.

In the business of making people more beautiful, it did not hurt to be attractive yourself. If much of that was genetics, well, it was not his fault.

He still used Navarra products—soap, cologne, skin care, shampoo—and he would always maintain, to who-ever would listen, that they benefited him greatly.

Now he sat in the back of the limousine with his projec-tions and printouts, and studied the focus-group informa-tion for the newest line of products NC was bringing out this fall. He was pleased with what he saw. Very pleased.

He was not, it should be noted, pleased with the agency that had sent this girl over. She was the fourth model he'd seen this morning, and though they'd finally got it right, he was angry that it had taken four attempts to get the correct combination of innocence and sex appeal that he'd desired for this ad campaign.

He was selling freshness and beauty, not a prepackaged look that many of the models he'd seen recently came with. They had a hard edge about them, something that looked out from their eyes and said that, while they might appear innocent, they had actually left innocence in the rearview mirror a thousand miles ago.

This girl, however...

He looked up, met her gaze boldly, appraisingly. She dropped her eyes quickly, a pink stain spreading over her cheeks. A sharp feeling knifed into him, stunning him. He had a visceral reaction to that display of sweetness, his body hardening in a way it hadn't in quite some time. Oh, he'd had sex—plenty of it—but it had become more of a box to check off in his day rather than an escape or a way to relax.

His reaction just now interested him. His gaze slipped over her again, appraised what he saw, as he had the first time. She was dressed in a cheap suit, though it fit her well. Her shoes were tall, pink suede—and brand-new, he realized, looking at the sole of one where she'd turned her legs to the side. The price tag was still on the shoe. He tilted his head.

$49.99

Not Jimmy Choo shoes or Manolo Blahnik shoes, certainly. He didn't expect her to be wearing thousand-dollar shoes, or even the latest designer fashions, but he had rather expected she would be more...polished.

Which was odd, considering that polish was precisely what he did not want. Still, she was a model with a highly respected New York City firm. He'd have thought she might be a bit more prepared. On the other hand, perhaps she was fresh from the farm and they'd sent her over straightaway in desperation.

"How many of these jobs have you done before?" he asked.

She looked up again. Blinked. Her eyes were blue. Her hair was the most extraordinary shade of strawberry-blond, and a smattering of light freckles dotted her pale skin. He would have to tell the photographer not to erase those later. They added to her fresh look.

"Jobs?"

Drago suppressed a stab of impatience. "Modeling jobs, *cara*."

She blinked again. "Oh, I, um…"

"I'm not going to send you away if this is your first time," he snapped. "So long as the camera loves you, I couldn't care less if you've just come up from the family farm."

Her skin flushed again. This time, her chin came up. Her eyes flashed cool fire, and he found himself intrigued at the play of emotions across her face. It was almost as if she were arguing with herself.

"There's no need to be rude, you know," she snapped back. "Manners are still important, whether you've got a billion dollars or only one."

Drago had a sudden urge to laugh. It was as if a kitten had suddenly hissed and swatted him. And it had the effect of making some of his tension drain away.

"Then I apologize for being rude," he said, amused.

She folded her arms over her breasts and tried to look stern. "Well, then. Thank you."

He set the papers down on the seat beside him. "Is this your first time to New York?"

Her tongue darted out to moisten her lower lip. A slice of sensation knifed into his groin. "Yes," she said.

"And where are you from?"

"Louisiana."

He leaned forward then, suddenly quite certain he needed to make her feel comfortable if he was going to get what he wanted out of this shoot. "You'll do a fine job," he said. "Just be yourself in front of the camera. Don't try to act glamorous."

She dropped her gaze away and slid her fingers along the hem of her jacket. "Mr. Di Navarra—"

"Drago," he said.

She looked up again. Her blue eyes were worried. He had a sudden urge to kiss her, to wipe away that worried look and put a different kind of look there. He gave himself a mental shake. Highly uncharacteristic of him. Not that he didn't date the models—he did sometimes—but this one wasn't his usual type. He liked the tall, elegant ones. The ones who looked as if ice cubes wouldn't melt in their mouths.

The ones who didn't make him think of wide-eyed idealists who chased after dreams—and kept chasing them even when they led down self-destructive paths. Women like this one were so easily corruptible in the wrong hands. His protective instincts came to the fore, made him want to send her back to Louisiana before she even stepped in front of the camera.

He wanted her to go home, to stop chasing after New York dreams of fame and fortune. This world would only disappoint her. In a few months, she'd be shooting drugs, drinking alcohol and throwing up her food in order to lose that extra pound some idiotic industry type had told her made her look fat.

Before he could say anything of what he was thinking, the car came to a halt. The door swung open immediately. "Sir, thank goodness," the location manager said. "The girl isn't here and—"

"I have her," Drago said. The other man's head swung

around until his gaze landed on the girl—Holly, was it?
Now he wished he'd paid more attention when he'd first
seen her outside his office.

"Excellent." The man wiggled his fingers at her. "Come
along, then. Let's get you into makeup."

She looked terrified. Drago smiled encouragingly. "Go,
Holly," he said, trying the name he was fairly certain was
correct. He didn't miss the slight widening of her eyes,
and knew he'd got it right. Clearly, she hadn't expected
him to remember. "I will see you again when this is over."

She looked almost relieved as her eyes darted between
him and the location manager. "Y-you will?"

She seemed very alone in that moment. Something inside him rose to the fore, made him ask a question he knew
he shouldn't. "Are you busy for dinner?"

She shook her head.

Drago smiled. He shouldn't do this, he knew it, and yet
he was going to anyway. "Then consider yourself busy
now."

Holly had never been to a fancy restaurant in her life, but
she was in one now—in a private room, no less—sitting
across from a man who might just be the most handsome
man she'd ever seen in her life. The longer she spent in
Drago di Navarra's company, the more fascinated she was.

Oh, he hadn't started out well, that was for sure—but
he'd improved tremendously upon further acquaintance.
He'd actually turned out to be…nice.

There was only one problem. Holly frowned as she listened to him talk about the photo shoot earlier. She wasn't a
model, but she'd stood there in Central Park and let people
fuss over her, dress her in a flowing purple gown, paint
her with makeup, tease her hair—and then she'd stepped
in front of the camera and froze, wondering how she'd let
this thing go so far.

She'd only wanted a chance to tell Drago di Navarra about her perfumes, but she hadn't known where they were going or what he expected until it was too late. She'd choked when she should have explained. But she'd been worried that if she explained who she was and what she wanted, he would be angry with her.

And that wasn't going to work, was it?

Still, as she'd stood there, frozen, she'd known it was over. Her dream was dead, because she was going to have to explain to all these people watching her that she truly had no idea what she was doing.

But then Drago had walked onto the shoot and smiled at her. She'd smiled back, and suddenly the photographer was happy. She was certain she'd still been awkward and out of place, but everyone had seemed delighted with her. They'd changed her clothes, her hair, her makeup several times. And she'd stood in front of that camera, thinking of her perfumes and wondering how on earth she was going to explain herself to Drago, until someone finally told her they were done.

Then Drago had whisked her off for dinner and she'd clammed up like a frightened schoolgirl. She was still wearing the last dress they'd put on her, a pretty, silky sheath in eggplant and a pair of gold Christian Louboutin pumps. This entire experience was a fantasy come to life in many ways. She was in New York City, being wined and dined by one of the most eligible bachelors in the world, and she wanted to remember every moment of it.

And yet everything about this day was wrong, because she'd come here to pitch her perfume, not model for Navarra Cosmetics. How could she tell him? How could she find the perfect moment to say "Oh, Drago, thank you for the dinner, but what I really want to talk to you about is my perfume"?

Still, she had to. And soon. But every time she tried to

open her mouth and tell him, something stopped her. There were interruptions, distractions. When he reached across the table and took her hand in his, every last thought in her head flew out the window.

"You were fabulous today, Holly," he said. And then he lifted her hand to his lips and pressed them against the back of her hand. A sizzle of electricity shot through her, gathered in her feminine core and made her ache in ways she'd never quite experienced before.

She'd had a boyfriend back home. She'd been kissed. They'd even gone further than that—but she'd never felt the moment was right to go all the way.

And then he'd broken up with her. Taken up with that catty Lisa Tate instead. It still stung.

You're too selfish, Holly, he'd said. *Too focused on your damn perfume.*

Yes, she was focused. Holly dragged herself back to the present, tried so hard to ignore the skittering of her pulse and the throbbing deep in her core. She knew what this was. She might not have had sex before, but she wasn't stupid. She'd experienced desire with Colin, but she'd just never got to the point where she'd tumbled over the edge into hedonism.

She could imagine it with this man. Her heart skipped as she met Drago di Navarra's smoky gray eyes. *Tell him, Holly. Tell him now....*

"Thank you," she said, dropping her gaze from the intensity of his as her pulse shot forward again.

"You're quite a natural. I predict you will go far in this business if you don't allow yourself to be corrupted by it."

She opened her mouth to speak, but his cell phone rang. He glanced down at the display, and then said something in Italian that could have been a curse.

"You must excuse me," he said, picking up the phone. "This is important."

"Of course," she replied, but he'd already answered the call. She sat with her hands in her lap and waited for him to finish.

Holly gazed at the silk wallpaper and the gilt fixtures, and felt as if she'd landed on another planet. What was she doing here? How had she ended up in the company of a billionaire, having dinner with him as if it were a daily occurrence?

Everything about her trip to New York thus far was so different from her usual experience that she could hardly get her bearings.

Why couldn't she seem to say what she needed to say? She'd feel better if she had her samples. With those, she could find her way through this strange landscape. But her samples were in her case, which was stowed in his car. That had given her pause, but he'd convinced her that her belongings would be fine while they ate dinner.

If only she had her case, she could open it up and pull out her samples. She could explain her concepts, sell him on the beauty of Colette, the last perfume she and her grandmother had worked on together. It was the best one, though her ideas for others were infinite. She got a tingle of excitement just thinking about the blend of smooth essences, water and alcohol that produced the final product.

Drago finished his call and apologized for the interruption. "Forgive me, *bella mia*," he said. "But the beauty industry never sleeps."

"It's fine," she told him, smiling. Her heart was beating fast again, but she'd finally settled on a plan of action. Once she was reunited with her case, she would explain to this man why she was really here. She was certain he couldn't say no once she'd given him a whiff of Colette.

Their dinner came then, and Holly found herself relaxing in Drago's company. He was completely charming. He was attentive, sending most of his calls to voice mail, and interested in what she had to say.

She told him about Louisiana, about her grandmother—without mentioning perfume, since that had to wait for her samples—and about the trip to New York on the bus.

He blinked. "You came all this way on a bus?"

Holly dropped her gaze to her plate as heat seared her cheeks. "I couldn't afford to fly," she said. But she had spent nearly everything she had scraping together the money for this brief trip. Just to talk to this man, for pity's sake.

Which she was doing, but not in the way she needed to. Not yet. She took a sip of her white wine and let it sit on her tongue for a moment while she sorted the flavors—the base notes were of wood and smoke while the top notes were floral. Delicious. Her nose was far better than her taste buds, but she could still sort flavors fairly well by taste.

"You really are fresh off the family farm," he said.

But it wasn't an insult, not this time, and she didn't take it as such. He seemed rather…wondering, truthfully. "I suppose I am," she replied.

"With big New York dreams." His tone was a bit less friendly this time, but she didn't let it bother her. Or maybe it was the wine that didn't let it bother her.

She shrugged. "Doesn't everyone have dreams?"

His gaze slipped over her face, and she felt heat curling in her belly, her toes. Oh, how she never wanted this night to end. She wanted to drink champagne under the stars, and she wanted to dance in his arms until dawn.

His hand settled over hers, and a shiver prickled down her spine. A delicious shiver. Her entire body seemed to cant toward him, like a flower turning to the sun. His fingers skimmed along her bare arm. Fire danced in their wake, and Holly wasn't certain she could pull in her next breath.

"I have a dream," he said softly, his body so close to hers now, his beautiful mouth within reach if only she leaned a bit farther forward. His fingers slid along her cheek, into her hair, and she felt as if she were melting. She ached and wanted and didn't care what tomorrow brought so long as this man kissed her now. Tonight.

His lips hovered over hers and her eyes slid closed. Her heart was beating so hard he must surely see the pulse in her throat. But she didn't care. She was too caught up in the beauty, the wonder, the perfection of this night. It was like a fairy tale, and she was the princess who'd finally been found by the prince.

His laugh was soft and deep. It vibrated through her, made her shudder with longing.

And then his mouth claimed hers in a tender kiss that stole her breath away. It was so sweet, so perfect—

But she wanted more. She leaned closer, and he laughed again, in his throat this time, before he parted her lips and thrust his tongue into her mouth. Holly couldn't stop the moan that vibrated in her throat.

The kiss suddenly changed, turned more demanding then as his mouth took hers in a hot, possessive kiss unlike anything she'd ever experienced before. Their tongues met, tangled, dueled. She could feel the strength of that kiss in her nipples, between her legs. Her sex throbbed and her panties grew damp.

She wanted to be closer to him. Needed to be closer. She wrapped her arms around his neck, clinging to him, losing herself in this kiss, this moment.

Drago finally dragged himself up, away from her, breaking the kiss. Her mouth tingled with the memory of his. Her eyes settled on his mouth, and a thrill went through her.

"My dream," he said, his voice a sensual purr in her ear, "is that you will accompany me back to my apartment."

Holly could only stare at him as he stood and held his hand out. Everything in her wanted to be with him. She wasn't ready for this night to end, no matter that a tiny corner of her soul urged her to be cautious. She wanted more of this excitement, this exhilaration.

More of Drago.

Holly put her hand in his, and her skin sizzled at the contact. This was right, she knew it deep down. So very right.

"Yes," she said shyly. "I want that, too."

CHAPTER TWO

One year later...

"I DON'T KNOW why you don't march right into his office and demand he help you out."

Holly looked up at her best friend and roommate. Gabriella was holding little Nicholas, rocking him back and forth. He was, thankfully, asleep for a change. Poor Gabi was such a saint, considering that Nicky hadn't slept a whole night through since Holly had brought him home from the hospital.

Holly picked up a tester and sniffed it. Attar of roses. It filled her mind with a profusion of fat red blooms like the ones that her gran had grown. Bushes that now belonged to someone else, since she'd lost the property months ago. Her mouth twisted as bitterness flooded her throat with scalding acid.

She set the tester down and pushed back from the table where she mixed her fragrances. "I can't go to him, Gabi. He made it very clear that he wanted nothing more to do with me."

Holly still felt the sting of Drago di Navarra's rejection as if it was yesterday. She also—damn him—felt the utter perfection of his lovemaking as if it had happened only hours ago. Why did her body still insist on a physical response at the thought of that single night they'd shared?

At least her brain was on the right track. The only response her brain had was rage. No, that wasn't quite true. Her mental response was like a fine perfume. The top note was rage. The middle, or heart note, was self-loathing. And the base note, the one that had never yet evaporated, was shame.

How had she let herself be so damn naive and needy? How had she fallen into Drago's arms as if it were the easiest thing in the world when it was nothing like her to do so? Holly pressed her teeth together. She would never be that foolish again. She'd learned her lesson, thanks to Drago, and she would never forget it.

She'd been so easily led, so gullible and trusting. She hated thinking about it, and yet she couldn't quite stop. And maybe that was a good thing, because it meant she would never be that foolish again. The world was a cold, hard, mean place—and she was a survivor. Drago had taught her that.

He'd taught her to be suspicious and careful, to question people's motives—especially men's. He'd made her into this cold, guarded creature, and she hated him for it.

But as she looked at her son in her friend's arms, she was overcome with a sudden rush of love. Nicky was perfect. He made her world full and bright and wonderful. Every single inch of him was amazing, regardless that his father was an arrogant, evil, heartless bastard. Drago might have been the worst thing to ever happen to her, but Nicky was the best.

Irony at its most potent.

"But if he knew about Nicky," Gabi started.

"No." Holly knew her voice was hard. Thinking about Drago did that to her. But she couldn't take it out on Gabi. She tried again, sighing softly, spreading her hands wide in supplication. "I tried to tell him. His secretary said he did not want to speak to me. Ever. I wrote a letter, but I never got a reply."

Gabi looked militant. "These are the modern ages, honey bun," she said. "Put it on Facebook. Tweet the crap out of it. He'll see it and come."

Holly shuddered. As if she would expose herself that way. "He won't. Not only that, but do you want me to die of shame?" She shook her head emphatically. "No way. He had his chance."

Gabi gazed down at the cherubic face of Holly's son. "I know. But this little guy ought to have the best that money can buy."

Holly felt the truth of that statement like a barb. She couldn't help but look around their tiny apartment. Tears pricked her eyes. Since returning home to New Hope, she'd lost Gran's home, failed in her goal to become a respected perfumer and had to move sixty miles away to New Orleans so she could support herself. She'd taken a job as a cocktail waitress in a casino. It wasn't ideal, but the tips were good.

Gabi had moved last year, before Gran had died, and when Holly found out she was pregnant, Gabi had encouraged Holly to come join her.

Holly had gratefully done so.

There was no way she could stay in New Hope. Her grandmother had been a well-respected member of the community. And though Gran would have stood beside her if she'd still been alive, she wasn't. And Holly wouldn't shame her memory by causing the tongues of New Hope's citizenry to wag.

In New Hope, everyone knew everyone. And they didn't hesitate to talk about anyone so silly as to fall from grace in such a spectacular manner. Besides, no way was she subjecting Nicky to the town's censure when there was absolutely no reason for it. This was the twenty-first century, but there were those in her hometown who acted as if a single mother was a disgrace.

"I'm doing the best I can," Holly said.

Gabi's big blue eyes widened. "Oh, honey, of course you are. I'm sorry for being such an insensitive bitch." She kissed Nicky's tiny forehead. "I just forgot myself in my fury for this precious little thing. What a stupid father he has. Hopefully, when he grows up one day to be president of the United States, he won't be hampered by that side of the family tree."

Holly laughed. Leave it to Gabi to find just the thing to make her giggle when she was so angry. She went over and squeezed her friend's arm. "You're the best, Gabi. I'm not mad at you, believe me. It'll all be fine. I'm going to make a fragrance that knocks *someone's* socks off, and then I'm going to get noticed. Drago di Navarra isn't the only cosmetic king in the world, no matter what he might think."

"He messed up when he sent you home without sampling your fragrance."

The heat of shame bloomed inside her chest again. Yes, he'd sent her home without even sampling the first fragrance. After their gorgeous night together, he'd made her breakfast and served it to her in bed. She'd felt so happy, so perfectly wonderful. They'd talked and eaten and then he'd had her case delivered to her when she'd remembered to ask for it. That was when he'd noticed the scent.

"What is this, *cara*?" he'd asked, his beautiful brows drawn down in confusion as he'd studied the case in his hands.

"Those are my samples," she'd said, her heart beginning to trip in excitement.

"Samples?"

"Yes, my fragrances. I make perfume."

She'd missed the dangerous gleam in his eye as he'd set the case down and opened it. He'd drawn out a bottle of Colette and held it up, his gray eyes narrowed as he'd studied the golden fragrance.

"Explain," he'd said, his voice tight.

She'd been somewhat confused, but she had done so. Because they'd spent a beautiful night together and she knew he wasn't really an ogre. He was a passionate, sensual, good man who felt things deeply and who didn't open up easily.

Holly resisted the urge to clutch her hand over her heart, to try to contain the sharp slice of pain she still felt every time she thought of what had happened next. Of how stupid she'd been not to see it coming. She could still see his handsome face drawn up in rage, his eyes flashing hot as his jaw worked. She'd been alarmed and confused all at once.

Then he'd dropped the bottle back into the case with a clink and shoved it toward her.

"Get out," he'd said, his voice low and hard and utterly frightening.

"But, Drago—"

"Get the hell out of my home and don't come back." And then, before she could say another word, he'd stalked from the room, doors slamming behind him until she knew he was gone. A few minutes later, a uniformed maid had come in, her brow pleated in mute apology. She'd had Holly's suit—the suit she'd worn to see Drago in the first place—on a hanger, which she'd hung on a nearby hook.

It had seemed even shabbier and sadder than it had the day before.

"When you are ready, miss, Barnes will take you back to your lodgings."

Holly closed her eyes as she remembered that moment of utter shame. That moment when she'd realized he wasn't coming back, and that she'd failed spectacularly in her task to convince him of her worth as a perfumer.

Because she'd let herself get distracted. Because she'd been a mouse and a pushover and a foolish, foolish idiot.

She'd let Drago di Navarra make love to her, the first man ever to do so, and she'd gotten caught up in the fantasy of it. She'd believed that their chemistry was special, that the things she'd felt with him were unique, and that he'd felt them, too.

Fool.

But he'd kicked her out of his house as though she'd been a common prostitute.

And hadn't you?

A little voice always asked her that question. She wasn't blameless, after all. She'd spent close to twenty-four hours pretending to be something she wasn't in the single hope of convincing the high and mighty CEO of Navarra Cosmetics that she had what it took to design a signature perfume for his company.

She'd had opportunity enough to tell him why she was really there, and she'd kept silent each and every time. She'd treated it all like an adventure. The country mouse goes to the city and gets caught up in a comedy of errors. Except, she wasn't a mouse and she had a voice.

Worse, she'd complicated everything when she'd fallen for his seduction. She knew very well how it must have looked to him, a powerful man who held the key to her dream in his hand.

He'd thought her the worst kind of liar and gold digger—and the evidence had been stacked against her.

She gazed at her son and her heart felt so full with all the love swelling inside it. Yes, she should have told Drago who she was and what she wanted. But if she'd opened her mouth sooner, she wouldn't have Nicky. What a thought that was. Life might have been easier, but it certainly wouldn't have been sweeter.

Holly's eyes prickled with tears. Gran would have told

her that the past was just that and it did no good to dwell on it, because you couldn't change it without a time machine. Holly knuckled her tears away with a little laugh—but then her gaze caught on the digital display on the microwave.

"I have to get to work," she said to Gabi. "Will you be all right until Mrs. Turner comes to collect him?"

Gabi looked up from where she was still cradling Nicky. "It's a couple of hours before my shift yet. Don't worry."

Holly always worried, but she didn't say that to Gabi. She worried about providing for her baby, worried that he was only three months old and she had to work so much. She worried that she'd been unable to breast-feed him—some women couldn't, the nurse had told her after the zillionth failed attempt—and he had to drink formula, and she worried that he needed so many things and she could barely provide any of them.

Holly kissed her son's sweet soft skin before changing into her uniform of white shirt, bow tie and tight black skirt. Then she stuffed her heels into her duffel and slipped on her tennis shoes. She made it to the bus stop in record time. With twenty minutes to spare, she got to the casino, put on her heels and touched up her makeup before stashing her things and heading to the floor for her shift.

In all her wildest imaginings, she'd never pictured herself serving drinks in a casino. But here she was, arranging her tray with cocktail napkins, pen and pad, stirrers, and then gliding through the crowd of people hovering around tables and machines, asking for drink orders—and enduring a few pats to the bottom in the process.

Holly gritted her teeth, hating that part of the job but unwilling to react, because she needed the money too badly. The rent was due next week, and it was always a struggle to make up her portion along with buying diapers and formula and groceries.

Holly pushed a hand through her hair, anchoring it behind her ears, and approached the group of men hovering around one of the baccarat tables. They were rapt on the game, and most especially on a man who sat at one end of the table, a dark-haired beauty hanging over his shoulder and whispering something in his ear. His face was remarkable, beautiful and perfectly formed—and all too familiar.

For a moment, Holly was stunned into immobility. What were the chances Drago di Navarra would walk into this casino and sit at a table in her section? She'd have guessed they were something like a million to one—but here he was in all his arrogant, rotten glory.

Just her miserable luck. She glanced behind her, looking for Phyllis, hoping to ask the other waitress to take this table. Holly's belly churned and panic rose in her throat at the thought of waiting on Drago and his mistress.

But Phyllis was nowhere to be seen, and Holly had no choice. The moment she accepted that, another feeling began to boil inside her: anger.

She suddenly wanted to march over to Drago's side and slap his handsome face. She'd endured a twenty-three-hour labor, with Gabi as the only friend by her side. Other women had happy husbands in the delivery room, and masses of family in the waiting room. But not her. She'd been alone, with only Gabi holding her hand and coaching her through.

By the time Nicky had been born and someone handed him to her, she'd felt as if the little crying bundle was an alien life-form. But she'd fallen into deep love in the next moment. She had seen Drago in her son's face, and she'd felt a keen despair that he'd tossed her out the way he had. That he'd refused to take her calls. He was missing out on something amazing and perfect, and he would never know it.

Now, seeing him in this casino, sitting there so arrogant and sure with a woman hanging on him, all Holly felt was righteous anger. Her heart throbbed in her chest. Her blood beat in her brain. She knew she should turn around and walk away, find Phyllis no matter how long these people had to wait for drinks, but she couldn't seem to do it. Instead, she moved around the table until she was standing beside the man who sat at a right angle to Drago.

"Something from the bar, sir?" she asked when the play had finished. She pitched her voice louder than she normally would and looked over at Drago. The woman with him sensed a disturbance in the perfumed air around her—much too heavy a scent, Holly thought derisively, like something one would use in a brothel to cover the smells of sex and sweat—and brought her head up to meet Holly's stare.

Sweat and sex. Holly swallowed as a pinprick of hot jealousy speared into her at the thought of this woman and Drago tangling together in a bed.

Holly sniffed. No, not jealousy. As if she cared. *Honestly.*

She was irritated, that was what. Irritated by the haughty look of this woman, and the outrageous presence of the man sitting at the table, oblivious to the currents whipping in the air around him.

The woman's dark eyes raked over her. And then she did the one thing Holly had both hoped and feared she would do. She said something to Drago. He looked up, his gaze colliding with Holly's. Her heart dived into her toes at the intensity of that gray stare. A hot well of hate bubbled inside her soul. It took everything she had not to throw her tray at him and curse him for the arrogant bastard he was.

"Dry martini," the man beside her said, and Holly dragged her attention back to him.

"Yes, sir," she said, writing the drink on her pad.

When she looked up again, Drago was still looking at

her, his brows drawn together as if he were trying to place her. He didn't know her? He couldn't remember?

That was not at all the reaction she'd expected, and it pierced her to the core. She'd had his baby, and he couldn't even remember her face....

That, Holly decided, stiffening her spine, was the last straw. She turned and marched away from the table, perilously close to hyperventilating because she was so angry—and because the adrenaline rush of fear was still swirling inside her. She went over to the bar and placed her orders, telling herself to calm down and breathe.

So he didn't recognize her. So what? Had she really thought he would?

Yes.

She shook her head angrily. He was a rich, arrogant, low-down, lying son of a bitch anyway. He'd wined her and dined her and seduced her. Yes, she'd fallen for it. She wasn't blameless.

But he'd promised to take care of the birth control, and she'd trusted him to do it right. But he must have done something wrong, because she'd gotten pregnant. And he hadn't cared enough about the possibility to take her calls.

Rotten, selfish, self-serving *bastard!*

Holly grabbed her tray once the drinks were ready. She would march back over there and deliver her drinks as usual. She would *not* pour them in Drago's lap, no matter how much she wanted to.

"Thanks, Jerry," she said to the bartender. She turned to go—and nearly collided with the slickly expensive fabric of Drago di Navarra's tailored suit.

Drago's nostrils flared as he looked at the woman before him. The color in her cheeks was high as she righted her tray before spilling the contents down the front of his

Savile Row suit. Her eyes snapped fire at him and her mouth twisted in a frown.

"If you will excuse me, sir, I have drinks to deliver."

Her voice was harder than he remembered it. Her face and body were plumper, but in a good way. She'd needed to round out her curves, though he'd thought she was perfectly well formed at the time. This extra weight, however, made her into a sultry, beautiful woman rather than a naive girl.

A girl who'd tried to trick him. He hadn't forgotten that part. His jaw hardened as he remembered the way she'd so blissfully confessed her deception to him. She'd come to New York armed with perfume samples that she hoped to sell to his company, and she'd cost him valuable time and money with her pretense. It wasn't the first time a woman had tried to use him for her own ends, but it had been a pretty spectacular failure on his part. He'd had to scrap every picture from the photo shoot and start again with a new model, which had been a shame when he'd seen the photos and realized how perfect she'd been in the role.

He'd wondered in the weeks after she'd gone if he'd overreacted. But she'd scraped a raw nerve inside him, a nerve that had never healed, and throwing her out had been the right thing to do. How dare she remind him of the things he most wanted to forget?

Still, it had taken him weeks to find the right model. Even then, he hadn't actually been the one to do it. He'd been so discouraged that he'd delegated the task to his marketing director. It wasn't like him to let anything derail him for long, but every time he'd tried to find someone, he kept thinking about this woman and how she'd nearly made a fool of him.

How she'd taken him back to a dark, lonely place in his life, for the barest of moments, and made him remember what it was like to be a pawn in another's game. He shook those feelings off and studied her.

The model they'd hired to replace her was beautiful, and the fragrance was selling well, but he still wasn't satisfied. He should be, but he wasn't.

There was something about this woman. Something he hadn't quite forgotten over the past year. Even now, his body responded with a mild current of heat that he did not feel when Bridgett, whom he'd left fuming at the baccarat table, draped herself over him.

"The perfume business did not work out for you, I take it?" he asked mildly, his veins humming with predatory excitement. She was still beautiful, still the perfect woman for his ad campaign. It irritated him immensely.

And intrigued him, as well.

Her pretty blue eyes were hard beneath the dark eye makeup and black liner, but they widened when he spoke. She narrowed them again. "Not yet," she said coolly. "I'm surprised you remembered."

"I never forget a face." He let his gaze fall to her lush breasts, straining beneath the fabric of the tight white shirt the casino made her wear. "Or a body."

Her chin lifted imperiously. He would have laughed had he not sensed the loathing behind that gaze. Her plan hadn't worked and now she hated him. How droll.

"Well, isn't that fortunate for you?" she said, her Southern accent drawing out the word *you*. "If you will excuse me, sir, I have work to do."

"Still angry with me, *cara?* How odd."

She blinked. "Odd? You seduced me," she said, lowering her voice to a hiss. "And then you threw me out."

Drago lifted an eyebrow. She was a daring little thing. "You cost me a lot of money with your deception, *bella mia.* I also had to throw out a day's worth of photos and

start over. Far more regrettable than tossing you out the
door, I must admit."

The corners of her mouth looked pinched. But then she
snorted. "I'm waiting tables in a casino and you talk to me
about money? Please."

"Money is still money," he said. "And I don't like to
lose it."

She was trembling, but he knew it wasn't fear that
caused it. "Let me tell you something, Mr. Di Navarra," she
began in a diamond-edged voice. "I made a mistake, but it
cost me far more than it cost you. When you spend every
last penny you have to get somewhere, because you've
staked your entire future on one meeting with someone
important, and then you fail in your goal and lose your
home, and then have to provide for your—"

She stopped, closed her eyes and swallowed. When she
opened them again, they were hot and glittering. "When
you fail so spectacularly that you've lost everything and
then find yourself at rock bottom, working in a casino to
make ends meet, then you can be indignant, okay? Until
then, spare me your wounded act."

She brushed past him, her tray balanced on one hand
as she navigated the crowd to deliver her drinks. Drago
watched her go, his blood sizzling. She was hot and beautiful and defiant, and she intrigued him more than he cared
to admit.

In fact, she excited him in a way that Bridgett, and any
of the other women he'd dated recently, did not. And, damn
her, she was still perfect for the ad campaign. She wasn't
quite as fresh-faced as she'd been a year ago, but she now
had something more. Some quality he couldn't quite place
his finger on but that he wanted nevertheless.

And he always got what he wanted, no matter the cost.
He stood there with eyes narrowed, watching her deliver
drinks with a false smile pasted on her face. There was

something appealing about Holly Craig, something exciting.

He intended to find out what it was. And then he intended to harness it for his own purposes.

CHAPTER THREE

HOLLY'S SHIFT ENDED at one in the morning. She changed her shoes and grabbed her duffel before heading out to catch the streetcar. Once she'd ridden the streetcar as far as she could go, she would catch the bus the rest of the way home. It was a long, tiring ride, but she had no choice. It was what she could afford.

She exited the casino and started down the street. A car passed her, and then another pulled alongside. Her heart picked up, but she refused to look. The streetcar wasn't far and she didn't want to cause trouble for herself by glaring at a jerk in a sedan. It wasn't the first time some guy thought he could pick her up, and it probably wouldn't be the last.

"Would you like a ride?"

Holly's heart lurched. She stopped and turned to stare at the occupant of the gleaming limousine. He sat in the back, the window down, an arm resting casually on the sill.

"No," she said, starting to walk again. Her blood simmered. So many things she'd wanted to say to this arrogant bastard earlier, but she'd held her tongue.

Which was necessary, she realized. It would do no good to antagonize Drago di Navarra. Not only that, but there was also a little prickle of dread growing in her belly at the thought of him learning about Nicky. No doubt he would think she'd done that on purpose, too.

Which was ridiculous, considering he'd been the one to assure her that birth control was taken care of.

"It's late and you must be tired," he said, his voice so smooth and cultured. Oh, how she hated those dulcet Italian tones!

"I am tired," she told him without looking at him. The limo kept pace with her as she walked, and it irritated her to think of him sitting there so comfortably while she trod on aching feet across the pavement. "But I'm tired every night and I manage. So thanks anyway."

Drago laughed softly. "So spirited, Holly. Nothing at all like the girl who came to New York with starry-eyed dreams of success."

A bubble of helpless anger popped low in her belly. She stopped and spun around, marching over to the car. It was completely unlike her, but she couldn't seem to stop herself. The urge to confront him was unbearable. The limo halted.

"I might have been naive then, but I'm not now. I know the world is a cruel place and that some people who have absolutely everything they could ever want are even crueler than that." She tossed a stray lock of hair over her shoulder with trembling fingers. "So if I'm *spirited*, as you say, I had to learn to be that way. It's a dog-eat-dog world, and I don't want to be eaten."

Spirited? She hardly thought of herself that way at all. No, more like she was a survivor because she had to be. Because someone else depended on her. Someone tiny and helpless.

Drago opened the car door and stepped out, and Holly took a step back. He was so tall, so broad, so perfect.

No, not perfect. A jerk!

"Get in the car, Holly," he said, his voice deep and commanding. "Don't be so stubborn."

Holly folded her arms beneath her breasts and cocked a

hip. "I don't have to do what you order me to do, Drago," she said, using his name on purpose. Reminding him they'd once been intimate and that she wasn't an employee—or, heaven forbid, a girlfriend—to be ordered around. It felt bold and wicked and brave, and that was precisely what she needed to be in order to face him right now. "Besides, won't your lady friend be angry if you drag me along for the ride?"

His nostrils flared in irritation. One thing she remembered about Drago di Navarra was that he was not accustomed to anything less than blind obedience. It gave her a sense of supreme satisfaction to thwart that expectation.

"Bridgett is no longer an issue," he said haughtily, and Holly laughed. He looked surprised.

"Poor Bridgett, tossed out on her gorgeous derriere without a clue as to what she did wrong."

Drago left the door open and came over to her. He was so tall she had to tilt her head back to look up at him. Her first instinct was to flee, but she refused to give in to it. Not happening. She'd been through too much to run away at the first sign of trouble. She told herself that she was far stronger than she'd been a year ago. She had to be.

She *was*.

"Get in the car, Holly, or I'll pick you up and toss you in it," he growled. It surprised her to realize that she could smell his anger. It was sharp and hot, with the distinct smell of a lit match.

"I'd like to see you try," she threw at him, heedless of the sizzle in his glare. "This is America, buddy, and you can't just kidnap people off the street."

Holly didn't quite know what happened next, but suddenly she was in the air, slung over his shoulder before she could do a thing to stop him.

"Put me down!" she yelled, beating her fists against his back as he carried her over to the car. The next instant, she was tilting downward again, and she clung to him as if he was going to drop her. But he tossed her into the car instead, tossed her bag in after her, and then he was inside and the door slammed shut.

Holly flung herself at the opposite door, but it was locked tight. The limo began to speed down Canal Street. Holly turned and slammed her back against the seat, glaring at the arrogant Italian billionaire sitting at the opposite end. He looked smug. And he didn't have a hair out of place, while she had to scrape a tangle of hair from her face and shove it back over her ears.

"How dare you?" she seethed. Her heart pounded and adrenaline shoved itself into her limbs, her nerves, until she felt as if she were wound so tight she would split at the seams. If his anger was a lit match, hers was a raging fire. "If anyone saw that, you're in big trouble."

"I doubt it," he said. He leaned forward then, gray eyes glittering in the darkened car. "Now, tell me where you live, Holly Craig, and my driver will take you home. Much easier, *no*?"

Holly glared.

"Come, Holly. It's late and you look tired."

She wanted to refuse—but then she rattled off her address. What choice did she have? It *was* late, she *was* tired, and she needed to get Nicky from Mrs. Turner. If she had to let this man take her there, so be it. At least she would arrive far earlier than if she took the bus. And that would make Mrs. Turner happy, no doubt.

"Do you have a guilty conscience?" she asked when he'd given the driver the address.

He laughed. "Hardly."

That stung, but she told herself she should hardly be surprised. He'd thrown her out without a shred of remorse, and then refused all attempts to contact him. Heartless man.

"Then why the sudden chivalrous offer of a ride home?"

His gaze slid over her, and her skin prickled with telltale heat. She gritted her teeth, determined not to feel even a sliver of attraction for this man. Before she'd met Drago di Navarra, she'd thought she was a sensible woman in control of her own emotions. He'd rather exploded that notion in her face.

And continued to explode it as her body reacted to his presence without regard to her feelings for him. Feelings of loathing, she reminded herself. Feelings of sheer dislike.

Her body didn't care.

"Because I need you, *cara mia*."

She swallowed the sudden lump in her throat. He'd said something similar to her that night in his apartment. And she, like an idiot, had believed him. Worse, she'd wanted it to be true. Well, she wasn't that naive anymore. Italian billionaires did not fall in love with simple, unsophisticated virgins in the space of an evening.

They didn't fall in love at all.

"Sorry, but the answer is no."

His long elegant fingers were steepled together in his lap. "You have not yet heard the proposition."

"I'm still sure the answer is no," she said. "I've been propositioned by you before, and I know how that works out for me."

He shook his head as if he were disappointed in her. "I liked you better in New York."

Her skin stung with heat. "Of course you did. I was a mouse who did whatever you told me to do. I've learned better now."

And she was determined to prove it.

"You like being a cocktail waitress, *bella*? You like men touching you, rubbing up against you, thinking you're for sale along with the drinks and the chips?"

The heat in her cheeks spread, suffusing her with an

angry glow. "No, I don't. But it's just about all I'm quali-
fied for."

"And if I were to offer you something else? A better
way to earn your money?"

Her stomach was beginning to churn. "I won't be your
mistress."

He blinked at her. And then he laughed again, and she
felt the hot, sticky slide of embarrassment in her veins. Oh,
for pity's sake. After the way the woman he'd been with tonight looked, did she truly think he was interested in her?

But he had been once. She hadn't dreamed it. Nicky
was proof she had not.

"Charming, Holly. But I don't need to pay a woman
to be my mistress. If I were to choose you for that...posi-
tion...I am certain you would not refuse."

Holly could only gape at his utter self-confidence. "It's
a wonder you bother with casinos when you have such bad
instincts. I'm surprised you haven't lost everything when
you reason like that in the face of such overwhelming evidence to the contrary."

"*Dio*," he said, "but you are a stubborn woman. How did
we end up in bed together again?" He didn't wait for her
reply. He nodded sagely as if answering his own question.
"Ah, yes, that's right. You were deceiving me."

Shame suffused her at that mention of their night together. But she didn't bother to deny it. He wouldn't believe it anyway. "Clearly, you like your women to shut up
and do as they're told."

"Which you seem to be incapable of doing," he growled.

"Fine," she snapped. "Tell me what you want so I can
say no."

His stare was unnerving. But not because it made her
uncomfortable. More likely because she wanted to drown
in it. "I want you to model for the Sky campaign."

Holly's mouth went dry. Sky was the signature fragrance from NC, the one she'd modeled for in New York when she hadn't been able to tell Drago why she was really there. "That's not funny," she said tightly.

His expression was dead serious. "I'm not joking, Holly. I want you for Sky."

"I did that already," she said. "It didn't work out, as I recall."

He shrugged. "A mistake. One we can rectify now."

The trembling in her belly wasn't going away. It was spreading through her limbs, making her teeth chatter. She clamped her jaw tight and tried not to let it show. Thankfully, the car was dark and the lights from the city didn't penetrate the tinted windows quite as well as they otherwise would have.

"I don't think it's possible," she said. And it wasn't. How would she go to New York with a three-month-old baby in tow? She didn't think that was what Drago had in mind at all.

"Of course it is. I will pay you far more than you earn in that casino. You will do the shoot and any appearances that are needed, and you will be handsomely rewarded. It's a win for you, Holly."

She thought of her baby in his secondhand crib, of the tiny, dingy apartment she shared with Gabi. The air conditioner was one window unit that rattled and coughed so badly she was never certain it would keep working. The carpet was faded and torn, and the appliances were always one usage away from needing repairs.

It was a dump, a dive, and she would do just about anything to get out of there and take her baby to a better life.

But what if he didn't mean it? What if he was toying with her? What if this was simply another way to punish her for not telling him the truth in New York?

She wouldn't put it past him. A man who threw her out and then refused all contact? Who didn't know he had a son, because he was so damn arrogant as to think she would want to contact him for any other reason than to tell him something important?

He was capable of it. More than capable.

"I want a contract," she said. "I want everything spelled out, legal and binding, and if it's legit, then I'll do it."

Because what choice did she have? She wasn't stupid, and she wasn't going to turn this opportunity down when it could mean everything to her child. Once she had a contract, signed and ironclad, she would feel much more in control.

"Fine."

Holly blinked. She hadn't expected him to agree to that.

"I hope you're certain about this," she said, unable to help herself when her teeth were still chattering and her body still trembling. What if this was a mistake? What if she were opening up Pandora's box with this act? How could she *not* be opening Pandora's box, when she had a three-month-old baby, and this man didn't know he was a father? "You know I'm not a model. I have no idea what I'm doing."

"Which is precisely why you're correct for the campaign. Sky is for the real woman who wants to recapture a certain something about her life. Her youth, her innocence, her sex appeal."

Irritation slid into her veins. "I've smelled Sky. It's not bad, but it's not all that, either."

The match-scent of anger rolled from him again. Why, oh, why did she feel the need to antagonize him? *Just take the money and shut up*, she told herself. The silence between them was palpable. And then he spoke. "Ah, yes, because you are an expert perfumer, correct?"

Sarcasm laced his voice. It made her madder than she already was, regardless that she knew she shouldn't push him.

"You have no idea. As I recall, you threw me out before I could show you."

He sat back in the limo then, his long limbs relaxing as if he were about to take a nap. She knew better, though. He was more like a panther, stretching out and pretending to relax when what he really planned was to bring down a gazelle.

"It takes years to learn how to blend perfumes. It also takes very intense training, and a certain sensitivity to smell. While you may have enjoyed mixing up essences you've ordered off the internet for all your friends, and while many of them may have told you how fabulous you are, that's hardly the right sort of training to create perfume for a multinational conglomerate, now, is it?"

Rage burned low in her belly, along with a healthy dose of uncertainty. It wasn't that she wasn't good, but she often felt the inadequacy of her origins in the business. She had no curriculum vitae, no discernable job experience. How could she communicate to anyone that she was worthy of a chance without backing it up with fragrance samples?

She glanced out the window, but they weren't quite to her neighborhood yet. So she turned back to him and tried very hard not to tell him to go to hell. He was so arrogant, so certain of himself.

And she suddenly burned to let him know it.

"It's gratifying that you know so much about me already," she said, a razor edge to her voice. "But perhaps you didn't know that my grandmother was born in Grasse and trained there for years before she met her husband and moved to Louisiana. She gave up her dreams of working for a big house, but she never gave up the art. And she taught it to me."

It wasn't the kind of formal instruction he would expect, but Gran had been extremely good at what she did. And Holly was, too.

She heard him pull in a breath. "That may be, but it still does not make you an expert, *bella mia.*"

The accusation smarted. "Again, until you've tried my scents, you can't really know that, can you?" She crossed her arms and tilted up her chin. Hell, why not go for it? What did she have to lose? "In fact, I want that in the contract. You will allow me to present my work to you if I model for your campaign."

He laughed softly. The sound scraped along her nerve endings. But not quite in a bad way. No, it was more like heated fingers stroking her sensitive skin. She wanted more.

"You realize that I will say yes to this, don't you? But why not? It costs me nothing. I can still say no to your fragrances, even if I agree to let you show them to me."

"I'm aware of that."

She believed him to be too good a businessman to turn her fragrances away out of spite. He hadn't built Navarra Cosmetics into what it was today by being shortsighted. She was counting on that.

And yet there was much more at risk here, wasn't there? They were getting closer and closer to her home, and she had a baby that was one half of his DNA.

But why should that matter?

He was the sperm donor. *She* was the one who'd sacrificed everything to take care of her child. She was the one who'd gone through her entire pregnancy alone and with only a friend for support. She was the one who'd brought him into the world, and the one who sat up with him at night, who worried about him and who loved him completely.

This man hadn't cared enough about the possibility of a child to allow her even to contact him. He'd thrown her out and self-importantly gone about his life as if she'd never existed.

A life that had included many trysts with models and actresses. Oh, yes, she'd known all about that even when she hadn't wanted to. His beautiful, deceptive face had stared out at her from the pages of the tabloids in the checkout line. While she'd been buying the few necessities she could afford to keep herself alive and healthy, he'd been wining and dining supermodels in Cannes and Milan and Venice.

She'd despised him for so long that to be with him now, in this car, was rather surreal. She had a baby with him, but she didn't think he'd like that at all. And she wasn't going to tell him. He'd done nothing to deserve to know.

Nothing except father Nicky.

She shoved that thought down deep and slapped a lid on it. Yes, she absolutely believed that a man ought to know he had a child. But she couldn't quite get there with Drago di Navarra. He wasn't just any man.

Worse, he'd probably decide she was trying to deceive him again, and then her chances of earning any money to take care of her baby would be nullified before she ever stepped in front of a camera. He'd throw her and Nicky to the wolves without a second thought, and then he'd step into his fancy limo and be ferried away to the next amazingly expensive location on his To See list.

No, she couldn't tell him. She couldn't take the chance when there was finally a light at the end of the tunnel.

The car pulled to a stop in front of her shabby apartment building. Drago looked out the window—at the yellow lights staining everything in a sickly glow, the fresh graffiti sprayed across the wall of a building opposite, the overflowing garbage bins waiting for tomorrow's pickup, the skinny dog pulling trash from one of them—and stiffened.

"You cannot stay here," he said, his voice low and filled with horror.

Holly sucked in a humiliated breath. It looked bad, yes, but the residents here were good, honest people. There

were drugs in the neighborhood, but not in this building.
Mr. Boudreaux ran it with an iron fist. It was the safest
thing she could afford. Shame crawled down her spine at
the look on Drago's face.

"I *am* staying here," she said quietly. "And I thank you
for the ride home."

His gaze swung toward her. "It's not safe here, *bella
mia*."

Holly gritted her teeth. "I've been living here for the
past seven months," she said. "It's where I live. It's what I
can afford. And you have no idea about safe. You're only
assuming it's not because it's not a fancy New York neighborhood like you're used to."

He studied her for a long moment. And then he pressed
an intercom button and spoke to the driver in Italian. After
that, he swung the door open and stepped out.

"Come then. I will walk you to your apartment."

"You don't have to do that," she protested, joining him
on the pavement with her duffel in tow. "The door is right
here."

The building was two stories tall, with three entrances
along its front. Each stairwell had two apartments on each
floor. Hers was on the second floor, center stairwell. And
the driver had parked the limo right in front of it. A dog
barked—not the one in the garbage, but a different one—
and a curtain slid back. She could see Mrs. Landry's face
peering outside. When her gaze landed on the limousine,
the light switched out and Holly knew the old woman had
turned it off so she could see better.

She was a nosy lady, but a sweet one.

"I insist," Drago said, and Holly's heart skipped a beat.
She had to take her things to her apartment, and then she
had to go to Mrs. Turner's across the hall and get Nicky.

"Fine," she said, realizing he wasn't going away otherwise. If she let him walk her to the door, he'd be satisfied,

even if he walked her up the steps to her apartment. And it wasn't as if her baby was home.

She turned and led the way to the door. She reached to yank it open, but he was there first, pulling it wide and motioning for her to go inside.

"Better be careful you don't get your fancy suit dirty coming inside here," she said.

"I know a good cleaner," he replied, and she started up the stairs—quietly, so as not to alert Mrs. Turner, who might just come to the door with her baby if she heard Holly arrive.

He followed her in silence until she reached the landing and turned around to face him. He was two steps behind her, and it put him on eye level with her. The light from the stairwell was sickly, but she didn't think there was a light on this earth that wouldn't love Drago di Navarra. It caressed his cheekbones, the aristocratic blade of his nose, shone off the dark curls of his hair. His mouth was flat and sensual, his lips full, and she remembered with a jolt what it had felt like to press her lips to his.

Dammit.

"This is it," she whispered. "You can go now."

He didn't move. "Open the door, Holly. I want to make certain you get inside."

He didn't whisper, and she shot a worried glance at Mrs. Turner's door. She could hear the television, and she knew her neighbor was awake.

"Shh," she told him. "People are sleeping. These walls are thin, which I am sure you aren't accustomed to, but—"

He moved then, startling her into silence as he came up to the landing and took her key from her limp hand. "You'd be surprised what I have been accustomed to, *cara*," he said shortly. "Now, tell me which door before I choose one."

Her skin burned. She pointed to her door and stood

silently by while he unlocked it and stepped inside. Humiliation was a sharp dagger in her gut then. A year ago, he'd dressed her in beautiful clothes, made her the center of attention, taken her to a restaurant she could never in a million years afford and then taken her back to his amazing Park Avenue apartment with the expansive view of Central Park. None of those things was even remotely like what he would see inside her apartment and she burned with mortification at what he must be thinking.

He turned back to her, his silvery eyes giving nothing away. "It appears to be safe," he told her, standing back so she could enter her own home. A home that, she knew, would have fit into the foyer of his New York apartment.

She slid the door quietly closed behind her, not because she wanted to shut him in, but because she wanted to keep her presence from Mrs. Turner until he was gone.

Fury slid into her bones, permeating her, making her shake with its force. She spun on him and jerked her keys from his hand. "How dare you?" she sputtered. "How dare you assume that because I live in a place that doesn't meet with your approval, you have a right to think I need your help to enter my own home?"

"Just because you've entered without incident in the past doesn't mean there won't come a night when someone has broken in to wait for you," he grated. "You're on the second floor, *cara*. You're a beautiful woman, living alone, and—" here he pointed "—these windows aren't precisely security windows, are they? So forgive me if I wanted to make sure you were safe. I could no more allow you to come in here alone than I could jump out that window and fly. It's not what a man does."

"First of all, I don't see why you care. And second, I don't live alone," she grated in return, her heart thrumming at everything he'd just said.

He blinked. "You have a boyfriend?"

"A best friend, if you must know. And she's at work right now."

He glanced around the room again. Gabi had left a lamp burning, as she always did, but it was a dim one in order to save electricity. Drago flicked a switch on the wall, and the overhead light popped on, revealing the apartment in all its shabby glory.

It was clean, but worn. And there was no way to hide that. His gaze slid over the room—and landed squarely on the package of diapers and jars of baby food sitting on the dinette. Holly closed her eyes and cursed herself for not putting everything away this afternoon. She'd been too caught up with her fragrances in the little free time she'd had after returning from the store.

Drago's brows drew down as he turned his head toward her. "You have a baby in this apartment?"

Before she could answer him, tell him she was collecting for charity or something, there was a knock on the door.

"Holly?" Mrs. Turner called. "Are you home, sweetie?"

CHAPTER FOUR

DRAGO WATCHED AS the color drained from Holly Craig's face. She pushed her hair behind her ear and turned away from him, toward the door.

"Coming, Mrs. Turner," she said sweetly, and he felt a flicker of annoyance. She'd been nothing but cross with him since the moment he'd first spoken to her in the casino. He understood why she would be angry with him, since he'd ruined her plans last year, but she should be perfectly amenable now that he was offering her the job of modeling for Sky. If she was ambitious, and she must be to undergo the deception she had, why wasn't she softening toward him?

His gaze landed on a table tucked into one corner of the room. It was lined with testers and other paraphernalia she must use to make her fragrance. Clearly, she was serious about it. And her grandmother was from Grasse, the perfume capital of the world. That didn't mean the woman had had any talent, or that she'd been a *nez*. Those were highly prized. If she'd been a nose, she would have gone to work in the industry, husband or no.

But Holly was certainly convinced she had what it took to succeed in his business. He glanced at the shabby furnishings and wasn't persuaded. If she had talent, why was she here? Why hadn't she kept trying even after he'd turned her down? There were other companies, other opportunities. They weren't the best, but they were a leg up.

Which she desperately seemed to need, he admitted. He refused to feel any remorse for that. She might have spent all her money coming to New York, but he was not responsible for her choices.

And yet, this place depressed him. Made him feel jumpy and angry and insignificant in ways he'd thought he'd forgotten long ago. He hadn't always lived the way he did now—with everything money could buy at his fingertips— and this dingy apartment was far too familiar. He thought of his mother and her insane quest for something he'd never understood—something she'd never understood, either, he'd finally come to realize years after the fact.

Donatella Benedetti had been looking for enlightenment, the best he could figure. And she'd been willing to drag her only son from foreign location to foreign location, some of them without electricity or running water or any means of communicating with the world at large. He'd held a hat while she'd busked on the streets, playing a violin with adequate-enough skill to gain a few coins for a meal. He'd curled up in a canoe while they'd floated down an Asian river, moving toward a village of mud huts and deprivation. He'd learned to beg for money by looking pitiful and small and hungry. He'd known how to count coins before he'd ever learned to read.

Holly took a deep breath and opened the door to greet an older woman standing on the other side. The woman held a baby carrier, presumably containing a baby, if the way Holly bent down and looked at it was any indication.

The beginnings of a headache started to throb in Drago's temple. Babies were definitely not his thing. They were tiny and mysterious and needy, and he hadn't a clue what to do with them.

"I thought I heard you come up," the woman was saying. "He was a good baby tonight. Such a sweetie."

"Thank you, Mrs. Turner. I really appreciate you helping out like this."

The other woman waved a hand. "Pish. You know I'm a night owl. It's no problem to keep him while you work." She looked up then, her gaze landing on him. Drago inclined his head while her eyes drifted over him. "Oh, my, I didn't know you had company," she said.

Holly turned briefly and then waved a hand as if to dismiss him. "Just an old acquaintance I ran into tonight. He's leaving now."

He was not leaving, but he didn't bother to tell her that. Or, he was leaving, but not just yet. Not until he figured out what was happening here.

There was a baby, in a carrier, and Holly was taking it from the woman. Was it her baby? Or her roommate's? And did it matter? So long as she modeled for Sky, did he care?

"Go ahead and take care of the baby," he said evenly. "I can go in a moment, once everything is settled."

The woman she'd called Mrs. Turner nodded approvingly. "Excellent idea. Get the little pumpkin settled first."

Mrs. Turner handed over a diaper bag, as well as the carrier, and Drago stepped forward to take the bag from Holly. She didn't protest, but she didn't look at him, either. A few more seconds passed as Holly and Mrs. Turner said their goodbyes, and then the door closed and they were alone.

Or, strike that, there were three of them where there'd been four. Drago gazed at the baby carrier as the child inside cooed and stretched.

"He's hungry," Holly said. "I have to feed him."

"Don't let me stop you."

She gazed at him with barely disguised hatred. "I'd

prefer you go," she said tightly. "It's late, and we need to get to bed."

"Whose baby is this?" he asked curiously. He thought of her in New York, sweet and innocent and so responsive to his caresses, and hated the idea she could have been with another man. He'd been her first. Yet another thing about her that had fooled him into thinking she hadn't had ulterior motives.

Drago tried very hard not to remember her expression of wonder when he'd entered her fully for the first time. She'd clung to him so sweetly, her body opening to him like a flower, and he'd felt an overwhelming sense of honor and protectiveness toward her. Something she'd been counting on, no doubt.

Dio, she had fooled him but good. She'd gotten past all his defenses and made him care, however briefly. Anger spun up inside him. But there were other feelings, too, desire being chief among them. It rather surprised him how sharp that feeling was, as if he'd not had sex in months rather than hours. Quite simply, he wanted to spear his hands into her hair and tilt her mouth up for his pleasure.

And then he wanted to strip her naked and explore every inch of her skin the way he once had, and let the consequences be damned.

Her expression was hard as she looked at him, and he wondered if she knew what he was thinking. Then she walked over to the couch—a distance of about four steps—and set the baby carrier on the floor. She grabbed the diaper bag from him and began to rummage in it. Soon, she had a bottle in her hands and she took the baby out of the carrier and began to feed it.

Drago watched the entire episode, a skein of discomfort uncoiling inside him as she deliberately did not answer his question.

It wasn't a hard question, but she looked down at the

baby and made faces, talking in a high voice and ignoring him completely. Her long reddish-blond hair draped over one shoulder, but she didn't push it back. He let his gaze wander her features, so pretty in a simple way, and yet earthy somehow, too.

She had not been earthy before. Now she bent over the child, holding the bottle, her full breasts threatening to burst from the white shirt, her legs long and lean beneath the tight skirt of the casino uniform. The only incongruous items of clothing were the tennis shoes she'd changed into.

Drago suddenly felt out of his element. Holly Craig nursed a child and turned every bit of love and affection she had on it, when all she could spare for him was contempt. Watching her with the baby, he had a visceral reaction that left a hole in the center of his chest. Had his mother ever focused every ounce of attention she had on him? Had she ever looked at him with such love? Or had she only ever looked at him as a burden and a means to an end?

"Holly," he said, his voice tight, and she looked up at him, her gaze defiant and hard. If he'd been a lesser man, he would have stumbled backward under that knife-edged gaze of hers. He was not a lesser man. "Whose child is that?"

He asked the question, but he was pretty certain he knew the answer by now.

"Not that it's any of your business," she told him airily, "but Nicky is mine. If this changes your plan to have me model for Sky, then I'd appreciate it if you'd get out and leave us alone."

Holly's heart hammered double-time in her chest. She hadn't wanted him to know about Nicky at all, not yet, not until the contract he'd agreed to provide was signed and she knew she'd get her money for doing the Sky campaign at the very least.

But of course her luck had run out months ago. First, she'd gone to New York, spent every dime she had and come home empty-handed. Then she'd lost the house and property—and found out she was pregnant. God, she could still remember her utter shock when her period hadn't started and she'd finally worked up the courage to buy a pregnancy test.

And she'd driven two towns over to do so, not wanting *anyone* in New Hope to wonder why she needed a pregnancy test.

She looked down at the sweet, soft baby in her arms now and knew for a fact he was not a mistake. But he'd definitely been a shock on top of everything else she'd had to deal with just then.

And now, of course, when all she wanted was the absolute best for him, when she needed to protect him and provide for him and keep him secret until she had this job sewn up, Mrs. Turner had heard her come home and brought him to her. What if Drago figured it out? What would happen then? She'd lose the opportunity to provide a better life for her baby.

Drago was looking at her with a mixture of disdain and what she thought might be utter horror. Resignation settled over her. She'd already lost the opportunity then.

But you can still tell him the truth.

Would he ignore his child's needs if he knew? Could she take that chance?

"How old is the child?" he asked, brows drawn low, and her heart did that funny squeeze thing it did when she was scared.

"A couple of months," she said vaguely, ignoring the voice. She couldn't tell him. How could she take the chance after everything that had happened? Not only that, but why did he deserve to know when he'd thrown her out and left her to fend for herself?

Guilt and fear swirled into a hot mess inside her belly. She'd always done the right thing. But what was the right thing now?

"You wasted no time, I see," he said coolly.

"I'm sorry?"

He looked hard and cool, remote. "Finding another lover," he spat at her.

A hard knot of something tightened right beneath her breastbone. Of course he thought she'd gone home and gotten pregnant by someone else. Of course he did. Holly closed her eyes and willed herself to be calm.

It didn't work.

My God, the man was arrogant beyond belief! Resentment flared to life in her gut, a hot bright fire that seared into her. "Why should I have waited? Thanks for showing me what I'd been missing, by the way. It was ever so easy to go home and climb back on the horse."

She gazed down at Nicky, who was sucking the bottle for all he was worth, and willed the irrational tears gathering behind her eyelids to melt away. Drago di Navarra not only thought she'd intended to use her body to get what she wanted out of him, but he also thought she'd been so promiscuous as to run straight home and get pregnant by another man. As if she could have borne another man's touch after she'd had his.

"Perhaps you should have been more careful," he said, and a fresh wave of hatred pounded into her. Her head snapped up. She didn't care what he saw in her gaze now.

"How dare you?" she said, her voice low and tight. "You know nothing about me. *Nothing!*" She sucked in a shaky breath. "Nicky is a gift, however he got here. I wouldn't trade him for a million Sky contracts, so you can take your disdain and your contempt and get the hell out of my home."

She was shaking, she realized, and Nicky felt it. He started to kick his little arms and legs, and his face scrunched up. The bottle popped out of his mouth, but before she could get it back in, he turned his head and started to wail.

"Shush, sweetie, Mommy's here," she crooned, her eyes stinging with tears and gritty from lack of sleep. She just wanted to put her head down and not get up again for a good long time.

But that wasn't possible. It wasn't ever possible these days.

"Forgive me. I shouldn't have said that."

Holly cuddled Nicky, rocking him softly, and looked up at Drago. Shock coursed through her system at those quiet words, uttered with sincerity. It was a glimpse of the man she'd found so compelling last year, the one who'd made her feel safe and who'd made her laugh and sigh and then shatter in his arms.

She'd liked that man, right up until the moment he'd proven he didn't really have a heart after all. And while she told herself not to be fooled now, she was moved by the apology. Or maybe she was just too exhausted to keep up the anger.

Nicky continued to wail, and Holly stood and bounced him up and down in her arms. "Hush, baby. It's okay."

"You need help," Drago said.

She didn't look at him. "I have help. You saw Mrs. Turner. Gabi helps, too. It's my turn now."

"You're tired, Holly. You should get some sleep."

"I can't sleep until he does." She paced the floor, giving Drago as wide a berth as possible in the small room. "You should probably go. Your driver will be wondering if I bashed you over the head and took your wallet."

"I doubt it," he said. He eyed the room again and she could feel the strength of his contempt for their surroundings.

"Drago." He looked at her, his nostrils flaring. He was acting as if he'd been caught with his hand in the cookie jar. "You should go. We'll be fine. We've been fine for months. Nicky will fall asleep soon, and then I'm going to crash, too. I have another shift tomorrow at noon."

"I'm afraid I can't do that," he said, and her stomach flipped. He took a step closer to her and she bounced Nicky a little more frantically. It seemed he didn't mind the movement at all. His little eyes were starting to close.

"Of course you can," she said. "You can't stay here, for God's sake. Nor would you want to, I'm sure. I'm afraid we don't have silk sheets, milord, or room service—"

"Shut up, Holly, and listen to me," he commanded.

And, as much as she wanted to tell him to go to hell, she did as he told her. Because she was tired. And scared he would walk out and take her last opportunity with him.

"I'm listening," she said when he didn't immediately continue.

"I'm returning to New York in the morning. You're coming with me."

Reflexively, she held Nicky a little tighter. "I'm not leaving my baby. Nor am I going anywhere without a contract," she said tightly. Because she didn't trust him. Because, as much as she wanted it to be true, she was too accustomed to bad luck to believe it was finally turning around for her.

Drago di Navarra wasn't suddenly being nice and accommodating for no reason. Did he suspect? Or was he just planning to drop her from an even greater height than he had the last time?

"No, you aren't leaving him," Drago said. "And you aren't returning to that casino, either. Pack what you need for the night. I'll send someone by for the rest of your things tomorrow."

Holly could only gape at him, her skin flushing hot with hope and fear and shame all rolled into one. *Don't trust him, don't trust him....*

And yet she wanted to. Needed to. He was the only way out of this hellhole.

Except, she had obligations.

"I can't just leave," she said. "This is my home. Gabi isn't even here. I can't quit the casino without notice—"

"You can," he said firmly. "You will."

Pressure was building behind her forehead. What should she do? What would Gran have said? Thoughts of Gran threatened to bring a fresh flood of tears, so she bit down on her lip and pushed them deep. *Think, Holly.*

"You're asking me to turn my life upside down for nothing more than a promise," she said. "How do I know you aren't planning some elaborate scheme to put me in my place once more?"

He blinked. And then he laughed, while she felt her skin turn even redder. "Honestly, *cara*, do you think I've spent a year plotting how to pay you back for deceiving me in New York? Until tonight, I had not given you another thought."

Well, all righty, then.

His words stung in ways she hadn't imagined possible. There wasn't a day since he'd thrown her out that she hadn't thought about him in some capacity or other—and here he was telling her so offhandedly that he hadn't thought of her at all.

"How flattering," she murmured, keeping her eyes on her baby so as not to reveal her hurt.

"It's not personal," he told her, all gorgeous Italian playboy. "I am a busy man. But when I saw you again, I remembered those photos and how right you were in them. All I want is your face on my campaign."

Nicky was finally asleep now. Holly turned and took him into her bedroom, where she placed him in his crib near her bed. When she straightened, Drago was standing in the door.

"I'll go," she told him quietly, making her decision. "But not tonight." She turned to look back at her baby before gazing at Drago again. "He can't be moved right now. It'll wake him up. And I'm too tired to pack a thing."

She joined Drago in the entry to her room. He was gazing down at her in frustration, his brows drawn down over his beautiful gray eyes.

"You're a very stubborn woman, Holly Craig," he said softly, his eyes dipping to her mouth before coming back up again. Her lips tingled. She told herself it was because she'd been biting them.

"I will always do what's best for my baby," she said. "He comes first. I'm sorry if you find that inconvenient."

She could feel the heat of Drago's body enveloping her, smell the cool scent of his cologne—a home run for Navarra Cosmetics, at least where he was concerned. Scents smelled different on different people, but this one seemed tailored to him. It was light, so light she'd not really noticed it before now, but it was also intoxicating.

There was sandalwood, which was to be expected in male cologne. But there were also pears, which was surprising, as well as moss. It was fresh and clean and she liked it. And she would forever associate the smell of NC's signature male cologne with its ruthless CEO.

Drago's mouth flattened for a moment, as if he were annoyed. But then he shook his head slightly.

"An admirable trait in a mother, I imagine," he said, and there was a piercing pain in her heart that she did not understand. Did he sound wistful just then? Lonely? Lost?

"I will send a car for you in the morning, *cara.* Say your goodbyes and pack your things. You won't need to return to this dwelling ever again."

Her heart hammered. "I can't leave Gabi in the lurch. She will need enough money to cover a couple of months' rent at least."

He didn't even blink. "I will take care of it."

And then he was gone, his footsteps echoing in the stairwell as he left her life once more.

CHAPTER FIVE

DRAGO'S APARTMENT IN New York was somehow even grander than she remembered it. Holly lay back on a bed that was almost as big as her entire room had been in New Orleans and stared up at a ceiling that had actual frescoes painted on it. Frescoes, as if this were a grand church instead of a personal dwelling.

Stunning. And completely surreal.

It was late afternoon and she needed to get out of bed, but she didn't want to. Early this morning—far earlier than she would have liked—Nicky had been awake and ready for his bottle. While she'd fed her baby, she'd done a pretty good job of convincing herself that Drago wasn't coming back. That she'd dreamed the whole thing.

Gabi had stumbled home at six, and Holly had told her the whole story—including the part where she was supposed to leave New Orleans and never have to worry about living in squalor again.

Gabi's face had lit up like the Fourth of July. "Oh, my God, Holly, that's amazing! You have to go! You *are* going, right?"

Holly had frowned. "I'm not sure." Then she'd raked a hand through her tangle of hair. "I mean, last night I was pretty sure. But how can I leave you? And how can I possibly deal with that man again? He's not nice, Gabi. He's selfish and arrogant and only concerned with his bottom line and—"

"And handsome as sin," Gabi had interrupted. "As well as richer than God. Not to mention he's the father of your baby."

Holly had frowned. "That's what worries me the most."

Gabi had sat down and taken her hand, squeezing it. Her blue eyes had been so serious. "This is a once-in-a-lifetime opportunity, Holly. You have to go. There's a reason this is happening now, and you have to go see what it is."

In the end, Holly had gone. Drago had arrived at eight, and by then Holly had packed everything she needed into three suitcases and a diaper bag. It was everything she owned. Drago had looked over her belongings coldly, and then his driver had carried them all down to the limo. Holly had hugged Gabi goodbye, crying and promising to call. She'd been terrified to leave her friend alone, but Drago had handed Gabi a fat envelope and told her to use it wisely.

Holly had bitten her lip to keep from saying something she might regret. It was up to Gabi to accept or decline the money, and in the end she'd accepted. She'd had no choice, really. Without Holly to help with expenses, she would have had to hustle to find another roommate or take on extra hours at work. The money was the better choice.

Within an hour, they'd been on a plane to New York. Within two hours, they'd landed. And, an hour later, she'd found herself in this room. She didn't know what she'd expected, but staying at Drago's had not been it. When she'd turned to him, he'd known what she was going to say, because he'd preempted her.

"There's no sense putting you in a hotel with a baby when this place is so big."

Nicky was in an adjoining room—the situation was going to take some getting used to. He had a nice crib and a play area with plenty of appropriate toys for a young baby. When she'd put him down for his afternoon nap, she'd come straight in here and climbed into bed. She always tried to snatch a few moments' sleep while Nicky was out—but he usually woke her before she was fully rested.

A prickle of alarm began to grow in her belly as she reached for her cell phone. She blinked at the display, certain she wasn't seeing it right. Because, if she was, that meant she'd been asleep for nearly three hours now.

Holly scrambled off the bed and ran into the adjoining room. Panic slammed into her when she realized Nicky was not in the crib. She tore open the door and raced down the hall, skidding into the palatial living area, with its huge windows overlooking Central Park. A woman sat on the floor and played with her baby. Nicky was on his belly, twisting the knobs of a toy, and the woman made encouraging noises as he did so.

"Who are you?" Holly demanded. She was trembling as she stood there. Part of her wanted to snatch her baby up and take him away from this woman, but the rational part told her not to alarm him when he was perfectly happy with what he was doing. And clearly safe and well.

The woman got to her feet and smiled. She was older, a bit plain, dressed in jeans and a T-shirt. She held out her hand. "I'm Sylvia. Mr. Di Navarra hired me to help with your son."

Holly's throat tightened painfully. She would *not* allow him to interfere. "I don't need help," she said. "He made a mistake."

Sylvia frowned. "I apologize, Miss Craig, but Mr. Di Navarra seems to think you do."

"I will speak to Mr. Di Navarra," she said tightly.

"Speak to me about what?"

Holly spun to find Drago standing in the door. Her heart did that little skip thing she wished it wouldn't do at the sight of him. But he was beautiful, as always, and she couldn't help herself. How had this splendid creature ever been interested in her for even a moment? How had they managed to make a baby together when she was so clearly not the class of woman he was accustomed to?

He wore faded jeans that she knew were artfully faded rather than work faded, and a dark shirt that molded to the broad muscles of his chest. His feet were bare. Something about that detail made her heart skitter wildly.

"I don't need help to take care of my son," she said. "You've wasted this woman's time."

He came into the room then and she saw he was holding a newspaper at his side. He tossed it onto a table and kept walking.

"I beg your pardon." He was all arrogance and disdain once more. "But you definitely do."

He stopped in front of her and put two fingers under her chin. She flinched. And then he turned her head gently this way and that, his eyes raking over her.

"I intend to pay a lot of money for this face to grace my ads. I'd prefer if you truly are rested instead of having you edited to look that way."

She pulled out of his grip and glared at him. Of course he was concerned about the campaign. What had she expected? That he'd hired a nanny because he cared? He didn't care. He had never cared.

Strike that: he only cared about himself.

"You could have asked me. I didn't appreciate waking up and finding my baby gone."

"My mistake, then," he said, his eyes searching hers. "I told Sylvia to take him when he cried. I knew you didn't get enough sleep last night."

Holly didn't dare think the fact he'd noticed she didn't get enough sleep meant anything other than he wanted to protect his investment. But she couldn't remember the last time someone had paid attention to how much sleep she was getting. It made a lump form in her throat. Gabi would have noticed if she weren't in the same boat.

Gran would have, too. Gran would have put her to bed and taken the baby for as long as she needed. Holly bit the inside of her lip to stop a little sob from escaping. It wasn't even eighteen months since Gran had died, and it still hurt her at the oddest times.

Holly glanced at Sylvia, who had gotten back down on the floor to entice Nicky with a new toy. There was a tightness in her chest as she watched her baby play. She'd greatly appreciated Mrs. Turner's help, and she was certain the woman was kind and gentle, but she was almost positive Mrs. Turner had spent her time watching television instead of playing on the floor with Nicky.

Sylvia clearly knew what she was doing—in fact, Holly thought sadly, the woman seemed to know more than she did, if the way she encouraged Nicky to play with different shapes was any indication. Holly had been satisfied when he'd been occupied and happy. She'd never really considered his play to be a teaching moment.

Holly put a hand to her forehead and drew in a deep breath. She wasn't a bad mother, was she? She was simply an overworked and exhausted one, but she loved her son beyond reason. He was the only thing of value she had.

"You need to eat," Drago said, and Holly looked up at him.

"I'm not hungry." As if to prove her a liar, her stomach growled. Drago arched an eyebrow. "Fine," she said, "I guess I am after all."

"Come to the kitchen and let the cook fix you something."

Holly looked doubtfully at her baby and Sylvia. It wasn't that she didn't trust the woman, but she didn't know her. And she was nervous, she had to admit, with this change in circumstances. The last time she'd been here, it had all been ripped away from her without warning. She wasn't certain it wouldn't be again. "I'd rather stay here."

Drago frowned. "He's not going anywhere, Holly. He'll be perfectly fine."

Holly closed her eyes. She was being unreasonable. She'd left Nicky with Mrs. Turner for hours while she rode a bus and a streetcar halfway across town and went to work. Was it really such a stretch to go into another room and leave this woman alone with her child?

"All right," she said. Drago led her not to the kitchen but to a rooftop terrace with tables and chairs and grass— actual grass on a rooftop in New York City. The terrace was lined with potted trees and blossoming flowers, and while she could hear the city sounds below, her view was entirely of sky and plants and the buildings across the tree-tops in Central Park. Astounding, and beautiful in a way she found surprising.

"This is not the kitchen," she said inanely.

Drago laughed. "No. I decided this was more appropriate."

They sat down and a maid appeared with a tray laden with small appetizers—olives, sliced meats, tiny pastries filled with cheese, cucumber sandwiches, ham sandwiches and delicate chocolates to finish. It wasn't much, but it was precisely the kind of thing she needed just now.

Holly dug in to the food, filling her plate and taking careful bites so as not to seem like a ravenous animal. She might not be accustomed to fancy New York society, but her grandmother had at least taught her the art of being graceful. The maid appeared again with a bottle of wine. Holly started to protest, but Drago shushed her. Then he poured the beautiful deep red liquid into two glasses.

"You should appreciate this," he said. "A Château Margaux of excellent vintage."

As if she even knew what that meant. But she did understand scents and flavors. Holly lifted the wine and swirled it before sniffing the bowl. The wine was rich and full and delicious to the nose. She took a sip, expecting perfection. It was there. And she knew, as she set the glass down again, it was the sort of thing she could never afford.

When she glanced up, Drago was watching her. His gray eyes were piercing, assessing, and she met them evenly. So unlike the Holly of a year ago, who'd stammered and gulped and been a nervous wreck in his presence. It took a lot to meet that stare and not fold, but she was getting better at it.

"Describe the wine to me," he said, his voice smooth and commanding. As if he were accustomed to telling people what to do and then having them do it. Which, of course, he was.

Holly bristled, though it was a simple request. She was tired and stressed and not in the mood to play games with him. Not in the mood to be devoured like a frightened rabbit.

"Taste it yourself," she said. "I'm sure you can figure it out."

She didn't expect him to laugh. "You have made it your mission in life to argue with me, it seems."

"I wouldn't say it's a mission, as that implies I give you a lot of thought. But I'm not quite the same person you ordered around last year. I won't pretend I am."

She was still more of that person than she wanted to be, but she was working very hard on being bold and brave. On not letting his overwhelming force of a personality dominate her will.

Not that he needed to know that.

He leaned back and sipped his wine. "I didn't force you to do anything you didn't want to do, Holly. As I recall, you wanted to do the same things I did. Very much, in fact."

Holly tried to suppress the heat flaring in her cheeks. Impossible, of course. They were red and he would know it. "The wine is delicious," she said, picking up the glass and studying the color. "The top notes are blackberry and cassis. The middle might be rose, while the bottom hints at oak and coffee." A small furrow appeared between Drago's brows.

"Ah, you are embarrassed by what happened between us," he said softly.

Her heart skipped a beat. "Embarrassed? No. But I see no need in discussing it. It's in the past and I'd like to just forget the whole thing."

As if she could.

His nostrils flared, as if he didn't quite like that pronouncement. "Forget? Why would you want to forget something so magnificent, Holly?"

She picked up the wine and took another sip, kept her eyes on the red liquid instead of on him. "Why not? You did. You refused to listen to me and threw me out. I'm sure you promptly forgot about me once I was gone."

His handsome face creased in a frown. "That doesn't mean I didn't enjoy our evening together."

"I really don't want to talk about this," she said. Because it hurt, and because it made her think of her innocent child in the other room and the fact that his father sat here with her now and didn't even know it. Hadn't managed to even consider the possibility.

No, he thought she'd spent the night with him in order to sell her fragrances. And then, when that didn't work, he thought she'd run home and got pregnant right after. As if she had the sense of a goat and the morals of an alley cat.

Yes, she could tell him the truth…but she didn't know him, didn't trust him. And Nicky was too precious to her to take that kind of chance with.

"What you see here is not who I have always been," he

said, spreading an arm to encompass the roof with its expensive greenery. "It may appear as if I were born with money, but I assure you I was not. I know what it's like to work hard, and what it's like to want something so badly you'd sell your soul for it. I've seen it again and again."

Holly licked suddenly dry lips. Was he actually sharing something with her? Something important? Or was he simply trying to intimidate her in another way? "But Navarra Cosmetics has been around for over fifty years," she said. "You are a Navarra."

He studied the wine in his glass. "Yes, I am a Navarra. That doesn't mean I was born with a silver spoon, as you Americans say. Far from it." He drew in a breath. "But I'm here now, and this is my life. And I do not appreciate those who try to take advantage of who I am for their own ends."

Holly's heart hardened. She knew what he was saying. What he meant. Her body began to tremble. She wanted to tell him how wrong he was. How blind. But, instead, she pushed her chair back and stood. She couldn't take another moment of his company, another moment of his smugness.

"I think I'm finished," she said, disappointment and fury thrashing together inside her.

Of course he wasn't telling her anything important. He was warning her. Maybe he hadn't been born rich, maybe he'd been adopted or something, but she didn't care. He was still a heartless bastard with a supreme sense of arrogance and self-importance. He could only see what he expected to see.

If she didn't need the money so much, she'd walk out on *him*. Let him be the one to suffer—not that he would suffer much if she didn't do the Sky campaign. He'd find another model, like he had last year, and he'd eventually give up the idea of her being the right person for the job.

No, the only one who would suffer if she walked out was Nicky. She wasn't walking out. But she wasn't putting up with this, either. She was going back inside and collecting her baby. Then she was going to her room and staying there for the evening.

Before she could walk away, Drago reached out and encircled her wrist with his strong fingers. They sizzled into her, sending sparks of molten heat to her core. Her body ached when he touched her, and it made her angry. Why hadn't she ached when Colin had touched her? Why hadn't she wanted him the way she wanted Drago di Navarra?

Life would be so much easier if she had. Lisa Tate would have never entered the picture. Nicky might be Colin's son, and they might be married and living in her cottage in New Hope while he worked his lawn-care business and she made perfume for the little shop she'd always wanted to open.

They could have been a happy little family and life could have been perfect. She might have never gotten a chance to sell her fragrances to a big company, but Gran would have understood. Gran had only ever wanted her to be happy. She knew that now. A year ago, she'd thought she had to succeed in order to carry on Gran's legacy. That Gran was counting on her somehow.

But she knew Gran wouldn't have wanted her to suffer. She wouldn't have wanted Holly to work so hard, to scrape and scrape and barely get by. She'd have wanted Holly happy, living in their cottage and making her perfumes.

Except that living in the cottage hadn't been an option, had it? Gran's health had suffered in the last few years and she'd had to borrow against the house to pay her bills. Holly had hoped to save the only home she'd ever known when she'd gone to New York.

What a fool she'd been. She'd left the big city broke and pregnant and alone.

"So long as we know where we stand, there's no need to get upset," Drago said, his voice smooth and silky and hateful to her all at once. "Sit. Finish eating. You'll need your strength for the coming days. I can't afford for you to get sick on me."

Her wrist burned in his grip. She wanted to pull away. And she wanted to slide into his lap and wrap her arms around his proud neck. Holly blinked. Was she insane? Had she learned absolutely nothing about this man?

She hated him. Despised him.

Wanted him.

Impossible. Wanting him was a threat to her well-being. To her baby's well-being.

Holly closed her eyes and stood there, gathering her strength. She would need every bit of it to resist his touch. So long as he didn't touch her, she could remain aloof. She could remember the hate. Feel it. Soak in it. That was how she would survive this. By remembering how it had felt when he'd kicked her out. How she'd felt when she'd lost everything and given birth with only Gabi and the medical staff for company.

There'd been no happy new father, no roses, no balloons for the baby. No joy, other than what she'd felt when she'd held Nicky.

"I am finished," she said coolly. "And I'd appreciate it if you'd let go of me."

Drago's jaw was tight. He looked as if he were assessing her. Cataloging her flaws and finding her lacking, no doubt. "Sit down, Holly. We have much to discuss."

"I'd rather not right now, thanks."

His grip tightened on her wrist. Then he let her go abruptly, cursing in Italian as he did so. "Go, then. Run away like a child. But we will have a discussion about what I want from you. And quite soon."

Holly gritted her teeth together and stared across the beautiful terrace to the sliding-glass doors. Freedom was almost hers. All she had to do was walk away. Just go and get Nicky and go to her room for the night.

But it was simply postponing the inevitable. She knew that. It was what she wanted to do, and yet she couldn't. She had to face this head-on. Had to fight for this opportunity before he changed his mind.

Holly Craig wanted to be the kind of woman who didn't back down.

She *would* be that kind of woman. She sank down in her chair like a queen and crossed her legs, in spite of her racing heart. Then she picked up the still-full wineglass and leveled a gaze at Drago.

"Fine. Talk. I'm listening."

CHAPTER SIX

DRAGO HAD NEVER met a more infuriating woman in his life. Holly Craig sat across from him at the table, with golden sunlight playing across her face and her pale hair, setting flame to the strands, and looked like a sweet, innocent goddess.

An illusion.

She was not sweet. She was most definitely not innocent. Remembering the ways in which she was not innocent threatened to make him hard, especially after he'd just had his hand on her soft skin. He forced the memory of making love to her from his mind and focused on the stubborn set of her jaw.

So determined, this woman. So different compared to last year. He sometimes had glimpses of that innocent girl under the veneer, but mostly she was hard and weary. Changed.

Or perhaps last year had been nothing more than an act. Perhaps she'd been just as hard then but had pretended not to be. He'd learned, over the years, that women would do much in an attempt to snare a wealthy man. Holly might have been a virgin, but that didn't mean she hadn't been a virgin with a plan. Innocence in sexual matters did not imply innocence overall.

Nevertheless, he still wanted her for Sky. She had the face he needed. An everywoman face, but pretty in the way every woman wanted to be. No, she was not perfect. She wasn't the sort of gorgeous that a top supermodel was.

But she was perfect for what he wanted her for.

And that was why he put up with her, he told himself. With her hostility and her loathing and her refusal to cooperate.

Drago had worked his way up the ladder at Navarra Cosmetics, because his uncle had insisted he start at the bottom to really know the business, but one of the things he'd always had—and had honed into a fine instrument these days—was a gut feeling for what was right for the company. Holly Craig was right for Sky, and he intended to have her.

Even if he had to suffer her hostility and a baby in his house. When they went to Italy, he would put her and the child in another wing of the estate. Then he would cheerfully forget about her until the shoot was completed and he went over the photos.

She took a sip of the wine and he thought of the way she'd described it to him. She'd never had Château Margaux, he'd bet on that, but she'd described it perfectly after one sip. She knew scents and flavors, he had to give her that.

Whether or not that made her a good perfumer was an entirely different matter.

"Tell me what you expected when you came to New York last year."

Her eyes widened. And then narrowed again, as if she were trying to figure out the trick.

"I'm not sure what you mean," she said carefully.

Her eyes dropped and a current of irritation sizzled into him. "Are you not? You had a case of perfume samples. You pretended to be a model. What was your intent? What did you think would happen once you had my undivided attention?"

She colored, her eyes flashing hot. He didn't know why, but that slice of temper intrigued him. "Because I had intent, right? You never gave me a chance to explain that morning, if I recall. It was a misunderstanding, but you didn't stay for that part."

He sipped the wine. "How did I misunderstand you, *cara*? You were not mute. You spent the entire evening with me. Not only that, but you stood in front of the cameras for two hours and never corrected the impression you were there to model."

Her color remained high. She closed her eyes for a moment. A second later, she was looking straight at him, her eyes shiny and big in her pale face. "I know. I should have. But you assumed I was a model, and I was too scared to say otherwise. Scared I'd lose my chance to talk to you."

"You had my undivided attention all evening," he bit out.

"Hardly undivided," she threw back at him. "You took a dozen phone calls at least. How anyone could have a conversation with you under those circumstances is beyond me."

"Ah, so this is your excuse. What about later, *cara*?"

He didn't think it possible, but her color heightened. Her cheeks were blazing now. She picked up her untouched glass of water and took a deep draft. Drago almost wanted to laugh, but he was too irritated. Still, her blushes made him think of how inexperienced she'd been—and how eager at the same time.

Basta, no. Not a good thing to think about.

"We were, um, busy later. I didn't think it was appropriate." Her head came up then and her eyes glittered. "Haven't you ever stopped to wonder how I could have possibly known you needed a model that day? How I just happened to be sitting there in your waiting room? It wasn't planned, Drago. I had an appointment." She cleared her throat. "Or I thought I did. A university friend of the mayor's wife said she knew you and could arrange a brief meeting. I was told the day and time and that I would have ten minutes. So I went."

It could be true, certainly. He had no recollection. But that did not change what she'd done. How she'd lied. "And yet you took advantage of the situation when I mistook you for the model."

She let out an exasperated breath. "I did. I admit it! But you ordered me to go with you and you didn't give me a chance to explain. I made a decision that it was best to go along with you until I could."

Drago studied her for a long moment. Did he really believe Holly Craig had masterminded the entire situation?

No, he didn't. But she had taken advantage of it. Of him. And that was unforgivable.

"It's possible you were on the schedule. But that was a bad day, as I recall. All the models were wrong. I told my secretary to reschedule the meetings."

She looked unhappy. "Since I didn't schedule it, it wasn't my contact information she would have had. Besides, I'd already come all that way. I couldn't go back without talking to you."

Yes, and she'd been sitting there in his waiting room, looking so fresh and out of place at the same time. He still remembered the black suit and the pink heels with the price tag. A twinge of something sliced into him, but he didn't want to examine it. And he definitely wasn't revisiting what had happened next. It might have been a mistake, but she'd had ample opportunity to tell him the truth.

Instead, she'd seen a way to gain advantage—and she'd taken it. Then she'd kept the pretense going until she'd thought she had him right where she wanted him. He could still see her face that morning, still see how pleased she'd been with herself when he'd questioned her about the case.

His reaction had been inevitable. He'd experienced all those old feelings of despair and fear and loneliness he'd had as a boy, and he'd hated her for doing that to him. For making him remember what he'd worked hard to bury. He'd had no choice but to walk out.

Because she'd blindsided him and he hadn't seen it coming. He'd thought she was someone she wasn't, and he'd felt something with her that he hadn't felt in a long time. He had almost—almost, but not quite—let himself relax with her. She'd been so guileless, unlike the women he usually dated. His fault for always choosing sophisticates, but until he'd experienced someone like Holly Craig, he'd not realized he might enjoy less artifice.

That she'd fooled him, that she'd been as scheming as the most seasoned gold digger, still rankled. He did not regret throwing her out.

But he did regret that he'd let her escape without first seeing the photos. He'd thought about tracking her down once she was gone, but he'd ultimately decided it was best if he did not.

"And what did you hope to gain from a meeting with me? A job?"

She shook her head. "I had hoped you would want Colette."

"Colette?"

"It's named after my grandmother. It's the last fragrance we created together. The finest, I might add. I had hoped you would buy it and market it."

"Surely you know this is not how huge companies work." He slid his fingers along the stem of his wineglass. "At Navarra, we employ several perfumers. We brainstorm concepts and give directions. The perfumers work to create something that meets our expectations. Sometimes, we create fragrances in tandem with celebrities. We do not, however, buy fragrances from individuals."

Her chin lifted. "Yes, but this one is good enough you might have. And I had to try."

He could almost admire her determination. Almost. "Why?"

She turned her head and put her fingers to her lips. He wondered if she was thinking about her answer, but when she turned back to him, he could see the sheen of moisture in her eyes. "Because my gran was gone and I didn't want to lose her house. I wanted to honor her memory and save my childhood home at the same time."

Inside, a tiny flicker of unease reared its head. "And did you lose the house?" He knew the answer because of how he'd found her. If she'd still had her childhood home, would she have been a cocktail waitress in a casino? Especially with a baby?

There were two fresh spots of color in her cheeks. "I did. I couldn't make the payments against the debt, so it was sold. A nice couple lives there now."

He hadn't had a childhood home. The thought made him feel raw inside. But he'd wanted one. He'd been eleven when his uncle had finally wrested him from his mother's capricious grip. Eleven when he'd first entered the Di Navarra estate in Tuscany. It was as close to a childhood home as he had.

Except, he had no memories of a mother's love or of warmth and belonging in a place. His uncle had been good to him, and he was grateful, but he'd spent a lot of time alone—or with tutors—because Uncle Paolo had spent so much time working.

"Where are your parents?" he asked her.

"I never knew them. My father is a mystery man, and my mother died when I was a baby." She said it so unemotionally, but he knew it had to hurt. He'd never known his father, though of course he knew his identity. He hadn't been that lucky with his mother. She had left her imprint deep. He was still trying to cover the scars of what she'd done to him.

"And what about the father of your child?" he asked, shaking away painful thoughts of his mother. "Why didn't he step up and help?"

Her lips flattened and she took a deep breath. "He didn't want to be burdened, I imagine," she finally said, her voice soft and brittle at once.

He imagined her pregnant and alone, without a home, and felt both anger and sympathy. Anger because she reminded him of his mother and sympathy because she'd lost so much. Was that what had happened to his mother? He'd never understood why she'd been so flighty, why she'd moved from place to place, always searching for something that eluded her.

She might have had to settle down if not for him. If not for the money he represented. The money his uncle gave for his care, but which she would spend taking him someplace remote and hiding him from the Di Navarras. When she would run out, she would emerge again, hand outstretched until Uncle Paolo filled it—and then they would disappear once more.

Clearly, Holly wasn't doing that with this child—but she had been living in that dingy building and leaving the baby with strangers. His mother had done the same thing, time and again. If Holly got money from the baby's father, would she spend it all recklessly in the pursuit of filling some emptiness inside herself? Or would she settle down and take care of the baby the way he should be taken care of?

"I am given to understand you can sue for child support in this country," he said mildly. "At the least, you could have gotten a bit of help for your child. I wonder that you did not do it."

Her eyes flashed hot. "You make it sound so simple.

But I would have needed money for a lawyer, wouldn't I? Since I couldn't afford to make the mortgage payments, I couldn't afford a lawyer, either."

"So you got a job as a cocktail waitress." There was condemnation in his tone. He knew it, and so did she. Certainly she could have found something else. Something safer for a child.

Her chin came up. "After I left New Hope, yes. I went to New Orleans and got a job in the casino. The tips were good and I needed the money."

"But not good enough to afford you a decent place to live."

"Not everyone is so fortunate as you."

"I have had nothing handed to me, *cara*. I worked for everything I have."

"Yes, but you had all the advantages."

"Not quite all," he said. For the first eleven years, he'd had no advantages. Hell, he hadn't even been able to read until Uncle Paolo had taken him away from his mother and gotten him an education that didn't require him to count out coins for supper. "Besides, when you are done here, you'll have enough money to take your baby somewhere safe."

"How dare you suggest I would put my baby in danger?" she said tightly. "Just because I couldn't afford a home that meets *your* standards, Your High and Mightiness, doesn't mean my son wasn't safe."

She was tightly strung, her body practically trembling with nervous energy. Her eyes flashed fire and her jaw was set in that stubborn angle he'd oddly come to enjoy. Such a firecracker, this girl.

They'd burned together before. What would it be like now?

He shoved the thought away and let his gaze slide over

her lovely face. She was going to make Navarra Cosmetics a lot of money, if his gut was any judge. And it usually was.

He didn't need to screw it up by getting involved with her again, however enticing the thought. Instead, he thought of where he'd found her, of the utter desolation of that apartment building, and his anger whipped higher.

"Do you really want your child to grow up there, Holly? Do you want Mrs. Turner keeping him every night, while he cries and asks where his mother is? Do you want him to only see you for a few minutes a day while you do whatever it is you plan to do with the money?"

She blinked at him, and he knew his voice had grown harsh. But he wouldn't take any of it back. She had to consider these things. She had to consider the child.

"Of course I don't want that," she said. "I want a house somewhere, and a good school. I want Nicky to have everything I had growing up. I intend to give it to him, too."

Everything inside him was tight, as if someone had stretched the thinnest membrane over the mouth of a volcano. He didn't know why she got to him so badly, but he didn't like it. Drago worked to push all the feelings she'd whipped up back under the lid of the box he kept them in.

"Perhaps you can give him those things," he finally said when he no longer felt so volatile. "Do you have any idea what the going rate is on a cosmetics campaign?"

She shook her head.

"It could be in the six figures, *cara*. But we'll need to see how the test shots go first." Because, no matter how bad he felt for her and the baby, he wouldn't hand over that kind of money for nothing. He'd go out of business if he allowed sympathy to get in the way of his decisions.

Her eyes were huge. Then she swallowed and fixed him with a determined look. "I expect to see that contract, spelling it all out, before anything happens."

Irritation lashed into him. "You don't trust me?" he asked, a dangerous edge to his voice.

She was nobody. She had nothing. She needed this job—and she needed his goodwill, after what she'd pulled last year.

But she didn't hesitate to push him. To demand her contract. He had to admit that a grudging part of him admired her tenacity even while she maddened him.

"Should I?" she said sweetly.

"Do you have a choice?"

Her jaw worked. Hardened. "No, I don't suppose I do."

"Precisely." He shoved back from the table and stood. "You will get your contract, Holly, because that is what businesses do."

Then he leaned down, both hands on the table, and fixed her with an even look. "And if you don't like the terms, you will be taken back to where I found you and left there without the possibility of ever seeing a dime."

Holly was restless. She was so accustomed to being on the go, to working hard for hours every day and then scrambling to get home and take care of her child, that being in this apartment with a nanny and no schedule felt surreal.

She'd tried to read a book. She'd tried to watch television—what was with all these people airing their private business in front of a TV judge for public consumption, anyway?—and she'd tried to listen to music. Nothing made her feel settled for more than a few moments.

She thought about going for a walk, but she was a little too intimidated by the prospect of roaming New York City streets alone. She'd walked the short distance from the casino to the streetcar stop in the dark—risky enough in some ways, but she'd never felt intimidated doing it.

Here, she thought if she went outside, she might never find her way back again.

So, she sat with the television remote and skipped through a variety of shows. And she finally had to admit to herself that the source of her restlessness wasn't just that her life had gone from two hundred miles an hour to a full stop in the space of a heartbeat.

No, it was also Drago di Navarra. He'd been angry at her earlier, and he'd threatened to drop her back in New Orleans, where he'd found her. The thought had chilled her. Yes, she was murderously furious with him—with his high-handedness and his arrogance and his certainty she'd been out to dupe him—but she couldn't let her anger get in the way of this job. She couldn't let him send her away before she'd earned that money.

It frightened her that she was suddenly so dependent on the promise of so much money. Yesterday, she'd nearly thrown a tray of drinks in his face. She'd been hostile to him and she'd wanted him gone—but he'd seduced her with words, with the promise of a better life for her child, and now she'd bought into it so thoroughly that the prospect of not having it threatened to make her physically ill.

She'd pushed him during their conversation. She'd been angry and she'd lashed out. Part of her regretted it—and part of her was glad. Damn him and his smug superiority anyway!

As if thinking of the devil conjured him, Drago walked into the living room, dressed in a tuxedo and looking every inch the gorgeous tycoon. Holly's heart thumped. Her jaw sagged and she snapped it closed again when she realized she was gaping at him.

Of course he was going out. Of course.

She didn't know where he was going, or who he was going with, but the thought of him out there dancing with some beautiful woman pierced her.

Why?

She did not care what he did. Holly lifted her chin and

stared at him, waiting for him to speak. Because, clearly, he'd come in here to say something to her. Perhaps he'd decided she wasn't worth the trouble after all. Perhaps he'd come to tell her to gather her things because a car was waiting to take her back to the airport.

"I have to go out," he said without preamble, and she let her gaze drop over him.

"I can see that. Have a wonderful time."

He ignored her and came over to perch on the arm of the chair facing where she sat. The TV was behind him, so she tried to focus on it.

Impossible, of course.

"We need to talk," he said, and her heart skipped. He was going to send her home. It was over. Well, she'd known it couldn't last. But he was going to have to pay her for her inconvenience, damn him. She'd left her job, for heaven's sake.

He lifted his arm, tugged the cuff of his sleeve. Adjusting. Making her wait for it. He was so cool, so unconcerned. His gaze lifted, bored into hers.

"Do you have a passport?" he asked, and Holly blinked.

"I— Um, no." Well, that wasn't what she'd expected.

He frowned. "Then we'll need to take care of it. As soon as possible."

"Why?"

"Because we are going to Italy, *cara*."

Italy? Her pulse throbbed with a sudden shot of fear. "Why?"

He looked annoyed. "Because this is where the Sky shoot will take place. Because I am the boss and I say so."

Holly shifted on the couch. "You aren't my boss," she pointed out, and then berated herself for doing so. But why should she let him get away with being so pointedly arrogant? He'd asked her to do the campaign. She'd said yes— but they hadn't started yet and she didn't have a contract.

He lifted one eyebrow. "Am I not? Somehow, I thought the one paying the salary would be in charge."

"You haven't paid me a single penny yet," she said.

"Haven't I? You did not get to New York by magic, Holly. Nor does Sylvia work for free."

Her ears felt hot. Well, yes, those things did cost money. "I did not ask you to hire her."

"No, but a baby on the hip was not quite what I had in mind for the ad."

"I won't go to Italy without a contract." She said it belligerently, and then winced at her tone. What was the matter with her? Did she want him to send her home? Back to nothing?

"These things take time to draft," he said coolly. "I don't keep a sheaf of contracts in my desk and whip one out as needed. Rest assured, Holly, you will get a contract. But you still need a passport, and so does the baby."

Her heart slid into her stomach. She'd never filled out paperwork for a passport before, but she imagined it required information she'd rather not share with Drago. Information that might make him ask questions.

"I don't understand why we can't do the shoot here. We did before. The park is lovely, and—"

"Because it's not what I want this time," he said. "Because I have a vision, and that vision takes place in Italy."

She dropped her gaze to the tips of her tennis shoes, where they rested on the ottoman in front of her. Jeez, he sat there in a tuxedo, and she was wearing jeans and tennis shoes as if she was still a teenager or something.

It reminded her starkly of the difference in their circumstances.

"It seems like a waste of money," she said softly. "The park is here, and it was so pretty the last time."

He stood and she could feel his imposing gaze on her. She looked up, and her heart turned over at the intensity of his stare. There was something in that gray-eyed gaze, something hot and secret and compelling.

Holly swallowed.

"I appreciate you thinking about the bottom line," he said with only the mildest hint of sarcasm, "but the fact is I can afford to do what I want. And what I want is you in Italy."

Holly twisted her fingers together in her lap. "Then I suppose we'll have to get passports."

"Yes," he said. "You shall. I'll make arrangements." He looked at his watch and frowned. "And now, if you will excuse me, I have a date."

A date.

Holly's stomach twisted, but she forced herself to give him a wan smile. Really, she didn't care at all—but being here made her remember what it had been like between them. The heat and passion and pleasure, the utter bliss of his possession.

Another woman would experience that tonight, while Holly lay in a bed in his apartment, only steps from the room where he'd first shown her what it was like between a man and a woman. She would twist and turn and imagine him with someone else. She would burn with longing, the way she'd done during the lonely nights when she hadn't been able to stop thinking about him no matter how much she'd wanted to.

Holly picked up the remote and flipped through the channels. She didn't see what was on the screen, couldn't have focused if her life depended on it, but it was something to do while she waited for him to walk out.

"Have fun," she said, because she had to say something.

He stood there a moment more, hands thrust in pockets. And then he turned and walked out and her heart slid to the bottom of her toes. Her eyes stung with unshed tears that she angrily slapped away.

She was furious because she was helpless. Because she had to do what he wanted or lose the money. That was the reason she wanted to cry.

The *only* reason.

Drago was not enjoying himself. He'd been expected to attend this event for the past month—a charity gala at the Met—but his attention was elsewhere. The woman on his arm—a beautiful heiress he'd met at a recent business dinner—bored him. He didn't remember her boring him when he'd met her only a few weeks ago. He remembered that he'd been interested.

She was lovely and articulate, and she had her fingers in many causes. But he saw beneath that veneer tonight. She had causes because she needed something to do with her money and her time.

She didn't care about the people she helped. She did it because it was expected of her. And because it brought her attention. He remembered seeing her in the paper only a couple of days ago, being interviewed about some fashion show she'd attended in Europe.

Even that wouldn't have been enough to make him think she didn't really care. No, it was her behavior tonight. Her need to be seen on his arm and her ongoing *catty* chatter about some of the other people in the room. As if she were better than them. As if he were, too, and needed to be warned about them.

The disconcerting thing was this: he wasn't quite certain any of these things would have truly bothered him just a few days ago. But now he thought of Holly sitting in that squalid apartment and feeding her baby a bottle, and a hot feeling bloomed in his chest.

Holly knew what it was like to struggle. To have almost nothing. She'd lost her home, and she'd gone to work as a waitress to make ends meet. His mother had done much the same, though for reasons of her own that had made no sense to anyone but her.

This woman—Danielle, was it?—wouldn't know the first thing about what struggling really meant.

He did. Even if he hadn't been a part of that world in a very long time, he knew what it was to have nothing. To rely on the kindness of strangers to eat. To beg and struggle and do things you didn't want to do, simply because you needed to survive. He'd only been a child, but the memory was imprinted deep. It was also usually buried deep—but not since Holly Craig had come back into his life.

"Drago, did you hear anything I said?"

He looked down at the glittering creature by his side—and a wave of disgust filled him. He didn't want this artifice. Not tonight. He didn't want to spend his time in the company of a woman who was superficial and selfish. She had millions, but she was still a user. A user of a different kind than his mother had been, but a user nonetheless. It dismayed him that he'd never seen it before.

Tonight, he wanted a woman who would look at him like he wasn't a god, a woman who would refuse to accept his pronouncements as if they were from some exalted place and, therefore, not to be questioned.

He wanted Holly. He wanted a woman who was direct with him. Oh, she hadn't always been. But she was now. She knew where she stood with him, so she was no longer trying to scam him. There was no need for pretense between them. She glared and huffed and stubbornly tried to get her way. She did not cajole. She spoke her mind.

No one spoke their mind to him. Not the way Holly did. She didn't even seem to like him much—but she did want him.

He knew that from the way her breath shortened when he was near, the way her eyes slid over him and then quickly away, as if she didn't want to be caught looking at him. Her skin grew pink and her breathing shallow.

That wasn't hatred, no matter what she claimed. It was desire.

"I heard you," he said to the woman at his side. "And I am terribly sorry, but I have to leave. I'm afraid I have another engagement tonight."

Danielle's mouth opened, as if she couldn't quite believe it. "But I thought…"

Drago lifted her limp, cool hand to his mouth and pressed a kiss there. "*Ciao, bella.* It was lovely to see you again."

And then, before she could utter another word, he strode from her side, out the front doors and down the sidewalk. His apartment wasn't far. His driver would have come to pick him up, but he wanted to walk. He needed to walk if he were to quench this strange fire for Holly Craig, before he stormed into his home and took her into his arms.

It was inconvenient to want a woman he'd once thrown out of his life. But he couldn't seem to stop himself.

He reached his building in less than fifteen minutes. The doorman swung the entry open with a cheery good-evening. Drago returned the greeting, and then he was in his private elevator and on his way up to the penthouse.

It was quiet when he let himself in. He glanced at his watch. It wasn't late, only nine-thirty. But his apartment was just as always. There was no television blaring, no one sitting in the living room, no baby on the floor surrounded by toys.

He found that oddly disappointing. He didn't care much for babies, but when he'd walked in earlier and seen Sylvia playing with the child while Holly made up a bottle, he'd had an odd rush of warmth in his chest. He'd dismissed it as something minor; a physical malady like acid reflux.

But now he felt strangely hollow, as if that warmth

would rush back if Holly were here with her son. He strode through the living room and toward the hall where the bedrooms were, his heart pounding. What if she'd left? What if she'd changed her mind and taken her opportunity to leave while he was out?

He'd taken the precaution of informing his driver—and the doorman—to alert him if she did, but no one had called. So why did he feel anxious?

A sound came from the direction of the kitchen, and he stopped, his heart thumping steadily as his ears strained to hear it again. It was late enough that the staff he employed would have gone home for the day, so he didn't expect to find any of them lurking about the kitchen.

He stopped abruptly as his gaze landed on the figure of a woman standing at the counter, her long blond hair caught in a loose ponytail. She was wearing yoga pants and a baggy T-shirt that looked as if it had been washed so frequently the color had faded to a flat red, one shade removed from pink.

She reached up to open the microwave and took out a bowl of something. Then she set a baby bottle inside it. Something about watching her warm the bottle hit him square in the gut. He'd never considered his life to be lacking, never felt as if he were missing out by not having a wife and children. He didn't know how to be close to anyone, not really, and he didn't know how to bridge that gap.

He'd always been on the outside looking in. And it had never bothered him until this moment. It was not a pleasant sensation to feel like an outsider in his own house.

But he did. And it made him feel empty in a way he had not in a very long time.

CHAPTER SEVEN

SOME SIXTH SENSE told Holly she wasn't alone. The skin on the back of her neck prickled and heat gathered in her core. She knew who it was. She didn't have to see him to know. She could feel him. Smell him.

She turned slowly, nonchalantly, her heart pounding in her breast. The sight of him in that tuxedo nearly made her heart stop. He was dark, beautiful, his gray eyes heated and intense as he watched her. He looked…broody, as if he'd had a bad evening. As if something had gone awry.

Was it wrong that her heart soared to think his date might not have worked out?

"You're back early," she said, keeping her voice as even as she could. Hoping he didn't hear the little catch in her throat.

"Perhaps I am not," he said, moving toward her, all hot handsome male. His hands were in his pockets and his jacket was open to reveal the perfect line of studs holding his shirt closed. His bow tie was still tight, as if he were going to an event instead of coming from one. "How would you know which it is?"

Holly turned to check the bottle. Not quite ready yet, so she dropped it back in the water. Then she shrugged. "I wouldn't. I'm just guessing. You don't strike me as the 'home and in bed by ten o'clock' type."

The moment she said it, she wished she could call the

words back. Heat flared in her cheeks, her throat, at the mention of Drago and a bed. Good grief, what was the matter with her?

Drago arched one eyebrow, and she knew he wasn't about to let her get away with that statement without comment.

"Oh, I most definitely am the 'home and in bed' type. Sometimes, I like to skip the evening out and go straight to bed."

Holly deliberately pretended not to understand. "How tragic for you. I would have thought the rich and dynamic CEO of a major corporation dedicated to making people beautiful would like to see and be seen."

"There's a time for everything, *cara mia*," he said, his voice low and sexy and relentless in the way it made vibrations of pleasure move through her body.

She'd spent the past few hours thinking about him. Wondering what he was doing tonight, if he was waltzing under the stars with some beauty, captivating her the way he'd once captivated Holly. He was a mesmerizing man when he set his mind to it. It had depressed her to think of him turning his charm onto another woman.

She told herself the only reason for her feelings was because she was here, in his apartment again, where he'd made love to her and created a baby. Her feelings were only natural in this setting. They would abate as soon as she was gone from this place.

He came closer, until she could smell him. Until her senses were wrapped in Drago di Navarra and the cool, clean, expensive fragrance of him. It wasn't just his cologne, which was subtle as always. It was him. *His* fragrance.

She wanted to turn and press her cheek to his chest, wanted to slide her fingers along the satin of his lapels, and just pretend for a moment that he was hers.

"Yes, and now it's time to feed Nicky," she said, her voice trembling more than she would have liked as she checked the bottle again. It was almost ready, but not quite. She set it back in the water with shaking fingers and then turned to lean against the marble counter. "So tell me all about your evening. Was it fun? Did you see anybody cool?"

He blinked. "Anybody cool?"

"You know. A movie star or something."

He shrugged. "There might have been. I wasn't paying attention."

Holly could only shake her head. Drago was a law unto himself, a man unimpressed with such fickle things as fame. It would take a very great deal to impress him, she imagined.

"Oh, yes, I suppose these things are ever so tedious for you," she said, with more than a little sarcasm. "Dress up in expensive finery, drink champagne, eat fancy hors d'oeuvres and hobnob with celebrities. What a life."

"Actually," he said, "it is tedious sometimes. Especially when the people one is with are shallow and self-absorbed."

Holly wanted to say something about how he was shallow and self-absorbed, but she suddenly couldn't do it. She should, but she couldn't seem to make the words come out. Because, right now, he looked a little lost. A little bleak. She wasn't sure why, but from the moment she'd turned around and seen him there, she'd been thinking of a lost and lonely soul.

Completely incongruous, since Drago di Navarra didn't *have* a soul. She tried to call up her anger with him, but it wouldn't surface.

She shrugged. "There are shallow people everywhere. I could tell you tales about the casino, believe me."

His eyes were hot and sharp. "And then there are people like you."

Her heart sped up. She swallowed the sudden lump in her throat. "What does that mean?"

He came and put his hands on her shoulders, stunning her. A shiver slid down her spine, a long slow lazy glide that left flame in its wake. Her body knew the touch of his. Craved it.

Holly felt frantic. *No, no, no.* It had hurt too much the last time she'd let him touch her. Not during, but after. When he'd sent her away. When she'd known she would never see him again. When he'd shattered her stupid, innocent heart into a million pieces. She hadn't been in love with him—how could she have been in only one night?—but he'd made her feel special, wonderful, beautiful. And she'd mourned because his rejection meant she hadn't been any of those things.

She could not endure those feelings again.

"What do you think it means?" he asked.

Holly sucked in a breath as doubt and confusion ricocheted through her head. "I think it means you're trying to seduce me again."

He laughed, and warmth curled deep inside her. She loved his laugh. He seemed a different man when he laughed. More open and carefree. He was too guarded, too cold otherwise. She could like him when he laughed.

"*Dio*, you amuse me, *cara*. Perhaps I was too hasty last year."

She refused to let those words warm her or vindicate her. "Perhaps you were," she said shakily.

His hands moved up and down her arms. Gently, sensually. She wanted to moan with everything he made her feel. "And yet here we are, with an entire evening to kill."

His voice was heady, deep and dark, and it made her think of tangled limbs and satiny skin. Of pleasure so intense she must have surely exaggerated it in her mind. Nothing could be that good. Could it?

Holly dug her fingernails into her palms, reminding herself there was pain in his proposition. Because it hadn't ended well the last time, and she didn't expect it would end any better now. She could take no risks.

"I'm sorry, but it's too late, Drago. You lost your chance to make me your sex slave. I am slave to only one man now, and he's pint-size and ready for his bottle."

Drago let his hands slide down her arms before he dropped them to his sides. Perversely, it stung her pride that he accepted her pronouncement so easily. As if he hadn't really wanted her after all.

"He's lucky to have a mother so dedicated."

Holly's pulse thumped. She let her gaze drop as a wave of hot shame rolled through her. "I do my best. I could probably do better."

Drago put a finger under her chin and lifted her gaze to his. His eyes bored into hers. "What makes you say this, Holly?"

Tears sprang to life behind her eyes and she closed them briefly, forcing herself to push them down again. She would not cry. She would not show a single moment of vulnerability to this man. She had to protect herself. To do that, she had to be strong. Immovable.

She wasn't so good at that, but she was learning. She had no room for softness anymore. Not for anyone but her son.

"I've worked so much," she said, her voice hoarse. "I haven't always been there for him. I hated leaving him with a babysitter every day. And I hated where we lived, Drago, but it was the best I could do."

He sighed again. "Things could have been far worse, believe me. You did what you had to do."

She didn't like the look in his eyes just then. Bleak. Desolate. As if he knew firsthand what those worse things were.

"I did the best I could. We weren't homeless and we had enough to eat."

A dark look crossed his face, and her heart squeezed in her chest. She almost reached up, almost put her palm on his jaw and caressed it as she'd done once before so long ago. But he took a step backward and put distance between them again.

"And now you are doing better. Working for me will give you a fresh start, Holly. You'll have more options."

She let out a shaky breath. "That's why I'm here."

He was frowning. Holly gripped the counter behind her until her fingers ached from the effort. She suddenly wanted to go to him, slip her arms around his waist. The only thing stopping her was the stone in her hands, anchoring her.

"You should have demanded help from his father," Drago said tightly. "He shouldn't have let you struggle so hard."

A shiver rolled through her then, stained her with the unmistakable brush of guilt. Oh God. "I couldn't," she choked out. "H-he made himself unavailable."

Drago looked suddenly angry. "Is he married, Holly?"

She was too stunned to react. And then, before her brain had quite caught up to her reflexes, she nodded once, quickly. A voice inside her shrieked in outrage. What was she doing? Why was she lying? Why didn't she just tell him the truth?

He would understand. He'd just said he knew she'd done her best. He would help her now, he would be a father to their child—

No. She knew none of those things. He was so intense, so powerful, and she had no idea what he would do if she told him the truth. What if he didn't believe her? What if he threw her out again, before she could earn the first cent? She needed this money too badly to risk it. And she needed to protect her child.

Until she had the contract, that ironclad promise of money, she couldn't risk the truth. She had to protect Nicky. He came first.

Drago's gaze was hard and her heart turned over in her chest. It ached so much she thought she might crumple to the floor in agony.

Your fault, her inner voice said.

"I'm sorry if that disappoints you," she told him, her voice on the edge of breaking. She shouldn't care what he thought, but she found that she did.

His eyebrows rose. "Disappoints me?" He shook his head. "I wasn't thinking that at all, Holly. I was thinking what a bastard this man is for leaving you so vulnerable."

Oh, goodness. He looked fierce, angry, as if he would go to battle for her and Nicky right this moment. It made the guilt inside her that much deeper, that much thicker and harder to shake off. She could endure him better when he was arrogant and bossy. She couldn't endure his empathy.

"I didn't tell him," she blurted, and Drago's expression turned to one of surprise.

She dropped her gaze to the floor. Holy cow, she was digging herself a hole, wasn't she? A giant hole from which she'd never escape.

"Didn't tell him? You mean, this man has no idea he has a son?"

She nodded, her heart pounding. "I tried, b-but he wouldn't listen. He didn't want to know."

Drago looked stunned, as if that thought had never occurred to him, and the quicksand under her feet shifted faster. Blindly, she turned and reached for the bottle. She couldn't stand here another minute. Couldn't sink deeper into the mire of lies and half-truths.

"I have to go feed Nicky."

She started to bolt from the room, but Drago's hand on her elbow caught her up short. "It's not too late to make this man meet his obligations—"

"It is," she said sharply. "It just is."

Drago sat at his desk and thought of Holly's face when she'd told him about the father of her baby the night before. She'd seemed so ashamed, so vulnerable. He'd wanted to pull her into his arms and tell her it was all right. Tell her she didn't need to worry. He'd considered, briefly, finding this man and forcing him to acknowledge his child.

But Holly's reaction told him everything he needed to know. She was scared of this man, whoever he might be. And as much as that angered him, as much as it made him want to find the bastard and thrash him for hurting her, Drago wasn't going to press the issue.

Besides, if this man came forward, there'd be someone else in Holly's life. Someone besides him. He wasn't quite sure why that thought bothered him, but it did. He didn't want to share her with another man.

Drago closed his eyes and pulled in a deep breath. No, it wasn't that he didn't want to share her. What an absurd thought. They'd had a hot night together, a fabulous night, but she had a baby now and he didn't see himself getting involved with a woman who had a baby.

The idea was fraught with pitfalls. Yes, he'd certainly like to have sex with her again. He wanted to take her to his bed and see if it was as good as he remembered.

But he couldn't. She'd shown him a vulnerability last night that had sliced into his chest and wrapped around his heart. She'd been frightened and confused—and worried. He didn't want or need that kind of intimacy. He wanted the physical without the emotional—and Holly Craig wasn't capable of that right now.

Drago ran both hands through his hair and turned to stare out across the city. He loved the city, loved the hustle and bustle, the sense of life that permeated the streets every hour of every day. New York City truly was the city that never slept.

But, right now, he wanted to be somewhere that slept. He wanted to be somewhere quieter, where life was more still. He wanted to take Holly and her infant to Italy.

But if he were going to get her to Italy, he had to get the passports taken care of. Drago opened an email from his secretary, who had informed him of what they would need to expedite the process. He made notes of what was required and went on to the next email.

This one contained sales figures for the quarter. Navarra Cosmetics was doing fabulously, thanks to a new skin-care line aimed at the middle-aged consumer. They had also debuted a new palette of colors for eyes, lips and cheeks that was doing quite well.

The numbers on fragrances were good. But Sky wasn't doing quite as well as he wanted for the new signature fragrance. Other CEOs would be perfectly happy with these numbers. But he wasn't. Because he *knew* they could be better.

Drago sat there a moment longer, thinking. And then he logged off his computer and informed his secretary he was leaving for the day. How could he concentrate when he was eager to revamp the Sky campaign? In order to do that, he needed passports for Holly and her child.

By the time Drago walked into his apartment, nearly half an hour later, he was no closer to understanding this strange pull Holly Craig had on him or why he was taking off in the middle of the day to do something he could have sent any number of assistants to do.

But when he strode into the living room and saw her on the floor with her baby, he got that same strange rush of warmth he'd had the first time. She looked up, her eyes wide and wounded, and his chest felt tight.

"*Ciao,* Holly," he said, dropping his briefcase on a nearby table.

She smiled, but it didn't reach her eyes. "I didn't expect to see you for hours," she said.

He shrugged. "I am the boss. I make my own hours."

She looked at her baby and smiled, only this time it was genuine. He tried not to let that bother him. "It must be nice," she said, her voice a little higher and singsongy as she directed it at the baby.

"Indeed."

The baby gurgled in response, his little lips spreading in a grin. Drago watched as he picked up a fuzzy toy cat and put the ear in his mouth. Drago had been around babies before, in the commune his mother had once dragged them to on some tiny island somewhere he'd tried to forget, but he'd never really had anything to do with them. The older children had been expected to take care of the babies while their parents worked in the vegetable gardens—and got high in the evenings—but Drago's one major act of rebellion, before his mother had left the commune and tried to use him to get money from the Di Navarras again, had been to refuse to help with the babies.

Instead, he'd had to pick vegetables and hoe rows. He suppressed a shudder and folded himself into a nearby chair. Holly's brows rose. And then she turned toward her baby and started to gather him up.

"Why don't I take Nicky and get out of your way—"

"No. Stay." She stiffened, and he sighed. "Please stay. I need to talk to you."

She let the baby go and he threw the cat. Then he picked up a toy banana and started to chew on that.

"I'm all ears," she said brightly, though her eyes were wary.

"Do you have a copy of his birth certificate?"

The color drained from her face. "Why?"

Drago felt there was something he was missing here, but he wasn't quite sure what it could be. "For his passport. We have to take him to the passport office and apply in person, because he is a baby and it's his first."

She dropped her gaze. "All right," she said quietly.

"Is his father named on the certificate?"

Her head snapped up again. There was definitely fear in those pretty blue eyes. A wave of violence washed over him. He wanted, more than anything in that moment, to make her feel safe from the bastard who'd abandoned her and her child.

"If he is, then he must approve of you taking the baby from the country," he explained. "If not, it does not matter."

Holly seemed to wilt as she shook her head. "No, he's not named. He would have had to be there to sign it, and that wasn't going to happen."

Drago smiled to reassure her. "Good. Then you are safe. All will be well."

"Yes, I—I suppose so."

She turned to look at her baby, and his heart pinched. She loved the child so much. What would it have been like to have a mother who'd loved him that way? A mother who did everything for his benefit instead of for her own?

He would never know.

"There's nothing to worry about, Holly," he said. "Everything will be fine."

"Of course," she said. But she didn't sound reassured.

CHAPTER EIGHT

EVERYTHING WAS NOT going to be fine. Holly sat in the limo with Drago, Nicky tucked into his carrier, as they whisked their way through the streets of New York City on the way to the passport office. In her bag, she had Nicky's birth certificate and the forms she'd filled out for their passports.

She could still see the box that had made her heart drop to her toes: parents' names. She'd filled in only her side, because in Louisiana a father had to sign the birth certificate in order to be named. Drago wasn't on Nicky's birth certificate. No one was.

Still, it made her nervous. What if the passport office wanted more information? What if Drago were sitting beside her when they demanded it? How would she answer? How *could* she?

Holly pressed a hand to her stomach and concentrated on breathing in and out. There was still no sign of a contract, and they were on their way to get passports. It could all fall apart here. She could find herself on a plane home in just a few hours.

She would never see Drago again. That thought twisted her belly tighter than before. The scent of her fear was sharp, like cold steel against her tongue. She tried to ignore it, tried to focus on the other scents in the car. Warm leather, soft powdery baby, sensuous man. She closed her eyes and savored that last one as if it would soon be gone.

"What's the matter, Holly?"

She whipped around to look at Drago. His sharp gaze raked her. Belatedly, she smiled, trying to cover her distress. "Nothing at all."

One eyebrow rose in that superior manner of his. "I don't believe you."

She clasped her hands together in her lap. "Believe what you like, but I'm fine."

His frown didn't go away. "Would it help you to know that my lawyers have finished drafting your contract?"

Her heart did a slow thump against her chest. The contract. If only she had that already signed, she wouldn't worry as much. *Wrong.* Of course she would. Because she'd been lying to Drago from the moment he'd walked back into her life.

And, as she knew from bitter experience, he didn't handle deception very well.

"Oh? That's good."

His brows drew down. "You don't sound very enthused. Considering how insistent you've been, I find this rather odd."

Holly swallowed. "I'm very enthused," she said with false brightness. "What do you want from me? A happy dance right here in my seat?"

"Not precisely."

She rolled her eyes, tried to play it off. "I'm happy, Drago. Ecstatic."

He watched her a moment more. "Fine," he said, before dropping his gaze to his tablet once more.

Holly turned to look out the window at the traffic, her heart thrumming. She had to tell him the truth. Not right now, certainly, but soon. It was the right thing to do, no matter how much it terrified her. Once she had the contract, once it made sense to do so, she would have to find a way.

Provided it didn't all fall apart before she got that far.

The car pulled to a stop in front of a building on Hudson Street, and Drago opened the door. When they were standing on the sidewalk, Holly holding Nicky's carrier, she looked over at Drago, who was getting the diaper bag from the limo.

"You can come back and get us," she said. "I'll call when I'm done."

He looked imposing as he straightened to his full height and gazed down at her. He was dressed in a custom suit, navy blue, with a crisp white shirt and no tie. The pale blue diaper bag with the smiling monkey on it looked completely out of place against that elegant backdrop.

And yet he held it as though he could care less that the rich and entitled CEO of one of the most important cosmetics companies in the world might look just a little ridiculous. Or a little too appealing for a tabloid photo.

Holly cast her gaze up and down the street, but nobody with a camera emerged to snap a shot. Thank goodness.

"I'm going with you," Drago said.

"I don't see why," she returned. "I can handle it alone. Or you could send a lackey. Surely you have work to do."

"I have a cell phone and a tablet, Holly. I can work, I assure you."

She tried to swallow down her fear. It tasted like bitter acid. "I won't run away, Drago, if that's what you're worried about."

A preposterous suggestion that he'd be worried about her leaving, but it was the only thing she could think of.

"Holly, for goodness' sake, just turn around and walk into the building. We have an appointment and you're going to make us late."

She glared at him a moment more, her stomach dancing with butterflies—and then she heaved a sigh. "Fine, but don't blame me if it takes six hours and you're bored silly. I told you not to come."

Thankfully, it did not take six hours. But Holly's fear refused to abate while they waited. When they were finally shown into an office and it was time to hand over the paperwork, Holly snatched the diaper bag from Drago and fished out the papers with trembling hands. Then she handed them directly to the clerk.

The clerk was a typical bureaucrat, going over everything in triplicate. At one point, the woman looked up at Drago. He was flipping through files on his tablet and didn't seem to notice, but Holly's heart climbed into her throat as she waited for the woman to say something.

Then the clerk met Holly's gaze for a long moment. Finally, she seemed to give a mental shrug, and the moment was over. A short while later, they were on their way back to Drago's apartment, the passports safely tucked away in Holly's purse.

Holly felt a little shell-shocked over the whole thing. When they arrived at Drago's, she took Nicky and put him down for his nap. Then she climbed into bed and lay there, staring at the ceiling, her stomach still churning with guilt and fear. It wound its way through her belly, her bones, her heart, curling and squeezing until she thought she would choke on it.

She'd overcome another obstacle, gotten one step closer to the goal. Her luck was holding, but for how much longer?

She needed to tell Drago the truth before her luck ran out, but she was caught in an infinite loop of her own making. There was no scenario in which she could envision telling him and it not exploding in her face.

Once she signed the contract, she would tell him. Once she had the guarantee that she'd have money to take care of her baby, she could admit the truth. And then, even if he threw her out again when it was over, it would be fine. Everything would be fine.

But she couldn't quite make herself believe it.

When Holly finally emerged from her room a couple of hours later, it was because she was hungry and couldn't stay hidden any longer. She hoped that Drago would have gone out for the evening, so she didn't have to face him right now, but of course nothing ever went the way she hoped.

He looked up as she tiptoed into the kitchen. Her stomach slid down to the marble floor and stayed there.

"I was just looking for something to eat," she said casually.

"There's Chinese takeout," he said. "It's in the warming drawer."

She couldn't help but look at him in surprise. "You eat Chinese takeout?"

He shrugged. "Doesn't everyone?"

Not billionaires, she thought. She expected they ate lofty meals in the kinds of restaurants he'd taken her to the last time she was in New York. Or meals prepared at home by their personal chefs. Which he did happen to have.

"I figured that would be too, um, basic for you."

He laughed and a trickle of warmth stirred inside her. She loved that laugh more than she should. He was sitting at the expansive kitchen island with papers arrayed around him and an open laptop off to one side. Just a tycoon and his paperwork. Quite a different picture from the one she usually made at her worn Formica table every month, trying to make too little money stretch too far.

Chinese takeout had been a luxury. And Gabi was usually the one who'd bought it, against Holly's protests.

Save your money, Gabi. Don't waste it on me.

It's not a waste. Eat.

The memory of her and Gabi perched on the sofa in

front of the television, eating from containers, made her feel wistful. And lonely.

"Holly, I'm a man like any other," Drago said. "I like lobster and champagne, I like Kobe beef, I like truffles—but I also like Chinese takeout, hotdogs from a cart and gyros sliced fresh at a street fair."

She very much doubted he was like other men. But the idea of him eating a hot dog he'd bought from one of the carts lining the city streets fanned the warmth inside her into a glow.

"Next you'll be telling me you like funnel cakes and deep-fried candy bars."

"Funnel cakes, yes. Candy bars, no."

She pictured him tearing off bites of funnel cake, powdered sugar dusting his lips, and fresh butterflies swirled low in her belly. "Will wonders never cease?"

He grinned and then stood and walked over to the warming drawer. He wore faded jeans and a dark T-shirt, and his feet were bare. It was entirely too intimate and sexy, especially since the sky was dark and the city lights sparkled like diamonds tossed across the horizon.

She didn't know why that made it more intimate, but it did.

Drago pulled open the drawer and took out several containers of food. "There's a variety here. Mu shu pork, sweet-and-sour chicken, Mongolian beef, kung pao shrimp, black-pepper fish, lo mein, fried rice…"

Holly could only gape at him. "Gracious, was there a party tonight and I missed it?"

He shrugged, completely unselfconscious. "I didn't know what you liked, so I ordered several different things."

He set the containers on the counter, and Holly walked over to peer at the contents. Her stomach rumbled. It all looked—and smelled—wonderful. Drago set a plate and some wooden chopsticks on the counter.

"Thank you," she said softly. And then, though it embarrassed her, "But I'll need a fork."

He pulled open a drawer and took out a variety of silverware—forks and spoons so she could dip out the food—and set them down without a word about her inability to use chopsticks. It was a silly thing, but she was ridiculously grateful that he didn't tease her about it.

He walked back to his seat at the island, and Holly started to fill her plate. She thought about retreating to her room with the food, but he'd been so nice to order it all and she didn't want to be rude.

Holly turned and set the plate on the island. But instead of sitting, she stood and dug her fork into the kung pao shrimp. The flavors exploded on her tongue—spice and tang and freshness. Far better than anything she'd ever had from the lone Chinese restaurant in New Hope, where everything was either hidden under too much breading or soaked in sauce.

"I have your contract here," Drago said softly, and her belly clenched. "When you're done, we'll go over it."

She wanted to shove the food away and see it now, but she forced herself to keep chewing. She'd been unable to eat breakfast or lunch and now she was starving. If she didn't eat now, she didn't know if she would be able to. Her nerves swirled and popped like ice dropped on a hot grill. She was so close to having security for her baby. So close.

She put the fork down. "I have to see it now," she said. "I'll never be able to wait."

Drago frowned. "Only if you promise to keep eating," he said, picking up a sheaf of papers from the pile next to him.

"I will."

He came over and stood beside her, and her body was suddenly made of rubber. She wanted to lean into him, into his heat, and rest there while he explained what was in the papers. But she didn't. She forced herself to remain stiff, forced herself to keep forking food into her mouth while Drago pulled up the top sheet and laid it down.

"This is a basic contract," he said. "You'll appear in the ads, if all goes well with the test shots, for the next year. You'll be available for appearances to promote the perfume—industry functions, parties, etc.—and for more shoots as necessary. In exchange, you'll receive five hundred thousand dollars—"

Holly nearly choked on a bite of Mongolian beef. Drago glanced down at her, one brow lifted curiously.

"Sorry," she said a few moments later, after she'd gulped water from her glass and coughed enough to embarrass herself thoroughly.

"If the test shots aren't good," Drago continued while she mentally reeled over the sum he'd just named, "if we decide you aren't right after all, you'll receive a fifty-thousand-dollar severance fee and all your expenses for returning home."

Fifty thousand was still a lot of money. She could do something with fifty thousand. She could find a decent job, afford a better apartment. But half a million? Heavens above.

It was far more than she'd hoped—and yet a part of her was oddly disappointed. This wasn't how she'd envisioned her future. She wanted to work for a top company like Navarra Cosmetics. But she didn't want to stand in front of a camera and be the face of a fragrance. She wanted to *create* the fragrance.

But she had no choice. Since Nicky had come into her life, her desires took a backseat.

"What about my perfume?" she asked.

He flipped a couple of pages and tapped his finger on a line. "It's here. You get a half-hour appointment. Nothing more, and there are no guarantees."

"Do I get the appointment even if you decide not to keep me for the campaign?"

"Yes."

Her heart took up residence in her throat. "All right." She set down her fork and wiped her fingers on her napkin. "Can I read it?"

He pushed the contract toward her. "Take your time. But it needs to be signed tonight, *cara*. We leave for Italy tomorrow."

She'd thought her chest couldn't get any tighter, but she was wrong. "So soon?"

Drago looked so imposing standing there, hands in pockets, watching her. "*Sí*. There is no time to waste."

Holly perched on a bar stool and began to read the contract from beginning to end. There was a lot of legalese, but it was straightforward enough for her to understand. If the test shots went well, she got a lot of money. If they didn't, she still got money. And she got a chance to present her perfume to the head of Navarra Cosmetics, which was all she'd ever wanted in the first place.

When she finished reading, Drago laid a pen down in front of her. She glanced up at him, met his gaze. He seemed...very self-satisfied. The heated look on his face sent a sizzle of sensation straight to her core.

Her body softened, her insides melting as if she'd drunk a glass of wine. She felt fluid, languid. And intensely in need of his touch.

Holly picked up the pen, concentrated on the warm, smooth feel of the expensive barrel in her fingers. Anything that would take her attention from Drago. Anything that would make her heart stop tripping along as though it was running a marathon. Finally, she took a deep breath and pushed the pen across the signature line. Then she laid it on the table.

"*Grazie, cara,*" Drago said, reaching for the documents.

He shoved them into an envelope and then made a quick call to someone. A moment later, a man appeared in the doorway to the kitchen. Holly blinked as Drago handed him the envelope.

"You had someone waiting?" she asked when the man was gone.

"It is a courier, and yes, he was waiting to take these back to my attorney."

"But I was in my room," she said inanely.

"This I know," he replied. "But he only just arrived before you came out. I was coming to get you in five more minutes."

"Oh."

He was still looking at her, his gaze somehow both hot and assessing at the same time. "Feel better?" he asked.

Holly swallowed. Her mouth was dry. "Truthfully, I'm not sure. I'm not a model," she added, as if he didn't know.

His eyes sparkled with humor as he went back to his seat. "What is a model, except someone who advertises a product? You are not a professional, no. But you will learn."

"I don't want to be a model," she told him truthfully. "I want to make perfume."

She wondered if he was irritated with her for mentioning it, because he picked up his pen and tapped it on the island. "Ah, yes. And I have promised to let you present your fragrances to me. It seems to me as if you are gaining your chance in exchange for your participation."

Her heart thumped and her skin tingled with a different kind of excitement. "You won't be sorry," she said. "I know you won't."

She wasn't arrogant, but she knew her fragrances were good. And she wanted him to know it, too. She was confident in her ability, even if sometimes she felt like a total failure on the business side of things.

And a total failure elsewhere, as well. A cloud of doubt and fear drifted through her happiness, and she shivered. He was the father of her child and he did not know it. And she didn't know how to tell him. If not for that, everything would be perfect.

The thought made her want to giggle hysterically.

"What is wrong, Holly?" Drago asked, and she realized that something of her mood must show on her face.

"It's nothing," she told him carefully. "Nerves. Just a few days ago, I was taking drink orders. Now I'm here, in New York City again. With you. I keep waiting for the bottom to fall out."

He reached across the island and touched her hand. A shockingly strong current of heat flashed through her. Skin on skin. It was heavenly. Her entire body concentrated its attention on the limited surface area where they touched. It wasn't enough, and it was too much.

When he traced his thumb over her knuckles, she thought she would moan. She bit her lip to keep it from happening. *It's just skin*, she told herself. But it was his skin, his hand.

"You worry too much, *cara mia*," he said, his voice a sensual rumble deep in her core. "We're tied to each other now. For the foreseeable future."

He was talking about the contract and the Sky campaign. Though, for a single dangerous moment, she envisioned a different kind of bond. A bond between two people who wanted to be together. Two people who shared a child.

Holly licked her lips nervously. Her chest rose and fell as her breath came in short bursts. She wanted to run. She wanted to shove back from the island and flee before she fell any deeper into the morass. Before the truth came out and everything fell apart again.

Her life had been on the brink of disaster since Gran had died. She was accustomed to it. She was not accustomed to having hope. It terrified her. She tugged her hand away and tucked it into her lap.

Storm clouds fought a battle in Drago's expression. He looked frustrated and confused, and then he looked angry, his eyes hardening by degrees. Finally he sat back again. Incongruously, she wanted to reach out to him, beg him to touch her again.

"You have no reason to be scared of me," Drago said, shoving his chair back and standing. "I'm not a monster."

She tilted her head up to meet his hard gaze. But it stunned her to realize there was something more in his eyes. He looked…lost, alone. Her breath razored into her lungs.

"I don't think you're a monster," she said softly.

"I'm not sure I believe you."

Impulsively, she put her hand on his arm. His skin was warm beneath his sleeve, the muscle solid. His eyes were hooded as he stared at her, and a wave of fire sizzled through her body, obliterating everything in its path except this feeling between them.

This hot, achy feeling that made her body sing.

She dropped her hand away, suddenly uncertain. Why did she want to tempt fate again? Why did she want to take the risk and immolate herself in his flame?

Drago tilted her chin up when she would have looked away. "I don't understand you, Holly Craig. You are hot and cold, fierce and frightened. One minute I think you want…" He shook his head. "But then you don't. And I'll be damned if I can figure it out."

She tried to drop her chin, but he wouldn't let her. He forced her to meet his gaze. It was unflinching, penetrating. She trembled inside, as if he were reaching deep inside her soul and ferreting out all her secrets.

Except, he wasn't. He couldn't know what she kept hidden.

"It didn't end so well the last time," she told him. "Maybe that's what scares me."

He blew out a breath and closed his eyes for a long moment. "I make no apologies for what happened, Holly. You lied to me."

"I know. And I'm sorry for it. But I already told you why."

"Yes, you did." He sank onto the stool beside her and rubbed his palms along his jeans. "I don't like being lied to. And I don't like being used."

She wondered if he could see her pulse throbbing in her throat. Her palms were damp, but she didn't dare to wipe them dry while he watched her.

"I understand," she said.

"I don't think you do," he replied. He picked up a glass of some kind of liquor that had been sitting beside his paperwork and took a drink. She watched the slide of his throat, wondered how on earth such a thing could make her gut clench with desire.

"I've always been a Navarra, but I haven't always lived as one," he said quietly, after a long moment of silence.

Holly wrapped her arms around herself, her gut aching with the loneliness of his words.

"My parents were not married. My father was a playboy, a wastrel. My mother was easily corrupted, I think. When he wouldn't marry her, she might have had a bit of a breakdown." He shrugged, and she wondered what he did not say. "They were together for a couple of years, at least. I was a baby when he left her. He died in a car accident not too long after that. And that's when my mother started trying to use me to get things from his family. She spent years trotting me out in front of my uncle, demanding money and then spending it all foolishly."

"Babies need a lot of things," she said. "Maybe she didn't have enough, and…"

The fire in his eyes made her words die. She swallowed, her soul hurting so much for him. And for the woman who'd tried to raise him alone.

"She had enough, Holly. But not enough for her to get what she wanted."

"What did she want?"

His throat worked. "I wish to hell I knew." He threaded a hand through his hair, dropped it to his side again. "My uncle offered to take me in, but she refused to give me up."

Holly's stomach tightened. "I understand that. I wouldn't give Nicky up, either."

Drago leaned toward her. His expression was filled with pain and confusion. "She refused because she knew what she had. I was the golden goose, and periodically I brought her a golden egg. Eventually, my uncle offered her enough to let me go."

Holly's heart thudded painfully for him. But she understood why a mother wouldn't give up her child. Why she tried and tried to make it work before she finally gave in. What must Drago's mother have felt when she'd realized she couldn't keep him? That he would be better off with the Di Navarras than with her?

And why wouldn't Drago's uncle take them both? Why didn't he provide them with a home instead of an unthinkable option for a mother?

"I'm so sorry, Drago." What else could she say?

His features were bleak, ravaged. She wanted to put her arms around him and hold him tight. But she didn't. She didn't know if he would welcome it. If she could be strong enough to do it without confessing her own sins.

Oh, God, how could she ever tell him about Nicky now? He would *never* comprehend why she'd kept it a secret.

"I don't like to be used, Holly. I don't like the way it makes me feel."

"I understand," she said, her throat aching, her eyes stinging with tears. "And I'm sorry."

For so many things.

He sighed again. And then he shook his head as if realizing how much he'd said. "You should finish your dinner."

She looked at the food congealing on the plate. There was no way she could eat another bite. "I'm finished."

He stood again, shoved his hands into his pockets. He looked more lost than she would have ever thought possible.

"Do you see your mother much now?" she asked tentatively, imagining him as a little boy who must have felt so alone and confused when his mother had finally given in to his uncle's demands.

His eyes glittered as he turned to look at her. "I have not seen her since I was eleven and my uncle finally convinced her to sign over custody. And I never will again. She committed suicide six years ago."

Holly's heart hurt. "I'm sorry."

He shrugged with a lightness he could not possibly feel. "This is life."

"But…your mother," she said, her throat aching.

He reached out and slid his finger over her cheek, softly, lightly. "I believe you are a good mother, Holly Craig. But not all women are as dedicated as you."

His words pierced her in ways he would never know. What kind of mother kept a son from his father? What kind of mother struggled to raise him, to provide for him, when he could be the heir to all of this wealth? When he could have everything?

"Drago, I—" But she couldn't say it. Her throat closed up and nothing would come out.

He smiled, but it was not a real smile. It didn't reach his eyes. "Go to bed, Holly. Tomorrow will be a long day."

Like a coward, she fled.

CHAPTER NINE

HOLLY DIDN'T SLEEP very well. She kept waking up for myriad reasons. First, she couldn't stop thinking about Drago telling her, his eyes stark and lonely, that his mother had given him to his uncle and that he'd never seen her again. Then she kept worrying about Nicky, wondering if he was safe in his crib or if he was awake and crying and feeling alone.

She knew he wasn't crying, because she had a baby monitor. But every time she'd drift off to sleep, she'd hear him crying. Lost little boy. Lonely little boy. So she'd pop awake to silence—or as silent as the city could be with the cars rolling by far below, the honk of horns and squealing of brakes reaching high into the sky and finding her ears even in this protected environment.

She thought about Drago and Nicky and wondered how she would ever—or could ever—broach that topic. And she thought about getting on a plane and flying across a vast ocean to a place she'd never been. A place where she knew no one. Where she would be as lost as if she'd been plunked down on another planet.

Finally, Holly gave up and got out of bed. She showered and dressed in her best pair of jeans and a silky top with a cardigan she could put over it if she got chilled. She looked at herself in the mirror and felt woefully inadequate in her simple clothes.

Unsophisticated. Plain.

She leaned closer to the mirror, peering into it, trying to figure out what it was about her face that Drago wanted for his perfume. Freckles? She had a few of those, but she thought of them as imperfections rather than characteristics.

Her nose was small and straight, her cheekbones were on the plump side these days, and her mouth wasn't exactly a supermodel mouth. Her lips weren't luscious. They were average. Two pink lines that formed a pretty pout if she pursed her lips.

Her eyes were blue, but not spectacular. They weren't cornflowers or sapphires or any of those other things. They were just blue. Maybe sky-blue. Maybe just plain blue.

Holly brushed her hair into a ponytail and went to check on Nicky. He was awake, looking up at the mobile above him and kicking his little legs. Holly took him out of his crib and went into the kitchen to fix his bottle.

Drago looked up as she entered. He was sitting at the tall table facing the view, drinking coffee and reading the newspaper. Her heart flipped at the sight of him. She was getting a little tired of reacting so strongly to him, but she knew it wasn't going away. It had been there from the first moment, and would likely always be there.

"*Buongiorno, cara,*" he said.

"Good morning," she replied. Nicky pumped his arms and made a loud noise, and she laughed, unable to help herself. When she looked at Drago, he was smiling, though he looked tired. Perhaps he'd had trouble sleeping, too.

"He is rather, uh, energetic, yes?"

Holly nodded. "Oh, yes. He keeps me on my toes."

She rummaged in the refrigerator for the formula she'd mixed in the wee hours. Nicky hadn't drunk it all, so she'd put it away. Now she needed to heat it up. Which was hard to do with a squirming baby in her arms. She tried to shift him around, but he kept wiggling.

"Let me," Drago said, coming over and holding out his hands.

Holly's heart skipped several beats as she gazed up at him. Then she handed over his son. It felt as if someone had wrenched her child from her arms, so much did it hurt to give him to Drago at this very moment.

A ridiculous notion, but there it was. And then it was gone as Drago stood there with Nicky in his arms, looking suddenly uncertain. He held the baby out from his body with both hands, and Nicky kicked his legs back and forth.

"You won't break him," Holly said. "Cradle him to your chest and be sure to support his head."

Drago dragged his gaze from the baby to her. "That's it?"

Holly nodded. "That's it."

Drago did as she said, and she turned back to the counter, getting a bowl and filling it with water. She popped it into the microwave to heat and turned back to where Drago stood, looking down at Nicky warily.

She would have laughed if her heart hadn't been breaking.

"He's so small," Drago said.

"But getting bigger every day."

Nicky started to fuss and Drago shot her a panicked look.

"Bounce up and down a little bit," she said. Drago looked doubtful, but then he started to do as she said, and Nicky quieted. Holly bit her lip to keep from smiling at the sight of strong, handsome Drago di Navarra—playboy, billionaire cosmetics king—bouncing awkwardly with a baby in his arms.

But then her smile faded when she considered that Nicky was *his* baby and she still needed to tell him so.

After last night, after she'd understood how lonely his life had been, it felt terribly wrong not to tell him he had a son.

But the moment had to be right. And it wasn't now.

She turned to the microwave and took the water out, setting the bottle inside and then reaching for her baby. Drago seemed relieved as he turned him over. Holly bounced Nicky and said nonsensical things to him while Drago went back to his coffee and paper. But rather than pick up the paper, he watched her. She met his gaze, saw the confusion and heat in his beautiful gray eyes.

"You make me want the strangest things, Holly Craig," he said softly, and a hot feeling bloomed in her belly, her core.

"It's probably just indigestion," she said flippantly, and he laughed. But her heart thrummed and her blood beat and a fine sheen of sweat broke out on her upper lip and between her breasts.

What she really wanted to know was what kind of things. That was the question she wanted to ask, but was too scared to. *Coward.*

Yes, she was a coward, at least where Drago was concerned. Because there was something about him, something she desperately desired. And if she angered him, if he sent her away, then she wouldn't get that thing, would she? It wasn't just sex, though it was that, too.

It was...*something*.

He folded the paper and sat back to sip his coffee with one arm folded over his body. He wore faded jeans and a dark button-down shirt, and his muscles bulged and flexed as he moved his arm. Her knees felt weak.

"Yes, perhaps you are right," he said. "Perhaps I just haven't had enough coffee yet." He glanced at his watch and frowned. "We need to leave for the airport in an hour. Will you be ready?"

Her stomach spun. "Yes."

"Good." He stood then. "I have some paperwork to attend to first. I'll let you know when it's time."

He left her in the kitchen alone, and she fed Nicky while looking out over the early-morning mist wreathing Central Park. She grabbed a cup of coffee and a bagel from the bag of fresh ones sitting on the counter.

Soon, they were in the car and on their way to JFK airport. Traffic was insane in New York and they spent a lot of time sitting still. Drago worked on his laptop, and Holly gazed out the window while Nicky slept.

She must have dozed, because suddenly Drago was shaking her awake and she was clawing back the fog in her brain while trying to process what he was saying.

"Passports," she finally heard him say. "I need your passports."

She fished in her bag and dug them out. Drago took them from her and then she leaned back and closed her eyes again. It was several minutes before the uneasy feeling in her belly finally grabbed her brain and shook hard enough to drag her into alertness.

But it was already too late. She sat up ramrod straight to find Drago looking at her, his gaze as hard as diamonds, his face some combination of both disgust and rage.

She'd had every chance in the world, and she'd blown it. Drago wasn't stupid. He would have realized by now she hadn't told him the truth. And he would never believe she hadn't meant to deceive him.

He held a blue passport in his hand, opened to the first page. He turned it toward her. She didn't need to look at it to know what it said.

"Tell me, Holly, precisely how old your child is again. And then I want you to tell me once more about this married man you had an affair with."

* * *

Drago felt as if someone had put a vise around his neck and started twisting. He couldn't breathe properly and he had to concentrate very, very hard on dragging each breath in and then letting it out again. It was the only thing keeping him from raging at her and demanding a definitive answer right this instant.

He held the passport in a cold grip and watched the play of emotions across her face. Her eyes were wide, the whites showing big and bright, and her skin was flushed. Her mouth was open, but there was no sound coming out.

Then she went deadly pale as all that heat drained away. He kept waiting for her to explain. To tell him why her baby was three months old and not two. Not that it meant anything that the child was three months old. It didn't make the boy his. He kept telling himself that.

Drago hadn't noticed the baby's real age at first. Hadn't realized the implications. She'd been soft and sleepy and he hadn't wanted to wake her, but he'd needed the passports for when they went through the checkpoint to reach the private jets. She'd handed them to him and gone back to her nap, and he'd flipped them open, studying the details as the car crawled closer to the guard stand. He was a detail-oriented man.

Holly was twenty-four, which he already knew, and she'd been born in Baton Rouge. Nicholas Adrian Craig had been born in New Orleans a little over three months ago.

That detail had meant nothing to him at first. Nothing until he started to think about how long ago it had been that he'd first met Holly when she'd come to New York. It was a year ago, he remembered that, because he remembered quite well when he'd had to scrap all the photos from the false shoot and start over. The numbers were imprinted on his brain.

Even then, he'd had a moment's pause while he'd pictured pretty, virginal Holly rushing home to Louisiana and falling into bed with another man. He didn't like the way that thought had made him feel.

But then, as he'd pondered it, as he'd watched her sleep and let his gaze slide over to the sleeping baby in his car seat—the baby with a head of black hair and impossibly long eyelashes—another thought had taken hold.

And when it did, Drago felt as if someone had punched him in the gut. He'd struggled to breathe for the longest moment.

There was no way. No way this child could be his. Black hair and long lashes meant nothing. He'd used protection. He always used protection.

But there'd been that one time when the condom had torn as he was removing it, and he started to wonder if it had perhaps torn earlier.

And as that thought spiraled and twisted in his brain, doubt ignited in his soul. If it were true, how could she do such a thing? How could anyone do such a thing?

But he did not know that she had, he reminded himself. He did not know.

"Whose child is he, Holly?" Drago demanded, his voice as icy cold and detached as he could make it. Because, if he did not, it would boil over with rage and hurt.

She'd lied to him. And she'd used him, used the opportunity to get what she wanted from him. He thought of the contract she'd insisted on, the money he'd agreed to pay her, and his blood ran cold.

Her gaze dropped and a sob broke from her. She crammed her fist against her mouth and breathed deeply, quickly. And then, far quicker than he'd have thought possible, she faced him. Her cheeks and nose were red, and her eyes were rimmed with moisture.

"I tried to tell you," she said, and his world cracked

open as she admitted the truth. Pain rushed in, filling all the dark and lonely corners of his soul. The walls he'd put up, the giant barriers to hurt and feeling—they tumbled down like bricks made of glass. They shattered at his feet, sliced deep into his soul.

"What does that mean?" he snapped, still hoping she would tell him it was a mistake, that this child was not his and she hadn't kept that fact hidden from him for the past three months. For nine long months before that.

But he already knew she wouldn't. He knew the answer as certainly as he knew his own name. This child was a Di Navarra, and Drago had done exactly as his father had done—he'd fathered a child and abandoned it to a mother who thought nothing of living in squalor and leaving her baby with strangers.

He wanted to reach out and shake her, but he forced himself to remain still.

"It means," she said, her voice soft and thready, "that I wrote you a letter. That I called. That you turned me away and refused all contact."

He was still reeling from her admission.

"And I will wager you didn't try hard enough," he growled. "I never got a letter."

It staggered him to think she'd spent all those months carrying his child, and he hadn't even known it. He hadn't specifically refused contact with her, but he had a long-standing policy of not accepting phone calls from people—especially women—not on his approved list of business associates. As for the letter, who knew if she'd even sent one?

"Well, I sent it. It's not my fault if you didn't get it."

His vision was black with rage. "How convenient for you," he ground out. "You say you sent a letter, but what proof do I have? You could be lying. And you could have done more, if you'd really wanted to."

"Why would I lie about this? I was alone! I needed help! And not only that, but what else would you have had me do?" she snapped tearfully. "Fly to New York with my non-existent credit cards and prostrate myself across the floor in front of your office? I tried to get in touch with you, but it was like trying to call the president of the United States. They don't just let anyone in—and no one was letting me in to you!"

The moment she finished, her voice rising until it crackled with anger, the baby started to cry. Drago looked at the child—Nicky, Nicholas Adrian—and felt a rush of confusion like he hadn't known since he was a boy, when his mother would come into his bedroom and tell him they were leaving whatever place he'd finally gotten settled into.

He didn't like that feeling. If they were still in the apartment, he would have stalked out and gone for a run in the park. Anything to put some distance between him and this lying, treacherous woman. But he was stuck in this car and his head was beginning to pound.

Holly bent over and started trying to soothe the baby, ignoring him as she did so. She talked in a high voice, offered the child a pacifier and made shushing noises. A tear slipped down her cheek, and then another, and her voice grew more frantic.

"Holly."

She looked up at him, her eyes so full of misery. He felt a rush of something akin to sympathy, but he shoved it down deep. Locked it in chains. How could he feel sympathy for her when she'd lied to him? When she'd used him?

He hated her. And he would *not* let her get away with keeping his child from him. Not any longer.

"Calm down," he ordered tightly. "He senses your distress."

"I know that," she snapped. She turned back to the baby—his son—and began to unbuckle the straps holding him in the seat. Then she pulled him out and cradled him against her, rocking and shushing until his tears lessened. Finally, he took a pacifier and Holly seemed to wilt in relief.

"You've been in my house for nearly a week now," Drago said, his voice so icy it made him cold. "And you've kept the truth from me. You had every chance to tell me, Holly. Every chance. Just like before."

She didn't look at him, and he wanted to shake her until she did. The violence whipping through his body frightened him, though he knew he would never give in to it.

But he'd never been this shocked, this betrayed, before. His mother had sold him in the end, sold him for money and freedom to do as she liked, and even the pain of that didn't quite compare to this.

He had a child, a baby, and the only reason he knew it was because he could do math. If he hadn't figured it out, would she have ever told him? Or would she have done the job, taken the money and disappeared with his child?

Until she'd spent it all and needed more....

Drago shook himself. "You have nothing to say to me?" he demanded. "You would sit there after what you've done and refuse to explain yourself?"

Her head came up then. Her eyes were red-rimmed. "I didn't know how to tell you. I thought you might throw me out again."

He reeled. She was unbelievable. A user. A schemer. First it was perfume; now it was a child.

He despised her.

"I might still," he growled. He wouldn't be as tender as his uncle had been. He knew what could happen when you let a woman keep a child she couldn't take care of properly, and he would never allow that to happen to his own son. He would use the might and money at his disposal to make sure she never saw this boy again.

Her eyes widened with fear. God help him, he relished it. He wanted her to wonder, wanted her to suffer as he was suffering.

"You would do that to your own son?" she asked, her voice wavering.

The violence in his soul whipped to a frenzy. "Not to him, Holly. To *you*."

Fear was an icy finger sliding down her spine. It sank into her body, wrapped around her heart and squeezed the breath from her. Drago sat beside her, his handsome face far colder than she'd ever seen it before.

He hated her. She could see it clearly, and her heart hurt with the knowledge that any sort of closeness they might have been building was lost. Crushed beneath the weight of this new reality.

She was frozen in place, frightened with the knowledge that he could kick her out of his life and keep her son. That he would even try.

And then, like the sun's rays sliding from behind the clouds to melt an ice-encrusted landscape, the first fingers of flame licked to life inside her belly. They were weak at first, vulnerable to being crushed out of existence.

But Nicky stretched and reached up to curl his fingers into the edge of her cardigan, and a wave of pure love flooded her with strength.

She met Drago's cold stare with a determined look of her own. Her heart was a fragile thing in her chest, but she didn't intend to let him know it. "You will not separate me from my son. Not ever."

"You forget who has the power here, *cara*," he said tightly.

"And you forget who Nicky's legal parent is," she threw back at him.

His jaw was a block of granite. "There are ways of remedying that," he said, and her stomach dropped through the floor.

"No," she choked out. "No. There's nothing you can do to change it."

She would fight him with every ounce of strength she had left in her body to prevent it. He would never take Nicky away. Never.

He was not the same man she'd spent the past few days with. This man was infinitely darker, more frightening. "Everyone has a price, Holly. Even you."

She hugged her baby's little body to her. "You're wrong, Drago. I'm sorry if you had a bad childhood, and I'm sorry you think your mother traded you for money. But I love my son and I'm not giving him up. You don't have enough money to even make me think about it, much less ever do it."

His eyes glittered and she shivered. "We'll see about that, *cara*."

He didn't say another word to her for the rest of the car trip. Instead, he got on the phone and started talking in rapid Italian. He made two or three calls before they reached the jet parked on the tarmac, and Holly's nerves were scraped raw by that time.

She wondered who he was talking to, what he was saying and what he planned to do. Was he talking to his lawyers? To someone who would bar her from the plane while he took Nicky and jetted off for Europe?

She held her baby tighter. She would never let him take this child from her. She wouldn't let anyone bar her from the plane and she would never accept money in exchange for Nicky.

There simply wasn't enough money in the world to make it worth her while.

When they reached the jet, Drago told her to hand Nicky over to Sylvia, who stood at the bottom of the stairs, smiling warmly. Holly cradled her baby close and refused, her heart hammering in spite of Sylvia's friendly greeting.

"You could fall on the steps," he said sharply, and her stomach banged with fear.

"I won't fall," she said. And then she started up the steps, one arm around her son, the other holding the metal railing until she was at the top and walking onto the plane. Drago was right behind her, so close she could smell his scent over the lingering aroma of jet fuel and the new smell of the plane's interior.

She could also smell the sharp scent of his anger, steely and cold. His body, however, was hot at her back, and she stepped away quickly, emerging into a spacious cabin.

The plane was much larger than the jet they'd flown on just a few days ago. This one was also incredibly luxurious. The interior gleamed with white leather, dark shiny wood finishes and chrome. There was a bar at one end, a couch with a television, and several other plush chairs.

"There are two bedrooms," Drago informed her. "And several bathrooms."

In the end, it turned out that one of the bathrooms was bigger than her entire bedroom had been in New Orleans. She knew Drago was wealthy—he was the head of a multinational corporation and heir to a cosmetics fortune— but she'd never quite realized the impact of all that money until this very moment, when she feared it was about to be arrayed against her. Yes, she'd signed a contract for half a million dollars, but she now realized how very tiny a drop in the ocean of wealth that was to a man like Drago di Navarra.

And it worried her. What if he did try to take Nicky away? She flinched as the door to the Jetway closed with a solid thump. Panic bloomed. She wanted off this plane. She wanted to take her baby—who she'd finally handed over to Sylvia now that they were firmly inside—and run down the stairs and into the terminal. Away from Drago. Away from the vessel that was about to take her across an ocean and put her somewhere she knew no one.

And had no power. Holly swallowed hard. She turned to go after Sylvia, to find her baby and at least be with him for the duration of the trip, since escape was now impossible.

But Drago was there, tall and commanding and so very distant as he gazed down at her, his handsome features set with disdain. An aching sadness unfolded itself within her as she thought back to last night and the Chinese food. She'd almost felt close to him then.

Almost.

"You will need to sit and buckle up," Drago said. "We'll be off the ground in a few minutes."

"I want to be with Nicky."

"Sylvia is taking care of him. That is what she is paid to do."

Holly tossed her ponytail over her shoulder. She could not let him see that he intimidated her, no matter how much he did. "My idea of how to raise a child isn't paying people to take care of him. Nicky needs me."

His eyes narrowed and she had a sudden, visceral feeling that she'd crossed a line somewhere.

"He will have only the best from now on, Holly. Sylvia is the best."

"And I am his mother," she said, her heart stinging with pain. She'd given Nicky everything she had, but of course it wasn't the best money could buy. She tilted her chin up. She had to be brave, assertive. "There's more to taking care of a child than money. He needs love and attention, and I give him that."

"Ah, yes," he said. "Such as when you dropped him with your neighbor and went to work in a casino. I'm sure he had plenty of love and attention then."

She felt as if he'd hit her. "I did the best I could," she

told him. "It wasn't as if you were there to help. And you weren't going to *be* there because I couldn't get in touch with you. You made it very clear that I was never to do so."

He shot up out of his seat and she took a step back instinctively. "To sell me perfume," he thundered. "You were never to contact me about your damn perfume!"

Her breath razored in and out of her lungs. "And how was I supposed to make sure you knew the difference if you'd already ordered your secretary to deny my calls?" she yelled back. "Was I supposed to send you mental signals and hope that did the trick?" She picked up a pretend phone and held it to her ear. "Oh, look," she mimicked, "it's Holly Craig calling. But this time it's *important*!"

His teeth ground together and anger clouded his features. Out of the corner of her eye, she saw a flight attendant moving carefully around them. That was when she realized they were making a spectacle.

She turned and flung herself down in a plush club chair and buckled her seat belt. Her cheeks sizzled with heat and her nerves snapped with tension. Her fingers trembled as she gripped the arms of the seat.

Drago dropped into a chair beside her, though there were plenty of other empty seats, and buckled himself in. Anger rolled off his body like fallout from a nuclear explosion.

"If you had wanted to tell me," he snarled, "you would have found a way. Instead, you let me believe this baby belonged to another man. A married man who abandoned you and left you to starve in the cold. You lied to me, Holly. And you would have kept on lying if I hadn't figured it out."

"I didn't say it was a married man. You *assumed*—"

"And you agreed!" he shot back. "What else was I to think, the way you acted?" His voice sliced into her. "You were worried about getting caught in your lies."

She whipped around to face him. "Yes, I was worried, Drago! I was worried because you promised me a way out of my situation. And if you learned the truth, and reacted the way you had the last time, I'd be back at square one. Only, this time I had my son to think about. And no way in hell was I letting you hurt *him*."

His eyes narrowed dangerously. She realized then, looking at him, that the roiling surface of his anger went far, far deeper than she'd ever thought. He was civilized—but barely.

"Did you ever consider for one moment, for one damn moment, that I might have a wholly different reaction to the knowledge I'd fathered a child? Especially when I told you about my own circumstances as a boy?"

She swallowed. "Not at first," she said. She'd endured the humiliation of being thrown out of his life before, when she'd done nothing wrong, and she couldn't take that chance with her child. "But I was going to tell you. I wanted the time to be right."

He leaned in toward her, his gray eyes hard and angry. "And why should I believe a word you say?"

Her eyes felt gritty. "No reason," she whispered.

"Precisely." He leaned back again, his body stiff with anger as the jet began to move. "You are going to regret your silence, Holly Craig," he told her. "You are going to regret it very much when I am through with you. This I promise."

CHAPTER TEN

THEY LANDED IN Italy late that night. It was dark and Holly couldn't see anything. She had no idea where they were, though she thought she'd read that the Di Navarras were from Tuscany. She didn't get a chance to ask Drago, because he got into a different car than she did. She was with Sylvia and Nicky, which was a great relief after the tension-filled flight over the Atlantic.

As soon as they'd been airborne, Drago had disappeared. He'd ripped open the seat belt and shot up from his chair like a hunted creature. Then he'd stalked toward the rear of the plane and hadn't returned. When she'd inquired of a flight attendant, she'd learned that Drago had an office. She didn't see him again until right before they landed.

He'd still glared at her with the same fury as he had hours before. His anger had not abated in the least, and that chilled her.

The cars wound their way through the night until they reached a grand estate that seemed to sit on a hill of its own. There were tall pencil pines and arbors of bougainvillea they passed on their way up the drive.

Holly wasn't even certain she'd been taken to the same place as Drago until she got out of the car and saw him gesturing to a man, who eventually bowed and then turned to give quick orders to the line of men and women standing behind him. Suitcases were hefted into many hands, and then they disappeared behind the tall double wooden doors of the villa.

Drago didn't spare her so much as a glance as he entered the house. Holly's heart pinched. And then she sniffed. She told herself that she did *not* miss the way he'd looked at her this morning when he'd told her she made him want things he'd never wanted before. It had been an illusion, nothing more. The sooner she forgot about it—the sooner she armed herself for this new reality—the better.

She was shown to a large corner room filled with antiques, Oriental carpets, gilded mirrors and overstuffed couches and chairs. There was a television in a cabinet, and a huge four-poster bed against one wall.

"I will need a crib," she said to the woman who was explaining how the television worked.

The woman blinked. "There is no need, Signorina Craig," she began in her perfect English. "The child is to stay in the nursery."

For the first time, Holly realized Sylvia was not right behind her, carrying Nicky. She'd been so tired, so lost in her own thoughts, that she hadn't noticed they were no longer with her. Holly's blood beat in her ears as fresh panic shot through her. "The nursery? And where is that?"

The woman, a pretty woman with dark hair coiled on her head, continued to smile. As if she'd been told to always be polite to the guests, no matter how frantic they sounded.

"It is not far," she said.

Ice formed in Holly's veins. "Not far? I'm afraid that's unacceptable."

The woman inclined her head in that slight manner that reeked of studied politeness. "Signore Di Navarra has ordered it, Signorina Craig. I cannot contravene *il padrone's* orders."

Holly didn't even bother to argue. She simply turned on her heel and strode from the room. There was a shocked silence behind her, and then the woman called her name, rushing after her. Holly picked up her pace, roving blindly through the corridors, taking turns that led into dead ends and empty rooms, doubling back on herself and trying again.

She didn't realize she was crying until she stopped in a hallway she'd already been in once before, looking right and left, and heard a sound like a sob. It took her a minute to realize the sound had come from her.

She squeezed her eyes shut, gritted her teeth. She would *not* lose control. She would not. She would find Nicky— or she would find Drago and give him a piece of her mind he wasn't likely to ever forget.

Holly came upon a set of stairs and dashed down them until she found herself in the huge circular entry. The foyer was quiet now, compared to just a few minutes ago, but she stood in the cavernous space until she heard a sound. A footstep, the clink of a glass, something. She moved toward it until it she heard a voice.

And then she burst into a room ringed with tall shelves that were lined with books. It took her a moment to realize the damn man had a library. A light burned softly on a desk, and a man stood behind it, his back to her, talking on a phone.

Drago.

Rage and longing filled her, rushing through her body in twin waves. She didn't understand how she could be so angry and so needy at the same time. How she could want to rage at him and hold him at once. She took a step forward, and Drago turned at the sound, his silvery eyes gleaming with anger when he saw her. He finished the call and set his phone on the desk.

"What do you want, Holly?"

She took another halting step forward, her lungs burning, her chest aching. "How dare you?" she spat. "How *dare* you!"

Drago looked bored. "How dare I what, *cara mia*? You must say what you mean. Or get out until you can."

"Nicky. You've put him in the nursery. Away from me." She could hardly get the words out she was so angry.

A muscle leaped in his jaw. "He is a baby. The nursery is where he belongs."

"He is my son, and I want him with me," she growled.

"He is my son, too, and I want him in the nursery. He is safe there."

Violence rocked through her. "Are you trying to say he's not safe with me?"

"And if I am?"

She couldn't answer that. Not without committing violence. "Why do you even have a nursery? You aren't married, you don't have children—"

The look on his face could have melted steel. "I do now, don't I?"

Holly swallowed. "You know what I mean."

"I do indeed."

She ignored the taunt in his voice. He was doing this deliberately. Trying to prove his mastery over her. His power. He wanted her scared. "How can you have a nursery?"

He came around the desk, too cool for words, and leaned against it. Then he folded his arms over his chest, and the fabric of his dark shirt bulged with muscles. Where had he gotten a physique like that? Clearly, he worked out— but she had no idea when he had the time, since he always seemed to be running his business.

Holly shook her head to clear it. She did *not* need to worry about Drago's muscles. They weren't hers to explore. Nor did she care.

"This estate has been in my family for generations,

cara. There has always been a nursery. It's been in disuse for quite some time, but a phone call fixed that. Did you think my son would have nowhere to stay once we arrived? Did you believe I would not even think to see to his comfort and care? Such a low—and dangerous, I might add—opinion you have of me."

There was menace in his voice. And heat. Oddly, it was the heat that interested her. She studied his face, the hard planes and angles of his perfectly sculpted features, and her pulse thrummed.

She needed to focus, and not just on this man before her. "I want my baby with me. He's not used to being alone."

"He is not alone, Holly. He has a nanny."

"He doesn't need a nanny," she blurted. "He only needs me."

Drago straightened to his full height. She wanted to take a step back, but she held her ground. "He needs more than a mother who struggles to make ends meet." His voice was like a whip. "More than a mother who leaves him with strangers while she works twelve to sixteen hours a day."

Pain exploded in her chest. She sucked in a deep breath and willed herself not to cry. Of course he would hit her where it hurt the most. Of course. "I gave him the best I could, Drago. I will always give him the best I can."

"Yet I can give him more. Better. How can you wish to deny him that?"

"I never said I did. But you will not separate us. Not ever."

His eyes narrowed. "Such conviction. And yet I wonder where this conviction stems from. Have you found your own golden goose, Holly? Will you cling to this child until you've bled as much money from his existence as you can?"

Holly didn't even think before reacting. The distance between them shrank too quickly for her to be aware of what she was doing. The next thing she knew, she was standing right in front of him and Drago was holding her wrist in an iron grip. Her open hand was scant inches from his face.

She jerked in his grasp, but he didn't let her go. Instead, he yanked her closer, until their bodies were pressed together, breast to belly to hip. It was the first time they'd been this close in a year, and the shock ricocheted through her.

Her palms came up to press against his chest—that hard, masculine chest that had filled her dreams for months. Holly forced herself to concentrate on her anger, not on the way it felt to be this close to Drago again—as if she'd come home after years away. As if she'd found water in the desert after going without for so long.

It was an illusion.

"You're a cruel bastard," she spat. "I love my son more than my own life. There is nothing I wouldn't do for him. *Nothing!*"

"Prove it."

She blinked up into his cold, handsome face. "What do you mean?"

"Walk away, Holly. Give him to me, and I will make sure he has the best money can buy for the rest of his life."

A shudder racked her. And then the heat of anger filled her. How dare he try to manipulate her emotions this way?

"I won't," she said. "No matter what you do to me, I won't."

His eyes glittered. One dark eyebrow lifted. "Are you certain?"

Her heart thumped. "Very."

Drago pushed her away and walked back around the desk. Then he sat down and opened a drawer, ignoring her for the moment. Her nerves stretched tight.

Finally he looked up, his handsome face cold and blank.

"There is a party tomorrow night for some industry people. You will attend."

Holly folded her arms across her chest, hugging herself as the wind dropped from her sails. "A party?"

His gaze was sharp, hard. "Yes. You signed a contract. You are the new face of Sky. You will be by my side tomorrow night."

Her throat ached. She couldn't very well refuse, and they both knew it. "Where is my son?"

Drago's look changed to one of supreme boredom. "The nursery is down the hall from your room. To the right. I imagine you went left when you departed, yes?"

She felt like a fool. How did he do that to her? "Yes."

His gaze dropped to his papers. "We are done. Good night."

When she was gone, Drago dropped his head into his hands and sat there at his desk, being very quiet and very still. Quite simply, she turned him upside down. This morning, his world had been right. He'd enjoyed having Holly in his home, oddly enough. He'd looked forward to talking to her. To watching her mother her baby.

His baby.

Drago swallowed. It felt like razor blades going down his throat. His entire day on the plane had been spent working in his office, making calls, viewing reports, talking until his voice gave out. He'd tried to distract himself, but all the while his chest had been tight and his eyes had stung and he'd wanted to go back into the main cabin and wrap his hands around Holly Craig's pretty neck.

And then he'd wanted to strip her naked and take her up against the wall. Bend her over a table. Lay her spread-eagled on the floor.

He hadn't cared how he would have her. He'd just wanted her.

And it angered him. How could he want a woman like her? A woman who'd lied to him, who'd kept his child hidden from him for the sake of a damn contract? She'd had every chance to tell him the truth, starting from the first moment when he'd walked into that hovel of an apartment and ending with the moment he'd discovered the truth for himself.

She hadn't done so, and he didn't believe she'd had any intention to—or at least not until it most benefited her. When she needed more money, when she'd spent everything she had, just like his mother had always done, she'd come with her hand out.

But even if she'd wanted to tell him, even if he gave her the benefit of the doubt, how could he forgive her for the lie for the past year? She said she'd written to him—who the hell wrote letters these days?—and tried to call.

He wasn't easy to get in touch with—but it wasn't impossible. Just last month, a woman he'd met at a party had managed to get a call through to his home number. He was not impossible to find. And Holly Craig had been to his home, unlike most of the women he went out with.

What if he'd never gone to New Orleans? When would she have come to him?

Drago shuddered. His mother hadn't taken him to his uncle for money until he'd been nearly four years old. He could still remember the look on Paolo's face when they'd shown up here at the villa. Shock, anger and confusion. And then Uncle Paolo and his mother had gone into his uncle's office while he was supposed to have played outside.

Instead, he'd stood in the foyer and listened to the raised voices. He'd been too young to know what they were fighting about, but he remembered the tension—and he remembered being scared and feeling as if it was his fault.

He would *never* allow his son to feel that way. As if he

was the source of everyone's problems. As though he was a commodity to be bartered again and again.

Drago shoved back from the desk and stood. One way or the other, he was taking control of his child's life immediately. Holly Craig had stood in his way long enough. No more.

He would own her completely—or he would send her away for good.

Holly was nervous. She stood just inside the house, listening to the sounds of laughter and music and chatter on the terrace outside, and felt as if her heart would pound from her chest. Drago had informed her only this morning that the party was taking place here, at his villa—and all her plans to beg out of the event with a headache or a stomachache or something else had come crashing down around her head.

She'd had no idea how she was supposed to attend a party when all she had were jeans and tennis shoes, but a tall, elegant woman—accompanied by three assistants—had arrived immediately after Drago's announcement with a selection of gowns and shoes and jewelry. Within two hours, Holly had a gown for the event and all the accessories to match—even down to the fine, lacy underwear.

She'd wanted to wear her own undergarments, but the woman—Giovanna—had looked at her in horror when she'd suggested it. When everything arrived that afternoon, Holly had still intended to wear her own things—until she'd taken a good look at the dress and realized the underwear was designed to go with it, and that her own would not be flattering to the cut of the gown at all. Vanity won out over stubbornness, and now she stood there in the shadows in a strapless flowing white gown, sewn with iridescent cream sequins, and felt so very out of her element that it frightened her.

She'd never worn anything so beautiful or expensive in her life. Her senses, already highly tuned, were sharpened tonight. Every scent bombarded her with sensation until she was afraid she'd have a pounding headache before the night was through. After she'd dressed, she'd taken one sniff of the bottle of Sky that Drago had sent up for her and knew she couldn't wear it.

There was nothing wrong with the fragrance, but it wasn't her. Instead, she spritzed on Colette and, head high and heart pounding, left her room and made the descent to the first level. She'd thought Drago would be waiting for her, but there was no one. The party was outside, in the glowing Tuscan evening. The sun was behind the horizon, but the sky was still golden and the landscape below undulated in darkening shadows of green and black.

Holly felt like a spy watching through the windows. And she felt as if she didn't belong. She wanted to go back upstairs to the nursery and curl up on the couch there with Nicky. Holly lifted her head. She was doing this for Nicky. For his future.

"I don't especially like crowds, either," a voice said, and Holly spun around to find a man standing behind her. He hadn't been in the room when she'd walked in. He was tall, handsome—not so handsome as Drago—and he was smiling at her. He held out his hand as he walked up. "I don't believe we've met. I am Santo Lazzari."

Holly held out her hand as butterflies swirled in her belly. Santo Lazzari of House of Lazzari was powerful in his own right. House of Lazzari wasn't a cosmetics firm, though they did sell a selection of designer perfumes in their stores to go along with their clothing and handbags. "Holly Craig. But how did you know…"

"That you weren't Italian?" He laughed. "My dear, Drago has spoken of nothing else since this party began."

His eyes narrowed as he studied her. "You are the new face of Sky."

Holly dropped her gaze as a blush spread over her cheeks. She was going to have to get used to this, even if she felt like an imposter. Even if she felt as if Santo Lazzari was mocking her, picking her apart and finding her lacking.

"I did tell Drago I'm not a model, but he seems to believe I'm what he wants." Her skin heated further as she realized what she'd said. "For the campaign," she added hastily.

Santo laughed. "Yes, Drago is like that." He took a step closer, sniffing the air around her. "Is this the perfume? It smells different from how I remembered."

"Um, well, no," she stammered. "I mean, yes, it's perfume. But it's not Sky."

Santo's gaze sharpened. "A new fragrance? Drago has not mentioned this before."

Beads of moisture rose on Holly's skin. Should she tell this man what she was wearing? Or should she change the subject? But how could she let a chance like this go by, especially when Drago was threatening to take her baby away? Telling Santo Lazzari about Colette could be insurance against the future. Drago was certain not to buy her perfume now, no matter that she had an ironclad appointment to pitch it to him.

"It's my own blend."

Santo's eyebrows lifted. "Is it, now?" His eyes gleamed with sudden interest. He held out his arm to her. "Come, Holly Craig, tell me more about this scent as we enter the party. I want to hear all about it."

Holly hesitated a moment longer. What would Drago think if she entered the party on another man's arm? But then the truth hit her, and it made her ache.

Drago would not care in the least. He despised her now.

No doubt he would think she was searching for another rich victim.

She told herself she did not care what he thought. She told herself it didn't matter, that the tentative closeness she'd thought they were building had been only an illusion. Drago did not care about her. He cared only about punishing her.

Holly smiled and put her arm through Santo's.

Drago stood with some of his best clients, telling them about his plans for Sky, when a collective hush fell over the gathering. Male eyes gleamed with appreciation as they gazed at a point beyond his shoulder. Drago turned to see what new arrival had caught their attention so thoroughly—

And gaped in stunned silence at the vision in white gliding across the terrazzo on the arm of Santo Lazzari. For a moment, he wondered who the woman was—but he knew. He knew it in his bones, his blood. He knew it in his soul.

Holly Craig did not look like the Holly Craig he knew. The Holly Craig he preferred, he realized with a jolt. No, this Holly was sleek and lovely, with her blond hair piled on her head to reveal her elegant neck, and her body-hugging dress shimmering in the torches that were beginning to glow on the perimeter of the terrazzo.

She moved like liquid silk. And she clung to Santo Lazzari in a way that made him see red. Her hand rested easily on Santo's arm and her head was turned to gaze up at Santo as if he was the most wonderful thing she'd ever seen.

Drago wanted to rip her from the other man's grip and claim her as his in front of all these people. So no man would dare to touch her again.

Instead, he tamped down on the urge to fight and strode toward the laughing couple. Holly sobered instantly when she glanced over and saw him, but Santo continued to gaze down at her for a long minute before he looked up to meet Drago's gaze.

"*Grazie, bella mia,*" Santo said as he took Holly's hand and kissed it. "It's been a pleasure talking with you."

"And you," she replied, her voice soft and sweet in a way it never was with him. With everyone else—Nicky, Sylvia, the passport clerk, a flight attendant—but never him. That thought grated on his mind as he took Holly's hand and gripped it tight.

"*Amore,*" he said. "I have been waiting for you to arrive."

She smiled, but he knew it was false. "And here I am."

"Yes, here you are."

He wanted to drag her back inside and lock her in her room, but instead he turned and led her into the gathering. He introduced her to many people as they circulated. He made sure she had wine and food, and he kept her moored at his side. Much of the time, her hand was anchored in his, until he could concentrate only on that small area of skin where they touched. Until his senses were overrun with sensation and desire.

As soon as he could do so without drawing attention, he dragged her through another door and into his office. He closed the door behind them and turned to face her. She stood in the darkness, her dress catching the light from outside and shimmering like white flame. He closed the distance between them, until he stood before her, dominating her space.

Her scent stole to him and he stiffened as he finally realized what had puzzled him for the past hour. "You are not wearing Sky."

"No."

"Why not?"

"Because I'm doing everything else you want of me."

"Everything else is not quite as good as everything," he grated.

She shrugged. "I will wear it the next time."

His blood beat in his ears. "How do you know there will be a next time?"

That made her pause. "I don't."

"What were you talking to Santo about?"

She seemed taken aback. "We talked about many things. You, the campaign, the weather."

His eyes narrowed. "That's all?"

Her chin lifted in the darkness. "Why do you care, Drago? You aren't interested in me as anything more than a face for your campaign, so what does it matter what I talk about with another man?"

"You are the mother of my child."

"Oh, so that's important to you now? I thought I was an obstacle, a situation to be dealt with."

The truth of her words slid beneath his skin. "And I will deal with you, *cara mia*. Whatever you thought before you came here, whatever ideas you might have had, you can forget. Nicky is my son, and my heir, and I will not allow you to withhold him from me or to use him to control me. Are we clear?"

"You're disgusting, do you know that?" She flung the words like poisoned darts. "I'm sorry for whatever hell you might have gone through in your life, but I am not your mother and I won't abandon my son. You can't buy me off, and you can't make me go away. I'll fight you, Drago. I'll fight you to the bitter end, and I won't do it cleanly. If you force me, I'll take to the internet. Then I'll call the media and I'll smear you and Navarra Cosmetics from one end of this planet to the other."

Fury rose to a dull roar inside him—but there was something else, too. Excitement. He recognized it in the way his body quivered, the way his nerve endings twitched and tingled.

Every cell in his being was attuned to her, attuned to her softness, her scent, her heat. He suddenly wanted to touch her. He wanted to thrust inside her body, wanted to feel her cling to him, shape herself around him, gasp and moan and shudder beneath him as he made her come again and again.

He dragged himself back from the brink, back from that irretrievable moment when he would claim her mouth for his own and then not cease until he'd had her body, too.

"Try it," he said. "I have the money to make it go away."

He could employ an entire team to counteract anything she tried online or with the media.

Sure, all it took was a sound bite and the idea that powerful, wealthy Drago di Navarra was being unfair to this poor woman, and he could suffer some bad publicity. But he'd weathered bad publicity before. He wasn't afraid of it.

"Of course you do," she said. "That's how you operate, isn't it? You buy people off. You threaten and yell and order, and people do what you want. Well, not me, Drago. We have a contract, and don't think I won't take you to court if you break it."

He could have laughed if he weren't so angry. She had no idea how powerless she was. How he could tie her up in court until she had nothing left to battle him with. She would win, but she would have nothing once she paid her lawyers.

Suddenly, he was tired of this. He was tired of battling with her—of battling with himself—when what he really wanted was to have her beneath him. There was no reason he could think of to fight this attraction a moment longer.

He reached for her and she gasped. But then he tugged her in close, until their bodies were pressed tightly together, his fingers spread across the skin of her back where the dress dipped down. She was warm, and his fingers tingled as if electricity flowed beneath her skin.

"Your threat is as frightening as a swat from a kitten," he murmured, his gaze focusing on her lips—those lush, pretty lips that had dropped open in surprise.

Her head tilted back, her eyes searching his. The heat of her burned into him. His cock leaped against the confines of his trousers, and he knew she felt it by the widening of her eyes. She did not try to move away, and he experienced a surge of triumph. Her palms on his chest became fistfuls of his shirt. Her eyes filled with sexual heat.

Oh, yes, he'd not read this wrong at all. She wanted him. Desperately.

"I'm not a kitten, Drago," she said, her gaze on his mouth. "I mean what I say."

"Yes," he said, his hands sliding down her back, cupping her bottom and pulling her in closer to the heat and hardness of his body. "I know you do."

She gasped. And then she moved her hips. It was a slight movement, the whisper of an arch, but he knew in that moment that she was lost. As lost and helpless to this pull between them as he was.

"I hate you," she said, the sound halfway to a moan as he held her to him and slid the hardness of his body along the sensitive heart of her.

"Yes," he said. "You hate me, *bella mia*. I can feel it so strongly."

She gasped again. "This is so wrong," she said. "I shouldn't feel like this, not after the things you've said...."

Neither should he. But he lowered his head and slid his mouth along the sweet curve of her jaw anyway. Her fingers flexed convulsively in his shirt.

"Don't think, Holly. Just feel. Feel what we do to each other...."

CHAPTER ELEVEN

A CORNER OF Holly's brain told her she needed to stop this. That she needed to push this man away and let him know, once and for all, that she was not his to command.

But she couldn't do it. Because she was his. She wanted him to command her, at least in this. She wanted to feel his heat and hardness and strength. Wanted to lose herself in him, in the way he made her feel.

He confused her, and excited her. He frightened her, and challenged her. She hated him—and she wanted him. She'd spent the past hour trying to focus on the conversations around her, trying to smile and be the Sky spokesmodel, but all her senses kept coming back to one immutable fact: Drago's hand on hers was driving her insane.

Now she had much more than his hand. His mouth moved along her jaw, slid to her ear. He nibbled the tender flesh of her earlobe, and she could feel the erotic pull all the way to her toes. She'd long since passed the mark where she was ready for him. Her sex felt heavy between her thighs, achy. She was wet and hot. She *needed*.

She slipped her arms around his neck and he rewarded her with a lick of his tongue on the tender flesh behind her ear.

Then he growled something in Italian and his hands went to her waist. He found the zipper at her back and slid it down slowly, until the bodice of her strapless dress gaped. His fingers found the clasp of her bra and then her breasts were free from their confinement.

Holly instinctively covered herself. "There are people outside," she said in a panic. "They will notice we've gone."

"Yes, they will notice. But they won't search for us, *bella mia*. They are well fed, plied with the best wines and dishes I have to offer. They will stay and listen to the musicians, they will eat and drink and talk. They will not follow us."

She felt so wicked standing here in his office, naked from the waist up, and hearing the strains of music and voices coming from the gardens. Drago covered her hands with his, gently pulled them away until her breasts were bare and gooseflesh rose on her skin.

Then his palms found them, shaped them, and her heart shuddered in her chest.

"So lovely," he said. "So tempting."

And then he dropped his head and took one tight nipple in his mouth. Holly thought she would come unglued right then. She clutched his head, cried out with the sweet torture of his lips and tongue and teeth on her breast. She hadn't been touched like this in a year. Not since he'd been the one to show her how beautiful and perfect it could be.

"Drago," she gasped. "I don't know—"

"I do," he said. Then he pressed her breasts together in his hands, moved between them, licking and sucking her nipples while she arched her back and thrust them into his hot mouth. She felt every tug, every pull between her legs, as if her nipples were somehow attached to her sex.

He made her utterly crazy. She shouldn't be doing this, shouldn't be succumbing to the sensual power he had— but she didn't want to stop. It had been too long, and she'd been too lonely.

If he wanted her this way, if he couldn't help himself,

either, then maybe there was a chance for them. A chance they could work out their differences and be good parents to their child for his sake.

"I want to touch you," she cried at the next sweet spike of pleasure.

"Then touch me."

Holly shoved his tuxedo jacket from his shoulders, then tugged his shirt from his waistband. Her hands slipped beneath the fabric until her palms were—finally, finally—on his hot flesh. His skin quivered beneath her touch, and it made her bold.

She found his nipples, pinched them between her thumbs and forefingers while he sucked on hers. He groaned low in his throat. And then he pushed her back, ripped open his tie and shirt, studs scattering across the floor.

His chest was so perfect, so beautiful. He wasn't muscle-bound, like a body builder who didn't know when to quit. But he had a hard physique that made her mouth water. His eyes, when she finally dragged her gaze away from his firm pectorals, sizzled into her.

"Do you want me, Holly?"

She should tell him no. She knew she should, but she couldn't. She nodded mutely.

"Then come to me." He opened his arms and she went into them. When their skin touched, she wanted to moan with the pleasure. Drago's fingers roamed over her flesh, his thumbs gliding over her sensitive nipples again and again. Holly spread her hands on his chest, slid her fingers over the firm planes of muscle.

She looked up, into his eyes, her heart turning over at the heat she saw there. She wanted him to kiss her. It was odd to think he'd had his mouth on her breasts, but had not yet kissed her. She moved restlessly in his arms, stretched up on tiptoes to find his mouth, but he dropped his lips to the side of her neck again.

The fire between them spun up quickly. Drago pushed the dress down her hips until it pooled at her feet. "It will wrinkle," she said.

"I don't care."

She reached for his zipper. It didn't take her a moment to free him from his trousers. She wrapped her hand around his hot, hard flesh, her heart thrumming hard, making her dizzy.

His groan made her want to do things she'd never done before. She dropped to her knees and put her mouth around him, her tongue curling and gliding over his hot flesh.

Drago swore. She glanced up at him, and his eyes were closed tight. His jaw flexed as if he were in pain.

But she knew it wasn't pain—or not the bad kind, anyway.

Still, he didn't let her explore him the way she wanted. Too soon, he dragged her up into his arms and speared his hand into her hair. This time—oh, yes, this time—his mouth came down on hers.

And that was when she knew that nothing in her life would ever be the same again.

Holly's knees buckled when Drago's tongue touched hers. It was a silly reaction, and yet she couldn't control it. She'd forgotten just how drugging his kisses were. How necessary.

He caught her around the waist, and then he lifted her and turned until she was sitting on his desk. The wood was cold on her bare bottom. She was still wearing the lacy thong that went with the dress, but it didn't protect her skin from the coolness.

Not that she wanted to be protected. It was a welcome coolness, since the heat of their bodies threatened to incinerate her.

Drago tugged at her panties until she lifted her bottom and he could yank them off. Then he spread her knees wide and stepped between them. Instinctively, Holly curled her legs around his waist. Together, they fell backward—she heard the crash of many things hitting the floor and realized that Drago had swept them away with his arm as he'd laid her down on the desk. She only hoped there was nothing breakable—

And then she didn't care. Drago's mouth was thorough, demanding. His hard erection rode the seam of her body, gliding against her wetness with the most deliciously pleasurable friction imaginable.

It wasn't enough. She wanted more, wanted him inside her. Her hands kneaded the flesh of his back, skated down his sides, over his hips. She tried to reach between them, tried to guide him into her, but he pulled back with a muttered curse.

"Condom," he said. And then somehow he found one in the desk. He pulled away and rolled it on. She lay on the desk and watched him, feasted her eyes on the sheer beauty of his body. He put his hand over the mound of her sex, and she bit her lip to keep from crying out. Then he slid a finger down, into all that wetness. He hissed, as if she'd burned him—and then he skimmed over her damp skin while she whimpered.

Drago traced her, the plumpness on the outside, the delicate ridges on the inside, and all the while her heart beat a crazy rhythm in her chest. When he touched her most sensitive spot again, she cried out as sensation rocked her.

"You're so ready for me, *cara*," he said. "And it is everything I can do not to take what you offer right this very moment."

Her eyes snapped open. "Take it. Please."

He shook his head, and her heart dropped. Was this some crazy act of revenge? Was he going to deny this heat between them now that they'd come so far? Was he going to send her away before anything happened?

Disappointment tasted bitter. So bitter.

But then he spoke and her heart soared once more. "Not yet. First, I want to make you come." He stroked her again, and she shuddered. "I want you to sob my name, Holly. I want you to beg me for release."

"I'll beg now," she told him, her body on fire. "I have no shame."

And she didn't. Not where he was concerned. The only shame she'd ever felt was when he'd kicked her out. She'd not felt one moment of guilt for what she'd done with him. She might not have always realized that, but it was the truth. There was no shame in these feelings, no shame in this fire between them.

He laughed, a deep sensual purr that reverberated through her. "Patience, *cara*. Some things are worth the wait."

"I've been waiting a year," she said heatedly, and his eyes darkened. But it wasn't an angry darkening. No, instead she sensed he was on the edge of control. He was every bit as eager as she was. He just didn't want to admit it. Or perhaps it was better to say that Drago di Navarra was accustomed to being in control. Taking his time meant he could govern his need. Meant that he was superhuman, not prey to the usual vicissitudes of emotion.

But Holly wanted him to lose control. She didn't know why it was important to her, but if she was committed to doing this with him—and she was—she wanted it to be something he couldn't shape into what he wanted it to be. She wanted it to be as wild and chaotic for him as it was for her.

Holly lifted herself on her elbows and reached for him. His breath hissed in when she closed her hand around him. He was so hot and hard that she wondered how he could stand it.

Because she could barely stand the empty ache in her core. The only way to ease that ache was to fill it with him.

"I'm begging you now, Drago," she said, hardly recognizing the note of desperation in her voice. "I'm begging you."

His eyes darkened again. Then he lowered his head slowly, so slowly, that she thought he would deny her. But then he kissed her, his lips fusing with hers so sweetly and perfectly that she let go of him and wrapped her arms around his neck.

The kiss was hotter than any she'd ever experienced with him. He took her mouth completely, utterly, and she gave herself up to him as if she'd been born to do so. Her legs went around his waist again, locked tight to keep him from leaving her.

But he had no intention of doing so. He found her entrance—and then he slid inside her. Slowly, but surely. Exquisitely. Holly gasped at the fullness of his possession. She hadn't remembered it being this way before, but of course it had been.

She closed her eyes. No, it would have been somewhat more intense simply because she'd been a virgin. She was no longer a virgin, and while she had no experience of sex beyond that single night with Drago, she was more than ready for this moment.

Drago groaned as he seated himself fully inside her. "Look at me, *bella*."

Holly opened her eyes again, met the intensity of his hot stare. The look on his face made her stomach flip. He was so intense, so beautiful. And, for this moment at least, he was hers.

"You excite me, Holly. You make me…"

Whatever he was going to say was lost as he closed his eyes and gripped her hips. His head tilted back, the muscles in his neck cording tight. And then he shifted his hips, withdrawing almost completely before slamming into her again.

Holly licked her lips as sensation bloomed in her core. A moment later, Drago was there, sucking her tongue into his mouth. She wrapped her arms around him and held on tight while he held her hips in two broad hands and pumped into her again and again.

She'd forgotten how amazing it was between them. How incredible. How necessary. The tension in her body wound tighter and tighter—until finally it snapped and flung her out over infinite space.

She fell forever, her body shuddering and trembling as she cried out her pleasure. Her senses were so keen, so sharp. She could smell their passion, a combination of flame and sweat and sex, and she could smell the flowers in the garden, the wine, the food, the mingled perfumes of dozens of people.

But, mostly, she smelled him—sandalwood, pears, moss and man. He was warm and hard and vibrant, and he owned her body in this moment.

When she thought she would never move again, when she was boneless and liquid in his arms, he withdrew from her body. And then he turned her so that she was sprawled over the desk, her bottom in the air, her breasts pressed against the wood.

She spread her arms and gripped either edge of the desk as Drago entered her again. It was different this time, though just as delicious. The pressure was exquisite as he stroked into her. She didn't think she could come again but he slid his hand around her body, found her sweet spot. Holly moaned and bucked against him as the spring began to tighten once more.

Too quickly, she shattered, coming in a hot, hard rush of feeling that left her limp and weak.

Drago rocked into her body again and again—and then

he stiffened. Her name was a broken groan in his throat. A moment later, his lips settled on her shoulder and a shiver went through her. He was still inside her, still hard. She tilted her hips up, and Drago gasped.

"*Dio*, Holly. What you do to me should be illegal."

She couldn't help but laugh, though it didn't sound like her usual laugh. No, this was the laugh of a sensual woman. A satisfied woman. It was low and sexy and sultry. She liked it. "Maybe it is illegal," she said. "Maybe I like it that way."

He withdrew from her body and helped her up, turning her until they were pressed together from breast to hip. Her heart beat hard, dizzily. Drago tilted her chin up with a finger and kissed her thoroughly.

Then he broke the kiss and pressed his forehead to hers. "I'm taking you to bed, Holly. *My* bed. Any complaints?"

She thought about the party in the garden, about her baby tucked away in his room, and about the man standing before her. "Not a single one," she said.

Drago grinned. "This is what I like to hear."

"Obedience?" she asked as she searched for her underwear in the darkened room. But she said it teasingly for once.

He laughed. "In this instance, absolutely." He came over and helped her into her dress, his mouth dropped to her shoulder as he slid her zipper up again. "But I promise to make it worth your while, *amore mia*."

Drago awoke in that early hour before dawn. Something felt different, and it took him a moment of lying there in the darkness and processing everything to realize what it was.

He was happy.

He frowned. But he shouldn't be happy. Not at all.

He should be murderously angry with the woman lying beside him. He had been angry. Violently so. But then he'd lost himself in her body and he hadn't been the same since. He couldn't seem to dredge up the fury he'd felt earlier. All he had now was hurt and sadness and desire. Plenty of desire.

Dio, what they'd done to each other last night. He was worn-out, sated. He couldn't remember the last time he'd felt so utterly drained after sex. Except, perhaps, the last time he'd been with her.

Drago threw the covers back and got out of bed. Quietly, so as not to wake Holly. She lay on her side, curled up, with her buttocks thrust toward him.

He had an urge to lean down and nip her.

Drago resolutely turned away from the woman in his bed and tugged on a pair of jeans he'd thrown over a chair when he'd been changing into his tuxedo. He had no idea when the party had ended or when the last guest had left. He was confident, however, they'd had a good time, regardless of his absence.

He left the room and padded down to the nursery, which was a few doors away on the same corridor. He'd originally planned to put Holly and her baby in another wing of the house—until he'd discovered the truth about the child.

Now the baby was his son and he had no idea what that meant to him other than it meant something important. He stepped into the nursery and walked over to the crib. The boy lay on his back, eyes closed, little chest rising and falling evenly.

Drago stood there and gazed down at the sleeping child while an emotional tornado whirled inside his soul. This was *his* flesh, *his* blood. He could see it now. In the dark hair, in the shape of the mouth, in the impossibly long lashes. This child was stamped with the Di Navarra signature traits like a piece of fine art was signed by the maker.

He felt a rush of feeling in his gut. He wanted to pick the boy up and hold him, but of course he wasn't about to do so. Even if he knew what he was doing, he didn't want to wake the baby when he slept so peacefully.

Drago might not know much about babies, but he knew they didn't sleep on command or at the convenience of others. If this one was asleep now, best to leave him that way. He watched the boy and thought of his own mother. Had she ever stood over him and felt this rush of emotion and protectiveness like he felt right now?

Probably not. What he didn't understand was how she couldn't feel those things. He didn't even know this child, not really, and he already knew he would never allow anyone to harm this baby. Not ever.

His eyes stung with tears. It stunned him, but he wiped them away and stood there a moment longer, clutching the sides of the crib and watching Nicky's little mouth move in his sleep. So beautiful. So perfect.

When he finally turned to leave, he drew up short. Holly stood in the doorway, her long reddish-blond hair hanging in disarray over her shoulders and down her back. She was bare-legged, having slipped into his discarded shirt. She looked so fresh and pretty, so innocent and sensual all at once.

Something twisted in his chest. He wanted to grab her and hold her close, but he didn't act on the urge.

"How is he?" she whispered.

"Asleep."

Holly glided over to his side and gazed down at her son. A smile curved the corners of her mouth and Drago felt a strong desire to kiss her. To own her and own that smile, too.

"He's so sweet," she said softly. "A very good baby." Then she looked up at him, and his heart clenched at the sadness on her face. It surprised him how much she affected him. How much he wanted to protect her and their baby, too.

He'd never felt this kind of possessiveness toward anyone. He knew it was because his feelings for her were all tangled up with the knowledge he'd fathered this child, but he couldn't quite seem to separate them.

He'd told her to walk away earlier. To take his money and walk away.

Now he couldn't imagine letting her go. He didn't *want* to let her go. And that frightened him.

Her brows drew together as she reached up and ran her hand along his jaw. "Don't worry," she said, and he knew that some of what he was feeling must have shown on his face. "You'll be fine with him. He will love you to pieces."

His heart seized. "I'm sure you're right," he said.

She slipped her arms around his waist and laid her head on his chest. "I am right. You'll see. Everything will be perfect."

He wanted to believe it, but he'd learned a long time ago that nothing was perfect.

CHAPTER TWELVE

TIME WAS FLUID. It moved like a river, rolling smoothly and inexorably forward. Sometimes there were rocks. Sometimes there weren't.

Holly sighed and looked up from her work. There had been no rocks for days now. She liked it this way. Life with Drago had been one long, immensely pleasurable ride along smooth water these past two weeks.

The days were pleasant—she played with Nicky, read books and mixed her perfumes. Drago had supplied her with everything she needed, just as he'd promised. He worked from home much of the time, though sometimes he got up early and took a helicopter to his office in Rome. She missed him when he wasn't at the house. Because when he was, he often came searching for her in the middle of the day.

They'd made frantic love against the wall of a closet once. He'd come looking for her and found her heading for her workroom. Instead of leading her back to the room they shared, he'd opened the nearest door—a closet—and dragged her inside. It had been incredibly erotic, fumbling with their clothes among the linens, mouth seeking mouth. He'd had to put his hand over her mouth to stop her cries when he'd buried himself deep inside her, their bodies sweating and writhing as they'd flown toward that perfect release. She'd bitten him, and he'd laughed.

There were other times, too, wonderful times, when they retreated to their room in the middle of the day and made love while the world moved by outside. She loved those moments, when it seemed as if they were the only two people who existed.

But of course she loved it when Drago came to play with Nicky, too. He'd been wary at first, nervous, but now he was a natural. And Nicky loved him, laughing whenever Drago picked him up and swooped him around the room, pretending he was a bird or a superhero.

She laughed, too, loving the sound of her two men enjoying each other's company.

But, as perfect as life had been lately, she wasn't worry-free. She and Drago avoided discussing anything to do with the future. What happened now?

She had no idea, and it worried her. For all her bravery, there were certain things she still couldn't manage to be vocal about. And the future was one of them.

There had been delays on the Sky campaign, so she'd told herself to stop thinking about it. Instead, she spent time working on her scents.

She tested the latest batch of Colette. Then she leaned back, satisfied it was perfect. She'd given some to the maids, and then she'd given some to the cook when she'd expressed an interest. Several of Drago's staff were now wearing her fragrances, not his. If he'd noticed, he hadn't said anything.

And she didn't think he could help but notice, since she wore the same fragrance herself. Colette was light, fresh and floral. There was lavender, verbena, vanilla, and a few secrets she wouldn't divulge to anyone. But it was unmistakable, and it tended to flatter most body chemistries. No one had been unable to wear it yet.

She sniffed the tester again, closing her eyes as she did so. It made her think of home, of Gran's lovely face. Of the fat blooms in Gran's garden, and the delicious gumbo on Gran's stove. She missed Gran so much.

A tear fell and she dashed it away, sniffling. She was happy, dammit. Happy.

She had a wonderful baby and a man she loved—

Holly froze. *Love?* How could she love Drago di Navarra? What they had was hot, physical and addictive. It was also volatile and chaotic in many ways.

But it wasn't emotional. It was sex.

When it was over, she could walk away and not miss a thing....

Holly hung her head as a sharp pain carved into her at the thought. Oh, dear heaven, it *was* emotional. For her anyway. Because the thought of leaving Drago, of not being a part of his life anymore, felt as if she were trying to slice off an arm or leg. She couldn't imagine life without him. Didn't want to.

That didn't mean it was love, though. He was the father of her baby, and it was inevitable she felt something tender for him, especially as they spent time together and as he doted on his son. In spite of his childhood, in spite of a mother who'd given him up and made him feel unloved, he was capable of so much love when it came to his little boy.

But what about her? How did he feel about her?

"Holly."

She turned at the sound of his voice, her heart leaping. A single tear spilled down her cheek and she hurriedly wiped it away.

"What's wrong?" he said, coming over to her side and kneeling down. He looked so concerned, and her heart turned over.

"I was thinking of Gran," she said huskily. It was true.

He reached up and wiped away another tear that escaped. "I'm sorry you lost her, Holly."

She shrugged, though she felt anything but lighthearted at the moment. "That's life, right?"

He stood and pulled her into his arms. She went willingly, burying her head against his chest and breathing him in. Oh, how she loved the smell of him. He wasn't wearing cologne today, but he still smelled like pears to her. Not sweet, but not tart, either. Delicious and crisp and inviting. That was Drago.

"It is life, but that doesn't make it hurt any less."

They stood that way for a long while, and then she pushed back and looked up at him, smiling through her tears. "I'm fine, Drago. I just miss her sometimes."

He took her hand and led her out onto the terrace. They sank onto a settee that was shaded from the sun by a vine-covered arbor. Fat grapes hung down, waiting for someone to pick them.

"Tell me about her," he commanded. She would have laughed at his imperious tone if she weren't touched by his desire to make her feel better.

"She raised me. I told you that before. I never knew my father, and my mother died when I was young. Gramps had died years before, so it was just me and Gran in her little cottage. She grew so many things, Drago. Vegetables, herbs and flowers. We ate well and we made essences. I had a wonderful childhood. I never thought I was missing out on anything."

"And then she died, and you couldn't keep her home."

She nodded. "Gran didn't have insurance, so when she got sick with cancer she had to borrow against the house. She didn't want to do it at first, but she really had no choice. And I was positive we'd find a way, once she was cured, to pay the money back."

She sucked in a pained breath. "But she wasn't cured, and I didn't find a way. After I buried her, there was hardly anything left. The cottage was repossessed. Someone else lives there now." She swallowed a fresh load of tears, her emotions whirling. "I just hope they love it the way I did."

His thumb skated rhythmically over the back of her hand. "I don't think they can, Holly. But I bet they love it in their own way."

Her throat was tight with emotion. He'd put it so perfectly. "Yes, I'm sure you're right. It would be impossible not to appreciate its beauty. The house isn't very big, but Gran had an acre of land and all of it planted and carefully tended. The wife was a gardener, so I'm sure she's in heaven with all the plants."

One of the maids came outside then and asked if they'd like something to drink. Drago asked for a bottle of wine and some water. Holly could smell the scent of Colette in the air. Drago watched the maid walk away.

"Don't think I haven't noticed that everyone smells similar to you," he said mildly.

She shrugged. "I was certain you must have. Are you angry?"

He laughed. "No one who works here is required to wear Navarra products, *cara*. For all I know, the housekeeper mixes up her own scents in her kitchen."

"She might, but that's not what she's wearing right now," Holly said.

"It's…different. I assume it's your Colette?"

Joy washed through her. "Yes. Gran and I made it together."

He looked thoughtful. "I think I like it. It's fresh, not overwhelming. Floral, but not cloying."

Holly nodded eagerly. "Yes, that's it exactly. I haven't found a woman yet whose body chemistry didn't complement the fragrance. It's different on everyone, but the same, too. If that makes sense."

He laughed. "You are talking to a man who hears a hundred different pitches a week for things that are the same but different. Sometimes it makes sense. Often, it's—how do you Americans say it?—bullshit."

"And is it bullshit this time?"

He pursed his lips in thought. "Perhaps not. But I will need more information." His gaze slid down her body, back up again, and she tingled everywhere he looked. "I will need a thorough, *private* demonstration, Holly Craig."

"I think I can arrange that," she told him. "Let me speak to the research-and-development department. I'll get back with you."

His eyes sparkled. "Mmm, and if I'm unwilling to wait that long?"

She tipped her head to the returning maid. "I think you must, Mr. Di Navarra. Your wine has arrived."

"Ah, but wine is portable," he said with a wink.

Drago was gone the next morning when Holly woke, off to Rome to tend to his business. She lay in the bed alone and thought about everything that had happened these past few weeks. She was happier than she'd have ever thought she could be, and she was frightened, too.

Drago did not talk about the future. Not ever. She had no idea what she meant to him, if anything. Oh, sure, they were lovers and she was the mother of his child—but what did that mean to him, beyond the here and now? He seemed to need her as much as she needed him—but he never said any tender words, never talked about what the future might hold for them.

She was under contract for a year, but only if the test shots went well. So far, there had been no test shots. There had been no shoot. Drago said it took time to do what he wanted and not to worry, but she worried nevertheless.

He did things like ask her about Gran and express his sorrow for her loss, and she wondered endlessly if that meant he felt something. Or if he was just being polite.

Yesterday, he'd said he'd needed more information about Colette. But once they'd been alone, perfume had been the furthest thing from his mind. He'd stripped her naked and made her mindless with pleasure. But when it was over, when they were sated and lying together in the bed, he'd pulled her close and fallen asleep. He'd not asked her one question about her fragrance.

She'd told herself it was ridiculous to be disappointed, especially after the way he'd held her and caressed her and wrung every drop of pleasure from her body, but she couldn't help herself. She wanted to be taken seriously, and Drago only wanted to use her body.

Not that she minded that part. But she wanted more. She wanted to know he thought about more than having sex with her. And she wanted to know what would happen when the campaign was over. Or if he didn't like the test shots and it never began.

He had to know she'd meant what she said about not giving up Nicky. But he had so much money and power. Did he really care what she said? He could fight her for custody. He might even win.

Holly's heart squeezed tight. She couldn't let that happen.

She flung the covers back and went to take a shower. After, she dressed in jeans and a T-shirt and went to find Sylvia and Nicky. They were in the garden, and Holly went to join them, her heart swelling with love for her baby. He sat on a blanket in the shade, playing with his toys, while Sylvia read a book. When he saw her coming, he threw the toy and began babbling excitedly. His little arms stretched up to her, and Holly bent to pick him up.

"Hello, precious," she said, sticking her nose against his neck and breathing in his soft baby scent.

She greeted Sylvia warmly, though she was still wary

of having anyone else take care of her son. It felt as if he wasn't hers as much, and she knew that was silly, but since Gran had died, she'd been so alone in the world with no other family. She had Gabi, of course, but Gabi didn't share DNA with her. This little guy, however, had become her world. She couldn't lose him. Not ever.

Holly spent the rest of the morning with Nicky and Sylvia, and then she put Nicky down for his nap and went to the room set up with her supplies. She had an idea for something new that she wanted to play with. When she'd been sitting in the grass earlier, the scent of sun-warmed cherries had seemed to waft over her from nowhere. They combined with the scent of the grapes in the arbor and the grass and soil beneath her to make her think of summer afternoons. It didn't mean she would get anything out of combining essences, but it was fun to play.

And it kept her mind occupied.

Sometime during the afternoon, there was a knock at her door. Her heart skipped when she thought it might be Drago, but then she realized he usually strode in without knocking.

"Yes," she called, and a maid opened the door.

"Signorina," she said, "there is a man here to see you."

Holly blinked. "Me? Are you certain?"

"Sí. It is Signore Lazzari, and he says he wishes to speak to you."

She hadn't thought about Santo Lazzari in two weeks, so to have him here now was a bit of a surprise. Still, she didn't have any reason not to see him. He knew she was the new face of Sky, and he was one of Drago's business associates.

"I'll be there in a minute," she said.

The maid inclined her head and left. Holly stoppered her essences, made a few quick notes and then went out to greet Santo.

* * *

Drago sat at his desk in his office in Rome and tried to concentrate on the numbers in front of him. But he couldn't seem to focus. He kept coming back to Holly, to the way she clung to him, the way she felt beneath him when their bodies were joined, the way he felt inside when he was with her.

She made him want to be a better man. She made him want to try to open his heart and trust someone. He'd never trusted anyone, not since he was little and had learned he could rely only on himself. That he was responsible for his own well-being instead of the woman who should have been taking care of him. He'd never had that freedom other kids had had, that freedom to play and have fun and not *think* about survival and belonging.

He'd always had to think about those things. About his place in his mother's world, and his place in the world at large. He had always been worth a lot of money. He still was, even more so now that he was in charge of it. His money enticed people to try to use him for their own purposes, to try to chip off just a little bit for themselves.

Holly had had his child, but she hadn't tried to get money from him. She hadn't shown up on his doorstep, threatening him with a paternity suit, threatening him with selling her story to the tabloids if he didn't pay up. She'd never tried to use Nicky to get anything from him.

She had kept him secret, though. And she had kept that knowledge hidden while she'd negotiated for a contract with him. She said it was because she wanted to secure her child's future. Because she was afraid he would kick her out again.

If he were honest with himself, she'd had every reason to think he might do just that.

He had not handled her betrayal quite so well the first time. In fact, he'd reacted in a way he never did. Blindly, emotionally. He'd thrown her out instead of listening to her pitch, politely telling her "no, thanks," and then sending her on her way.

But she'd blindsided him. Or, rather, his own feelings had blindsided him. In a single moment, Holly Craig had reminded him what it had felt like to be worth nothing as a person and everything as an entity. He'd hated her for making him feel that way.

And how did he feel now?

Drago sighed. That was the problem. He didn't know. He only knew that since taking her to his bed, he'd felt a sense of relief and joy that he hadn't experienced in a very long time. It made no sense, especially when he considered that she'd lied to him for so long—but maybe he was tired of being suspicious, tired of letting the past dictate the future.

He had a child with her, a wonderful, adorable child. And he wanted that child to have the things he hadn't had: a stable home, a father, love. Holly loved Nicky, and he loved Nicky. Shouldn't they work together to give their boy everything they could?

They hadn't had the best beginning, but they could have a good future together. All he had to do was take a chance. It took him a few more hours of thinking and considering and weighing all the options, but in the end he made a decision.

He picked up the phone and started to make a few calls. When he got home tonight, he would take the first step toward the future.

CHAPTER THIRTEEN

EXCITEMENT BUBBLED AND popped in Holly's veins like fine champagne poured into a crystal flute. Santo Lazzari wanted her to make perfume for House of Lazzari. He wanted to buy Colette. It was everything she'd ever dreamed, everything she'd wanted when she and Gran had been mixing their blends together—and then, after, when Gran was gone and Holly had been determined to save her home and introduce the world to Gran's perfume.

But there was also an undercurrent of sadness in her joy. Drago. She'd wanted *him* to want Colette. She'd wanted him to be the one who was excited about the possibilities, who praised her for her skill and who mapped out a potential campaign that showed what he could do with her fragrance.

Except, he didn't seem interested. Yesterday, she'd thought he finally would talk to her about it, but he'd kissed her instead. And then he'd taken her to bed and made love to her and all thoughts of perfume had flown out the window.

Now she stood in her workroom and waited for him to return from Rome. She'd told Santo she had to think about it overnight, but what she really wanted to know was how Drago felt. Did he want Colette? Or was that nothing more than a dead end?

Finally, when the shadows grew long on the tall pencil

pines, she heard the *whop-whop* of the rotors as Drago's helicopter returned. Her heart lodged in her throat as she went outside to greet him. He came walking up from the helipad, clad in a custom suit and handmade loafers, carrying a briefcase and looking lost in thought.

She watched him for a long moment, her breath catching at the sheer masculine beauty of him. Santo Lazzari was handsome, and he'd even flirted with her a little bit, but she'd been unmoved. When Drago walked across a room—or a lawn—she felt as if she were slowly burning up from the inside out. Every sense attuned to him. Every cell of her body ached for him.

He saw her, finally. His expression grew serious and her blood slowed to a crawl in her veins. What was he thinking?

"Holly," he said when he drew near. And then, before she could ask him what was on his mind, he dropped the briefcase and dragged her into his arms. He kissed her thoroughly, completely, until she was boneless in his embrace.

"I have something for you," he said when he finally lifted his head. His eyes sparked with heat and passion, and a throbbing ache set up shop in her core.

"I think I know what it is," she said teasingly, her heart thrumming fast.

He laughed. "I doubt it." Then he reached into his pocket and pulled out a small velvet box.

Holly's heart lodged in her throat. "What is it?"

"Open it."

No one had ever given her jewelry—and certainly not something in a velvet box. She knew the size, the shape, knew what it usually meant in commercials and movies. But what did it mean here?

Her hands stayed anchored at her sides as the world spun crazily around her. "I don't think I can."

He stood there so tall and handsome in the golden light. She could hear birds in the trees now that the helicopter was gone again. Inside the house, she heard the clink of dishes and knew the chef was preparing dinner. Drago's scent assailed her nostrils, along with the freshness of the evening breeze and the dampness of an approaching storm.

She felt everything so keenly, and she was afraid to move beyond this moment. Afraid it wouldn't mean what she wanted it to mean. Afraid it would end and she'd be brokenhearted again.

"Then I will do it for you," he said, flipping back the lid as he stood so close to her she could feel his heat enveloping her senses.

The ring wasn't huge by billionaire standards, but it was undoubtedly bigger than anything she'd ever thought she would have. And it was unmistakably an engagement ring. The center diamond was at least three carats, and the band held more diamonds, which enhanced the center and made it sparkle all the more. She didn't think the setting was white gold. Platinum most likely, unless there were a more rare metal she didn't know about.

"Marry me, Holly," he said. "We'll make a home for Nicky, and one day he'll inherit all of this."

Her chest ached as tears filled her eyes. "I don't know what to say."

He looked uncertain for a moment, as if he hadn't anticipated that answer. "Say yes."

She wanted to. Desperately. But she couldn't until she asked a question. He'd never given any indication of his feelings, and she needed to know. "Do you love me, Drago?"

He swallowed. "I care about you," he said, and her heart fell slowly, so slowly, until it hit the floor and shattered into a million pieces.

She told herself it was silly to feel sad or disappointed.

It was too soon to ask for more. He was proposing to her. Offering to make a home for Nicky, to give him a family. She knew how important that was to him. A man who'd never had a stable home life until he was nearly a teenager.

What more could she ask for right this moment? It was a start. And yet she was more hurt by his offer than cheered. She wanted *more*. She wanted him to feel the way she felt. She wanted him to feel as if he would burst trying to contain all these hot, bright feelings inside the shell of his skin, and she wanted him to care about the things she cared about.

She told herself this was enough, for now. But it wasn't.

"Santo Lazzari wants to buy Colette," she said on a whisper, because she couldn't say the other things she was thinking. She couldn't put her heart on the line when she was more and more certain he didn't feel the same way.

Drago's face changed. She watched the emotions crossing his features and knew she'd said the wrong thing. There was disbelief, hurt, loneliness and, finally, fury. He snapped the box closed and she jumped at the finality of the sound.

"And what does Lazzari have to do with this, Holly?" he gritted. "With what I am asking you right now? Are you hoping for a better offer from *him*?"

Shock hit her like a lightning bolt sizzling across a clear blue sky. "What? No! But you said you care about me, and this is something I care about. And you haven't spoken of it, though I keep waiting—"

His expression grew darker, if that were possible, more thunderous. His lips curled back from his teeth and she shrank away from him. "You think mentioning Lazzari to me will make me buy your perfume?" He held up the box in his clenched fist. His knuckles were white where he gripped it so hard. "I'm offering you more than you could have ever dreamed possible—money, position, even power—and you still care about your trite little scents?"

His words stabbed into her. *Trite little scents.* He thought her dreams were beneath his notice. No, he thought she wanted to make perfume only so she could make money. That she was driven by ambition and greed rather than joy and love.

He didn't really know her if he thought that. He'd spent these past few weeks with her, and he had no idea who she was. It hurt more than she'd ever thought possible.

Blindly, she turned away from him. Everything was blurry as she started across the terrace. She had to get away, or scream.

"Where are you going?" he thundered. "Holly? Holly!"

She didn't turn around. She didn't stop. She kept going until she was inside her room, the door locked to the outside. Until she could cry for everything she'd lost, and everything she would never have.

Drago went back to Rome. When he reached his apartment, he slammed inside and threw his briefcase on the couch. And then he took the velvet box from his trousers, where it had sat like a hard lump of marble, and wanted to howl in frustration.

He'd misjudged her again. He'd thought she wanted him, wanted this life, but she wanted him to buy her perfume and she didn't mind using Santo Lazzari to get him to do it. And she wanted him to proclaim his love for her, as if that would make a difference somehow.

Love. *Dio*, what kind of fool would love her?

Drago raked a hand through his hair. He didn't understand love. He didn't understand how anyone could let go enough to feel love. In his mind, it was a dangerous emotion that made people unstable. When you loved someone, you gave them the keys to your soul. The means with which to destroy you.

He'd spent years loving a mother who hadn't loved him back—or hadn't loved him enough. It had taken him years to get over the neglect, and he was not about to open himself up for that kind of experience ever again.

Holly knew, damn her. She *knew* how hard this was for him, how damaged a life he'd had. She knew and she insisted on pushing him.

Santo Lazzari. *Christo!* It had been only a few weeks, and they hadn't even begun the Sky shoot yet. Already she was scheming to get her perfume in front of another company. It infuriated him that she would betray him, that she would talk to Santo instead of to him.

Why hadn't she just asked him what he thought? Why hadn't she come to him instead of going behind his back?

The answer was obvious: because she didn't trust him.

Hot feelings swirled inside him. He wanted to punch something. Wanted to rage and howl and ask why he wasn't good enough for her.

He went over to the liquor cabinet and poured a shot of whiskey. His fingers shook as he poured and he stopped, stared at them. *Why wasn't he good enough for her?*

That was the kind of question he'd asked as a child. It was a question for his mother, not for Holly. He set the whiskey down and stared at a window across the street, a little lower than his. A man and woman danced together, the woman smiling up at him, the man saying something that made her smile.

Holly was not his mother. And she very likely hadn't gone to Santo. He remembered Santo escorting her onto the terrace a couple of weeks ago. Santo could have asked her about the scent she was wearing then. And she would have told him the truth.

And even if she'd pitched it herself, why should that matter to him?

If he were truthful with himself, he hadn't shown much interest, though he knew she worked hard on her fragrances. He'd been in the room she'd set up as a work area, he'd smelled her concoctions and he'd seen her notes. She was a professional. And she was good.

But he'd never told her that. *Why not?*

Drago stood in the darkness of his Rome apartment, with the city sounds wafting up from below and the lights of Rome's ancient ruins and sacred domes glittering before him, and felt more alone than he'd ever felt in his life.

What was he doing? Why was he here instead of back at his villa, with his beautiful son?

And with Holly.

A cold, sinking feeling started in his gut, spread through his limbs. What if he'd ruined it this time? What if he'd gone too far? He tried to imagine his life without her in it. Emptiness engulfed him.

It was more emptiness than he'd ever thought he could feel. Somehow, she had become important to him. To his life. If he had to live without her in it, how could he ever laugh again?

He was a fool. A blind fool, driven by things that had happened to him over twenty years ago instead of by the things that his life had become. Inside, he was still lost and alone and frightened. And he was waiting—waiting for betrayal. He expected it, looked for it, congratulated himself when it happened. Because it was what he knew was supposed to happen to him.

But what if it wasn't? What if the problem was all him? What if Holly was exactly what she seemed to be? A somewhat naive, trusting woman who'd had to learn how to survive on her own when she'd found herself pregnant and alone.

Drago turned away from the window, panic bubbling up from a well inside him that he'd kept capped for far too long. He was an idiot. And not for the reasons he'd supposed. No one had made him into a fool. He'd done it all by himself.

Holly woke in the middle of the night, her eyes swollen, her throat aching, and knew she had to leave. There could be no Sky. There could be no Drago. She would do whatever it took to arrange for him to see his son, but right now Nicky belonged to her and she wasn't leaving here without him.

She dressed in the dark, tossed some things into a bag and went to gather Nicky from his crib. Somehow she managed to get him into his carrier without waking him, and then she crept down the stairs and stood in the empty foyer, undecided about what to do. On the hall table, there were several sets of car keys in a box. She took one—a BMW—and went out to the garage.

It took her nearly forty-five minutes to get the car, find the nearest train station on the GPS and drive to it. She could have gone to the airport, but for now she figured she'd get a train to Rome, call Santo Lazzari and arrange to meet with him about Colette, and then get a one-way ticket back to Louisiana. If she could just get an advance, she'd be all right. She had some money, but not enough to get her very far.

Holly purchased a ticket to Rome and went to sit on a bench. She studied her ticket and studied the boards, hoping she'd found the right track. Her eyes were gritty and tired, and she suddenly just wanted to go back to sleep. Nicky stirred in his carrier, but he was too sleepy to wake just yet. She prepared a bottle and hoped it would keep him quiet once he did.

Eventually, her train arrived—or she hoped it was her train—and she boarded it, finding a seat in a corner and leaning her head against the window. It throbbed with the remnants of her crying fit, and the early-morning coolness felt good against her skin.

She dozed a bit and then the train lurched and started to glide down the tracks. Her heart ached with such a profound sadness that she could hardly acknowledge it. How could she go back to the life she'd left behind? How could she forget Drago this time?

The last time, she hadn't been in love with him—or maybe she had, but it had been so easy to convince herself she hated him instead. This time, her heart mourned for everything that could never be. They would see each other again. Because of Nicky. She couldn't get out of it and she didn't want to.

But she would have to figure out how to survive those moments when she had to face him for the sake of their child.

The train lurched again, and then began to slow. They hadn't quite made it out of the station when it stopped completely. The Italians on board seemed unperturbed about it all, but her pulse hummed along a little bit faster. She just wanted to get away, before Drago discovered she was gone. She figured she had time, since he'd presumably returned to Rome last night, but she was nervous nevertheless.

There was a commotion in the car behind her, raised voices, and she turned to look along with the other passengers. Her heart seemed to stop beating then. She could see Drago's face, determined and hard, and her legs turned to mush. She reached for her bag, slid out of her seat and grabbed the carrier. She was on her way down the car when the door behind her opened and a man shouted her name.

She spun, her hair whirling into her face, and confronted him—because there was no escape now.

"Go away, Drago," she said. "Just leave me alone."

He looked wild-eyed as he moved into the car. The

other passengers glanced between them with interest, eyes bouncing back and forth as if they were at a tennis match.

"Holly, please." He held his hand out, and she saw that it shook. She steeled her heart against him and shook her head. What a good actor he was.

"Stop it," she said coldly. "You're only pretending so these people won't think you're some kind of unfeeling monster. But we both know the truth, don't we?"

He looked taken aback. "No, that's not true." He tried to smile, but it wasn't a very good attempt. "Besides, since when do I care what anyone else thinks about me?"

He had a point there, but if she allowed it to penetrate, her shield would crumble. She had to be strong. For her baby. For herself.

"You don't care about anyone."

He took another step forward, one hand out in supplication. "I care about you."

Panic bloomed in her soul. "You don't. You're only saying that because I tried to leave. Well, guess what, Drago, you can't force me to stay! I won't prevent you from being a part of Nicky's life, but I won't stay here and let you ruin my life, either."

His hand dropped to his side. "I don't want to ruin your life, Holly. I want to make it better."

She laughed bitterly. "By locking me up in a gilded cage? By not trusting me? By belittling my dreams and my interests? By telling me I'll never be good enough for the likes of you?"

His expression was stark. And then he said something that stunned her. "You're too good for me, Holly. I'm the one who isn't good enough."

Anger seeped from her like air from a balloon. Confusion took up residence in her brain. She wanted to believe him, but how could she? "Is this a trick?"

He shook his head, and she finally saw that lost, lonely

man that lurked inside him. "It's not a trick. I'm a fool, Holly. I need you too much, and it scares me."

Holly stared at him for a long moment, studying his face. Her heart thundered and her blood pounded and her skin felt hot and tight.

"I think he tells the truth," a woman said, and Holly glanced over at her. She was a pretty woman, with dark hair and eyes shiny with tears. "It is *amore, signorina.*"

Holly's heart skipped. "Is that true, Drago? Do you love me? Or is this all an elaborate ruse to get me to go back with you so you can take our son away?"

He stood there before her, so tall and commanding—and then he drew in a sharp breath and she heard the pain in it.

"I don't know what love is, Holly. I loved my mother. I know I did, and yet she didn't seem to care. She left me. I meant nothing at all to her. What if I am incapable of love? Of being loved?"

There was a huge lump in her throat. "You aren't incapable of being loved."

His eyes were filled with so much pain. "How do you know?"

She felt a tear spill over, and then another. How could she let him think such a thing when she knew the truth?

"Because I love you." The words felt like razor blades coming up, but once they were free, she was glad she'd said them.

She didn't know what would happen, but he moved then, an inexorable wave coming for her. Then he swept her up in his arms, her and Nicky, and held them tight, burying his face against her neck.

"I don't know what love is," he said, his voice a broken whisper in her ear. "But if it's this feeling that I would die without you, then yes, I love you. If you leave me, Holly, I will be more alone than I've ever been in my life."

The tears flowed freely down her cheeks now, and the train's inhabitants clapped and cheered.

"I want to stay with you, Drago. But I'm afraid. You hurt me, and I'm afraid."

His grip didn't ease. "I know. I've been an ass, Holly. I want you to come home with me, and I want you to marry me. And I want Colette, and whatever other perfume you want to make for me. I want you to be happy, to do what you love—and I'm sorry I said it was trite. It's not. Nothing you do is trite. I was just…afraid."

Holly drew in a shaky breath. And then she pulled back and put her hand on his cheek—his beloved cheek—and caressed him. "I love you, Drago. You can't make me stop. It has nothing to do with your money or your stupid cosmetics company. Even if you had nothing, I would love you."

He wiped away the tears on her cheeks with shaky fingers. His eyes shimmered with moisture, though he grinned to try to hide it. "That's a pretty speech, considering I am worth somewhere in the neighborhood of eighty billion dollars. It's easy to love a rich man, *amore mia*."

She laughed then. "Perhaps it is, but not when that rich man is you. Do you have any idea what a pain in the ass you can be? Sometimes it would be easier to love a cactus."

His laugh was broken, and it tore her heart to hear it. "You are too much, Holly Craig. You and that smart mouth." He drew in a breath. "Please marry me. Please come home and bring our son and let me spend the rest of my life making it up to you for being so blind and stupid."

"Yes," she said simply. Because it was right. Because there was nowhere else she'd rather be than in this man's arms for the rest of her life.

His smile was filled with relief and tenderness. "Then let me do this right," he said. Before she knew what he was about, he pulled a box from his pocket and dropped to one knee. "Marry me, Holly Craig. Fill my life with light and happiness. Tease me, exasperate me, challenge me—and never give up on me."

"Do it, *signorina,*" the dark-haired woman urged.

Holly laughed. As if she could do anything else when she had the great Drago di Navarra on his knees in front of her. As if she wanted to.

"It's a deal," she said softly. "No contract required."

Drago slipped the ring on her finger. Then he got to his feet and kissed her right there in the middle of the train as everyone cheered.

EPILOGUE

DRAGO LOOKED UP from the photos he'd been studying and found his wife standing in his office, looking amazingly gorgeous in a simple dress and flats.

"I didn't hear you come in," he said.

"Obviously." She came and looked over his shoulder. And then she sighed. "Are you sure about these?"

"Of course. You are the most gorgeous model to ever grace a fragrance ad."

"I think your colleagues are going to think you've lost your mind," she grumbled.

He turned and put his hands on her waist. "Holly, you are precisely what I wanted for this campaign. You're gorgeous but approachable. Women will buy this perfume in droves."

She ran her hands through his hair. And then she kissed him. "I think they'll buy Colette in greater droves."

He laughed. "You could be right. I guess we'll see when we launch it in the spring, yes?"

She arranged herself on his lap. He did not mind. His arms went around her and held her tight. How had he ever, *ever* thought he could live without her?

"I'm perfectly confident," she said. And then she frowned. "But, Drago, I'm afraid I can't work in your fragrance development lab as first planned."

He studied her face, shocked at this news. "But you

insisted you wanted this. You've proved to me how good you are, and I've been counting on adding your expertise to the staff."

She toyed with the lapel of his collar. "Yes, well, you can still have that expertise. But I'm afraid the scents will be too much for me. In a lab. At home, I can do it when I'm feeling well. But all those scents? No, not happening."

Drago shook his head. She'd left him about a mile back, standing on the side of the road and staring at her dust cloud. "I'm not following you," he told her.

She leaned down and kissed his nose. "Oh, you darling man. No, I suppose it wouldn't make a lick of sense to you. The smells, my darling, will be too much for a woman in my condition."

He felt as if his brain was stuck in the mud, spinning tires—

And then he came unstuck and her meaning dawned. "You're pregnant?"

Her smile could have lit up the grid. "Yes."

Drago squeezed her tight, unable to say a word. And then he panicked and let her go again. "I'm sorry, was that too much?"

"No, of course not." She squeezed him back and they sat together, holding each other and laughing.

"I almost forgot," he said. He pulled open a drawer and took out some papers. "I just got these. I wanted to surprise you."

Holly took the papers and opened them. Tears filled her lovely blue eyes as she read the deed. "Gran's house."

"Your house," he said, the lump in his throat nearly too big to get the words past.

"*Our* house," she said, squeezing him tight. "Oh, Drago, thank you."

He pushed her hair back from her face, tucking it behind her ears. And then he drew her down and kissed her sweetly. "Anything for you, Holly. Anything."

She made his life complete. Her and Nicky. And this new baby, whoever he or she turned out to be. Drago's heart was full as he kissed her again. Life was full.

And it always would be. In that, he had complete faith.

* * * * *

BOUND BY THE
ITALIAN'S
CONTRACT

JANETTE KENNY

For as long as **Janette Kenny** can remember, plots and characters have taken up residence in her head. Her parents, both voracious readers, read her the classics when she was a child. That gave birth to a deep love of literature, and allowed her to travel to exotic locales – those found between the covers of books. Janette's artist mother encouraged her yen to write. As an adolescent she began creating cartoons featuring her dad as the hero, with plots that focused on the misadventures on their family farm, and she stuffed them in the nightly newspaper for him to find. To her frustration, her sketches paled in comparison with her captions.

Though she dabbled with articles, she didn't fully embrace her dream to write novels until years later, when she was a busy cosmetologist making a name for herself in her own salon. That was when she decided to write the type of stories she'd been reading – romances.

Once the writing bug bit, an incurable passion consumed her to create stories and people them. Still, it was seven more years and that many novels before she saw her first historical romance published. Now that she's also writing contemporary romances for Mills & Boon she finally knows that a full-time career in writing is closer to reality.

Janette shares her home and free time with a chow-shepherd mix pup she rescued from the pound, who aspires to be a lap dog. She invites you to visit her website at www.jankenny.com and she loves to hear from readers – e-mail her at janette@jankenny.com.

CHAPTER ONE

CAPRICE TREGORE WRAPPED her confidence around her like a protective cloak and strode into The Corbett, Aspen's newest five-star hotel, which a Russian billionaire had built one year ago to cater to the rich and famous. She surveyed the interior, her senses in overdrive.

It was a breathtaking, palatial design of marble pillars, gleaming granite floors and exquisite tapestries dressing massive walls. This lavish and elite winter hotspot was exactly what she had pointedly avoided the past seven years. If she didn't desperately need help, she wouldn't be setting foot in this playground for the rich and famous now.

She quickly circled the three-tiered castle fountain that dominated the center of the expansive lobby and scanned the myriad seating nooks tucked here and there for the handsome Italian she'd come here to meet. With rising annoyance, she realized not one man resembled him. Was he late? Had he stood her up?

"Punctual as always, Miss Tregore?"

That deep voice rumbling behind her, flavored with a distinct Italian accent, sent an electric shiver zinging through her. That was the last reaction she wanted this playboy to incite in her and she wouldn't tolerate another second of it!

"Punctuality is one of the cardinal business virtues,"

she said stiffly as she turned to face him with a professional smile she'd perfected.

For one second it threatened to slip as she stared into his riveting blue eyes framed in a face surely reserved for an archangel. Or the devil?

God knew either could apply to Luciano Duchelini. That reminder stiffened her spine and her resolve.

"A Don Marquis quotation, but you left the rest off," he said, not one iota of amusement ringing in that velvety voice that she'd once found incredibly attractive. "Always insist on it in your subordinates."

"I wasn't suggesting you were—"

"It doesn't matter. I watched you walk in five minutes ago," he said. "Your promptness is an asset."

That he knew exactly when she'd walked in the door spoke volumes. So did the fact he'd remained a bit hidden, making her seem the one a bit late and harried.

Not the impression she wanted to impart.

The Luciano she'd known had always run five to ten minutes late. It was a control thing and she'd accounted for it by arriving exactly on time. But he'd been here waiting.

That was a huge surprise. And a miscalculation on her part.

Seven years ago Luciano had been the world champion on the slopes, winning more gold medals than any Alpine skier before him, besting even his acclaimed father. The only things he was ever on time for were competitions.

It had been proven no man could beat him on the slopes. Rumors had flown that his ex-wife had captured his heart and taken it with her to her grave. That he no longer cared what anyone thought of him. That he lived for the moment, in sport and pleasure.

That no woman could reach the heart of the man.

Yet once she'd foolishly fallen for the champion, beset by a strong teenage crush. He was her idol. Her coach.

Her friend. Or so she'd thought.

He'd used her friendship, her naïveté, just as he'd done with his lovers. She'd hated him then for hurting her, and hated herself now because she knew better than to trust his type.

He was a celebrated playboy. Life had been a game to him and he'd played it to the hilt. He laughed. He partied. He took nothing seriously.

Not her. She'd assumed the role of a reckless flirt one time in her life. A stupid act of retaliation that she'd regretted every day since. That one horrific incident convinced her that she wasn't a player in that world.

"Thank you for agreeing to meet with me," she said, refusing to let him fluster her.

He smiled, though it appeared as practiced as hers. "My pleasure."

If only she could say the same. She had to strike a winning deal. A position she deeply resented.

She'd worked hard. Saved. Scrimped. Yet it hadn't been enough to save her when crisis struck. Now she needed this deal or she would lose Tregore Lodge, her heritage, her home, her livelihood.

"I've come prepared, Mr. Duchelini," she said, getting right to the point.

He laughed, a brief, rich contralto that set his blue eyes twinkling and carved his beautifully sculpted lips into a half smile he likely used to charm ladies. "You are a take-charge woman. I remember how expertly you cracked the whip to get me to those pre-event meetings on time."

She nearly smiled until she recalled how bitterly their last working relationship had ended. "It would have been easier if you hadn't been a night owl."

He simply shrugged, just like he'd done back then only lacking the teasing smile. Zero contrition. She expected no less from a rich womanizer who'd skirted conventions all of his life.

"Come," he said. "Let's go someplace private to talk."

Said the spider to the fly? Being anywhere private with him was the last thing she wanted to do, but she said, "I'm ready."

"As am I. This way," he said, and gestured to the elevators.

She fell into step beside him and tamped down her annoyance that he hadn't simply arranged for her to meet him at a set location for their meeting. The sooner this phase was over, the better. No, not over. Resolved, so she could move forward achieving her dream.

"I brought plans for the lodge and a prospectus for my program, Mr. Duchelini," she said, not wishing to waste a minute, not wanting to be here any longer than necessary.

"Please, you know me. Call me Luciano or Luc." He motioned to the open elevator and she stepped inside, then stood as far from him as she could though she may as well have not bothered.

The mirrored wall behind made the space loom larger, but it did that to her companion as well. Not that he needed any physical enhancements.

Luciano simply consumed any space he was in with his commanding presence, absorbing the energy of everything around him.

She knew most women would be content to stare at his gorgeous body and classically handsome features because years ago she'd fallen under his charismatic spell. Not now, though it was tempting to admire him. Thank God she was stronger than that, that she'd learned from her mistakes.

"Very well, Luciano," she said, refusing to use his nickname as she'd once done. That would be too familiar. "To be honest, I'm surprised you didn't send someone in your stead."

He shot her a frown, his gaze cool. "There is much business that I attend to personally."

"You never used to, unless it pertained to competition," she said, and it was the truth. "What I meant was I hadn't expected you to fly halfway around the world to speak with me."

"It was no bother to coordinate my schedule to come here," he said matter-of-factly. "I was already in Denver to interview a ski therapist, like yourself, when my assistant phoned to let me know you were seeking a financial backer."

In a second, the stakes skyrocketed with competition thrown into an already tense equation, but she remained calm and determined to win his bid. "Good. I'm eager to discuss business."

"As am I," he said with a bite of impatience.

Game on. Having a rival meant she had one way to proceed—full tilt.

"Please," he said as the elevator door whispered open, motioning her to precede him with a disarming smile that was likely meant to throw her equilibrium askew.

Immune to his charms, she returned his smile with a cool one of her own and stepped from lift. And came up short. She blinked, surprised to be standing in a short hallway with a single door at one end and carved double doors to her right.

"This way." Luciano escorted her toward the double doors, where he reached around her, swiped a key in the slot and knuckled the door open. "I trust you don't mind discussing business in my suite?"

"Not at all," she said, stepping inside to regain the buffer of personal space he'd come too close to crossing.

The amazing view of the mountains from his private suite drew her to the windows. She welcomed the calm their rugged beauty always gave her, this grounding to reality that gave her strength.

"Thank you for showing interest in my proposal," she said, turning to face Luciano, whose attention seemed riveted to a small laptop open on the desk. "If there's anything in particular you wish to know about the designs I've envisioned for Tregore Lodge…"

"Your property is small and in need of intense restoration," he cut in, not bothering to look at her.

She cursed the flush burning her face, a show of emotion that she'd never learned to control. "True. Tregore Lodge needs major updating to make it competitive again. But I believe it has much potential…"

"I don't," he said, rudely shooting down the momentum she needed to build before she had a chance to explain how she could establish a state-of-the-art rehabilitation facility there.

"If you feel that way, then why did you ask for this meeting?" she asked, the question burning holes in her patience despite her determination to maintain a business mien, despite the determination to finance her program.

"Simple. The only admirable investment on your property is you."

"Is this some kind of joke?" she asked, needing to know she hadn't misunderstood him.

"Not at all." He studied her with eyes that took everything in and gave absolutely no emotion away, eyes that touched her as intimately as a caress, bold and without apology. "You hold my interest, Caprice. I want you."

Seven years ago she would have fallen all over him, deliriously happy. But then she'd been innocent. Trusting.

She knew better than to trust a man now. Though this was the faintest glimmer of the playboy she'd known, passionate and direct, she took his remark as an insult.

"Look, I came here to discuss business that is near and dear to my heart, Mr. Duchelini. If you're not interested in hearing my proposal, then you're not interested in me." She turned and strode toward the double doors with calm, precise steps, determined to walk out with her head held high and in charge of her life.

"Stay," he said, the command soft yet persuasive.

She stopped, fingers tightening around the leather handle of her bag. "Why should I?"

"I've a proposal that will benefit us both," he said. "I can grant you what you want."

That was a fact she knew all too well. And really, could she afford to walk out without hearing his offer? No, she admitted.

"Then let's hear it," she said, whirling to face him.

"With pleasure," he said crisply, then strode back toward his desk. "Would you care for a glass of wine?"

"No, thank you."

She never mixed alcohol with business, and that had never been more crucial than now. Despite his wicked reputation, Luciano Duchelini was a superb businessman, and he would expect the same of her. He could take advantage of her and her lodge if she wasn't careful.

Caprice crossed to the sofa angled near the balcony with her composure intact and her mind fixed fully on securing a means to fund her program. That was all she wanted from him.

"Tregore Lodge. Tell me your plans for it," he said, as he dropped onto a leather office chair and twirled it to face her, his long fingers draped casually over the curved chair arms.

"Gladly," she said as she set her portfolio beside her and dug inside it. "I plan to renovate Tregore Lodge inside and out. Foremost is establishing my alternative program for those who have never skied as well as for people who possess varying levels of aptitude on the slopes."

"Your program is tiered then?" he asked.

"In its most basic form, as you'll see by these," she said, her confidence snapping into rapier-sharp focus as she handed him a copy of her carefully prepared prospectus.

He lounged back on the chair and thumbed through the papers, looking relaxed and in charge, the last thing about him that was still organic. But he'd changed.

Not in looks or physique. He was still disarmingly handsome. Still lean and fit. But he'd lost all trace of the flirtatious, teasing charmer she'd remembered so well and adopted the image of a serious businessman who detested wasting his time.

Or maybe he simply still wasn't attracted to her. Maybe he believed if he was too friendly, he'd have a repeat of the teenager with the monstrous crush on the star athlete. If that was the case, he need not worry.

She had no desire in him beyond securing a business deal. "Regardless of one's ability, I slant the program to the individual's needs."

"Just what I wanted to hear," he said at last. "This is why I am interested in you."

"I'm flattered," she said, relieved he was referring to her program.

"As was intended," he said with a bow of his head. "Do you recall my brother?"

"Julian? Yes, I do." Quite well, in fact. "Years ago, he crashed often in your suite."

She'd immediately liked the boisterous Italian who took great pleasure needling and teasing his champion older brother. And the world had gloried in the upstart's daring exploits on the slopes, expecting Julian to set new world records, breaking those set by his father and Luciano despite his undisciplined ways.

But rumor had it Julian had kept his slot on the Italian team only because of his brother's lead position. Whether that was true or not she never knew. One month after the World Cup, Julian had broken his neck in a tragic ski accident and ended up bound to a wheelchair for life.

"Julian is lucky to be alive," she said and meant it.

He gave an abrupt nod, jaw snapping taut. "My brother doesn't think so."

"I'm not surprised. Paralysis is difficult for average patients to cope with. It tends to devastate top athletes." And Julian had been a new star on the horizon. "Recurrent bouts of depression are understandable in cases such as his. That is why adaptive skiing works," she said. "It boosts confidence both on and off the slopes, strengthens physical ability and agility, and provides a means to broaden social skills."

"Unfortunately Julian has gained less than desirable results with alternative skiing and given up the effort," he said. "Even more troubling, none of the therapists I've hired have a program as individualized as yours. He needs your help, Caprice. I believe he will respond to any challenge you put before him."

She blinked, his effusive praise at odds with his earlier criticism of her plans for her lodge. "Wait a minute. If you believe my program is that beneficial, then why are you hesitant to finance the renovation of Tregore Lodge?"

"It is too small a facility to sustain a program of your scope."

A fact she couldn't deny. Still, the lodge was hers and she could expand in time if she wished. "It's all I can manage." All she could afford.

"Alone, perhaps." He pushed to his feet and paced before the windows, his stride gracefully masculine. "You need to expand your scope. What you have envisioned has global appeal. Run with it."

He couldn't be serious. Just the idea of taking her program into the world market had her head spinning. She didn't want to run something that huge.

"You're talking incorporation and I want none of that," she said.

"Why?"

"I want the lodge to remain controllable, and I can do that by keeping it family oriented," she said.

He tapped one long finger on the side of his glass and studied her so long that dread lay like a lead ball in her stomach. "You want to police every aspect of your program. That's why you balk at courting the après-ski set. The expansion would be too great and you would have to delegate, to trust others, and you can't do that."

She stiffened, disliking that he thought her that intractable. "My reputation is on the line here. I don't want to slap my name on programs around the world, even if I personally train every therapist I hire. There is more to it than technique. The personal connection I strive to achieve with clients is what makes my program unique."

"Are you sure you aren't equating small with safe?" Luciano asked.

"I simply want to renovate my lodge into an alternative ski facility and launch my program," she repeated. "That's why I need a backer."

He pushed to his feet and crossed to the bar. "You want

my money and nothing more from me, and you don't want to take a risk," he said over the clink of glasses.

"Basically, yes," she said. "Is that a problem?"

"It could be one for you." He strode toward the sofa with two glasses of decadently red wine and handed one to her, his gaze hot on hers, probing, assessing. "Everything has risks to some degree."

Like being here alone with him. Like courting his interest and financial support, which was all she wanted from him.

"I'm cautious, Luciano," she said, taking the wine at last but hesitant to taste it.

Challenge glinted in his eyes. "Be bold."

"I am." *To a point.* "What's your proposal?" she asked, mindful of the disastrous turn her life had taken the last time she'd acted boldly.

"Ignite my brother's love of life again with your program. It is my hope that he will regain his desire to ski and develop his own line of adaptive equipment."

All built under the la Duchi logo of course.

It was a logical sound business move that would surely make Luciano millions. That he was going to great lengths for his brother spoke volumes.

"I can't promise that therapy will totally heal him," she said honestly. "Julian must want my help as well."

He sat on the sofa, so close to her she saw flecks of silver flare in his eyes. "Give him a reason to. In exchange for your tireless effort and expertise, I will completely finance the renovation of Tregore Lodge to your specifications. Anything you want. Do we have a deal?"

She shook her head, refusing to agree to any verbal agreement, no matter how tempting. "It can't be that simple. What's the catch?"

"No catch," he said, his gaze riveted on hers, hot and

intense. "I will finance the renovation and equipment for the launch of your adaptive ski program if you agree to come to my Alpine lodge and do all in your power to help Julian regain his life."

"Why is this so important to you?"

"He's my brother and has all but given up hope of having any normalcy of life," he said. "Look around. There are far too many like him similarly afflicted. I have the means to give him that new start. You have the knowledge to reach and motivate him."

She bit her lower lip, thinking. Her program would gain huge accolades if it helped Julian. But even if it didn't, she liked him and wanted to help. And she did need to cinch this deal with Luciano.

"What you're expecting of me is massive," she said. "The chance for failure is great. You must realize that."

His frown deepened but he gave an abrupt nod, troubled eyes meeting hers. And for a heartbeat she was lost in them. Lost in the emotional pain that flickered a nanosecond in his eyes before vanishing behind that same blank wall.

"I understand the risk," he said. "But it is worth it if Julian will one day lead a productive life again."

"That's admirable of you." Touching.

He shrugged, his blue eyes as turbulent as a restive sea. "As I said, I care about my brother."

She didn't doubt that. But something else was bothering him deeply. What was it?

This vulnerability of his to the travails of others was another change, a huge switch from the ruthless, competitive champion she remembered. Could a man change that much in seven years?

Her father had taught her that a leopard never changed its spots. Yet this stern businessman she faced now was nothing like the rash playboy she'd known. Nothing similar to the man she'd expected to deal with.

This Luciano was all business. Serious, driven, and clearly tormented. What had caused this transformation? His bitter divorce? The accident? Or did it run deeper than that?

Hard to guess as she rarely read anything about him in the tabloids either. It was as if he'd dropped out of sight. She rose from the sofa and walked to the stunning vista offered by the windows. She needed the space between them to think.

"Will Julian's transformation free you to live your life again?" she asked.

His jaw clenched. "My life is as I wish it. Your answer, Caprice," he said, his intense gaze locked with hers in silent challenge again.

She nodded, mentally kicking herself for getting sidetracked over the state of Luciano's health instead of getting on with her business with him. But she wasn't fool enough to accept his word at face value and snap up the chance to work with him, forgetting the slights.

"If we agree to this on paper, you've got a deal," she said and extended her hand just like she would to wrap up any business deal.

His lips curved in a rare smile that brought back memories of the fun-loving man she'd known. Just as quickly it vanished behind that wall of indifference that he wore so well.

"Excellent. I'll arrange for us to meet with my interior design team as soon as possible. Once they are made aware of what we require, they will be able to come up with a plan for my lodge by the end of next week."

"Whoa! I thought I was to decide how my program should be designed and implemented at your lodge."

"You'll have a voice at the meeting."

A voice she intended to use. "I suppose you plan to sit in on the design meeting for Tregore Lodge as well?"

"Of course I am. I'm financing it," he snapped, brows drawn in a dark frown. "Why are you being so contrary?"

"I don't mean to be difficult. It's just that this is all very important to me."

"Do you think it isn't for me as well?"

"I really don't know *what* you're thinking."

He muttered something she didn't catch, rose and strode toward her, his long legs moving with fluid grace, the broad width of his shoulders a shifting wall of lean muscle. Each step exuded power and masculine grace and purpose, like a cougar stalking the canyon rim in search of prey.

She stepped back, startled by the power that was all Luciano. He was a force to be reckoned with and she would do well to keep that in mind at all times.

He stopped, his larger hand grasping hers in a warm, but clipped shake. "I am thinking I made a very savvy deal with a very smart woman who I admire."

"Thank you," she said, pulling her hand back and hoping it didn't appear as if his touch disturbed her. "To our mutual success."

"It will be."

"You're that sure of yourself?"

His smile was brief but oh so cocky, just like the man. "I play to win, Caprice. In everything."

She nodded, not needing to be reminded of that. "This isn't a game to me either. It's business. It's what I've wanted to do for years and have put all my efforts into."

"Your business is your life," he said, his features hardening into a benign mask.

"I've put a lot of time into the lodge while my father was ill," she said, hoping he understood. "The past year it demanded most of my attention because my program is a fledgling operation and I couldn't afford a mistake."

"If you hope to succeed, you need to learn how to delegate," he said, advice she'd received before and ignored.

"Nobody knows my business like I do," she shot back in defense.

He frowned. "Still the same need for control, Caprice?"

If only this wasn't the first time she'd been accused of that, she thought, face burning. "I have to be picky when my reputation as a therapist is on the line."

One dark brow lifted. "You need to learn how to play the game."

That word again.

She had no doubts that he referred to business *and* pleasure, her heart kicking up its pace at the thought of the latter, which was totally unacceptable. Under no circumstances would she fall victim to his charm again.

So what if her business was her life? It was her choice, though she didn't expect him to understand what she had gone through to get where she was at now.

"I've told you before and I'll tell you again. This isn't a game to me, Luciano. This is my future. My dream. I couldn't have gotten this far with the few resources I have available if I hadn't focused on getting my program started," she said, gaze fixed on his.

He huffed a breath, shaking his head. "I do understand."

He couldn't. Not that it mattered. She wasn't looking for friendship with Luciano Duchelini. Wasn't looking for pity. All she needed, wanted, from him was a fat check for setting up her program in Italy and renovating Tregore Lodge before she returned to Colorado.

She needed his business acumen and financial support. Her best chance to get both was to remain immune to his charismatic charm as she solidified this deal. She couldn't let her judgment be clouded by emotions she had no intentions of pursuing.

"Where do you suggest I start delegating?" she asked, determined to move forward.

"Now. Let me be in charge of the renovations from start to finish," he said.

She stiffened at the idea of handing over control to him. "You don't want my input in my own lodge?"

"Your ideas are welcome," he said, though the impatience creeping back into his voice belied it. "But there is no need for you to remain in Colorado to oversee the project."

He was right. She couldn't devote full attention to her ski program if she had to deal with the building issues at the lodge. "You must understand that there are certain structural specifics I need in place to make my program work—"

"I get that," he interrupted, tossing his hands upward. "As I said before, you will sit down with my design team and list what is needed. When the plans are drawn up, you will see them again to ensure all your needs are met."

"I get final approval?"

"Of course."

She bit her lip, searching for a shadow to pick apart and finding none. "That sounds good." Perfect, actually.

"It is. I will bring this renovation of your lodge to fruition." He leaned forward, riveting gaze locked with hers, mesmerizing yet commanding. "Trust me."

"That's hard for me to do again."

He spread his arms wide. "Why? I was nothing but honest with you."

And he had been. It was she who'd raised her expectations.

My God, had she been that starved for love that she

had grasped for scraps? Was she still that emotionally deficient?

"I ended up hurt the last time I put my faith and trust in someone," she said simply. *By my mother first. By you, lastly.*

To her surprise, a ruddy flush streaked across his olive-hued cheekbones. "Believe me when I tell you I never intended to hurt you. I was—" he made a face, accented with a sharp upward jerk of one hand "—behaving abominably before the end. I regret hurting you, Caprice."

Dare she believe him? She wanted to continue thinking he didn't care about anything but himself.

Except that really wasn't true. He had come here to enlist her aid to turn his brother's life around. He was offering her a golden opportunity, albeit with him pulling all the strings.

"It doesn't matter," she said. Not now and it didn't. It couldn't.

"You have my word it won't happen again," he said.

She swallowed hard. Those were just the words she'd vowed to herself, with the added caveat to avoid Luciano's company. Now here she was, straddling the fence about taking his offer when she'd already decided this was her best bet. He was a genius at what he did. In that, she had to trust him.

"Then I will take you at your word," she said.

"Good." His magnetic eyes grew more intense. "The length of time the lodge is closed will depend on how long it will take you to establish your program at my Alpine facility as well as my brother's progress. A month is a generous estimate, considering Julian's manner of late."

She shook her head, saddened. "Julian may have appeared laid-back, but I remember him being a force of pure energy," she said. "He was always moving."

"People change, Caprice. My brother isn't the man you remember."

She would be stunned if the crippling fall *hadn't* changed the daring young skier. "I'm aware how an accident can affect an athlete physically and mentally. But I'm an optimist."

He stared at her, his features vague, unreadable. "I'm a realist. By proceeding with renovations here at top speed and avoiding problems, it will take at least two months to turn Tregore Lodge around."

Not what she wanted to hear, but there was nothing she could do to change it. Her lodge needed intense work and she needed Luciano's backing.

"I still intend to return to Colorado within a month when I'm finished with my part of our deal." She would find a friend to crash with until her lodge was completed.

"An aggressive prediction," he said, his intense scrutiny stretching the moment and her nerves to the max again. "The timeline doesn't matter to me. I want my brother to have the chance and drive to live life again."

"I'll do what I can to help him, but he must put forth the effort as well," she said.

"Therein lies the challenge." He shook his head, firm lips pressed in an unyielding line.

She blinked, unsure what to say. In her profession she had been quick to teach that a family member shouldn't set the bar so high. Each patient must enter into the rehabilitation process because they wanted change.

Whether that was the case or not, it boiled down to two things. She couldn't renovate her business without Luciano's help. Nor could she ignore this opportunity to help his brother.

Julian had been there for her once when she'd needed a friend, helping her get away quickly and quietly. She owed him, at least in her mind. It was time to cease arguing with Luciano over minor points and repay his brother's kindness.

"Okay. When do we start?" she asked.

"Now. I'll get the team in place here, then we leave for Italy immediately."

CHAPTER TWO

SHE WANTED HIM for his connections and his money.

Luc dug his fingers into the leather-covered steering wheel and shot Caprice a pointed glance. She perched beside him in his rented Mercedes, attention trained on the netbook on her lap, oblivious of his annoyance. And why should he pay him any mind?

She'd gotten exactly what she'd wanted from him—a financial backer with the added bonus of using his name and reputation in connection with her lodge. In that regard, she was just like Isabella, using him to better her own lot in life.

The comparison had him clenching his jaw so hard it ached.

Seven years ago he'd put Caprice from his mind for one reason. Her congratulatory kiss had stirred feelings in him that mirrored those he'd felt for Isabella. Feelings he'd buried with his wife and refused to ever revisit again.

Now that Caprice had reentered his life, the image of the bright-eyed young woman he clearly recalled was replaced by a determined businesswoman who sought to align with him for her own benefit. Nothing more, nothing less.

Strictly business. He got that. Understood it. Respected her for her drive.

He shouldn't find her attractive in the least. But he did.

It was her aloofness and passion for her program and her old lodge. That was the only plausible explanation for his fascination with her.

The only difference between Caprice and the score of women hoping to snare him into marriage was the simple fact she could help his brother. That was why he'd agreed to meet with her. That's the only reason why he didn't stop this car now and call the whole thing off.

He needed her to help Julian as much as she needed his money and the connections his name would lend to Tregore Lodge and her program. From a business standpoint, theirs was a win-win situation. As long as he kept her at arm's length, everything would be fine.

No problem, as she'd made it clear she wanted nothing personal to do with him. Their association was all business. Good. That's all he wanted from her as well.

As they headed toward the airport and Italy, she appeared content to immerse herself in her miniature laptop before the flurry of their combined work began. Unlike his previous traveling companions, she showed no interest in making small talk during the past three hours as they prepared to leave Colorado.

Not that he was complaining.

He just wanted to get home to Italy and back to business while she delved into doing what he'd hired her to do. With space between them, he could find peace of mind.

That was what he wanted. It remained to be seen if he would achieve it after putting himself through so much personal hell.

Caprice stared out the window, more frazzled over being secluded with Luciano than she was unnerved by the Denver traffic they whipped past. Seven years had passed since she'd spent this much time alone with a man.

She'd vowed never to leave herself vulnerable again. Yet here she was, traveling for over an hour with him. So close she could reach over and touch him.

Not that she would. Even if she had the desire to do so, there was absolutely nothing welcoming about his stern expression.

Which was just as well. Too much was riding on the success of their mutual deal for her to relax.

She wanted this job done as soon as possible. Only then could she return home.

If Tregore Lodge was still under construction, she would cope with the inconvenience. Heavens knew she had a lot of details to see to before the launch of her renovated facility and a return to total independence.

No matter what faced her in Italy, she *would* see it through. And really would her being in Luciano's company again be that bad?

Difficult to guess, she decided as she stole a glance at him behind the wheel of the gleaming silver Mercedes he'd rented. As they reached the brighter lights leading to the airport, his deceptively relaxed pose was at odds with his hard-as-nails expression.

He'd always been demanding, a fact she attributed to his aggressive personality and his station. But he'd changed as well and she couldn't tell if it was for the better.

One thing was for sure, she would be right back in the thick of the elite world. Just like she was now, arriving at the private airport terminal in a rental car worth well over what she made in a year, scheduled to fly out on a private jet that cost at least a billion dollars.

He swerved to pass a slower car, and she noticed the imperceptible way he favored his right shoulder. Had he always done that?

At the lodge, she'd blamed his obvious discomfort on

the hurried way he'd loaded her baggage into the car. Now it was obvious his shoulder was bothering him.

"What's wrong?" she asked, noticing his chiseled features were more haggard under the flash of streetlights as he whizzed around the curved interior airport roads with the ease of a racing car driver.

"Nothing," was his clipped reply.

A lie, she was certain, if she'd read correctly that terse tone and body language that screamed pain. "Something is bothering you."

He wheeled into a parking space and cut her a scowl. "I have had very little sleep in nearly two days."

And lack of sleep had never bothered him before. But it clearly did now.

Luciano looked physically drained. Given his wicked reputation, she assumed it was from a combination of overindulgence and mental exertion while he was touring the U.S.

"How long have you been in Denver?" she asked.

"My plane landed at seven-thirty this morning, your time," he said.

She blinked. That only gave him four hours before their meeting, and he'd admitted to having an appointment before hers. "You flew here from Italy and went straight to a meeting?"

"I did not wish to waste time in the States."

That wasn't the Luciano she remembered. He was a party animal. The playboy who had the stamina to keep late hours and still perform with championship precision.

"Let me signal a skycap," she said as she followed him to the opened trunk of the Mercedes.

"Don't bother, I've got it." Yet, as he removed her bags, his movements seemed stiffer and his olive skin paled considerably.

She doubted his condition had anything to do with him loading her two suitcases into the rental and driving them to the Denver airport tonight. Nor was it the result of anything recent.

Under the brilliant glow cast by the private parking lot, she studied the lines of strain marring his handsome face, etching deep grooves around his piercing eyes and sensual mouth. Toss his terse attitude into the mix and it equaled a man who'd grown used to living with pain and hating it. Lingering pain. Reoccurring pain. Phantom pain.

She saw enough of it in her profession to be able to recognize it after a few minutes of observation. Luciano was gripped with the first two. Considering he'd been a world-class champion with a reputation for taking daring jumps and going at lightning speed down the slopes, it wasn't unusual it had left him with tangible scars from his years of fierce competition.

All of that abuse had come before the accident that had ended his career.

"I can read the signs, Luciano," she said, slinging her carry-on over her shoulder before he could add it to the wheeled cases he seemed intent on maneuvering alone. "The muscle in your left shoulder is cramped and the fingers of your right hand have gone numb, or at least they are in some sort of tingling paralysis. Right?"

He threw her a frown—no, a scowl befitting a warrior. "Again, my error is forgetting how perceptive you are."

She took the backhanded compliment with a smile. "It's my profession to recognize these problems with my patients."

"Which I am not," he said with a good deal of heat. "You've agreed to lend your professional services to my brother. He's the only Duchelini you will be attending."

"I wasn't offering to take you on as a client," she

snapped back, which wasn't true because if she could help him…oh, what did it matter? "I understand athletes detest showing weakness. The majority of them I've encountered consider pain from an injury a weakness to overcome. Am I right?"

"Yes," he hissed out. His long legs carried him across the drive toward the terminal with her two cases in tow. Then he stopped and cast her another impatient look. "Come on. The plane is waiting."

No surprise he wanted the subject dropped now, she thought as she beat him to the door and opened it for him, determined to have her say. "For one thing, you're wrong. Pain is not a weakness. Second thing—I believe you could benefit from therapy."

"I don't," he spat, every viral inch of him rigid with anger. "There is nothing that can be done to help me. Nothing."

The words plummeted like granite slabs on the concrete, shattering her tenuous confidence. She hadn't just touched the surface of a major sore spot with him. She'd raked over it with claws and flung salt into the wounds.

Crawling back into her protective shell and keeping her thoughts to herself would be smart. But she knew how the body reacted to pain, both physically and mentally. To a degree, she knew Luciano Duchelini—at least she knew the fiercely competitive athlete he had been.

"Okay. You've explored all avenues to alleviate your pain and nothing worked," she went on doggedly, just like she would with her patients. "But you've said it yourself. My program is different from the standard. If you utilized it to the fullest, there could be a chance for you to see physical improvement."

He bit off something in Italian, likely a curse aimed at

her. "Not enough to waste my time trying. I have learned to accept my limitations, Caprice. There is a difference."

"So that's it? You just give up?"

"This isn't about me. It's about Julian, and his injuries are life altering. All of the reports and reviews I've read about your program are glowing, and the professional techniques you've implemented are revolutionary. Focus on helping him with them." He motioned her inside, a muscle pulsing wildly in his jaw. "After you."

She looked away from his probing gaze and hurried through the doorway. Maybe he was right. Even with the best therapeutic programs out there, recovery from injuries hit a wall at some point. She knew that. Taught it often. So why was she pushing the issue with him? Why was she eager to discover his injuries?

The answer eluded her as she moved past him into the spacious waiting area of the airport with its welcoming chairs and scattering of passengers. She hadn't been here in fifteen years, but it hadn't changed except for an upgrade in the interior design.

She looked out the expanse of glass spanning the outer wall of the private concourse that lent a fabulous view of the private planes waiting to be boarded or disembarked by the rich or famous or a combination of both. The only time she'd been here was when she was twelve, and she was still haunted by the painful memory from her childhood leading up to that first trip to Denver.

She's of the age to be sent to boarding school, her mother's latest lover for the past six months had said one day as they'd readied for a trip to Jamaica.

Fine. Pay her tuition and I'll sign the papers, her mother had shot back.

She's not my daughter, he'd said. *Let her father assume her support or remain with her.*

And at that ultimatum, her mother had packed up Caprice and her possessions and flown to Colorado. She would never forget the shock twisting the reserved man's face when her mother marched her into Tregore Lodge, announced that Caprice was his daughter and ceremoniously dumped her into his care. She would never forget the sense of abandonment that haunted her still, despite the fact her father had accepted his responsibility and raised her well.

"This way," Luciano said, her body jolting as he pressed his right palm to her back.

For an insane moment, she wanted to lean into him. Wanted the heat radiating from his touch to melt the chill locked deep inside her. Wanted to feel needed and coddled just once in her life.

Sanity prevailed and she stumbled forward, breaking the odd hold. Already, being with him felt too familiar, too personal.

She moved to the aisle, walking slowly and purposefully when part of her screamed to run from the vortex of emotions swirling inside her. But there was no escape from memories, she knew as she continued toward the attendant standing by the door.

The woman's hungry gaze touched briefly on Caprice before devouring Luciano. The fact he always got that response from women didn't surprise her. The sudden tension and annoyance bubbling up inside her did, catching her unaware.

A denial screamed inside her brain. She wasn't jealous. She couldn't be. She wouldn't let herself be.

"Good evening, Mr. Duchelini," the attendant said in a soft purr. "Your plane is ready. If there's anything else I can do…"

"*Grazie,*" he said, and pressed several bills in her hand.

The woman loosed a throaty laugh that set Caprice's

teeth on edge. "If you ever need another assistant for your fleet, or anything else," she added, stepping closer to him, "please let me know."

"I will bear that in mind," he said.

Caprice had no doubt that he would. There was never a shortage of willing, beautiful women in Luciano's world.

She took a step away from the pair only to be caught by a strong yet gentle hand on her arm. Her gaze lifted to his, questioning.

"We must leave," he said, his crushed-velvet voice warm against her ear.

She shivered, her breath catching in her throat. "Sure. Fine," she managed to get out.

In moments he hustled her across the tarmac to the waiting jet. This gleaming plane dwarfed the local charter ones she'd taken with the ski team from one regional airport to another. The Duchelini jet was close in size to the spacious connection planes she'd taken on short jaunts between major terminals.

"She was hot for you," she said.

"She was overtly forward and looking to feather her nest."

"I'm sure you're used to that," she said, well remembering that he'd always had a bevy of beauties at his beck and call, many literally hanging on his strong arms.

"The falseness? Yes," he said, his lip curling. "Women like that have their place, but I am done with them."

Which meant what exactly? She chose not to pry because she knew the type of woman he referred to, and because it was none of her business or concern.

She followed him to the skirted ramp rising to a gleaming white jet, the belly and tail embellished with vibrant swaths of red and blue that faded into a muted spray of color. The la Duchi logo, the same one she'd seen brandished on the most elite skis and winter gear worldwide.

Her stomach clenched as she gripped the rail and ran up the steps, palm gliding up the cool metal. A whisper of chilled air greeted her at the top.

Fragmented memories of her childhood flickered before her like a black-and-white movie, faces and names of people long forgotten or barely known. Nannies, the score of men her mother had romanced and the array of beautiful people who had played with their set in that glamorous world.

Caprice recalled few details, but remembered one thing perfectly clearly. She'd always felt alone in her mother's elite world.

Even now, there was loneliness deep in her.

The old uncertainty and fear closed in around her, holding her in the past. For a moment, she paused to take a breath and push those unpleasant memories from her mind.

She didn't doubt going with Luciano was the right thing, nor did she hold any more qualms over their business deal. Still, a second's hesitation needled over her skin, a last warning that the moment she stepped into the spacious Duchelini jet there would be no turning back.

"What is the matter now?" he asked, his breath warm on her nape, the press of his palm to her back, firm and hot, and stirring feelings in her that made her want so much more. Dangerous yearnings that she still hadn't been able to quell yet.

She didn't need the conflict of working closely with him. She was the professional here. She would find a way to cope.

"Nothing more than the initial shock of stepping into air-conditioning," she said, slamming the door on her past and childish longings.

She'd expected the interior to reflect a masculine and sterile tone. But the rich burgundy and cream seating, glass-topped walnut tables and warm lighting gave the cabin a welcoming feel. Like coming home after a long, tiring trip.

"Then I'll have Larissa bring you a wrap," he said with a beckoning curl of his fingers, and a trim woman with a kind face appeared from behind a curved wooden divider midcabin with a gorgeous pale cream blanket draped over her arm. "The cabin gets quite cool when we reach cruising speed."

"Thanks," she said, taking the offered wrap and moving to a plush swivel seat by the window.

Luciano strode to the stocked bar, his movements noticeably stiffer. Ice clinked in a glass, the sound loud in the spacious cabin.

"You should take something for the pain," she said to his broad back.

"I intend to. Bunnahabhain on the rocks."

"From Islay," she said, remembering his preferred Scotch.

He saluted her with a heavy goblet half filled with the amber liquor. "Do you still drink it or have you adopted a different taste?"

The fact he remembered she'd drank it at all stunned her, but she hid it well, just like she hid the dark moments of her life. His accurate memory was nothing more than an attempt at polite conversation.

"I did once." She couldn't lie to him because games had never been her style, her one attempt having ended disastrously. "Actually, I haven't tasted Scotch since Val d'Isère."

He studied her, features tight and unreadable. "You enjoyed it."

"At the time," she said. But she'd enjoyed his company as well. Far too much.

The week before he'd swept the events, they'd talked of their future plans in life, sitting alone by a fire sharing a Scotch. He'd never spoken of his ex-wife and she'd never summoned up the courage to ask.

She hadn't wished to sour his mood, immaturely sure they would finally cross the line between star athlete and volunteer. When he'd swept the events, she'd finally gotten the courage to kiss him with all the feelings bubbling in her heart.

And for a heartbeat he'd returned her affection. Then he'd cursed and pulled away from her, scowling, anger flaring like live embers in his eyes as he turned on a heel and stalked away from her.

Confusion and embarrassment had tumbled inside her like leaves caught in a wind. Rejection. Her first from a man, but far from the first time she'd been passed over.

Still, it had hurt and left her confused. When she'd finally gone after him, she'd found him lounging on a sofa in the bar with a beautiful woman in his arms, their lips locked together in a passionate kiss.

That's when she'd run from him with one intention—finding a means to ease the heartbreak.

"What's wrong?" he asked, the question jarring her from the past.

"Nothing," she said.

"You're lying."

She met his intense gaze with a spark of hostility. "I was thinking about the last time we shared a Scotch and how wretchedly it ended."

The muscle along his jaw snapped taut, which only fueled her own annoyance. Then, as now, she'd meant nothing to him, which was fine by her.

"What happened that made it such a bad memory?" he asked.

"You rebuffed my congratulatory kiss," she said, because that's what had started it.

What had happened after that would forever haunt her. Her dark secret.

He snorted. "That was not what your kiss implied."

"You can't know that." He couldn't have known she'd been wearing her heart on her sleeve. That she'd slowly fallen for him.

He nodded and splashed Scotch into two heavy glasses. "You were very young, Caprice. Nineteen?"

"Twenty." Barely.

"I did you a favor by walking away from you instead of taking you straight to my bed."

How different her life might have been if he only had. What was done was done. She couldn't change things now, but she could remember the lesson well.

"I'm sure you're right," she said.

He nodded. Frowned. "Now that we've settled that, will you join me for a Scotch? Or would you prefer something else?"

"No. Scotch is fine," she said as she took the heavy glass from him, the brush of their fingers jolting her again. This time she couldn't hide her flush.

He lifted one eyebrow. "Something else is bothering you."

"No. I'm just tired." She took a sip and caught her breath as the slightly spiced heavy liquor warmed her tongue and throat. "I forgot how good this was."

He smiled but kept his gaze on her, and the barely leashed energy pulsing between them had her tension strung high. "It will get better if you let it."

She blinked, unsure if he meant the liquor, this tenuous

rapport they struggled to hold on to, or something else, and chose to believe it was the former.

"Yes, I think it will, too," she said, trying for a similar nonchalance.

"Count on it." He finished his drink and poured another. Instead of taking himself off to a private location, he eased down into the chair across from her.

The rev of the jets increased and she felt the tiniest vibration just before the pilot's voice filled the cabin, the sound far less tinny than in a commercial airliner. "Ready when you are, sir."

"Get us home" was Luciano's reply as he snapped his seat belt into place, the la Duchi logo on the custom gold buckle screaming of the quiet wealth that was spent on details.

The interior lights lowered to an intimate glow for take-off and the engines rumbled. She grabbed the burgundy strap and snapped her own belt into place, chancing another quick look at Luciano. His drawn features were more pronounced with his eyes pinched closed.

Concern welled inside her even stronger than before. He was obviously still in pain even after downing pain meds with two drinks that had likely packed a punch. At least the few mouthfuls she'd taken of her drink were making her head spin.

Even so, what he consumed hadn't been enough to affect him in the least. He was hurting inside, and her training told her it wasn't totally physical.

"What really happened that day on the mountain?" she asked, broaching the subject at last.

Silence roared over the monotone of the engines as the plane gained altitude, then leveled out, yet her stomach still felt suspended in midair. The details of that accident had been well hidden by the family. Why, she couldn't guess, but it was obvious Luciano wasn't eager to divulge anything.

"Luciano, I need to know everything in order to help Julian recover," she said when she couldn't stand the tense silence any longer. "There are psychological reasons as well as physical ones that impede recovery. If I can find a workaround for his internal obstacle, I stand a better chance of helping him." And Luciano as well?

Two champion brothers on skis. One horrific accident that had changed both their lives. Only they knew what had happened.

A muscle, or maybe a nerve, pulled hard in his cheek, puckering his olive skin. "The media provided a plausible version of our rescue and injuries."

She flinched, feeling the sting of his pain ricochet through her. Yes, she'd heard reports. Watched the news. Yet it was likely just what he'd said. A plausible version.

"Yes, I know where Julian and you were found, and I'm aware of the extent of his physical injures," she said, having hung on every word of the reports with the hope that Julian and Luciano would have full recoveries. "Now I need to understand the scope of your brother's psychological ones as well. The best place to start is knowing why two of the best skiers in the world chose to tackle one of the most hazardous runs in the Alps during less than hospitable conditions."

Luc drove his fingers through his hair and swore. How the hell could he satisfy her curiosity about the accident without revealing too much of his own emotional wounds? "It is the way of brothers who have spent their lives competing with each other in everything."

"There must be more to it than sibling rivalry."

There was. Too much baggage. Too much guilt.

He tossed back his drink and grimaced, hesitant to bear

his black soul to her. "Look, Julian is a Duchelini, second in line to a company that makes the best ski equipment in the world, youngest in a long line of Duchelini champions. It was a duty and privilege for him to compete in Alpine and win. Quitting was not an option."

"It was his choice to make."

"It was selfish, which is why Father froze his allowance," he said. "He thought when the money stopped, Julian would abandon his reckless bent and focus on the team."

"But that wasn't the case," she said, voice rising in question as she likely remembered how tensions had run high between the Duchelini brothers throughout the games.

"No. It was just the opposite, so Father charged me to intervene and get him back on track," he said, feeling removed from himself now, as if he were talking about a stranger instead of himself. "Julian was the reckless one without ties or obligations while I accepted my duty and became a champion skier and suitably married man with a day-to-day hand in the family business."

And perhaps he would have remained content in that role if his marriage hadn't crumbled in his hands.

"Did you resent your role?" she asked calmly reminding him of counselors he'd seen to no avail.

If she only knew the details, Luc thought sourly. But she couldn't and it wasn't a subject he wished to go into great detail.

"I did after my ex-wife died," he admitted, hungry for the punishment a free, grueling lifestyle promised.

She swallowed, going still. "You loved her."

"Very much so." He pressed his head against the seat, eyes closed as he allowed old memories and their pain to intrude. "With a bit of pressure, I was able to secure Julian a spot on the Italian ski team. But he didn't care about Alpine. Extreme ski drove him. Challenged him."

"Then why did he agree to participate in Alpine?"

"Father exerted his muscle," Luc said. "Adding to the pressure, the sports world jumped on Julian's natural ability, touting him as the faster and more daring Duchelini. It was a challenge few men could walk away from."

"Was he really that good?" she asked.

"Better than good. Off the record, he beat me most of the time." He fisted his hands on the chair, remembering how jealous he'd been of his brother's bravado and skill. His freedom. "All champions know it is a matter of time before their records will be broken. I shattered my father's records and Julian had the potential to best mine, but his heart remained in extreme ski, which is why he turned in such a poor performance at the World Cup."

"Is that why Julian seemed so upset the day I left?"

He leaned back in his chair and rubbed his knuckles along his jawline, glaring at the ceiling as the jet leveled off at cruising altitude. "No. I realized he got a tremendous high from extreme skiing and told him I, too, was going to compete against him there. He threw a fit. Said I wasn't prepared. That I hadn't practiced the quicksilver moves needed to attempt the extreme ski."

She wet her lips, eyes narrowed and breathing shallow, looking vulnerable, pensive, concerned. That last one got him in the gut like a blow.

"Why? You were a four-time Alpine champion, skilled in tackling the toughest slopes in ungodly conditions. At the World Cup I remember you attacking the slopes with reckless abandon, earning gold in everything you entered."

He loosed a bitter laugh at his carnal failings then and now, recalling that dark period in his life. If only he could alter time and go back, he might have been able to prevent the tragedy.

"Why doesn't matter," he said bitterly. "Alpine no longer thrilled me. But Julian refused to let up. So I challenged him to a race to decide my future. If he won, I would bow out of extreme ski."

"And if you won, you would compete against your brother in the sport he excelled in."

"Exactly. So I arranged the meet," he said, regretting the fool's bet every day.

"Wow." She blew out a breath, then another, and he only just stopped himself from reaching over to her, touching her, holding her. "Why did you pick the most treacherous slope in Austria for your challenge?"

"The Hahnenkamm was the best test of our abilities," he bit out. "I dreaded that mountain as most do and was grateful that winning my yearly race there was behind me. But it tests the best and that's what this challenge was about. Julian readily agreed, knowing it was beyond reckless to attempt it at the same time. But he lived to test himself and saw this as his means to best me."

"But he failed," she said softly.

He closed his eyes and watched that moment unfold in his memory, feeling the amazing rush, the choking fear and the crippling pain that never ended, that rolled on and on like a monster avalanche, clearing everything in its path. "He could have won."

"Then why didn't he?"

"It was my fault." He took a deep breath and huffed it out, gaze trained on the opaque wall but seeing nothing but blinding snow. Hearing nothing but the howl of the wind as he shot over the edge behind his brother and realized he was too low, that he hadn't launched off as Julian had. "I was behind him by a good twenty seconds when we took a dangerous jump. I miscalculated the distance and lost a ski and the race. And my brother—" He hung his head and broke off, swallowing hard, face carved in anguish.

"Don't go there," she said softly, reaching over to lay a hand on his clenched one.

He turned his arm and grabbed her hand, squeezing it like it was a lifeline. "He shouldn't have looked back. He should have kept flying down the mountain toward the next jump and proved he was the best. But he didn't. He ignored the most basic rule and glanced back at me sprawled in the snow. I looked up just as he skidded out of control and shot over the precipice."

"My God," she whispered as she laid her hand atop his arm. "You can't blame yourself for what happened."

"I can do anything I want."

"Let me help you—"

For one fleeting moment he wanted to accept her help. But that opened another avenue he wasn't about to travel with a good woman.

"Helping Julian will help me," he said, gruffly.

"There are other treatments—"

"No! What is done is done." He shook his head, accepting his penance, his guilt. "I have had surgeries, followed by long sessions with top physical therapists around the world. My rehabilitation dragged on for two years before I put an end to it. They can do no more."

"Are you always this intractable?"

"Stop being so optimistic," he said, and without giving her time to reply, he barked out, "I brought you to Italy to give Julian a chance at a fuller life. You're under contract do that and no more. In exchange, I will make sure you have an updated, state-of-the-art lodge for your therapy program in your quaint Colorado Rocky Mountains. Remember that."

"How could I ever forget?"

He hoped to hell she didn't. Hoped he could find that sweet spot that blinded him to the errors he'd made in the past. But then, in truth, he didn't want to ease the misery.

It was the penance he lived every day. His due.

Nothing would change that. Nothing.

CHAPTER THREE

THE MAN HAD absolutely no concept of failure, she fumed, welcoming the sleep that finally overtook her during the long flight.

At least it spared her from listening to any more of Luciano's vitriol. She'd made an error attempting to help him. Hadn't she learned years ago that he never wanted that of her?

Okay, fine. Lesson learned now. She would never again be the fool with that Italian who was clearly packing more baggage than a short line rail car. As he so clearly put it, she would finish her job and leave Italy as soon as possible. She silently swore not to give his physical pain, or a means to ease it, another thought as the plane finally touched down in Italy.

She pulled in a long breath, then another. For the next few weeks, possibly a month, she would need a surfeit of patience. If she focused on what she would gain, she could make it through this without a problem.

That thought stayed with her as they began the process of departing the plane and passing through customs. Thankfully it went so fast that Caprice barely had time to register she was standing on Italian soil before Luciano hustled her onto the tarmac.

"This way," he said, his features devoid of pain, his expression anxious, and then he was off.

She practically ran to keep marginally close to him, thanks to his long, sure strides. Obviously the long flight with scant physical activity benefited him. In fact she had to jog to stay behind his fast pace as he headed toward two chauffeur-driven sedans parked side by side.

Two cars? Did he mean for them to travel separately? God, she hoped so, having endured as much of his prickly company as she could tolerate.

But he was too far ahead for her to attempt asking, not that it really mattered. She was in for the long haul, no matter the discomfort.

Just before they reached the cars, the rear door on the one farthest away opened and a tall, elderly gentleman stepped out. He took a sentry stance, his strong features unreadable. Yet he was very recognizable to her, reflecting so much of the man ahead of her.

"Is it typical for your father to greet you at the airport?" she asked, finally coming abreast of him.

"Never." Luciano released a muffled curse and continued walking to the other sedan at a sedate pace that she could keep up with. "We haven't spoken in months."

"By choice or chance?"

"Both." He shook his head. "It's complicated."

A family state she knew intimately, she thought sourly. "I know what you mean."

His intense blue gaze swung to her, brow furrowed. "Do you?"

"I've been estranged from my mother for the bulk of my life," she admitted.

"You never told me."

"You never let us get that close," she said.

He stopped and grasped her hand, and just like that she

was gone, caught up in the river of fire gushing through her veins. She tried to block the power and pulse of him but failed, soaking him in like rain on the desert. And she hated the sensations as much as she thirsted on them, but finally managed to jerk free with a shaky smile.

"It's okay. I'm long over it." *And you.* Or was she? *Don't go there,* she told herself, focusing instead on what had shaped her. "When my dad passed away, my mother didn't bother to send me a note or flowers, or even call to check on my welfare."

"Perhaps she wasn't aware of his death."

"She knew," she said, not bothering to soften the bitterness that hardened her voice. "My mother is just as self-centered as she has always been. The day after my dad's funeral, she told the paparazzi she was out of sorts because her first husband had just passed on."

"She is a selfish woman."

"Very."

He nodded, walking at a more sedate pace toward the sedans again, tension radiating off him as hot as the heat rising from the asphalt tarmac. "You are nothing like her."

"That is the greatest compliment you could ever give me," she said, keeping stride with him as they headed toward his waiting father. "You don't know how much I envied people who had a normal family."

"Normal?" He snorted, the strong line of his jaw going taut. "Mine was far from it."

"Come on, you had a mother and father who were married and lived together. My God, you and Julian had everything money could buy. Even after your mother's death, you told me that your father ensured his sons got the very best education and opportunities available."

"True. But don't confuse a privileged lifestyle with a

perfect one," he said. "'Money can't buy happiness' is a very true saying."

A saying her mother would strongly disagree with. "I know."

They reached the sedan at the same time the elder Duchelini crossed to intercept them. Hard lines dug grooves into the older man's tanned features, but they merely enhanced his rugged good looks.

"Father," Luciano said, pulling her close. "This is Caprice Tregore, rehabilitation therapist extraordinaire."

Certainly not the tag she would add to her name, but it would embarrass her make to make a fuss out of his exaggerated praise. She managed a smile. "Hello."

"Good to meet you," Mr. Duchelini said, and lifted each hand in turn and bestowed a kiss on each. The gesture was so old and charming she couldn't take offense, yet she felt Luciano stiffening beside her. "Welcome to Italy. I hope your stay proves entertaining."

"Thank you, but this is a business trip for me," she said.

The older man frowned, looking from her to his son before landing on Luciano. "What is this?"

"Caprice will be setting up her program at our new lodge," Luciano said.

Again, she was treated to another exacting perusal from Luciano's father. "Ah, a beautiful woman and a smart one as well. A dangerous combination," he said to his son.

"Yes, she is," Luciano said.

And what was that supposed to mean? The only danger she saw was the powerful draw of Luciano that she constantly fought to ignore.

"What brings you here, Father?"

"A problem." His dark gaze swung to her, assessing she was certain. "If you will excuse us, I need a moment alone with my son."

"Certainly," she said and moved to get in the sedan, only to have Luciano open the door for her and offer an apologetic smile.

"This won't take long," he said.

"It's okay. Take your time." She busied herself fishing her netbook from her tote and hoped he didn't see how her hand shook.

Several strained seconds passed before the door closed. Only then did she take a breath and glance out the window. The two men squared off between the two sedans, looking obstinate and commanding. Father and son. So much alike in that regard yet something was driving them apart.

She didn't want to guess what it was. She didn't even want to know details. She only wanted to find a way she and Luciano could work together for the next month without tearing each other apart. And without her losing her heart to him all over again.

It wasn't going to be easy.

"What is this urgent business?" Luc asked his father, having no patience for this interruption to his own plans.

"Victore wants to do business with us at the new lodge. I can't refuse them."

"I can," Luc said with heat.

His father bit off a ripe curse. "Carlos Victore has been a friend of mine for fifty years. It would be a slap in the face to refuse to meet with his son because of past issues you have with Carlos's eldest son."

"Past issues?" Luc said, balling his fingers into fists. "His son had an affair with my wife while he was doing business with me. He's not to be trusted."

His father stared at him, unmoved. "Let it go."

"I most certainly will not let it go. I will *never* do business with a Victore."

And he most certainly would not stand here while his father tried to strong-arm him into dealing with the man who ruined his marriage. He stormed toward the waiting sedan.

"Wait," his father barked.

"I've nothing more to say on the subject. I'm considering Mario Godolphin as the architect." He wrenched open the car door and dropped in beside her. "Go," he told his driver as he reached for the door.

His father positioned himself in the door's opening and the driver noticed and remained parked. Stubborn old fool!

"Our families have done business for decades," his father said. "We are like family!"

"Family that stabs one another in the back," Luc spat.

His father slashed the air with a hand. "What proof do you have for such a claim? None, other than your wife and Carlos's eldest son dying in a horrific motor accident. Think, Luciano. We can make this work to our advantage. What do I tell Carlos and his son?"

"Tell them both to go to hell."

Luc pulled at the door and his father backed out of the way with a scowl that screamed retribution. He didn't want to have this talk and he sure as hell didn't want Caprice privy to the details of his family's scandal. "Drive."

The big sedan jolted forward, slamming Caprice against the plush cushions. Heat seeped from Luciano and tension pulsed inside the car. Her heart raced. Should she ask what was wrong? No. This wasn't her business. Wasn't her concern.

So why was her heart still pounding? Why were her fingers numb from clenching her hands together tightly?

"That was not pleasant," he said at last.

"Is there a problem with la Duchi?" she asked, the most logical thing that popped into her mind.

He barked a laugh that lacked humor. "My father wouldn't know one way or the other. He held a small figurehead role at la Duchi for years because of his impressive records and because my grandfather insisted on it. But Father's only gift was his supreme athletic ability regarding equipment design and an overload of *savoir faire*. As far as business acumen, he was doubly cursed."

"While you were blessed with all three," she said, genuinely meaning the compliment to the champion who'd come up with innovative designs and who could also run an empire.

"That blessing sometimes is a curse," he said.

"Everything has a price."

"Sometimes a price that pains us to pay."

"Do you want to talk about it?" she asked.

"No. There is nothing to discuss. I like my life the way it is," he said, his crisp tone and intent gaze on the road dissuading further comment.

"As do I," she said.

She had a home, business and profession all crammed into one. Her employees were trustworthy. Her few friends were loyal.

And so what if her love life was nonexistent? It was her choice. She'd never received any pleasure from a man.

Alone she was independent. In charge of her own fate and pleasure.

If she ever got the crazy idea to indulge in an intimacy, she would choose the time and place. She'd never let herself be victimized again.

And she wouldn't dream of entertaining close company with a man like Luciano Duchelini! When she'd known him years ago he had been an athlete at the top of his game. The champion. Arrogant beyond belief.

Everyone had wanted a piece of him, from the vast endorsements clambering for his approval to the women who hoped to win his heart. Even her, and look where that had got her.

Caprice pushed those dark memories again to the back of her head, preferring to let her gaze wander the land so very different from Colorado. Though they were on the southern perimeter of the Alps, well into Italy, place names were an intriguing mix of Italian and Germanic. Soft romantic sounds interspersed with hard guttural ones.

The mountains here were just as unyielding as the Rockies with bold limestone cliffs that screamed danger. Just like the man beside her.

He was the predator, a champion in winter sports and high-stakes business. She'd watched him dominate the slopes, and she was certain he attacked business with the same fierceness.

But she refused to let his bravado or his business prowess scare her into meek compliance. Though she never earned a medal, she did earn a degree. She was an expert in her field and was insulted by the fact he expected her to play by *his* rules.

He would soon learn that she refused to be the puppet dancing on his strings, she vowed as they reached the village close to an hour later. It looked more like an Alpine village than a ski area. The panoramic vista that seemed to stretch forever into the horizon literally took her breath away.

It was a hidden place of treacherous cliffs and lush hidden vales amid the backdrop of soaring snow-capped peaks. Shadows and amazing lights. Light and dark. Soft and hard. Like Luciano, who clearly had roots here.

Deep roots would be mandatory here. Clustered against the hills and nested on the flats were charming Alpine structures anointed with cream stucco walls and tiled roofs that gleamed a rich patina under an intense high mountain sun. It silently offered beauty and solitude. Yet for all its apparent quaintness an upbeat atmosphere pulsed in the air, as if the area were being prepped for an event.

Robust villagers waved as they passed, many shouting out warm greetings to Luciano, who returned each with a very broad, very relaxed smile that she'd never seen before. The transformation was miraculous. She blinked, certain she must have imagined the change in him from stoic traveling companion to congenial resident of this bustling settlement tucked in the Italian Alps.

Right now he was beyond handsome. Boyish. Open.

This was the man she'd caught a rare glimpse of years ago. A man she'd thought she shared much in common with. But she'd been wrong. She hadn't known him then and she certainly didn't know him now. Nor did she wish to.

The village might be a world apart from the après-ski scene she'd associated him with, but Luciano was the same cunning man. This show of relaxation was just another mask for him to don at will.

She wasn't about to be fooled by him this time. But she would give herself over to admiring this amazing village. Every building held its own Old World charm. Except for the mammoth glass and log structure that rose high above the village. The clouds shifted and rays of sun illuminated its soaring glass facade as well as the hints of dangerous runs streaking the surrounding mountains.

It was a curious combination of danger and opulence, just like the man beside her.

"Is that your lodge?" she asked, shielding her eyes as she pointed to it.

He slid on a pair of Louis Vuitton sunglasses, but the hint of a smile pulling at his mouth boasted pure pride. "Yes, that is la Duchi Royal."

Fingers of panic reached out to her from the shadows of her mind as he wound the car through the narrow cobbled streets toward the premier lodge overlooking the valley. She'd expected wealth unlike she'd ever seen before, but this went far beyond her imagination.

"It's fabulous." An understatement, but words failed her.

"It is unique." He glanced at her and smiled, and her heart did a crazy thump in her chest. "Like your program."

Her cheeks burned. "You don't have to keep saying that."

He shrugged. "It is the truth."

She tore her gaze from his and swallowed hard, shaken that his compliments affected her so deeply. Was she that needy for attention?

No. That was her mother's penchant.

She thrived on work and being totally independent. She had to be in control. Yet his compliments had begun to fluster her, and that wasn't normal.

Luciano was right. She was only comfortable when she was in control of her business and her life. Right now both were hanging in limbo, leaving her feeling on edge.

Once she immersed herself in this project, she would draw strength and confidence. She couldn't settle for any other outcome, no matter how much she was tempted.

Luc shook off the last of his tension like water and gave the sedan more gas, trying like hell to put the woman beside him from his mind. She was far too intriguing. Far too attractive, and that was a signal that he'd been away from his business for too long. But soon they'd be at the lodge and he could delve into much-needed work while Caprice did the same.

Apart. Maybe then he wouldn't be tempted to touch her. To see if her skin was as smooth as it looked, to explore how much of her well-toned body was tanned.

Seven years ago, her allure hadn't been that strong. He'd been able to resist her simply because she'd seemed more innocent. More playful. More inquisitive.

Now she was a woman in control. A very desirable woman. Far too tempting to him.

The last few hours he'd longed for sanctuary. If Caprice hadn't been with him, he would have whizzed past the exclusive lodge and hit the trail that wound higher to his private *rifugio* nestled on a mountain ledge.

But he would not take her to his hideaway. Besides, the luxury car would never make the journey and he wasn't about to stop to trade out vehicles. The designers were waiting for them to arrive for the meeting and that was what they would do.

As usual, he had no time for anything but business. But wasn't that what he wanted?

"The village isn't what I expected," she said, breaking the silence.

"And that would be?"

"Trendy. Busy," she said, nose wrinkling.

"A hotspot for tourists or more specifically, the haute rich," he said, taking a wild guess at her thoughts and sensing her discomfort.

"Yes. But it's just the opposite."

"It was planned that way to set it apart from the party havens," he said, quickly leaving the cluster of aged buildings behind. "Decades ago, my family chose to maintain the Old World charm of the village while keeping all the services up to date. They purchased the majority of the chalets, renovated them and hired full staffs. They immediately appealed to those who wanted exclusivity and were able to afford the cost of it. The village hasn't changed much in decades. The chalets are rarely unoccupied for more than two weeks out of the year."

"A getaway for the wealthy," she said, capturing a yawn with her palm. "Do you also own or hold interest in the local businesses as well?"

"Several are la Duchi holdings. They were bought up when the previous owners wished to sell," he said, hoping that put an end to her inquiry. "You are free to visit them after I give you a tour of the new facility and we have met with the designers."

"I'm anxious to see it and get started."

So was he, only for different reasons than hers, he suspected. "Good. We'll be there in a few moments."

She blinked. "You mean the meeting is now?"

"I told you we would meet the designers when we arrived here."

"Well, yes, I remember," she said and bit her lower lip.

"Is that a problem?"

"No," she said and sat up straighter. "But I haven't seen the place where you plan to house the therapy unit. After that I'll need a little time to gather my thoughts before I can discuss detailed designs. Even then, some things may need to be changed."

"I realize that," he said as he eased the car through the short tunnel to the arched portico where a valet waited. "We'll tour the area set aside for the therapy pod and go from there, if you have no objections."

She shook her head. "None at all."

Even though he had expected it of her, again she surprised him by being ready to dive in at a moment's notice. It was a trait that would suit her well in her business. A trait he admired.

He climbed out at the same time the valet jumped to open Caprice's door. By the time he'd rounded the hood, she'd fetched her bag from the trunk.

"If you please." He motioned for her to precede him though massive glass doors into the lobby.

"Thanks." She took half a dozen steps inside and stopped. "Wow."

He savored that moment, admiring her lovely backside before she turned, her eyes alight with pleasure, her gaze dancing over the native granite wall behind the bank of glass reception desks to the stand of trees that towered in the central rotunda.

"This is absolutely fabulous," she said, her face capturing her awe. "Who designed this?"

His chest swelled as he, too, surveyed the fluid modernity style that had already garnered three prestigious awards for the designer. "Valvechete of France. I commissioned him because my architect was off exploring some island in South America and I was too inpatient for him to return. Valvechete immediately stepped in and developed a design that was elegant yet fluid. Something that incorporated the location yet was innovative. In my opinion, this is by far his most stunning work. If not for my loyalty to my friend, I would use him exclusively for all my projects."

"Sometimes you just have to go with the better man," she said. "I've never seen anything remotely like this before. It's breathtaking."

"That was the idea." He made to press his hand to the inviting small of her back but stopped short. Touching her might ignite the need he'd so far managed to tamp down. Might suggest an intimacy to her that he definitely wasn't about to explore, even though he was sorely tempted. "Come. Let me show you the space allocated for your therapy program."

The short walk down the central corridor gave a commanding view of the valley, thanks to the walls of glass to their left. "It feels as if we are strolling along a mountain path," she said, face wreathed in a smile that erased the weariness he'd noticed earlier.

He ran his palm over the massive log wall to his right, proud of the rich patina it had developed over the past year. "I thought that would be a benefit to those who came here exclusively for therapy."

"Very clever," she said.

His face warmed uncomfortably. "Far from that."

She paused in the glass-walled rotunda to stare out on the ski village and the verdant valley below, the perfect picture to advertise the area. "I disagree. This view is riveting."

Not as captivating as her, he admitted. "Very much so."

He tore his gaze from her and focused on the mountain. When he built the lodge, he'd commissioned a top photographer to capture this vista from differing seasons, a job that had taken a year. But the end product had been worth the wait.

And yet for all its grandeur and appeal, owning this premier lodge failed to assuage the guilt that ate at him day and night. At times it actually made him feel worse.

"Time to tour the therapy pod," he said.

They walked side by side down the long corridor in silence. Sunlight spilled through the glass, brushing her hair with gold. Yet the excitement in her eyes was far brighter as she gazed out the expansive windows in turn.

"No matter where you look you see ski runs," she said.

"That's an enticement for those who come here for reha-bilitation."

"It's good you feel the same way," he said, and this time let her praise seep into him, allowing himself that plea-sure. "The wider pistes are designed for alternative skiers. The elevator off the therapy wing opens into their equip-ment room. From there, special lifts take them to the top of the slopes."

"Your idea?" she asked, finally glancing back at him.

He shrugged. "It seemed logical."

"It is. Like the view from here."

He dipped his chin and smiled. "Do you approve?"

"Very much, but then as I said your design up to now has been very clever indeed," she said. "I expect the pod you've created for my program will live up to or exceed that standard."

"If it doesn't," he said with a grin, "you will tell me."

"Oh, you can bet on it."

He had no doubts she would feel free to express her opinion. That was what he wanted. Not someone who'd agree to everything he suggested but someone who would actually brainstorm with him to create the best possible facility.

She was perfect for his needs. His wants. His desires, he admitted, and tried to block out how much he desired her as they crossed the glass-domed walkway specially floored with a mat that absorbed sound as well as cush-ioning one's step. When had she become such an alluring woman? Why hadn't he seen this in her years ago? Or had he and blacked it out because of his disastrous marriage?

No answers trotted forth. He knew better than to let a woman's praise go to his head, even if hers was from a professional standpoint.

"How long did it take you to see this completed?" she

asked, breaking the silence as they neared the glass doors at the end of the corridor.

"The major structures, lifts and runs took two years to finish." He glanced up at the mountain on which he once had loved to test his prowess and frowned. "Now it's time to add the final touches to it and take the facility to the next level."

For himself as well? No, he'd given up all thoughts of pursuing sports after the accident and had funneled his daredevil edge and drive into business. He wouldn't dwell on regrets either. But he vowed to open doors for his brother, and Caprice was the key he needed.

"You certainly couldn't charge exorbitant prices unless the facility was the best worldwide," she said.

He opened the pod door and motioned her to precede him. "Yes, it must make a profit, but as I told you before, I'm doing this for Julian."

She stopped a few feet into the room, her slender back to him. "That's noble, but I suspect there's a deeper reason besides brotherly love that drives you to do this." She faced him then, eyes questioning. "Care to share?"

He felt the tension snap through his shoulders, and knew she would keep picking away until she got to the truth. Perhaps it was best to tell her everything. "Knowing that it is my fault Julian is paralyzed, do you really need to ask?"

Caprice stared at him, seeming not to know what to say to that. "He accepted your challenge."

"Of course. He is a Duchelini."

She walked the length of the room in silence, the slap of her slender flats the only sound other than the rasp of his breath. Finally she faced him again.

"What does that mean? Duchelinis don't back down?"

He smiled. "It is a matter of pride."

"Pride." She shook her head and resumed her study of the massive pod. *"Pride goeth before the fall."*

The old saying ricocheted off the walls and pierced his heart, drawing emotional blood. She had no idea how living with that knowledge pained him. No idea that seven years ago he'd pushed her away from him out of self-loathing because her kiss had touched on feelings he'd felt for his wife. Tender emotions that Isabella had shredded with her deceit. Stronger emotions because his wife's death had changed him.

Her death froze his heart and loosed a restless spirit.

Therein lied the regret that haunted him day and night.

The fall, as Caprice poetically put it, had severed his family in two. It had cut off any further efforts of his on the slopes.

After the fall, he'd given up what he loved because he'd lost all he loved. His unfaithful wife. His brother, as only a shell of a man seemed to survive.

His fingers fisted, his muscles tensing tightly down his side to taunt the injury that reminded him daily of his stupidity. His pride. Taunting him over what he could have had if he'd just been forgiving. As if staring into his brother's eyes weren't enough to scar him!

He ached to shout a biting comeback, but words failed him. At least cordial words. Not a single one came to mind.

"I'll leave you alone to decide what you need to present to the design team. Meet me in my office in an hour," he managed to bite out as he strode toward the open door without looking back to see her reaction.

What she thought didn't matter. This part of their planning would be done his way, and she would just have to deal with it.

CHAPTER FOUR

WITHOUT A DOUBT, Luciano Duchelini was the most infuriating man she had ever met. How dare he immediately haul her off the plane and expect her to formulate a workable plan for a state-of-the-art adaptive ski and rehabilitation facility that would bear her name. And on limited sleep at that!

Did he think he could best her? Or did he believe she really was that prepared to launch right into work off the plane?

The fact that was she semi ready was a major benefit. And that she wanted this job done as quickly as possible was another added incentive for her to focus on this instead of the promise of rest.

She could sleep when this job was finished.

With that in mind, she crossed to the bank of windows that opened to face the mountains and drank in the amazing view. Luciano had been wise choosing this wing for the therapy pod. She would give him that, and she would certainly optimize this vista that was key to her program's success.

It took twenty minutes to roughly sketch the placement of necessary equipment and another ten to adjust the initial list she'd used in her presentation package. A thorough edit and tweaking of minor details and she was ready to meet the design team.

If only she could say the same about being in Luciano's company again.

As she made her way to his office with five minutes to spare, she admitted that on a physical level, she was attracted to him. The unwelcome feeling grabbed her unbidden and caused her stomach to pinch tight.

She didn't know how to squash it. But she would.

The last thing she wanted or needed was a man in her life. Tolerating this stubborn Italian through the completion of their contract was all she ever wished to manage.

She paused outside his office suite and took several deep breaths. Game on. Affecting a smile, she pushed through the door. His secretary's head snapped up, the woman's attention switching from the neat stack of papers on the desk to her.

"Caprice Tregore to see Mr. Duchelini," she said

"Right on time," Luciano said, before the secretary could open her mouth.

Caprice whirled to find him standing in a doorway that had been closed a heartbeat ago, one broad shoulder propped against the doorjamb, perfectly sculpted lips pressed firmly together. Those intense eyes made one lazy sweep of her length, but this time there was something besides anger or challenge lighting his eyes.

A shiver of anticipation streaked through her, awakening that part of her that had slept for far too long. Pure animal attraction that she refused to act on, now or ever.

"Is the design team here?" she asked stiffly.

"No. Please, come in." He motioned her inside his office, but instead of stepping back to free the doorway, he stood like a sentinel with his back to the jamb.

If this was some tactic of his meant to intimidate her,

he had wasted his time and effort. She gripped her portfolio and squeezed past him, cursing him for his mulishness and hating how her nipples tightened.

"Where should I set up?" she asked, struggling with the nervous fear that kept her stomach queasy and her palms damp.

"To the left of my desk," he said, coming toward her. "Let me help you."

"Thanks, but I can manage."

He took the easel from her before she could stop him. "I didn't say you couldn't, but this way you will be ready in short order and time is of the essence."

Arguing with him would leave her in the wrong state of mind for giving the best presentation, and he did set it up in the ideal spot, so she bit her tongue and suffered his help in silence.

"Is there anything you need?" he asked.

A break from his close presence, which she knew wouldn't happen soon enough. "Nothing," she said and sent up a prayer as the door opened and his secretary poked her head in.

"Germaine and Fuseli are here to meet with you," the woman said.

"Buono," Luciano said. "Send them in."

In moments, a dapper man and a tall, elegant woman joined them, the man toting an expensive portfolio while the woman clutched a netbook. Luciano quickly made introductions.

Caprice stepped forward and extended her hand toward the elder of the pair, making it clear she wished to take charge of her program. If Luciano took offense at her boldness, he certainly masked it well. In fact, he appeared as eager as her to get past this phase.

"Nice to meet you both," Caprice said. "Luciano promised you were the best designers for my program."

"We strive to please," Mr. Fuseli said, and his partner nodded in agreement.

"Which you do to perfection," Luciano said to the designers. "Caprice has developed a unique and amazing program. It is up to you two to determine her needs so this facility exceeds her expectations."

"We're ready whenever Ms. Tregore is," Ms. Germaine said, her accent bearing a hint of French.

Caprice looked for a place to sit that was far from Luciano and his desk. Too late, his gaze snared hers again, and this time she felt the burn of desire scorch her soul. Curse him for doing this to her now when she needed to be on.

She tore her gaze away and settled on a stuffed chair in the sitting area that gave an enviable view of a startlingly challenging ski run. Pushing him from her mind, she fetched her notebook from her bag, all the while mentally reviewing her specific needs. A few clicks and she pulled up the file that detailed her program. "I'm ready."

"Excellent," Mr. Fuseli said and nodded to the elegant Ms. Germaine, who immediately began shooting her questions.

Twenty minutes later Caprice had answered them all. She ended by handing them rough sketches for the placement of equipment and a furnishing list.

The designers huddled together to review her drawings. Germaine shot her an excited smile. "I can see this in grays and blacks highlighted with reds and glass."

"Yes, it is perfect for a European theme with clean lines. Monochromatic with the occasional splash of intense color to define," Fuseli chimed in. "We can have a fully scaled mock-up done in a week for your approval."

"Nothing sooner?" Caprice asked.

Fuseli stroked his narrow chin with thumb and forefinger. "Perhaps by a day."

"And if I don't care for this design?" Caprice asked.

Luciano threw his hands in the air. "You will. But if you don't, then they will produce another for your perusal."

"That's all well and good except for the fact we'll fall another week behind schedule while the designers create a new mock-up." Which meant she would be in Luciano's company that much longer.

Ms. Germaine frowned, glancing at Luciano. "If time is crucial, then why don't you show her your *rifugio*?"

"Yes, yes, good question. That design is exactly what we envision for here. But perhaps you've sold the property," Fuseli quickly added.

Luciano stiffened. "I haven't sold it, but taking Miss Tregore there is out of the question."

The designers nodded, but Caprice could only stare at Luciano. Why was he balking at showing her the design? Whatever the reason, she wouldn't have it.

"Luciano, could I have a moment alone with you before we go any further?" she asked.

He fixed a cool stare on her, his blue eyes snapping with irritation. "Is this necessary?"

"Only if you expect me to proceed with the program."

His jawline hardened, but he gave a nod and addressed the pair. "If you please, would you mind stepping into the outer office for moment?"

"Not at all," Fuseli said, and the pair hurried out, closing the door in their wake.

"Do they seriously expect me to copy a known design of yours?" she asked, keeping her voice low.

"This is *my* design and is known only to a select few that have seen my *rifugio*," he said dismissively.

She frowned, her muzzy mind struggling to grasp the

meaning of the word, but the way it rolled off his tongue made the place sound sensual and relaxed. Intimate. Exactly the place she never wished to go with him.

"How far is it from here?"

"A day's journey and back at the most," he said, irritation sharpening his words. "Why do you ask?"

"I want to see it."

"Out of the question."

She bracketed her hands on her hips. "Why? What is this place?"

"It was an old refuge for shepherds and skiers caught out in inclement weather, built just below the snowline like all the *rifugios* that dot the Dolomites. I've turned it into my private retreat."

A hideaway. "On the order of Rocky Mountain line cabins," she said more to herself, becoming less convinced anything remotely similar to that would suit her needs. "What makes you so sure I will like the design?"

"I paid attention to your body language when we met in Denver, while we were at your lodge and when we arrived here as well. I listened as you talked with the designers about what you wanted. You've yet to feel totally comfortable," he said.

She wanted to dispute him but couldn't. "You're right. I want a plan that is clean and open, but I don't want stark modernism, nor do I want classic elegance, or Western themed."

"As I thought. You wish to keep the integrity of your historic old lodge, yet you don't want the interior to be rustic, ultra-modern or lavish."

He was trying to sell her on a design sight unseen, but she wasn't about to cave in. Time was too crucial.

"Am I right?" he pressed.

"Yes."

He smiled. "Good. May I bring the designers back in so we can finish this?"

"Please do."

Stay strong! The only way she knew how to do that was to take control now before this totally spiraled out of hand.

"You are all convinced I will love this design done at the *rifugio*. Correct?" Caprice asked when the designers stepped back into the office.

The designers nodded, but Luciano raised a questioning brow. "Caprice," he said in a warning tone.

But she ignored him and pressed on. "Then I insist we save time and energy. Take me to the *rifugio*."

"Splendid idea," Ms. Germaine said, gaining a nod of approval from her partner. "We shall still start the second design idea, but will await your approval on the first. You are both in agreement?"

"Well?" Caprice asked, arms crossed over her bosom, joining the designers to stare at Luciano.

His chest heaved and his blue eyes went black. "You insist on seeing it? Fine," he said, throwing his hands in the air for the second, or perhaps third time, and the designers quickly left, leaving her alone with a very irate, very intense Italian.

She took a steadying breath and blew it out, determined to see this through, well knowing the consequences and the chances to gain. Her mind was set. Do-or-die time. She wanted this over and done with.

"When do we leave?" Caprice asked.

He combed his fingers through his hair and paced the room, clearly agitated. "I will take you there tomorrow."

"Why waste the time? Can't someone take me now?" she pressed, aware she was pushing him, aware this could go badly for her as it had the last time she'd pushed buttons she had no business pushing.

He whirled and stalked toward her, clearly furious. Panic nipped along her nerves, touching on old fears. She tried slipping behind the protection of the divan, but she wasn't quick enough.

His big palms cupped her cheeks and her mind fizzed like champagne uncorked too quickly. Panic bubbled in her as well and she grasped his wrists, her gaze meeting his. And her tension popped, her fears gearing down to nothing. This was Luciano, the man she'd shared a room with sans sex. The man who was financing her dream. The man who'd moved the mountain of doubts and fears in her far too easily, expecting only one thing she was certain of—her compliance.

Easily won right now because she could drown in those fathomless blue eyes. If she let herself...

"Caprice, my *rifugio* is on a high, remote step to the north of us," he said in a gruff voice that feathered along her skin. "It is near the Austrian border and will take an hour over a rough track to get there."

She swallowed hard, debating the wisdom of spending the rest of the afternoon with him, especially as she knew how much his nearness affected her. How weak she could be with him if she let go. And that was the key. She couldn't let go. She had to keep pushing forward, pushing hard for what she wanted. What she believed herself capable of doing.

What better reason could there be for wanting to take this reckless course?

None. At least not for her.

The longer she dawdled here following Luciano's relaxed schedule, the more personal torment she would endure. She looked toward the day that she would put a period on this project and walk away with her head held proud. She would not slink off in the night as she'd done before.

"It's still early, right?" she said, carefully extracting

herself from his light hold to glance at the clock, pretending she was totally unaffected by him. "So if we leave now, it'll take an hour to drive up. Even if we waste thirty minutes there, we would still be back at la Duchi Royal before five p.m."

He snorted. "I don't want to hear any complaints about the bumpy drive."

"Hey, I grew up in the rugged Rockies. Rough mountains tracks and roads are home to me," she said, meaning it.

"You're sure of this?"

"Positive." Never mind that it all sounded heavenly and inviting and far too dangerous a place to be secluded with him.

"Fine. We'll go now."

He ushered her out the door without ceremony toward his private elevator. Yet as the door swished open and she stepped inside, she felt his power throb and grow, felt the pulse of the man beating in her veins as well. Her heart pounded in rhythm and felt expectation ripple through her.

How stupid could she get! Luciano was nothing more than her business associate. Old friend. Never lover. Never. She willed that vow to embed itself in her mind and sucked in air, but that only drew the spicy scent of him deeper into her lungs and her blood.

"Are you all right?" he asked.

She feared she'd never be all right again, but nodded. "I'm just anxious to see the design of your *rifugio*." Anxious to get this leg over with, return to the lodge and have a moment's peace without Luciano.

"Soon."

Having dressed in appropriate gear, they arrived in a garage lined with a dazzling array of cars, all high octane and high dollar, she was certain.

Instead of going for the sedan they'd arrived in or the Land Rover, he ducked his head under the open canopy and swung his long, muscled leg over the black padded seat of an impressively large all-terrain vehicle. "Climb on. I would prefer getting there before it turns dark or storms."

She looked at the sky and shivered. Though a good distance from them, a dark cloud bank was moments away from blocking out the sun and her avenue of daylight.

Being in the mountains after dark didn't bother her nearly as much as the thought of getting caught out in bad weather. His handsome face, carved in impatient lines with a critical inspection of the rugged ATV tires, got her moving forward. She swung on behind him just as he fired up the powerful engine, sending an unsettling vibration through her nerves and her blood that she had so longed for.

"Is anything wrong?"

"Nothing. Hang on," came his clipped order as he shifted gears and backed them from the massive garage.

Caprice spent a millisecond running her palms down the passenger grab bars before she pressed her spine against the plush seat back. The war between hanging on to to the bars or simply relishing reckless freedom darted within her.

Luciano barked an order. "Buckle up or hang on."

His muscled physique was inviting. Too inviting.

She fastened the black web belt over her flat belly with a snap because she wasn't about to wrap her arms around him. No matter the allure. No matter how much a part of her wanted to touch him, feel him, taste him. She wasn't about to do any of that.

He gave her one quick look back before he sent the ATV in motion and took a trail that wound above the massive manicured lawn of the lodge to a rugged track that angled away from the ski village. The harsh beauty of the mountains called to her soul while the sensual pulse of the man before her threatened to tempt her heart.

In what seemed like moments, the ATV swerved and jolted up the uneven mountain trail that ran parallel to a rushing stream littered with rocks, climbing higher at an angle that took them so far from the ski village she couldn't even see those roofs now. Each yard they traveled threatened to slam her against his broad back. She resisted, staying strong. Away from him.

The air was thinner at this elevation and deep snow still hid in crevices and shadowed nooks on the northern slopes high above the trail. Really, it was similar to the terrain in Colorado, where hearty trees struggled for survival on the unforgiving terrain of rocks and soil. The occasional alteration in the track below bore swaths that screamed danger, clear evidence of massive slides of soil and rock likely brought down the slope by heavy slabs of snow.

Her unease compounded as the wind tormented her with his spicy scent, forcing her to breathe him in with each breath she took, to feel the man on her skin and in her blood. The uneven terrain conspired against her battle to keep a careful distance.

"Hold on. It gets rough for the next few kilometers," he said after they'd been on the trail a good thirty minutes.

Halfway point, she hoped. Yet this was an exhilarating slice of heaven she wouldn't have wanted to miss. The vistas were incredible, dwarfing the Rockies with their beauty.

Just as she was getting into her stride the heavy ATV busted over the uneven track with another, larger, bared slope rising to the summit. Clearly a small avalanche had scrubbed a narrow pathway, leaving gullies and massive boulders clinging to the face. The ATV bucked and sprayed gravel, sand and slush in a rooster's fantail that covered their trail over this rugged patch. Then the route evened with thick trees on the slope and a swift running stream to their right.

On the other side of the stream rose a smaller ledge of firs that flattened out into a dense stand of trees. It made the area they traveled more a wedge of safety than a valley, and by no means eliminated them from danger. In fact she couldn't imagine this route being used at all during the winter months. Isolated? Chillingly so, she thought on a shiver.

A mile or perhaps more up the winding rising track, the surface turned dangerously rocky. Luciano geared down and took it slower over the track, which rose unevenly. Instinctively she looked up the towering slope to the slab of deep snow suspended in above them, stretching across the face near the summit.

"Has it been cool here?" she asked in a near shout.

She felt him tense and peer up the slope as well. "It had been, but my groundsman alerted me to the sudden spike in temperatures yesterday and today, coupled with above-freezing numbers at the summit."

Her stomach clenched painfully, her heart kicking up pace. "Avalanche danger."

"It's a possibility," he said. "That is why I was hesitant to come up here today."

It wouldn't take much for that ridge of snow to turn deadly. Above-freezing temperatures at night. Hot days. Rain. Any combination could send that mass of ice and slush tumbling down the slope, wiping out everything in its path.

"Why didn't you say so at the lodge?" she asked.

He snorted. "*You* wanted this done with, and I do as well."

Was she that transparent to him? Was he that anxious to be free of her?

Her palms skimmed over the grab bars until a burst of speed up the tree-lined track jolted her. She wrapped her arms around his lean waist and leaned against his strong back. Cooler air buffeted her face and back while the heat of the man seeped into her length.

"Hang on. We're almost there. See the green roof on the far ledge?" he shouted over the rev of the engine that tormented the tender flesh between her legs in a sinfully delicious way. "That is my *rifugio*."

She caught a glimpse of the chalet-like structure before the winding trail took the ATV speeding down a sharp, curving dip in the trail. She buried her face against his broad back for a millisecond, then looked up.

Excitement hummed through her, her heart accelerating with each rev of the engine that gave a sensual jolt of her body against his broad back. Feeling his muscles tighten was a delicious torment that she had never felt on a pleasurable level, but she wanted more, wanted to explore those feelings.

Don't pursue it, the rational part of her brain warned as the ATV all but crawled over the rough track, the dips and jolts creating a delicious torture she hadn't anticipated.

A sound like thunder turned her blood cold and yanked her attention from the man to the mountain. Snow sprayed over a high ledge into the air, quickly tumbling downward. The wide surf of tumbling, sliding white snow flung rocks ahead of it, the mass turning browner as it gathered more snow, soil and trees. A new fear skittered up her spine.

"Avalanche!" she screamed.

"Hang on," he ordered at the same time as he boosted the ATV to a reckless speed.

She splayed her fingers on his chest and held tight, heart

pounding in rapid tandem with the beat of his against her palm. The roar up the slope increased and a glance up proved the snow slide was gaining more speed than they were. My God, they'd get eaten alive by the snow.

"Go faster," she implored.

"We're at top speed now," he shouted back.

Not fast enough. That realization played over and over in her mind, a litany of doom to come. One by one, the trees disappeared under a wall of snow and soil, the crack and splintering louder than violent cracks of lightning over the hum and rev of the ATV. Massive boulders vanished, torn from their mooring of earth only to shoot out amid sprays of ice and dirt ahead of the wall of dirty white, tumbling into a hellish maelstrom that raced toward them.

"Can we outrun it?" she gasped, holding on to him for dear life, heart in her throat.

He flicked a glance back at the deathly gray slope, blue eyes hard as flint and tinged with terror. "I hope to hell so. If not…"

She knew from her last glance that the horrendous slide was too close. The tumbling tide of snow in front of the avalanche was less than twenty feet from engulfing them and gaining fast. Too fast. A glance ahead had her guessing how far they were from the safe zone.

They had a fifty-fifty chance. *If that much.*

The fear and horror of her past paled in comparison to this horror. No terror compared to the nanosecond the spray slammed into them, tossing them off track.

Luciano spat a curse and the ATV revved and roared, swerving and bucking for a heart-stopping moment. She couldn't make out any details, not even the man she clung to. Snow and mud rained down on them, soaking her with muck and fear. Stones pummeled her head, her back so much she wanted to scream out the pain.

Somewhere came the crash of snow and trees. Deafening deadly sounds. Ice pellets pounded her back and arms and head. It soaked her in seconds, matting her hair to her head. Each labored breath was torture.

Something hard, a limb, or perhaps rocks slammed into the back of the ATV. She whimpered, eyes blurring, at the same time Luciano swore violently. Her fingers scrambled to find purchase on his soaked clothes, her head spinning and aching.

Tired. She was so damned tired of clinging to him. And afraid, more than she'd ever been in her life. Their chances of outrunning an avalanche had been slim. Surviving one was a rarity.

"Hold tight!" Luciano shouted.

She jerked and did just that, plastering herself against his broad back, knowing he was taking the brunt of the fallout, wildly thinking this was what clothes felt like tossed in a washing machine. Soaked. Wrung out. Limp.

She took a breath and gagged. Tasted the mud on her lips.

The ATV engine whined and roared, shooting them through a wall of muck that blinded her. The tight pinch to her stomach and heightened rev of the engine told her they'd propelled into the air. Into what? Would they get buried under a massive drift of snow-covered debris? Would the force slam them into boulders or the jagged ledge? Or would they end up propelled over the mountain's edge?

Was death imminent? Was this her last moment?

She didn't want to die. Didn't want Luciano to either. Didn't want either of them hurt. But it was out of her hands and his.

Please, God, she prayed. *Please!*

The ATV dropped with a jolt and reared, but somehow

Luciano kept it speeding forward. She swallowed a scream and clung to him, unable to see anything ahead of them under the pummeling waterfall of snow and mud.

In a blink they shot out into open space.

She swiped at the grime on her face and stared ahead. Fingers of tumbling snow and debris reached ahead of them. Further ahead were whole trees and unspoiled land. Was safety that close?

The promise of escape barely registered before the ATV plunged into a roiling finger of snow and debris. She cringed as her body was peppered again with God knew what. Inside that maelstrom she couldn't even see Luciano before her, yet she felt his muscles bunch and clamp down as the ATV tipped on its rear axel. She clung to him over the manic rev of the engine and wheels spinning frantically without purchase. Crashing was imminent and her hands were so sore and slickened by snow and sludge that she could barely hang on.

The debris tormented them for long seconds that felt like hours before the ATV rocketed out from the far fringe of the avalanche tide. The unspoiled track and treed slope she'd glimpsed before was right ahead. Was she dreaming? Had they survived?

Luciano maneuvered the ATV between a tight stand of trees, dropping down and away from the ledge of snow. Something about the surety of man in the face of danger called to her as nothing else ever had.

It was comforting. Strengthening. Seductive.

Danger pulsed in her heart and cried in her soul, danger that had everything to do with nearly losing her life and her heart to this bold, reckless man. She didn't want either to happen, but she'd never felt this heart-stopping adrenaline rush before.

The ATV sped up the trail along the sloped woods. She

held tight to the grab bars with hands that were near numb and peered over her shoulder at the cascading tumble of snow and debris that still raced down the slope. The heart of the avalanche bulldozed across the track they'd narrowly just traveled and dumped into the stream in a mixture of muck mingled with boulders and trees torn from the earth.

In seconds, the trail was blocked, she realized with a sinking heart as the area between the slope and the ridge beyond the stream filled in, burying the trail and damming the stream.

Her breath came short and fast, and her heart thundered in her chest. They'd barely escaped getting buried alive beneath a mountain of earth, stones and crusted snow. They'd cheated death. But how would they get back to the village?

Luciano pulled to a stop at the hillocks summit and swung off the ATV, his breathing labored and eyes unnaturally bright. "All you all right?"

All right? No, she was far from it, but she nodded anyway and got off barely standing on shaky legs, her entire body still riding the wave of charged danger.

It was preternaturally quiet. "Is it over?"

"That one is," he said, staring at the mountains with critical eyes.

She wanted to cry. Wanted to give up, but she did neither. They were alive. Wet. Filthy. Cold. But alive.

He pulled a blanket from the small boot on the ATV and wrapped it around her without ceremony. "You're shivering."

"So are you," she said and clutched the blanket under her chin. "Thank you."

He shrugged. "There is always one packed in the ATV."

"I didn't mean the blanket. I meant… You did it," she said in a near sob as she threw her arms around Luciano. "You saved our lives."

Luc held her in a crushing hug that made his heart pound all the harder, his face pressed to hers for a long, silent moment as the experience brought memories of his brother's crippling accident to the surface. One near miss with catastrophe was enough in one lifetime. If he'd lost his own life, so be it. But if anything had happened to her under his watch, he never would forgive himself.

They'd cheated death, yet an avalanche of need he couldn't escape raced within him. He wanted to ride the adrenaline rush to its fullest and run his palms over her breasts, skim them down her torso, her trim waist, the inviting curve of her hip.

Need, more powerful than he'd felt in years, pounded hot and heavy in him. He ached to celebrate life and crush his lips to hers. Break down the walls of her resistance and unleash the passion he knew surged within her. He wanted to plunge his hard length into her and ride the storm of passion to its fullest.

More than anything, he wanted to break his vow to keep her at arm's length and make her his. Make them one. And that was the last thing he should do.

"That was too close for comfort," he said, voice hoarse with emotion, his mind muddled with duty and desire.

Caprice swallowed hard, hesitant to pull away from the comfort of his embrace. "God, yes. I've never been so terrified in my life."

He gave a rough laugh and set her back from him, holding her at arm's length, his expression intense. "That is the dangerous allure of extreme sports."

The dangerous allure of the man as well? Without a doubt, she decided.

"It's not for me," she said, meaning both.

His lips pressed into a thin line and put distance between them. "Or me."

"The trail is blocked, isn't it?" she asked, knowing the answer before he nodded.

"It will take days to move the ice and rubble."

"But we can get back to the village," she pressed.

"Not today," he said and pointed to the dark clouds roiling over the mountains. "Let's get out of here."

Darkness and perhaps a storm would descend on them soon. They could be stuck here at a remote *rifugio* for tonight. Maybe another day before the track could be cleared. Maybe more. And for once she had left her netbook and papers in her portfolio in her room.

She had nothing to occupy her time except the company of her host, and nobody to blame for being here except herself. She'd insisted on coming up here today because she'd been intent on getting this job done quickly. Her obstinacy had nearly cost them their lives.

They reached another shelf that was far smaller than the other one. "Welcome to my refuge from the world," he shouted.

Her gaze landed on a red-roofed stone building perched on a rocky ledge she estimated was the length of a football field from them. "Finally," she said, teeth chattering.

"Are you all right?" he asked, wrenching around to look at her, brows drawn, eyes dark.

She shook her head. "I'm cold."

"We'll be there soon. Can you hang on a while longer?"

She nodded and slid her arms around his lean waist, pressing close to his body and welcome heat, not caring if he liked it or not. He sighed. Or was it a groan?

Moments that seemed like hours passed before he parked the ATV on the cliff side of the building next to a small stone wall that snaked along the edge of the slope. He vaulted off and helped her dismount, then wrapped an arm around her shoulders and guided her through the gate.

It swung open soundlessly and she preceded him through it onto a paved stone walkway that led to a large wooden deck. Only one door was visible on the side and she headed toward the heavy wooden panel, her wet shoes pounding a weary beat on the deck that wrapped around the front V of the *rifugio*.

He unlocked and opened the door for her, his palm to her back as they hurried inside. "I'll start a fire."

"Okay," she said, hugging herself. "Is there a shower?"

"*Si*, in the bedroom down the hall. Can you manage?"

"I think so." But once she was there, her numb fingers couldn't twist the knob.

Without a word, he opened the door wide, then swept her into his arms, slamming the door behind him. "You are chilled to the bone."

She heard a gruff curse in Italian and felt herself pulled into the corner of the wet room.

Blessed warm water pelted her through her clothes as he slammed his back against the wall, still holding her tight in his arms. She gasped a breath and flung her head back, her fingers clasped behind his neck, glorying in the hot water washing away the grime and cold and fear from her.

He shifted and the hot spray plastered her hair to her head. She turned her head from the force, watching the streaks of brown mire from them both rush across the white tile floor toward the drain.

If only bad memories could be erased that easily.

Her face lifted to the hot spray, the jets washing over her body just like they had done seven years ago as she'd tried to scrub the taint of her attacker's seed and smell from her body. She hadn't thought it important to wash that beast from her soul as well.

She and Luciano had just escaped death. He'd done it at least once before, but this was her first close call. In all the years she'd skied in competition and for fun, she'd never experienced anything that threatened physical devastation or worse. Yet for the past couple of years she'd treated those who had. Dealt with men and women who'd lost the most basic vital functions of mobility.

All of these years she'd thought she understood how her patients must feel because she'd experienced her own demoralizing fear. She'd lost something precious, something she would never have back again. This time, she could have lost more—her life or Luciano's.

Yet she had buried a vital part of her seven years ago.

Rape was death, whether bodily or mentally. It was the last rites of one's innocence. The total stripping of will, power and control. That violation victimized and punished, leaving scars that ran soul deep for years, that haunted the survivor long into the nights to come. It remained the stain that couldn't be washed away, couldn't be removed, couldn't be forgotten.

It victimized, sentencing the wronged to a living hell. It was the prisoners' brand only invisible to the eye, but still she'd hidden the truth from the world out of fear and shame. And just like a devastating accident that sentenced the victims to wheelchairs for life, her rape had left her scarred emotionally.

She had tried then to scrub that stain from her body, but it remained. The mark she couldn't wash away, couldn't forget. It had clung to her for years, just like her sopping clothes did now.

Dirt was dirt and she'd wallowed in that particular filth long enough. She pulled at her T-shirt, at his, desperate to be free of constrictions, of phobias, of pain.

This was her call. Her choice. A beautiful, haunted man held her in his arms. Wanting her on a purely carnal level, judging by the strong hands that held her so tightly, by the hard, rigid length of his anatomy that prodded her hip through her sopping jeans.

She wanted to be rid of them. Wanted to feel the man naked and willing.

For seven years she'd pulled into a shell, refusing to date, refusing even to go out with the girls. She was sick and tired of hiding, of jumping at shadows. She wanted to confront life again. Wanted to be intimate with a man because it was her choice.

All she had to do was reach for what she wanted most. Right now.

She turned in his embrace and wiggled her legs free, slithering down his long legs like a serpent. "What if I said I'd changed my mind?" she said, straddling the edge of flippant.

"About?"

"Sex. Us. Now."

He pulled back, water pouring over his head and streaming down his face as his eyes searched, assessed. "That's the shock of surviving danger talking."

"You don't feel it, too?" she asked, voice hoarse. "God, I feel it," she said, breathless. "But what difference does that make? I want you. Need you now. What more can I say?"

"Nothing. In the end you will expect more than that. An affair, commitment."

She shook her head. "Not anymore. No ties. No promises."

His eyes narrowed, and his hopes and desires soared. "You want my financial backing *and* sex?"

"Yes. We are bound together by a contract, there's no changing that. But when the job is finished, so are we."

"Of course," he replied, his eyes dark and unreadable.

Then his beautiful lips curled in a wolfish smile and he pulled her into his arms, his mouth brushing hers once, twice, before settling in for a lengthy melding of lips and tongue that poured live coals on her desire. The passion burning in his eyes melted her heart, and the heat curling off his body threatened to set hers on fire with raw need.

She moved against him with feline grace, her hands boldly stroking his broad shoulders, the long line of his spine and lean hips, before her fingers splayed over his firm buttocks. He jerked, his erection sliding between her thighs and gracing her core through her clothes. A moan tore from her as the friction of wet bodies moving together stoked the ache pulsing low in her belly.

God, how she wanted this man. Wanted to experience uninhibited sex with him. Wanted this moment to blot out the ugly memory that haunted her deep into the night.

This was her choice. No promises. No regrets. No shame.

The only way to escape the demons in her past was to plunge headlong into the future because she wanted this. She deserved it. She would take it.

CHAPTER FIVE

LUC HADN'T FELT this exhilarated, this alive in years, this impassioned to make love to a woman. And not just any woman.

He wanted Caprice. Wanted her without strings attached. Wanted her now without a thought to tomorrow.

In the course of a few hours she'd changed from businesswoman to an enchanting vixen hungry for sex, nothing more. All the passion she'd infused into her program now fueled her intent to satisfy her needs.

It was sexy as hell. Liberating.

How the hell could he turn his back on that proposition?

He couldn't. He would be the man who satisfied her needs as well as his own.

Without ceremony, he grasped her slender shoulders and levered her away from him, peeling off her wet clothes to reveal a toned body rosy with passion. "You are beautiful. Perfect."

She blinked, lips soft and dewy. Inviting lips. Lips that could pleasure a man, and God knew he selfishly wanted that from her now.

His body pressed her against the tiles, his palms slapping the cool marble while hot water pounded his head and shoulders and streamed over them creating an erotic steam bath of writhing bodies, dueling tongues and sizzling need.

Sweet and spicy. Hot. She was more provocative than any woman he'd kissed, enflaming his desire more than before, nudging deeper feelings in him that had screwed up his mind and his life once before. He shoved those dark thoughts of Isabella away and focused on Caprice, taking everything she would give him before he turned the tables on her and made her whimper and beg for more.

He removed his clothes and circled her slender shoulders in his arms, pulling her closer, tucking her against his rock-hard erection. Her gasp was proof she knew what would come next. That she was ready for his possession.

"Now," he ground out as his erection probed between her legs, desperate to be inside her.

She shifted and his penis grazed her belly, away from the core he ached to explore. He sucked in a sharp breath, his blood fizzing with passion. Was she evading him?

The thought of seducing her quickly shorted and sparked as her hot lips pressed a trail down his chest and her fingernails raked over the taut abdomen, enflaming a blaze of passion that defied the water streaming over them.

"So good," she murmured against his belly, sliding lower.

"Bella," he breathed.

His hands tangled in her wet hair as her sensual fingers stroked him and her hungry mouth ravished and licked and sucked his entire hard length until he was certain he could hold back no longer. He tossed his head back and welcomed the punishing pings of cooler water on his shoulders and face, struggling to hold back his release that threatened to erupt any second, wanting this sensual torture to go on and on. It would be easier to hold the sea in his palms.

"Caprice," he shouted, surrendering to the sweet sensual torture he'd hungered for, barely able to think beyond savoring the exquisite pleasure of her mouth settling over his engorged tip.

Her lips pressed a hot wet trail upward, her knowing hands gliding up his torso in a sultry caress that sparked embers to his semi-sated desire. He wouldn't have guessed this depth of sensuality from her, yet why not?

She was passionate in her work, passionate in her sensuality.

Yes, she was using him for pleasure as much as he was using her, but she had been upfront with him from the start. She'd made clear what she wanted going into their contract as well as the changes she wanted in their arrangement now.

Her professional mind was brilliant, sharp, open. Sex with her would be incredible, addictive.

They could do this, have an affair and walk away without regret or reservations.

He flicked off the shower that had grown cool and sucked in great drafts of air, his body quivering with pleasure from that one taste that left him hungry for more. Since his divorce, he'd had women with little conscious thought, feeling nothing but carnal satisfaction when a fling was over because that's all he'd wanted from them. He would feel the same when his "contract" with Caprice ended.

Theirs was the perfect situation. She was the saving grace for his brother, and for his own choking guilt. He was the means to an end for her. Rich means to finance her new venture. Something she wanted so badly that she'd agreed to share her intuitive knowledge, and now her bed with him. She'd been honest about it. And he would take great satisfaction in making it as pleasurable for them both in work *and* in play.

His palms skimmed down her spine, which was tight

with muscle and tension. His ego swelled as she moaned and pressed closer. Needy. Trusting. Giving.

His lips captured hers and he drank the passion still wet on her lips, a drugging sensual brew that tossed hot embers on the emotions banked in his heart and soul. Whatever her reasons for pleasuring him first were, they were hers. He was grateful for the amazing rush, and he would repay the favor. In fact he looked forward it.

"I am the reflection of you at this moment," he said, sliding his arm around her slender shoulders, tucking her close and relishing the feel of her in his arms.

Her hushed laugh was bells on the wind, soft and fleeting. "I don't believe it."

He smoothed her wet hair back and cupped her face in his palms, staring into eyes that never stayed locked with his for long, as if hiding something and afraid he'd discover her secrets. Like his wife?

"Why do you doubt me?" he asked, pushing thoughts of Isabella away, not wanting her dark memory to shadow this pleasure he felt now.

"You're a man, operating on a different level than women. You take what you want when you want it without reservations or regrets."

"As you just did with me."

Her cheeks turned pink, an odd reaction for a woman who'd just taken the initiative to indulge in fellatio. But then Caprice was unlike any woman he'd ever known.

Her chin came up and her palm skimmed down his bare belly, stopping inches from where he throbbed for her touch. "I took what I wanted without regrets."

"And now it is my turn, *bella*," he said.

"What if I've had enough?" she asked.

He grabbed a soft bath sheet and wrapped it around her beautifully naked body, drawing her flush against him.

Then he slipped his leg between hers and caught the quiver of need that shot through her. "You haven't."

A provocative look and a promising smile was all it took to enflame his desire to a fever pitch again. It had been a long time since he'd taken this much time and pleasure with a woman, despite what the tabloids boasted. His choice, just as this was his decision to make now. He wanted more from her. He'd have it.

She'd invaded his sanctuary. He'd never allowed another woman to do that and had sworn on the drive up that he wouldn't tolerate it happening again.

This was a onetime shot. It was nothing beyond the duration of their contract.

His lips adored her closed eyelids, teased the curve of her ears and cooled cheeks, still charmingly rosy, before capturing her sweet lips in a long, drugging kiss that left his head spinning. His hunger for her consumed him, but he took care lowering her to the carpeted floor and following her down, lounging beside her when his body demanded he plunge into her hot depths and find his satiation now.

His palm took a meandering route up her torso to full creamy breasts bearing hard nipples with dark rose areolae that puckered from the change of temperature from hot shower to marginally cooler chamber. He lowered his head to nuzzle and kiss and adore the soft flesh under both breasts in turn, lifting them closer with cupped palms to the torment of his tongue and mouth.

Her lithe body twisted and arched; the soft sounds she was making were invitations to take her right now.

And he would, laying a wet trail of kisses down her tight torso and flat belly, his tongue circling her navel once, twice, before settling down at the juncture of her thighs.

A skim of his fingers over her bare folds told him she was still wet and ready. And his!

"Luciano!"

"Bella, amore mio."

He dipped his head to taste her lightly, then treated her to a deep, sensual kiss. Her back arched off the floor, fingernails digging into his shoulders, a high keen coming from her softly parted lips. A guttural moan of satisfaction escaped him as he kissed her, stroked her, probed her depths to the limits, his own body tight and throbbing with the need to release.

Again he was struck by the rightness of being with her. Had he ever felt this intense before? Had it ever felt this perfect?

And once again his mind was blank of everything except the woman in his arms. He needed her. Needed to get his fill of her so he would be free of her memory.

He slid his palms under her soft bottom and held her to him, loving her deeply, her fingers grasping his shoulders, his hair, only fueling his rising passion to a crashing crescendo. She arched again, her body trembling with spasm after spasm. Her climax peaked not one second too late before his own need threatened to explode.

In one smooth push, he entered her, sliding up over her body, satisfied as her legs parted wide to welcome him home. And that was just what it felt like as he thrust into her again and again, struggling to hold back his release until she shattered into another climax. He held her tight and let go, his body violently jerking as he reached for his own summit.

Drained, sated, he collapsed on her, his head resting on her shoulder, numb with pleasure. A sense of completeness pulsed around them.

This was right. Perfect.

No! She was right. Perfect. He'd needed this. Needed her at this moment.

That was all. He could still walk away from her at any time without regrets.

Caprice ran her palms up his damp back, her fingers skimming the hard muscles that were now lax and felt boneless herself. Complete. She hadn't expected this afterglow to hum through her softly, lulling her more deeply into relaxation like she'd never known before.

"That was amazing," she whispered against his shoulder.

He shifted enough to look down on her, hand gliding down her side, igniting that slow burn of desire all over again. "You are amazing."

She laughed at his compliment, not believing it for a moment.

"What's wrong?" he asked.

"Nobody has ever told me that before."

"Then your previous lovers were all fools."

She sobered at that. "I've only had sex once before," she said, and wanted to bite her tongue off for admitting that much.

He shifted to look at her, and she averted her eyes, preferring to stare at the dark whorls of hair on his muscled chest. "Once?"

She nodded, not daring to look up.

"Not a memorable experience?"

"Not one I care to bring to mind," she said, hating that memories of that night threatened to rush back to life, to taint the pleasure she'd just experienced.

She shook her head, willing the dark past to retreat into the recesses of her mind. But the voices remained, a low nagging whisper of pleas and cries and threats, a living reminder of that night, that man's total domination over her, and the ugly violation she'd lived with for years.

A woman never forgot being raped. She'd become an expert at keeping people at arm's length until Luciano came back into her life.

He grasped her chin and forced her to face him, blue eyes intent on hers. "You will tell me someday, yes?"

That was the last thing she would do, now or ever. But admitting that would only prompt him to pester her for details she never wanted to reveal.

"Someday," she lied.

She'd told no one she'd been raped by Luciano's friend, afraid to challenge the threat her attacker had issued, wanting the whole thing buried. Forgotten. She intended to keep it that way.

And she had to believe that man had done the same. She'd certainly never heard any rumors connecting them, and Luciano seemed ignorant of the entire thing. Of all people, she would think he would have known and was so glad he didn't.

For her, it would always be the black day in her life, over and done with but she would never forget. After seven years, nothing would be served by telling anyone, especially Luciano. She'd moved on. Hopefully she would never cross paths with that horrible man again.

"I have given you one good memory, but that isn't enough, *bella*." He dropped a kiss on her forehead, her cheeks, his lips hovering over hers. "Let's make more for both of us."

"Yes," she breathed before his lips captured hers in a long, lazy kiss that sparked fire in the desire banked inside her, making her feel wanted, needed.

"Yes," she whispered again between breaths, locking the door on the past and opening wide the portal to the present. She welcomed Luciano into her arms, her heart, as they plunged into the warm surf of passion, wanting to remember it when the darkness and fears intruded.

He was a drug in her veins and her blood fizzed, her control spiraling downward into a tide pool of passion. For one split second she nearly pulled back into her protective shell. But another searing kiss, coupled with the hot possessive glide of his hands up and down her back, banished the urge, making her want more of his touch, his kiss, his possession.

Her hands sought and found the hard, pulsing length of him. He groaned, rocking into her palm, as if begging her fingers to explore him. She did, stroking the silk-over-steel erection that grew in her palm. Her heartbeat quickened, the core of her wet and throbbing with want.

Her other hand slid down his thigh, the muscles there hard and powerful to a point. And then…she stilled, frowning as her fingers recognized the change in skin and the uneven shape. A scar, and a very deep one, she suspected.

"Enough playing," he said, dragging her exploring hand to his chest.

His fingers found her core, stroking, teasing, and the questions that had ballooned to her mind popped. Each stroke strummed a lover's song that whispered around them like silken ribbons, the melody intoxicating to her senses.

She'd dreamed of being loved like this for years, not believing it could ever come true. That sex with a man could only be better if she imagined it.

Now she knew that wasn't true. Now that Luciano was literally in the palm of her hands, she would savor this forever. Her timidity and hard-learned caution diminished as desire and awareness of her own sensuality increased.

There was power in sex. Power in her own needs. Power in satisfying his as well.

She would deal with the consequences of embarking on an affair tomorrow, or the next day, or whenever they returned to the real world. For now she just wanted to savor the pleasure.

Luc lay on his back, staring at the ceiling. The lull of her even breathing and relaxed body tempted him to sleep as well. Yet old demons chose now to haunt him and remind him how close he'd come again to letting tender emotions blind him.

He was right there on the edge, enjoying this special moment with Caprice, wanting to believe she was nearly innocent. But how could he? Was it possible for a vibrant, passionate woman to have had experienced sex once yet satisfy a man of his experience?

His heart said yes but his cynical mind warned something was off, that she was not being straight with him.

He'd learned to distrust women from the best.

Isabella had been a very convincing liar. She'd said all the right words and done all the right things. His charming, deceitful wife had had great fun with the lofty position marriage to him had afforded her and had enjoyed spending his money on her every whim.

She'd relished using him.

Tension tightened his muscles and glazed his heart in ice, for he'd never denied her anything.

Isabella had been the supreme actress, sleeping in his bed and his arms every night. Professing her love.

A damned lie. She'd sneaked away during the day to be with her lover.

The hell of it was he hadn't known, hadn't suspected. Perhaps he never would have if he hadn't spontaneously decided to fly to London and surprise her there during one of her solo shopping trips.

That was the end of his marriage. Divorce was the expected outcome, and she hadn't fought it, seeking only a fat settlement.

Looking back on it now, he wondered if he should have gone through his life loving her, loving any children produced of their marriage. If he could have found contentment, she would be alive today. But he'd sent her away. Shamed. Scorned.

And she'd died in a horrible auto accident.

Guilt was a horrible thing to bear. His wife's death. His brother's crippling accident. Both could be laid at his door.

Those events had changed him. Hardened him.

Right now they were tainting a good moment in his life with Caprice that he wanted to preserve in memory. Yet how could he when he suspected she was lying to him about something in her past?

It would be impossible until he got to the truth.

That would come. He would uncover her secrets before he made another costly mistake with a woman.

Caprice wasn't sure who fell asleep first, or who awakened first. One moment she was sated and warm lying in his arms on the floor. The next he was gently tipping her face to his and staring at her with eyes that always saw too much.

"Are you okay?" he asked, his voice rough.

"Yes. Fine." Better than she thought she'd be, and that alone told her she'd made the right decision.

"Why didn't you tell me you had only had one lover before me?"

Because she hadn't had a lover. Her attacker didn't deserve that title.

"What difference does it make?" she asked.

He heaved a sigh. "None, I guess. I just thought…you'd had more experience. Hell, I thought you'd had experience when I met you at the World Cup."

"I admit I was naive but fearless." To her own peril.

"I have thought long and hard about how poorly I treated you in the past," he bit out, as if hating to admit that much.

"It's okay. I was too young to understand that relationships were all a game to you." Too young to realize that some men were only out to use and abuse.

She reached up to cup his jaw, desperate to connect with the man who'd just pleasured her beyond belief. Had granite ever felt this hard? She chanced a peek at him. Had blue eyes ever looked so icy cold?

He grasped her hand and pulled it away, and she felt the distancing yawn between them, felt the old rejection nip at her nerves. "I did you a favor, *bella*."

"It didn't feel like it at the time." She rolled away and got to her feet, wrapping the towel around her naked body, breaking the physical contact, but still plagued with a jumble of good and bad memories.

"I was in the wake of a bitter divorce. You knew that."

She nodded. "I heard rumors surrounding the end of your marriage and none of it put you in a good light. Is it true you threatened divorce unless your wife got a paternity test?"

He got to his feet, unabashedly naked. "Yes, which she refused to do. If you knew that, then why didn't you ask me if it was true?"

"I didn't believe you would do such a thing to your family." Even now she had trouble accepting his matter-of-fact confession.

"You'd heard the truth and yet you flirted with me." He shook his head. "My God, you were naive."

"I call it trusting and loyal," she added. And she still was in many respects.

"Yes, you have always been that way to me," he said, eyes drilling into her so intimately she felt as if he were touching her still. "But that is not why I wanted you now."

"You've made it clear from the start that you simply wanted rights to my therapy program," she said. "I don't have a problem with that or what just happened between us."

She knew any relationship with him would simply be carnal lust. No emotional ties. No commitments. No promises.

His women were conveniences. Well paid, if the rumors were true. And well loved, if only physically. Now she was one of them.

"Good." He stalked to the door and paused to look back at her. "You should be able to find suitable clothes in the closet. When you're dressed, meet me in the great room."

Then he was gone, not giving her the option to agree or balk. But then why would she?

She'd gotten what she asked for. No more. It was time to view this amazing design that may, or may not, be suitable for the therapy pod. Then she would get back to the lodge and reality.

Solitude. That's what she needed to put all of this back into perspective, and soon.

Fifteen minutes later she found jeans and jerseys, still bearing tags, hanging in the closet. Considering she had nothing to wear, and refusing to belabor the point of wearing something intended for another woman, she rid them of the tags and dressed, then finished towel-drying her hair.

She was clean and incredibly charged with energy, considering the day's events, when she walked into the great room. And stopped.

The amazing expanse of glass on either side of the massive stone fireplace, complete with roaring fire, made it feel as if they were suspended over a fathomless gorge, as if she were hanging on to this primitive ledge. She couldn't image a more perfect view.

"I've never quite seen anything like this," she said, near breathless.

"Is that good or bad?" he asked, the warmth of his body against hers telling her he was far too near again.

"Good. Has this place been in your family for long?"

Again, the crooked smile that made her skin tingle and her stomach tighten. "No. I acquired it after my first World Cup win with intention of restoring it to a quality *rifugio*."

"But you didn't," she guessed.

He shook his head, his smile disappearing like the clouds that suddenly shrouded the jagged peaks in the distance. "Because of the disrepair here, it took undue time restoring it. So long, in fact, that I'd begun to long for a secret place to get away from the world. But the wait was worth it."

She took it all in, understanding his need for a retreat and finding this very nice, very relaxing and cozy. "Is this the design that you thought I would love?"

"No, that is upstairs. After you," he said, making a sweeping motion toward the multiple landings of the long staircase that separated the great room from the galley area, suddenly treating her as a guest.

The low risers between the trio of landings said more about his need for rest than any explanation could convey. Each landing provided a place to pause with an arresting vista that differed from the one before it. They were a reminder of the majestic mountains and challenging runs that would call to any accomplished skier.

Yet Luciano hadn't gone back. This was the retreat he'd

designed for himself. Where he could hide and heal his broken body. But what about his troubled soul? she wondered.

That question troubled her as she reached the top level. It took her a moment to scan the massive space. *Peaceful* was the only word that came to mind. The furnishings were dressed in variant blues and browns and whites, colors that melded in with artistic murals and the living landscape vista just beyond the two walls of glass, which opened naturally onto the vast sky and rugged mountain range.

"This is it," he said, pride and something indefinable resonating in his voice.

He didn't have to tell her this was his bedroom. She knew it the second she walked in.

The entire space felt as vast as the rugged range, dominated by a bed that screamed pleasure. And she knew that was exactly what she would find there.

She looked away from it, body burning and tingling anew. What had happened to the instinctual warning that heartache would be the end result of an affair? Was the promised pleasure worth the pain that would come?

"This is beyond unique," she said, focusing on the design again instead of the arresting man who threatened to dominate her thoughts, who made her trust him, want him. "The architectural and interior design make the entire space seem as if I am standing on the mountain."

"Yes." He remained by the window, his back to her now. "This place helped heal me."

"After the accident?"

He nodded. "My ex-wife's death as well. Can you understand that?"

"Yes, I think so. You loved her. Grieved her death."

He scrubbed a hand along his nape and sighed. "It is

true. Many of my friends could not understand why I cared, why I shut myself away after her death."

"Who asked for the divorce?"

"I did." He braced an arm on the window and stared out at the vista. "Does that surprise you?"

She wouldn't lie. "In a way."

He faced her then, back to the window and arms locked over his chest, a wall keeping anyone from getting too close. "I found her in bed, in the arms of another man. It was an ugly confrontation with passions and tempers running high. Finally she admitted that he was her lover and their affair had been going on long before our marriage."

She pressed her fingertips to her mouth, unable to imagine how awful it would be to catch your loved one cheating. "You must have been heartbroken."

"Yes, but I was furious over her betrayal," he said, his voice dark.

"If she had a lover she refused to leave, why did she marry you?"

"Marriage afforded her a lavish allowance, the bulk of which ended up funneled to him, I suspect." He drummed his fingers on the glass panel, his expression remote. "They were expecting a child."

She cringed at the added pain Luciano went through. "So you divorced her."

"As quickly and quietly as possible."

She shook her head, stunned that the ugly rumors she'd heard about Isabella Duchelini were true. Betrayal like Luciano had received at his wife's hand cut to the heart and drew blood that stained a soul.

In many ways he was starting over, but only partially.

"Why didn't you return to skiing?" she asked.

His shoulders shifted into such a tight line she was surprised she didn't hear the twang of muscles and tendons snap and break. "I had my reasons." He faced her, all warmth gone from his features, making it clear he wasn't going to share those reasons with her, so she forced herself to change the subject. "You paid more attention to tactile detail, which in turn reflected the mood that resonated with you."

"Good, you see it, too," he said, and she nodded. "I didn't realize how very much I needed a retreat until the accident."

She certainly understood the desperate need to escape a horrible incident. Her refuge had been her lodge and a redirection of her life. Taking control again, if only in baby steps.

In time, the personal attack she'd suffered receded to the back of her mind. It was rarely recalled, yet the pain and shame were never forgotten.

No, she didn't have to ask how much his loss and his terrible accident pained him emotionally and physically. One look at his drawn features proved he suffered deeply on both levels.

"I wish I would have been able to help you then," she said, hesitating before laying her hand atop his.

But on what level could she have helped? Emotionally? Maybe. Physically? Not likely considering what she'd endured.

She would like to think she could have put her own feelings aside, but in all honesty she wasn't sure. It had taken her years to recover to this stage. And besides, the point was moot as that was the time she'd delved deeper into her studies, putting her degree first in her life and taking that vow to go it alone.

He brushed off her hand and stormed to the window. "I couldn't think beyond my own need to be alone. Secluded." He shook his head. "I don't expect you to understand."

"But I do," she said, batting at the unwelcome tears stinging her eyes, debating if she should tell him what had happened that night he'd left her.

Why? What good would it serve? None.

"I have lived with shame and fear and the desperate need to escape the world my mother adored," she said instead.

He hung his head, jaw clenched. "I didn't know that pained you so much, but then I was too wrapped up in my own problems and needs. What else can I say to convince you that I am truly sorry for my past behavior?"

"Nothing. Explanations aren't necessary." *For either of them.* She shook her head, shelving that dark past where it belonged. "Did you hire me because you regretted how you treated me in the past?"

"No. I told you it was because you are the best at what you do and I meant it. The past had nothing to do with it." He grasped her hand and she could have sworn she saw sparks fly from the contact. God knew she felt the burn to the depths of her soul. "What can I do to ease your mind, Caprice? Tell me."

"You're doing it." She forced a smile, grateful she could still feel the trembles deep inside her.

"Good." He rubbed his hands together and smiled, a far more relaxed expression than she thought him capable of. "Am I right then? Do you like this and feel it is the perfect design for the adaptive program?"

She turned in a slow circle, absorbing the pulse of this amazing space, liking it. No, she loved it. Felt the energy flowing here. "You're right. It's amazing—this design makes me feel strong and capable of doing anything."

"It is the inspiration I covet." He took a deep breath and blew it out. "I'm loath to share it, but because it will benefit others, I give it to you."

For a long moment she studied his solemn expression, judging if he was sincere. If relinquishing his private design somehow took the beauty and serenity from him.

"I accept this with pride and honor and thanks." She entwined her fingers and drank in this sense of calmness and power again, not ever wanting to lose that. "I'm anxious to get going on this. Will we be able to leave tomorrow?"

He barked a laugh. "If we're lucky."

She sobered. "Are you kidding?"

"It could take days to clear the destruction left by the avalanche."

She nodded, exuberance slouching a bit. "You're sure?"

"Yes. It has happened before." He crossed to her and clasped her shoulders, his blue eyes turning seductively smoky. "For now, we wait for word when the road is cleared."

"And do what?" she asked.

His wolfish smile was answer enough.

Caprice opened her eyes slowly, every muscle in her body deliciously relaxed. It was too dark to guess the time, but at some point he'd taken her to bed. And they'd never left it.

She smiled and stretched, feeling a bit wicked being naked beneath the silk sheet with his scent on her, around her, the heat of him so near she remained comfortably warm. "Are you asleep?"

"No," he said gruffly in a sleep-roughened voice. "I'm too hungry. Are you?"

Her stomach answered in a low rumble and they both laughed. "Definitely. And this time for something besides sex."

"Can you cook?"

"Sure. I help out in my kitchen at the lodge all the time," she said, a bit confused. "Why do you ask?"

"While we were sleeping, I received a text from my housekeeper. She tried to bring the monthly supplies to the *rifugio*, and discovered the trail blocked, so they went back to la Duchi Royal."

"So someone knows we're up here?"

"That was never an issue. Anyway, they are safe in the village and wanted to make sure we'd escaped the avalanche." He pulled her from the bed and draped his shirt around her shoulders, his own long, lean body beautifully naked and aroused in the arrows of moonlight that targeted him. "Come on. Let's raid the kitchen."

She shrugged her arms into his shirt and rolled the sleeves up to her wrists, enjoying the glimpse of him thrusting long, strong legs into jeans that rode decadently low on his hips. "The ATV is low on petrol and my housekeeper assured me there was none to be found here, so seeking a route higher up is out of the question."

"We can't get down the mountain and nobody can get up it. And supplies here are obviously limited," she said, the isolation of being here with him finally sinking in. "How long will it take before the trail is cleared?"

"Typically the crews have the route reopened in less than a week," he said, his frown saying otherwise. "But this was an exceptionally wicked avalanche. It could take longer."

"I suppose attempting to descend the mountain on skis is out of the question?"

"That would be too dangerous to attempt."

Was she really hearing this from the man who thrived to test the limits on the slopes? "But—"

"We'll wait for the trail to be cleared," he cut in, his brow pulled into a dark scowl that dared her to argue.

Not that she would.

Taking an off-piste route around the avalanche was too

risky to attempt for anyone who wasn't a top skier. Her skills were higher than most, but nothing to compare to him. Or at least to the skier he'd been. Now? If he couldn't attempt the run with full confidence, then they were right in staying here until the trail was safe to travel.

"Okay," she said, content to follow him down the wide hallway until she noticed that he favored his right leg. The same limb where her fingers had skimmed a ridge of skin before he'd pulled her hand away. "Your right side took the brunt of the injury when you fell that day on the Hahnenkamm. That's why you don't ski."

He came to a dead stop and looked back at her, eyes glacial hard again. "I wondered how long it would take you to notice."

"It's not that obvious," she said, and when he raised a questioning eyebrow, she shrugged. "I'm trained to catch things the average person wouldn't see."

"As I said before, you are extremely astute. But you're wrong about one thing. My injuries are not why I quit skiing." He continued down the hall without explaining more, leaving her to wonder the real reason.

She entered a large kitchen that boasted an array of copper pots and skillets, their shiny surfaces gleaming from the sun streaming through the bank of windows. "But your abilities were diminished by the accident?"

He nodded. "My injuries were severe. As soon as I was able, I began rebuilding muscle tone. But the right side didn't fully return, leaving me with one-sided strength. I can ski. Do pretty much anything I want," he said, his gaze skimming over her body once, twice, as if reminding her of the pleasure they'd just shared, before settling on her eyes again. "But I would be a fool to attempt competition again."

"You could ski for pleasure," she said.

"I skied to win. Now it's over." He spread his arms and turned in the center of the large kitchen. "Let's see how good you are at concocting a meal out of thin provisions."

And just like that, he had swiftly changed topic again. Normally she'd never have given up this easily with a client, but then, as he'd reminded her, he wasn't her patient.

"Your chef has excellent taste in cookware."

He laughed as he rummaged through a massive twin-door refrigerator that looked rather stark. "The cookware is my preference."

"Seriously? You cook?" she asked, and bit back adding, *more than a box meal*.

"Of course I can. I love good food and have always known how most can be best prepared," he said, kissing the pinched tips of his forefinger and thumb in such an exaggerated, theatrical way she laughed, thoroughly enjoying this freedom with a man. "It seemed logical that I learned how to prepare these dishes as well. One lesson from a chef in Tuscany and I was hooked on cooking."

She shook her head and smiled, liking this playful, relaxed side of Luciano. Liking it a bit too much perhaps. But she'd come this far. She might as well enjoy this companionship with a man while it lasted.

"I had no idea you possessed such hidden talents," she teased.

He laughed, a rich contralto that hummed within her. "Are you hungry, *bella*?"

"Ravenous." She moved to him and stroked a hand down his chest, feeling far bolder than she ever had with a man.

"Hmm, would you like Italian?"

She trailed a fingernail down his breastbone and had the satisfaction of hearing him draw a sharp breath, his blue eyes darkening to near black. "Are we talking food or the man?"

"Both." He bent close, capturing her lips for a kiss that was far too brief. "What would the lady like first?"

Her stomach chose that moment to release a low growl. Or had that sound bubbled from her throat?

"I get my choice between a fantastic meal or you?"

"But of course. It is always your choice."

"Then I choose you," she said against his lips.

He drew her flush against his length, his mouth teasing the corners of her mouth, her nose, her eyes before melding over her, lips, tongue flicking her teeth, tasting and taunting. His hands explored her shoulders, his palms smooth, the fingers strong as they trailed down her back, over her hips before cupping her bottom and sweeping her up in his arms. Any protest she made, not that she could utter more than a gasp, was stopped by the slow, erotic thrust of his tongue against her own.

"Bella, mio amore," he said, flicking the buttons open on the shirt to free her breasts, his palm cupping one and brushing a thumb over the nipple before his mouth captured it, nuzzling and drawing it in deeply, doing the same to its twin in turn.

Fire raged through her blood, a sensual inferno that could only be put out by his possession. She dug her fingernails into his back, lost to desire, not caring how or where he took her as long as it was now.

"Love me," she husked against his head, threading her fingers through the dampening strands of his hair and pressing closer to his ravishing mouth, feeling his blood pulsing in his temples and the tension vibrating in his arms.

"With pleasure," he husked out, taking her down on the counter, his weight barely suspended above her, his hot, hard erection probing her swollen flesh that was damp with desire for him again.

This time there was no hesitation, no sense of awkwardness alive in her. The trust she'd once had returned, along with the longing she'd held close for him. But that longing had come alive at his touch, and she reveled in being wanton in his arms, consumed by the promise of pleasure that blazed in his blue eyes, a promise she'd tasted once and hungered for again.

He rocked forward above her and she lifted her hips to meet his downward thrust. She gasped as they smoothly became one. He released a grunt of pure masculine satisfaction and held her tightly, still and hard within her, hearts thundering from the storm raging within them.

In that moment, suspended in passion, she thought she could stay like this forever and yet knew she could barely take another moment of this sensual torment, tasted but far from sated. And then, thankfully, artfully, erotically he moved, slowly pulling back from her core before thrusting into her so hard and deeply she saw stars flickering behind her closed eyes. Heaven. She was but a breath from it and it was far more glorious than she'd dreamed it could be.

"Look at me," he ordered. "Look at me when you climax, *bella*."

She did, blinking until her eyes focused. Her breath caught in her throat as his gaze bore into her, holding her tighter than any bond could.

"I could drown in your eyes," she said.

"If you did," he gasped as he moved inside her with deliciously torturing thrusts, "I would follow you down and bring you back to me."

Tears stung her eyes and she swallowed hard, engulfed in passion, emotion, confusion. He couldn't mean that.

"Why?" she asked on a caught breath, staring into his

eyes dark with passion, fingernails digging into his powerful upper arms.

"For this." He grasped her hips and pushed hard into her, features strained, cords in his neck standing like ropes.

She arched her back, rubbing her hot body against his scorching one, muscles clenched in her core, encasing his erection. A shout, or was it a scream, tore through the air. She didn't know. Didn't care. Only this moment mattered with their bodies joined. His hot seed spilled inside her, his erection rubbing the sensitive nub that he'd brought to life.

A rainbow of light flickered behind her eyes and her breath caught, her senses soaring into the stratosphere. Time had no meaning as she gloried in the sensations.

One last delicious spasm rippled through her and she collapsed, savoring the high of passion. Nothing compared. Not even taking to the air on skis with only the wind beneath her.

His weight came down on her, muscles slowly relaxing, body still burning hot. Both welcome. She needed his warmth. Needed the grounding of slowly returning to the present.

Tension pulled at her, threatening to erode this bliss.

His shoulders and head lifted off her, his brow furrowed, his gaze boring into hers. "What is wrong? Am I too heavy for you?"

"No! I just—" She shook her head and looked away, not wanting to admit the concern this need for him caused her now.

He cupped her chin, forcing her to look at him. "What? Tell me."

"I…working together, if this ends badly…"

"This was a mutual surrender to passion," he said, guessing at her concern, his lips curling into a seductive smile. "Nothing more, nothing less."

Her words in their most basic form. "You're right."

"Don't look for the bad to happen." He took her hand and held it. "Not here, not now."

She nodded, but she didn't trust him, couldn't trust him, any more than she did her ability to control her desires around him. Being lovers for the time she was in Italy was inevitable. She wouldn't argue that point. Nor would she deny him or herself that wondrous pleasure, but she wouldn't play the fool, believing every promise, every sweet lie that tumbled from a lover's lips.

With Luciano she would take what he offered. Savor it. Revel in the pleasure. She would enjoy the present and not worry about the future.

CHAPTER SIX

LUC STOOD ON the deck overlooking the precipice and welcomed the sun beating down on his face, staring out over the vast Alps yet not focusing on anything. His mind was elsewhere, just as it had been the past three days.

It seemed ironic that he'd balked over bringing Caprice to his *rifugio* and now dreaded the thought of leaving here. His reasons were purely selfish.

He'd had the pleasure of having her in his bed surrendering to passion and didn't want it to end. When was the last time he'd spent this much time alone with a woman and enjoyed it?

He shook his head, unable to recall one. Even when he was married, he and Isabella had never spent much more than a day together without it ending in an argument.

But while his compatibility with Caprice was stronger than what he'd had with his wife, he well understood she was using him just the same. The only difference was that he'd known going into it that Caprice was only interested in his money.

He scraped his fingers through his windblown hair and swore. If he was honest with himself, he was more than fond of Caprice. He admired her. Cared deeply for her. Lusted for her.

Though he'd been sure that once he'd tasted her passion

his ardor would cool, his craving for her this morning disproved that theory. She'd quickly become the wildfire in his blood, and sex only fanned the flames. As did thinking about making love with her, he thought sourly, which was happening too frequently.

Their affair was short-term at best. So what if her reasons for being with him were selfish? He could be that way as well, wanting her only for the incredible sex.

That did not have to change when they returned to the lodge, which would be soon. As of an hour ago, the track was cleared and his housekeeper and caretaker had started back to the *rifugio*.

There was no reason for him and Caprice to remain here when their careers and obligations demanded they return to the lodge. Once there, he saw no reason why they couldn't continue their affair for the duration of the contract.

It would simply be convenient. A mutual give and take. They would both get what they wanted without worry over lasting entanglements. Surely she would not object to that.

He whirled on a heel and entered to the bedroom. If they hurried they could be on the road in thirty minutes or less, giving them plenty of time to return to the lodge before dark.

The bed was empty, save the pile of crumpled bedding that streamed from the bed to the floor. "Caprice?"

"I'm here."

He spun around to find her standing in the en suite doorway, eyes wide and sheet clutched to her bosom. The mirror behind her showcased her firm spine and feminine curves of a near-perfect body. Not model perfect. She was "seductive woman" perfect.

"Did you want something?" she asked, clutching the bath sheet tighter, which only emphasized the enticing globes of her bottom.

Her show of modesty made him smile.

"I got a text from my housekeeper. The track is clear."

Her eyes brightened. "We can leave then?"

"As soon as we can."

"Great," she said, moving toward the clothes she'd been wearing off and on for days, though in reality they had been more off of late. "I need to get to work quickly on the project if I'm to have it completed in a month or less."

He crossed to her and took her in his arms, loosely caging her there as he bent for a kiss. Sweet as honey. "The time frame is totally up to you. I am not rushing you."

She planted her palms on his chest and sighed, her gaze pausing at his chin before lifting to meet his eyes. "I know, but I want to finish your contract so I can get busy on Tregore Lodge. There's much to do there."

"You are anxious to return home."

"Of course," she said, chin coming up. "I've never hidden that fact."

"No, you haven't."

She'd stated her priorities up front. How could he argue with that?

"We will leave when you are ready," he said, striding to the door. "I'll wait for you in the great room."

Within an hour, his housekeeper had arrived with supplies and petrol for the ATV and Caprice was ready to leave. Her anxiousness annoyed him, despite the fact he'd expected her to react just as she had. He'd had no doubts she would abide by their contract, but what of their relationship? Was it over in her eyes? Would he be able to seduce her into his bed again?

He would. Somehow, someway.

The drive back to the village was uneventful, save the brief pause he made at the site of the avalanche. Plows had cleared a wide path in the track and had heavy gravel packed on the roadbed. But it wouldn't last the winter.

To his surprise her arms crept around his waist, and she rested her head on his shoulder. "If not for your swift reactions, we would have died."

He nodded, feeling a chill pass through him. "If I'm the cat with nine lives, I had better start using caution as I've expended at least five of them."

"On the slopes?"

"Not all of them."

"Oh?"

He shrugged. "I went through a rather reckless phase in my life."

She sat up, denying him the pleasure of her closeness. "I suppose all boys do that, especially if they are athletes."

And especially if they suffered betrayal and deceit from the one person they loved and trusted. "It's a rite of passage for most, but I cannot blame my exploits on youth."

"Really?" she asked, her small hands resting on his shoulders, reminding him of how tightly she'd held on to him when she'd climaxed. "What spurred your recklessness?"

He sucked in a breath and blew it out, letting the pain of that period in his life knife through him, wanting to remember every single detail so he wouldn't repeat mistakes. "My divorce. It was messy at the end."

Silence echoed in the mountains before she finally broke it. "Want to talk about it?"

"No." Talking about his dead ex-wife with his current lover was the very last thing he ever wished to do. "We need to get moving."

And with that he threw the ATV into gear and sped back down the track, mindful of the woman behind him. Of the lack of contact he received from her now.

She was shelving him away. Her wild romance in the Alps was over for her. She would delve into her work, avoiding him whenever possible.

So would he, but he wasn't done with her yet. No, he'd barely begun. Before the week was out, he would have her in his arms again, willing and wild.

Caprice sat behind Luciano, refusing to grasp the rails for balance instead of the tall, strong man maneuvering the ATV with precision and speed down the rutted trail. Instead of the bracing odor of evergreens and fresh air, she was enveloped by the enticing scent of Luciano.

She supposed it had been inevitable that they fall into each other's arms, finally indulging in the passion that she'd felt toward him for years. For him she understood it was simply having sex.

Fine. She didn't want ties here. Didn't want to lose her heart. This was never supposed to be anything more than a fling. A chance encounter to explore passions. To replace horrible, ugly memories with something beautiful. Something that was her choice.

She had a life and career waiting for her in Colorado. She had aspirations of independence. Of having a peaceful, happy, fulfilled life.

Not once had she thought that she would let Luciano get to her heart again. But she had. Even now it was as if he were pulsing in her blood and stroking her skin. If she closed her eyes she felt him coursing thick and hot through her body, tugging and pushing her over the edge of passion when she least expected it.

He'd left her out of control. Reckless, not with her body but with her heart.

That was where she'd failed before. As an athlete she'd had a margin of upper edge over physical balance. But that training didn't carry over into emotional stability. It didn't shield her heart from the onslaught of emotions she couldn't stop or control.

And that terrified her.

She was comfortable when she was in control. When she was with Luciano, she was horribly off balance. And to think it had only taken him a few days to break down the barriers she'd built around her heart.

For three days and nights she'd made love with him every possible way. Her choice. She'd wanted pleasure from him. Perhaps if she was honest she wanted to revisit the past, to do over what had gone so horribly wrong one cold winter night.

But she hadn't wanted to involve her heart. Hadn't wanted to fall a bit more in love with him as the minutes passed. Love?

Ha! How could she love a man who'd rejected her before? Who only wanted her for sex now? Never mind that she'd told herself she wanted this affair with him for pure pleasure. She'd been the one to seduce him.

That realization left no room for complaints. They were getting what they wanted from each other at the moment. As she'd told him, when the job was over, so was their fling.

Those words reminded her that she was tied to him for the duration of their contract. She would still have him in her bed, his strong arms banding around her while his steely length pulsed inside her, filling her with heat and passion. Banishing the emptiness within her.

But staying here with him meant she wouldn't be free of the crazy nervous upheaval of emotions rioting within her. That wouldn't happen until she left Italy and Luciano. Then she'd be free.

She was strong enough to have an affair and walk away with only battered emotions. She would survive.

She would welcome these memories of Luciano over those that haunted her with his old friend.

That was the promise she made to herself as she lifted her face to the setting sun. When her job here was finished, she would dredge up the courage to walk away with her head held proud, no matter how much a part of her would stay with him forever.

Luciano topped another undulating rise and she spied the village just below. He whipped over one long easy slope and they were there in the thick of it. Shop owners paused to wave as they passed. And up on the high step rose the majestic la Duchi Royal.

She drank it all in and reveled in the sensory buzz that hummed like a swarm of happy bees. Here she could get back to work instead of chasing hot pursuits with Luciano. She would distance herself from him during the day. If timing permitted, she would spend time with him at night.

If not? So be it. She couldn't think any other way and remain sane.

Once she focused her thoughts on installing her program in Luciano's new facility, this hurt needling her heart would ease. At the least she wouldn't have time to dwell on herself, she thought as he wheeled the ATV under the lodge's *porte cochere*.

With the sun at their backs, the pale pink marble columns turned a warm apricot. An attendant rushed to help her off the ATV, but Luciano was quicker, swinging off and offering his hand to her. She stared at the strong hand that had touched her in places no other man had with warmth and passion, well aware that refusing it was an insult.

But her pride rode strong in her now, and she needed to strike independence, if only in a small way.

"Thanks, but I can manage," she said, and got off on the side opposite of Luciano.

His lips drew into a thin line. "Very well. I'll leave you to find your room."

He swung back onto the ATV and revved the engine, shooting off like a rocket. She hadn't intended to hurt his feelings, but judging by his actions, she had.

She stood there a long moment until she could no longer see him, then strode inside the lodge, trying not to feel sorry for her actions and failing. Spite was something she never felt, but Luciano brought emotions and feelings out in her that she'd never experienced before. This one she didn't like.

When she saw him again, she'd apologize. That was all she could do at this point.

She hurried inside, but instead of seeking her room, she walked to the therapy pod. Before she chased up the design team, she wanted to have another look at the space without Luciano. He had a way of muddling her thoughts and she needed a clear head for this. If she wanted changes made to the submitted plan, it would have to be decided today.

Without Luciano's presence, the therapy pod appeared far larger. She walked the space, envisioning how each area would look and function. One certainly worked hand in hand with the other in regard to therapy, a fact she'd leaned early in her training.

Nothing appeared off, yet she couldn't shake her sense of unease. What caused it?

She stepped around the wall into the last area, which boasted a turret-like charm to it, and smothered her surprised gasp with a hand pressed to her mouth. A man sat in a wheelchair, his back to her.

Her chest tightened. She instantly recognized the impressive width of broad shoulders and the arrogant cant of his head.

"Julian," she said softly.

He wheeled the chair around and flashed her that winning smile. "I see my brother was successful in contracting you to rehabilitate me. You've wasted your time."

So he was a hard case, just as Luciano had told her. "He hired me to establish my therapy program here," she said, hoping that would ease the former athlete's resentment. "I could use your help."

Instead of responding to that lure, Julian spun the chair around and returned his gaze to the mountains. "I suppose he chose this pod for that?"

"He did."

"Groomed pistes for the cripples," he said, his tone mocking again. "Oh, wait, you prefer the term 'alternative skier.'"

"Bitterness doesn't become you, Julian," she said.

He hung his head, a muscle twitching along his jaw. "Sorry. I've had a rough day."

As had she, tacked on to a whirlwind three days with Luciano in a mountain hideaway. But she couldn't voice that. In fact she was at a loss how to reach Julian.

"*Scusa*, Jules," came a cultured masculine voice behind her, a voice that scraped along her nerves to free a memory she'd locked away.

Her breath froze in her lungs and her skin crawled. It couldn't be!

She prayed she was hearing things as she followed Julian's gaze to the newcomer. No joke, no mistake. Less than sixteen feet from her stood the man from her nightmares. The lift of his head and narrowing of his eyes were proof that he recognized her.

Run, her instincts screamed. *Hide. Get as far from this*

animal as you can. But even if she could force her feet to move, that would give him the satisfaction of intimidating her again. Worse, it would raise questions, and she wanted her attack buried in a deep, dark pit.

She wouldn't show fear and she wouldn't cower to him, no matter how hellish it was to be in the same room with this beast. And being in the same room with this animal who had raped her was pure torture.

"Mario, you remember Caprice Tregore, Luc's assistant during the World Cup in Val d'Isère?" Julian asked, and a part of her died fearing what Mario Godolphin would say.

Her former attacker's mouth curled into a cruel smile, but his dark eyes remained narrowed. "Yes, I remember Miss Tregore. How good to see you again."

She mumbled something resembling an acknowledgement.

Bastard! Had she come to his mind as much as he'd tormented her nightmares for years? She hoped not! She hoped he couldn't remember the details that haunted her.

"Tell me, Mario. Has my brother secured your firm for the completion of the therapy pod?" Julian asked, and her blood froze at the insane thought of dealing with Mario.

"We are discussing things," he said in a noncommittal tone.

A shiver rocketed through her. There was no way she would tolerate this man designing her therapy unit. But how could she express that to Luciano without telling him the ugly truth?

"Please, think about what I asked," she said, pressing a hand to Julian's shoulder before she strode out the door, hoping her attacker wouldn't follow.

She made it halfway down the corridor before she stole a look behind her. She was alone. Mario had stayed there.

Mario. He'd altered her life completely, spurring her to leave the world she had once loved.

For days, weeks, months after her rape she'd dreaded running into him again. Her phobia was so great and her pain so crippling that she'd pulled out of competition.

And she was glad she had.

Soon after her retirement and the horrific accident that removed the Duchelini brothers from the chase for gold, Mario had stepped in to dominate the ski world. It was the logical way of things.

For years, the ski world had been abuzz over the duo Italian champions. Luciano always took first place while Mario snared the second slot.

They were a one-two punch on the slopes that nobody could best. When Luciano retired from competition, Mario had a short run of being the best.

She'd been aware of his dominance in the sport, his name batted about everywhere in Colorado, unknowingly tossing coals on the pain that burned in her.

Then, within four years, he'd faded from the news, which was a relief to her. In fact, she'd never once considered that she would ever cross paths with Mario. She'd certainly never entertained the idea of working with him, even remotely.

It just wasn't possible. The idea of forcing her to do so turned her stomach.

But whether that happened or not, she would return home as soon as possible. There was no way she could stay and finish what she'd barely started, even though abandoning her job would kill all plans for her lodge.

She had to retreat to her safe zone. And abandon her dream?

No! Running away would convince Mario he'd bested

her again. But how could she stay here, knowing he could come upon her any second?

Her mind whirled with a solution as she waited for the elevator door to open, but nothing was coming to mind. Nothing except the urge to find Luciano and throw herself into his arms. Strong fingers wrapped around her arm and held tight and her heart nearly stopped.

Had Mario found her? Was she in his grip again?

She tried to twist free, panic bubbling up her throat when she couldn't break his hold. "I'll scream if you don't let go of me."

"Bella," Luciano said, enfolding her trembling body against his, pulling her into his arms. "What has terrified you so?"

How was she supposed to answer that? Certainly not with the truth, not when her attacker was in the lodge, clearly a friend of Julian's and of Luciano's as well. Dear God, what a monumental mistake she'd made aligning herself with an Italian, even if he was a man she'd started to trust again.

She wanted to be strong and push him away, presenting a brave face. Wanted so desperately to shun his comfort. But held close against his muscled chest, where she heard the steady drum of his heart, she was lost, burrowing against him like a child in a storm, tears smarting her eyes.

If only the past hadn't happened. If only...

"Come." He escorted her down the hall to his private elevator and pressed his thumb on the security pad.

"I'm okay," she said as the door swished open seconds later.

"No, you are not." He ushered her inside and punched the up button, all the while keeping her caged in his embrace.

"Really, I'm fine. Maybe I'm still jumpy over the avalanche," she said, and yet she was reluctant to let go of him.

His sigh rumbled through her. "That was a horrific experience."

She loosed a nervous laugh. "One I never wish to repeat."

He clasped her shoulders and levered her from him, his shrewd gaze scrutinizing her. "I should have refused to take you up there."

"It happened, like most accidents do. It's over. If I have flashbacks they are mine to deal with."

"As well I know," he said bitterly, looking away.

She cupped his jaw and forced his gaze back to her. It was far easier to be the inquisitor than the one questioned. "You revisit the accident again and again?"

"Playing shrink again?" he asked.

"Being a friend. I care about you," she said and thought, *far too much at times.* "I know how the bad memories can haunt you."

One dark eyebrow lifted over a discerning blue eye. "Do you?"

His doubt was understandable. And really, why had she even brought her own problems into this mix?

"I don't know what it's like to experience what you and your brother did, but my life hasn't been devoid of heartache."

He clasped her hand and pulled her close, his other hand lifting to cup the back of her head, his long fingers gently massaging at the tension that gripped. "We have both had our trials and tribulations since birth. Wealth or lack of it made no difference. Agree?"

She filled her lungs and heaved out a breath, nodding. "Agree."

"Would you like a drink? Wine? Scotch?"

Liquor was the last thing she needed, as she wanted her wits sharp as tacks, yet as wound up as she was she doubted she would find any peace this night. "Scotch but light," she said at last.

He obliged with a nod, pressing a thick glass into her hand, before raising his own. "To the launch of your therapy program worldwide."

"To your astute help achieving it," she said and clinked her glass with his.

It should be just this simple, thanks to his financial assistance on the project she'd poured long hours into. But Mario's presence changed everything. It sullied her dream and left her too skittish to concentrate.

She simply couldn't get around it. That left her one choice. Get rid of the problem or bail, and she sure didn't want to run away again.

"I spoke briefly with Julian today," she said. "He mentioned you might have hired an architect to work at the lodge."

He frowned, staring into his half empty glass. "As of this point, I haven't decided whether I should go with Godolphin's firm."

She bit her lower lip, biting back what she wanted to say. This was her problem. Not his. And yet to think that Mario Godolphin would have his name tied to any part of her program made her sick.

"I thought he was a close friend of yours," she said, as if that was reason enough to hire him for the job.

"I've known him all my life, but he is a closer friend to Julian than to me." His frown deepened. "Mario was a rival on the slopes and has proven to be a challenging businessman, branching out from his initial architectural firm."

So there was a chance to oust him. "Are there other companies you're considering?"

"Several, including the firm that built the lodge."

"Not that you asked, but I'd suggest you stick with the same firm so the design is exact instead of similar," she said, then dropped the subject before she said too much. "Have you any idea when the rest of the equipment will arrive? It's imperative we get this done as quickly and efficiently as possible."

"You're that anxious to get away from me?"

"No, I…" She just wanted to put distance between herself and her attacker. Wanted desperately to slam the door on that dark moment in her past forever. "It's complicated."

He smiled and ran a hand up her arm, creating friction that hummed in her. "Want to talk about it?"

Her words thrown back at her. She shook her head, fighting tears of frustration. Revealing her past would solve nothing.

"There's nothing to talk about," she said. "I just want to get this job over and done with and go home."

He crossed both arms over his chest and stared at her, the silence crackling between them for a long, uncomfortable moment. She looked away with a shiver, afraid he could read too much into her mind. That he could uncover her deepest secret.

"Is it me you're bent on running away from?" he asked at last.

"No." She knew as soon as his blue eyes narrowed that her quick reply had revealed too much.

"Then why? Tell me why you are so desperate to leave here."

She pressed her fingers to her forehead, feeling the first tinge of a killing headache. Wasn't her heart hurting too much for her body to tolerate more?

"Drop it, Luciano."

"No. You're not leaving this room until you tell me what has upset you."

She peered at his resolute features and thought marble statues didn't look as hard or inflexible. "You can't lock me up."

"Want to bet?"

Not on her life. "You're being totally unreasonable."

One dark eyebrow arched. "You have that desperate look of a woman ready to hide from the world."

"I do not."

"I'm not blind," he said. "What are you trying to hide from?"

Tears threatened again, but she managed to hold them back. She wouldn't cry. Wouldn't give Godolphin the satisfaction of terrorizing her waking moments as well.

"Bella," Luciano murmured as he gathered her into his embrace, her weary resistance failing to deter him. "You can tell me anything. You know this."

"Not this time. Please."

The man who'd destroyed her innocence was his friend and business associate. He was here at la Duchi Royal, waiting to hear if he'd been chosen for the job. She couldn't involve Luciano in the mess that was her personal life.

And just admitting that loosed her tears. They came hot and miserably fast, burning trails of makeup down her cheeks that his tailored shirt soaked up.

"What happened? You must tell me that much," he insisted, keeping her encased within his arms, clearly not about to give up.

What was the use in holding her silence? He was right. She could tell him that much.

She sucked in a shaky breath and held it, willing the chills to stop yet knowing nothing would ever truly purge her of the hell she'd endured.

There was only one way to get through this. Tell the truth.

One more shaky inhalation and she blurted out, "I was raped."

CHAPTER SEVEN

LUC GRABBED HER forearms and held her in front of him, stunned—no, furious this horrible thing had happened to her. Rape. It was an ugly word depicting an abhorrent act. "When?"

"Years ago," she said.

"How many years?" he persisted.

She pinched her eyes shut and held her breath for several counts he was sure. "Seven."

"Seven?" The same year...as the last World Cup. Around the same time as his and Julian's accident. "Where did this happen, Caprice? How?"

"What difference does it make?"

"Tell me," he demanded.

Tears stung her eyes and she tried to wrench free, but he wasn't deterred, holding her close. "If you must know, it was a date gone horribly wrong at the World Cup. He was convinced I'd agreed to go out with him for sex, and turned deaf ears when I told him no. The next thing I knew he dragged me into an equipment storeroom and took what he wanted."

"You should have told me."

A reddish stain streaked up her neck and dotted her checks. "I couldn't come to you. You'd rejected me earlier that night."

He banged a fist on the door, furious he'd played a part in her turning to another and bitten with guilt that she'd thought her only recourse to take was to run away. "Did you at least summon the authorities?"

"And tell them what? Do you think they would believe me or assume I'd simply drank too much and changed my mind about having a quickie because I assure you that is exactly what *he* would have claimed," she said, her body trembling and her teary eyes stark with fear.

"So you just gave up?" he asked, ravenous for revenge and sickening fury eating at his insides.

"I was shamed beyond belief. And so terrified he'd come back and do it again," she said, tears streaming down her face, shoulders slumping. "That's why I left that night without saying a word to anyone."

"Mio Dio!" He stalked the perimeter of his office, furious this happened to her, disgusted that her attacker had never been brought to justice. That was something he intended to change. "Who the hell is he?"

"Why do you care? You dismissed me that night, wanting nothing more to do with me," she snapped back.

He slashed a hand through the air and swore again. "I turned you away because of that kiss. You touched something in me that I refused to explore further. My life was in such a turmoil then."

She blinked, eyes bright with moisture that he wanted to wipe away. Wipe away all her hurts, but he couldn't. "I wish I would have known that then. Wish I wouldn't have attempted to prove I was desirable to a man."

"As do I." He drove his fingers through his hair and swore, feeling the weight of guilt bear down on him again. "We can't change the past, but we can learn from it."

"A saying my father repeated often," she said, shaking her head, wide gaze lifting to his again. "I certainly learned the hard way about blindly trusting a man."

He took her cold hands in his, hating the shiver that coursed through her, hating her attacker more with each breath. "Bella, tell me his name. Let me settle this for you."

She shook her head violently. "It doesn't matter."

He gave her one terse shake. "It matters to me. Is there a connection between your attack and your aversion to remaining here?"

Her gaze lowered, her skin paling. "There isn't one."

He swore roundly again. "I don't believe you. You have seen him here, perhaps have spoken with him. Is he a guest? Employee? Someone who lives in the village? Tell me."

"Stop it, Luciano. What happened was in the past. Let it go."

His palms cupped her face, holding her still, as he kissed the tears from her cheeks. "I will not give up until you tell me his name."

Her shoulders slumped and her head bowed. "It was Mario."

"Mario Godolphin?" he asked, and at her nod, he dropped his hold on her, fingers bunched into fists, his rage towering higher than the mountains. "I'll kill him."

"No!" She gripped his wrists, complexion growing deathly pale. "Please, Luciano, I want that entire ugly night to remain forgotten."

"Why? You've never forgotten it," he said. "Even if you had, Mario laid his filthy hands on you. He hurt you. Now he must pay for those actions."

She tipped her head back and growled low in her throat. "It is his word against mine and I refuse to go into battle with a man who will deliberately make me look like I pursued him," she said, hysteria rising in her voice. "That publicity is too humiliating to face, let alone endure."

He combed his fingers though his hair and swore, sickened that he'd failed another person he cared about. If there was a chance he could make this right for her... If he could undo a wrong and bring someone to justice, he damned well would.

"You can't let him get away with this violation," he said.

"It is my choice to make," she said, voice cracking.

Had she ever felt this raw and exposed and rigorously furious? No, not even after the rape, after she'd fled home to Colorado, after she'd gone through weeks of worry until she was certain she wasn't pregnant.

This time she wasn't just fighting for her sanity and career. She was fighting for her independence, even though that hard-won gem might sever her from Luciano forever. But the business deal she struck with him and their affair would end soon anyway. She had to take this stand.

"Don't you see that if I *deny* anything happened between us, it diminishes Mario's hold over me?" she asked, desperate for him to understand her fears and phobias. "It gives me the power to choose."

He stared at her a long hard moment before he stalked to the window and stood with his broad back to her, which for all the world seemed an impenetrable wall. She resisted the impulse to cross to him and wrap her arms around his waist.

"What can I do to make this right for you?" he asked.

If only he could... "I need to know if Mario's firm is vital to la Duchi Royal."

He pulled a dark face. "It is true he's been the exclusive architect on all my projects."

She pressed a hand to her queasy stomach, her blood chilling. "He'll continue working with you then, right here."

"No. I am done with him."

Bubbles of panic popped inside her. "But if you sever ties with Mario now, he'll know I told you what happened."

"Who cares what he thinks?" he asked.

"I do and so should you. Think what he will do if you break your contract with him," she said. "There are legalities to face, and what about the ensuing publicity?"

"Mario won't be so foolish as to engage in a legal battle with me," he said.

She hugged herself but still couldn't stop her trembling. "What if you're wrong? What if he retaliates and spreads vicious lies about me? I can't have that black mark attached to my name or my program."

"I respect your decision to keep silent about this, but your way of dealing with it is to live in denial—and whilst that is your choice, I intend to take the direct and final approach." He snagged the phone off his desk. "Get legal on the phone now."

Panic clawed at her throat. "If you go through with this now, I'll be the one who'll end up with the tainted reputation."

"I won't allow that to happen." He slashed the air with his hand, features hard and cold. He spoke into the receiver. "Begin proceedings today to cancel all contracts with Mario Godolphin in all industries and business." He paused, listening for a response. "Yes, every single one of them, and see that he's barred from setting foot at this lodge."

He soundlessly laid the receiver in the cradle, but a black silence roared in the room.

She pressed her palms to her temples, chest heaving, her control close to snapping like a mighty pine under the force of an avalanche. "I've worked hard all of my life to ensure I had a clean name. Divulging the past now will ruin that. They'll believe every lie he tells."

He chewed out a curse, muscle thrumming madly in his lean cheek, eyes narrowed to angry slits. "And what if letting him get away with this leads him to force himself on another woman?"

She covered her face with her palms, feeling sick inside. Trapped. "I would never want this to happen to any woman."

"Neither do I," he said. "Severing all ties with Godolphin is the right thing for me to do. You must choose what you feel is the right thing to do for yourself. But, *bella,* Mario is the guilty party in this. He should be held accountable for harming you."

She sighed, so very tired of running, hiding, of closeting her emotions so they wouldn't leave her vulnerable to making the same mistake again. "Okay," she said at last. "I'll consider it, after my contract is completed."

"Good."

He crossed to an elaborate liquor cabinet, but instead of fixing a drink, he stood there like a statue. She wondered what to do. If there was anything she could or should do.

Hesitantly, she crossed to him and wrapped her arms around his stiff frame, desperate to feel his strength. To hide from reality if just a little while longer.

He remained cold and hard as steel for less than a heartbeat in her embrace. Then he heaved a sigh, grasped her wrists to stay her and turned to embrace her so tightly she feared she might break. She grabbed a breath, then another and held it tightly as his arms enveloped her, holding her close, his head finding a place on her shoulder to rest, his face millimeters from her neck with his breath so intensely hot that her chills finally, *finally* eased.

"I'm sorry," she whispered at last.

"Why? You've done nothing wrong," he said. "You're the one wronged by me and an old friend, damn his soul."

"It was partly my fault. I knew better, but I did it anyway," she said. "Let it go, Luciano. Retaliation isn't the answer."

"This is not your decision to make."

Panic stabbed through her like fallen icicles piercing the snow. "Isn't it? Your name is golden. It can withstand bad press. Mine can't, not when I'm so close to launching my program worldwide."

He fisted his hands at his sides, jaw rigid. "I can't let this go. He's hurt you because I failed you. A revelation of this scope could protect innocents, or at the very least shine light on his crime. And you are tied to me through our mutual contract. If he besmears our names, my attorneys will have him tied up in legalities in an hour or less."

She grabbed a breath, frustration pinching her soul, wanting this lifted from her conscience. He was right and she hated him for it. She wasn't selfish. The truth could protect women from Mario, but the consequences of having everyone know her own personal nightmare scared her to death.

"I don't know if I'm strong enough to face this," she said honestly.

"You aren't," he said, stepping closer, his strong arms coming around her. "Not alone. I'll be with you. Yes, there will be gossip tossed about, but I promise it will not have any ill effect on your lodge."

She rested her forehead on his chest, but his heat couldn't thaw the deep chill invading her soul. "How can you possibly promise that?" she asked, her deep fears sleeping just under the surface.

He pressed his lips to her forehead, her eyes, and nuzzled her head up to brush his lips over hers once, twice. "We will marry. He wouldn't dare sully your name then."

"What?" she squeaked, too stunned to make sense of his out-of-the-blue proposal. "You don't love me."

"Love," he muttered, shaking his head. "Our marriage would be a contract. You'd be under my protection with full access to a battery of la Duchi attorneys."

He was offering another business arrangement, only this one with sex. It certainly wasn't a marriage and wasn't for her, simply because love wasn't involved and never would be, at least not mutually. His heart would never be hers because he'd given it to his wife long ago, and she had taken it with her to her grave.

"Why are you doing this?" she asked.

"I failed to protect you the first time."

"I wasn't yours to protect," she said.

Not that his reasons or rationale mattered. There wouldn't be a sham marriage for her. She would have to be crazy or desperate or both to put herself through an emotional hell that would take her years to recover from. *If* she ever recovered.

"*Bella*, be reasonable."

"No! I refuse to marry under those circumstances," she said and headed for the door and fresh air. Freedom.

She would rather be alone and in control of her life than enter into a marriage of convenience.

"Don't reject this out of hand," he said.

"If you'll excuse me, I've got work to do," she said, and walked from his office with her head high and her heart heavy.

She'd rejected him. Rejected him.

For days the thought had haunted him. He was, in a sense, off the hook. Relief should wash over him instead of these needles of anxiety. He should brush it off instead of dwelling on her refusal. But he couldn't.

Annoyance pinged his taut nerves as he crossed to the window and stared out at the hard, unyielding mass of mountains, feeling cold and remote inside. This sense of aloofness closing around him wasn't new. He'd gladly embraced it after his divorce. He'd worn it like a shield, never wishing to cast it off.

He liked his life the way it was, without commitment, without a woman complicating his life. He'd proposed to Caprice to protect her. That's all.

Yet she'd refused him. And his protection.

He blew out a long sigh and hung his head, determined to get back on track. For weeks he'd tried to put Caprice in the same class as Isabella, out to get his money and entrée his name would lend. But she was nothing like his ex-wife.

Caprice had abided by the letter of their contract.

He would not complain about that.

She wanted a premier facility in Colorado and he would see that she got it. He could see now that she wanted to enjoy sex with him.

It had been good. Amazing for him. But was she able to say the same?

His intercom beeped. "Sorry to bother you, Luc, but you wanted to know when the therapy equipment had been set up."

"Thank you, Eva."

In a matter of minutes, he arrived at the therapy pod for a quick inspection, frowning as resonant clicks and whirs echoed from deep in the unit. Was someone using the equipment unsupervised?

He crossed to the sounds coming from the far room, only to pull back around the privacy wall. Julian was strapped into a harness that allowed him to stand on a massive machine while Caprice supervised.

"That's it," she said. "Stretch slow and steady again, holding when you reach the point of peak endurance."

A masculine grunt, then a loud clank. "I can't do this."

Luc peered around the corner, careful to remain hidden. The defeat on his brother's face stabbed at his heart. And then he looked at Caprice and saw the compassion glittering in her eyes as she patiently readjusted the straps on the pulleys and handed the ends to Julian.

"'Can't' isn't a word we use here," she said softly, pressing a palm to Julian's muscled bicep, as if encouraging him to try again. "It's going to pull, hurt and resist. You have to work at this. You have to want it."

Julian gave a short nod and began using the equipment again, face contorting as he exerted upper body strength. Slowly, minutely, his legs began moving back and forth, mimicking the motion of cross-country skiing.

Julian barked a laugh and Luc smiled. "I can't believe it. As my legs are worked, the tension in my shoulders eases."

"That's because your entire body is moving as it should in motion," she said. "You're doing great. But another minute then you stop for today, okay?"

"No problem. We'll do this again tomorrow, right?"

"Right," she said.

Luc stood there a moment longer, watched the satisfaction on Caprice's face reflected from the serious intent of Julian's. She wasn't all talk and no action. She was the perfect package, doing just as she said she would for his brother by implementing her unique program with specialized equipment.

Absently he rubbed the weak area of his leg. Was there a chance she could help him as well? Probably so, but he wasn't going to think of himself or of his brother.

Right now was about Caprice. He wanted to return the favor, do something special just for her.

A moment later he knew just what that would be. He would give her a night to remember. The perfect night she'd been denied.

Toward dusk, Luc strode down the executive hallway, a box of Noka chocolates and a bottle of Dom Perignon vintage brut champagne in one hand and a bloodred rose in the other. If it looked like an apology, so be it.

He hadn't been able to think of anything else, other than a diamond ring and undying professions of love, that would embody *amore* better than what he'd chosen. Besides, after his divorce, he'd vowed he would never risk his heart on a woman again.

So he decided to shower Caprice with romance. Indulge her passions. Prove to her she was a very desirable woman whom he respected and wanted.

He didn't count the sultry nights spent in each other's arms, indulging in sex. He certainly didn't want to revisit that first time, which had been a rushed, frenzied affair.

Every sexual encounter they'd shared had come before he'd known about her attack.

It became clear to him then that she deserved to be pampered and indulged. Made love to deeply and passionately, focusing on her wants and needs and desires instead of his own.

Which is what had brought him here bearing romantic gifts.

He rapped on her door, gripped with an odd nervousness he hadn't felt in years. Perhaps because doing this for her meant so much to him.

This was to be her night of decadent indulgence. This was to be the one she would remember instead of the painful one, and the harried times they'd made love. This would be the time that she was given all and expected to do nothing but savor each moment.

She swung the door open, her smile a bit uncertain. "You're right on time."

"And you are lovely," he said, visually caressing the blue dress that draped her full bosom before nipping in at her waist to hug her from hips to hem.

"Thanks. You look amazingly handsome as always," she said.

"For you." He handed her the rose and chocolates before lifting the bottle. "I thought this would be an excellent time to have a pre-celebration drink to toast the near completion of our therapy pod."

"Good idea. The work has been intense the past week but well worth the effort," she said, taking a leisurely inhalation of the rose and smiling. "Wow! I never expected this. Thank you, Luciano."

"My pleasure." He motioned her to precede him into the sitting room and waited until she'd chosen a seat, hiding his surprise and relief when she eased onto the sofa.

He uncorked the champagne, splashed some in two crystal flutes and joined her. "I've taken the liberty of reserving a table for us in the village."

She took the glass, her smile fading. "I'm not sure I'm up for going out tonight."

He moved closer and slipped an arm around her shoulders. "Are you worried you will run into Mario?"

She shrugged, staring at her lap, reverting to the restrained woman he preferred not to see tonight. "A bit."

"You won't find him here or in the village," he said, drawing her close and dropping a kiss on her forehead. "But if you really don't wish to go out, we can dine in. Your choice, *bella*."

Her brow puckered and she fidgeted with her fingers, her body far too tense to find pleasure in anything right now. "I won't let that man keep me a prisoner here or anywhere else. You've made the reservation so let's go."

He lifted his glass to hers, marveling again at this woman he'd underestimated. "Well said, *bella*. You are strong. Smart. Beautiful. To you and all you wish for."

"And you as well," she replied, clinking her glass to his, her smile quivering the slightest bit, as if she were fighting tears.

But she wouldn't cry. He knew that much about her. This moment didn't warrant tears. Within fifteen minutes they arrived at the *ristorante* in his limo and were promptly escorted to a private nook. The space was small and the lighting subdued. *Perfecto!*

Luc assisted her to her chair and took his own, still struggling with that odd sense of imbalance. "I've ordered a pinot grigio, but if you prefer something else…"

"That would be heavenly," she said, looking relaxed.

He tasted the wine and accepted it, then asked for a selection of appetizers, gaining Caprice's okay, which again came readily. And wasn't that exactly one of the things he liked most about her? They were in sync on preferred designs, adventurous palettes and the hunger of carnal pleasures, the latter being what he wished to explore leisurely with her tonight.

His wish was for her to walk away from him and Italy feeling very much in control of her mind and fully attuned to the needs and provocative charms of her body. Together they were a powerful aphrodisiac possessing the power to bring him down to his knees.

He jerked when her hand pressed over his. "Is everything okay?"

"Yes, fine," he said, closing the door on emotions stirring to escape.

His feelings had no place here. This was her night. The one she'd deserved from him seven years ago.

"I want this to be a good night you will recall with pleasure," he said. "Would you prefer a menu?"

She leaned back in her chair, her glass cradled in her hands, her gaze drinking him as if she were parched. "It seems you've designed this night for me. You decide, Luciano."

"To your pleasure," he said, just barely tipping his glass to her and liking this surety and boldness about her.

My God, he admired her strength. Whatever it took he would make this night very special for her.

They dined on a medley of vegetables, cheese and crusty breads reminiscent of Austria, and he placed their entrées along with another bottle of wine.

"This is fabulous," she said, scooping a generous portion of *parmesano polenta* dressed with wild mushrooms, sausage and tomatoes onto crusty bread.

She held it out, tempting him to lean close, to take it from her fingers.

And he did. Slowly. Ending with a swish of his tongue over pale skin that tasted sweet. "Delicious," he said.

Her tongue flicked over her lush lips; then she leaned forward, her grin challenging, her eyes sparkling with devilment. "My turn."

That remark crumbled any remaining awkwardness lingering between them. They ate. They drank. They flirted outrageously.

When the generous plate of carpaccio of beef and greens arrived, they laughed and ate and drank and let go, enjoying the moment. Laughter grew softer as did the few words spoken. And through it all the wine flowed.

"What is your dream?" he asked her when the plates were cleared and the dessert they would barely touch had been ordered.

She smiled and laughed, but the exuberance was gone. "Part of me will always long for a home and family. Normalcy. But with my career—" She shook her head, her laugh far too brief. "You were my dream, Luciano. Nothing will ever compare so I will never try. But would I anyway? You've made sure my career is set. I can't complain. Ever."

But did she want to? "You humble me when I don't deserve it."

"But you do." She looked away, pensive. "We come from different lives. Different wants and dreams. We end when the job ends because we must."

"Yes," he said, nodding yet unsettled she'd grasped what was obvious so easily. "You're right. It is the only way. So let's make the most of this night."

"I couldn't agree more."

The decadent dessert was left, as was an uncorked and untried bottle of wine. Luciano clasped her to his side and ushered her to the limo, pulling her into his arms.

"That was so good, so good," she said, lifting her face to his, her fingers tracing long, lazy figure eights on his back.

In what seemed a blip in time, they reached his lodge. "We'll take the back elevator up to my suite," he said, guiding her into the lift.

"You're just full of surprises," she said, pulling away from him and stepping back from the glass enclosure that offered a bird's-eye view of the lodge and the Alps.

He laughed. "It is one-way glass, *bella*. Come," he said when the doors whispered open.

In a moment, they were secluded in his suite. He pulled her into his arms, backing her into his bedroom, ravenous to taste her, to get drunk from her kisses.

His lips found hers in a melding of lips and tongues that was pure carnal abandonment. Hands joined in, lifting her onto his massive bed and following her down, fingers sneaking beneath the constraints of clothes, finding flesh that was hot and wet and wanting.

"Yes," she breathed when his forefinger skimmed the heat of her core while his thumb found her pleasure point.

"Oh, God," she moaned, arching her back, shivering with desire.

He peeled her thong away and pushed her skirt up, wanting only to pleasure her. Taste her. With seductive precision, he opened her to him with his tongue and finger before he thrust inside her, playing a game with her libido and his own, gambling which one of them could hold out. God, he could draw this moment out. Embed memories of a night that would never be triumphed.

She would remember her first lover, the first encounter with sex not counting because it had been taken. This was given to her.

He clasped her buttocks as she arched her back, surrendering the passion locked in her. So sweet. So tight. His gift.

What they shared was a moment she would bank away for the future if loneliness overcame her. He hoped she would remember the very good and not the bad, that those images of a beast abusing her would vanish. God knew he would banish them for good if he could.

Caprice was just rousing from her climax, supine and drowsy in his arms.

"That was beyond wonderful," she said. "Now I believe it is your turn."

He caught her before she could move, drinking from her lips until he was drunk on passion, until his own plans of setting her away from him seemed flawed.

"You make leaving difficult," she said.

"I could say the same."

Their mouths met and melded again in a moan, lips dueling an erotic melody while their hips swayed to the same wanton rhythm. Whatever time they had together, he would give her his all. He wouldn't regret this decision.

She deserved this from him and so much more.

And yet was this lovemaking that much different?

Yes, because his attitude was different. He'd given without expecting compensation.

Her head lulled back, a sigh whispering from her. "I feel boneless," she said, clearly basking in the sensations rocking through her while he did the same just knowing he'd given her this release.

He pulled her flush against him, the hard length of his erection pressed to her belly as he kissed her neck before his lips found her ear and his tongue traced the contours, pleasuring her until she cried his name. Only then did he look up into her face and catch her wide smile of pleasure.

And he smiled, knowing he'd succeeded, that she had indulged in passion. *Remember me*, he thought before he tucked her close and sought the same sleep she was quickly falling into.

CHAPTER EIGHT

CAPRICE STRETCHED IN the massive bed, silk sheet under her bosom, her mind clearing from the sensual haze she'd reveled in last night. Talk had been minimal after that last amazing joining of bodies and souls, or at least it had felt that strong and good for her.

Now her affair was closing. Luciano had said so in so many words. But she didn't balk. She had to get away from here and return home so she was grounded. Had to get away to where the likelihood of running into Mario was incredibly small.

She could manage. She had in the past seven years.

The bathroom door opened and he stalked inside, looking painfully contemplative. "What's wrong?"

"I need to return to Colorado," she said.

He swore and stormed toward her, towel cinched over his lean hips. "Why?" he said with a dismissive wave of his hand. "It would be safer if you stayed here awhile longer."

"Where I could run into Mario at any time?"

"I've barred him from coming to the lodge."

"But you can't keep him out of the village." She stared at the intricate swirls of blue and red that outlined the exquisite black geometric designs in the Turkish carpet, waiting for him to deny it. But he couldn't because it was true. "I can't stay here."

"Can't or won't?"

She signed, not wishing to delve into this discussion on the tail end of a marvelous night of celebration. "Won't. This isn't just about Mario. If I'm to make a success of my business, I need to complete my work here and return to Colorado."

He cupped her chin and forced her to look at him. Had blue eyes ever seemed so intense? This assertive? "The lodge isn't finished yet. Where will you go?"

She pulled back from the touch that felt too comforting and the eyes that probed far too deeply. "I have friends in Colorado that I can stay with until the lodge renovations are completed."

"You're certain?" Luciano asked, jaw set tight.

"Yes. As soon as my work here is done, I'll go home."

The following week Caprice saw little of Luciano. It was unbelievable how the time had zipped past in a flurry of last-minute details she had to attend to on the therapy pod. The grand opening was a week away. The first therapy guests would arrive in a few days.

She would return home to stay with friends. Yes, staying here in Italy would be easier, but wasn't that the problem? Everything she experienced here with Luciano wasn't real.

It wasn't love.

It wasn't commitment.

What they had together here was amazing sex. Nothing more.

That wasn't enough to keep her here. In fact it was the very reason she should go. Leaving here would break this addiction she had for Luciano and force her to take back control of her life and business.

She slid from the bed and slipped into a lovely satin robe

that had appeared the day she'd arrived. More clothes had been delivered since then. All were his choice. All were far too elegant for her to wear when she returned to Colorado and the real world. But for now they suited the role she was playing.

She walked barefoot into the adjacent salon where the *colazione* had been deposited on the sideboard. After pouring a cup of *caffè e latte* and selecting a *brioche,* she curled up on the divan just as the bedroom door opened and Luciano strode into the room, his lean muscled body bare except for a thick, knotted towel that rode low on his lean hips.

A different hunger stirred inside her until her gaze lifted to his remote features. "Is something wrong?"

"We need to talk," he said, pouring a rich coffee for himself before joining her on the divan with masculine grace.

"Sounds serious. Please tell me this has nothing to do with my lodge," she said, hoping she hadn't suffered any setbacks there.

He gave one abrupt shake of his head and stared at her with eyes that burned with fury. "My PA rang me yesterday. Mario scheduled a press conference in Milan tomorrow. According to sources he wants to set the record straight on why la Duchi has halted his company from further work at the lodge."

The bite of sweet brioche she'd just eaten soured in her stomach. "I was afraid he would defy any threat."

"He is an arrogant fool," he said. "I will not allow him to spew lies."

"There must be some other way to silence Mario. A payoff, maybe?" she asked, desperate to avoid scandal.

"He has money to burn. But he does rely heavily on the endorsement he's always gotten from being the architect of my projects, several that were still in the planning stage," he said, challenge darkening his eyes to a stormy blue. "Once legal measures are finalized and his current contracts with la Duchi are nullified, many businessmen will notice and follow suit, not wishing to do business with his sort."

"Do you really think you can ruin him?" she asked, not entirely convinced he wielded that much power.

He pulled her close and kissed her hard, possessively. "Yes. Trust me, *bella*."

"I do." At least she was trying to put all her faith in him.

"Continue with the plans here. I'll return before the opening. Promise," he said, and when she nodded he released her and found his clothes.

She allowed herself the pleasure of watching him thrust long legs into snug black jeans, the denim hugging his firm thighs and riding low on his lean hips. He pulled on a gray jersey and tugged it over the muscled slabs of his chest, tucking it in with an economy of movement.

Her heart swelled, even though sadness lurked in the back of her mind. He was hers to physically love for a week more at most. For the umpteenth time she asked herself if this heaven she reveled in now was worth the hell she'd sink into when they separated.

The answer was obvious. She was a career girl. She was determined to be independent of a man.

She could survive alone. But did she really want to?

No. But her relationship with Luciano was drawing to an end. The most she could hope for was a few more nights with him as his lover. Having her own business and being self-sufficient was what she had dreamed of for years. So why did she entertain doubts about every facet of her life?

"Are you all right?" he asked, startling her.

"I'm anxious about the grand opening for the therapy unit at your lodge."

"It will be fine. Perfect," he said. "You will be as well."

"I hope you're right."

She crossed to him with a smile and wrapped her arms around his neck, tilting her face to his, for the first time offering herself to him for whatever he wished to do. His sudden stiffening froze her to the spot.

"What's wrong?" she asked.

"My thoughts are on dealing with Mario," he said, grasping her wrists and gently setting her aside. "We'll talk at length when I return."

He strode out the door without a goodbye or kiss, his curt rejection cutting like a knife, bringing back unpleasant memories of how he'd been too involved in competition to have much courtesy for anything or anyone, especially her. How easily he'd dismissed her back then.

But then she'd been nothing but the volunteer helper. The starry-eyed young woman who'd had a too-big crush for the champion.

And now? She shook her head, admitting she hadn't escaped that yet. Sure she was his business associate as well as his convenient lover. But once the contract was finished, all of that would end.

It was what she wanted. What she'd demanded from the start. So she shouldn't feel melancholy now.

Luciano was never going to change, so it was useless to continue trying.

For the first time in weeks, she knew exactly what she had to do. After the grand opening at his lodge, she would return to Colorado and begin the lengthy process of putting him from her mind.

Hours later, Luc landed his private Eurocopter atop his towering glass and steel office building in Milano. He still got a special thrill seeing the helo's reflection on the structure's sides. This was his baby. The pinnacle of taking a million-dollar business that had gone stale and expanding it into a multibillion-dollar corporation.

He'd done it in less than a decade, which was much more than Mario could boast.

Mario. The detectives he'd hired confirmed his old friend had stayed in Milano, living and working out of his office. The fact he'd gotten away with rape still filled him with rage. But it wasn't his place to bring that revelation to the public.

Only one person could do that. Caprice. So far she wasn't inclined to do so.

He pounded across the helipad to the rooftop door, recalling the last time he'd rushed here on business was the morning after his ex-wife's fatal accident. The tabloids had been filled with truths and half-truths and lies.

Guilt had nipped at him for ending their marriage so swiftly. For giving her no chance to explain or apologize.

But that guilt wasn't near as biting as what he felt for the sweet young attendant he'd hired at the World Cup in Val d'Isère. Caprice had done everything he'd asked and anticipated his needs to the heartbeat. And she'd fallen into puppy love with him—a dog of a man.

Instead of putting her down gently, he'd dismissed her in the same manner he would fire a lazy employee. All because her kiss had stirred feelings in him that he'd only felt for his wife. The tender emotions that were a prequel to love.

That realization had scared the hell out of him. He'd vowed never to love again. Never to give his heart to another. He could not risk being around her.

So he'd left her vulnerable. And his friend Mario—*his damned friend, of all people!*—had taken advantage of her.

Luc remembered his treks down to the caretaker's house

to tempt Mario away from his chores. They'd been closer than brothers for years.

Before Luc had begun training vigorously for Alpine, he'd convinced his father to pay for Mario's way. They'd been an unbeatable duo on the slopes, and pursued by countless women across the globe.

But that had changed as well after the accident. Mario had remained in his life as a friend, and if not for Caprice's tearful confession, he never would have known the depths Mario was capable of sinking to.

Luc drove his fingers through his hair and swore. He would not repeat past mistakes and cause Caprice more grief. The fact he'd done so years ago made it even more difficult for him to face himself in the mirror. And to think he'd thought his father was a careless bastard!

The American saying "the apple doesn't fall far from the tree" certainly was true in Luc's case. He wasn't worthy of tying himself to a good woman. He'd already screwed up badly two times. He wouldn't do so a third time.

Caprice had done everything they'd agreed to. She'd established her premier program at his lodge, and she'd thankfully incited his brother's interest in life again.

The renovation he'd begun at her lodge in Colorado paled in comparison. She deserved much more.

He would see she received a hefty settlement so she would never want for money. So she could move forward with her life without financial worry. So he couldn't hurt her more. Then he would never trouble her again.

His driver was waiting below and made a quick twenty-minute drive to Mario's firm across the city. With instructions to his driver to wait, Luc exited his luxury Mercedes and marched into the Godolphin building Mario had designed and built from the ground up.

The express elevator sped him to the thirty-fifth floor

and a modicum of steps took him to Mario's outer office. "Signor Duchelini!" Mario's PA said, shooting to her feet. "Is Mario expecting you?"

"No," he said, storming past her. "It is a surprise visit."

He twisted the knob and entered his old friend's lair, slamming the door in the PA's face and twisting the lock, ensuring privacy. "Cancel your press conference."

Mario lounged in his chair and laced his fingers over his flat stomach, a sly grin touching his hard mouth. "A man must defend his honor."

"Don't speak to me about honor. You have none."

Mario sat up, sobering. "So you take the word of a woman and take legal measures to nullify Godolphin contracts with all la Duchi holdings."

"She told me what happened. Why did you do it?" Luc asked, desperate to know what had corrupted Mario's mind.

Mario leaped to his feet, dark eyes slitted and sweat dotting his upper lip. "You've got this all wrong. Caprice came to me. She asked for it."

He barely restrained himself from driving his fist into his old friend's face. "Enough lies! I'll never forgive myself for tossing her out of my life, leaving her vulnerable for a shark like you. I won't make that mistake again."

Mario had the gall to laugh. "Don't play martyr or gallant over a woman you hold no affection toward."

That remark was sharper than a knife that sank deep, drawing emotional blood. "I'm not leaving myself blameless, but I was your friend. You used an innocent girl!"

"How interesting that young girl is now your mistress. I've never known you to defend one before. Hell, you wouldn't do that for your wife."

"Don't ever speak ill of either woman again," he said, jabbing a finger at the man he now considered his enemy.

"I know you raped Caprice. Why, Mario? Why did you do it?"

Mario sneered and his eyes went jet black. "You're a rich boy with a family legacy on the slopes and everything you wanted at your fingertips. Not once did you or your family hide the fact I was the charity cause you took on. The 'friend' most saw as a hanger-on. No matter how I tried, you always won the top medals, secured the richest business deals and toyed with the most beautiful women. But I finally bested you. I had your sweet little American first."

Luc lunged across the desk, grabbed him by the collar and jerked him back across the desk, holding him so close that the red streaks in Mario's eyes stood out in bold relief. "If I ever catch you on any Duchelini holding or if you dare make any of our conversation public, I will come after you with enough legal guns to destroy you."

He shoved Mario away from him and stalked out the door. A few months ago he would have sought release of his rage through drink and a willing woman. Now his only thought was returning to Caprice.

But he had urgent business to settle here with his lawyers that would take days. He had to ensure Mario would never be a threat to any woman again. He had to safeguard Caprice.

No matter what it took, he couldn't fail her a second time.

"Yes, that's it," Caprice said, more to herself than the two workers.

It had been a hectic week ensuring everything was in place and going as planned, watching her advertisements go up in the newspapers and on television. Though she'd hoped for a good turnout, she hadn't expected she would get such a crowd. But Luciano's PA informed her that the lodge was booked to capacity for the grand opening.

Now, as the finishing touches were put into place, she stood aside, fingers entwined under her chin, watching, stomach alight with butterflies. Even after the workers slipped out the pod door, she didn't move, preferring to admire the high intensity of this room used for those almost ready to hit the slopes again. From the vibrant splashes of color on the walls to the living backdrop of rugged mountains capped with snow and the challenging green runs lying in wait for that first blanket of snow beyond the bay of windows…it was spectacular.

Her eyes misted and her heart swelled as the vision she'd dreamed of for years came to life before her eyes. "It's absolutely perfect."

"So are you," Luciano said, startling her.

She whirled to face him, cursing the fact her cheeks were flaming and her hands and knees trembled with that giddy excitement that still hit her whenever he was near. "When did you get back?"

"Just now. I came straight here."

"You look exhausted," she said, afraid to ask how it went, afraid that the news wouldn't be good.

Too much had gone right lately for her to believe it would continue. Her luck had never lasted that long.

He shrugged. "It's only been a week, but I've been assured that Mario's clients are dropping at a steady rate."

"He must be frantic. Furious with you. Me."

"Tough. He deserves to wallow in his own hell."

She bit her lip, agreeing but worried just the same. "Is there a chance he still might go to the press?"

"Sure, but he's a fool if he does." He straddled a weight bench, tested the pulleys and whistled. "These are good strength trainers."

"Thanks," she said, knowing she couldn't dwell on Mario and his threats with the opening tomorrow—with the man she loved here before her. "I designed these to build upper-body strength needed for downhill and endurance."

He tested them again and nodded. "Mind if I avail myself of them?"

"Anytime," she said with a smile, stepping close enough to smooth a hand over his muscled shoulder. "It's good to see you again."

He was off the bench and gathering her close in a heartbeat, lips closing over hers for one long, lusty kiss that chased her earlier weariness away. "It is good to be back with you as well, *bella*. A man could get used to this."

So could she. The question remained, should she? "So what happened? You know I've been on needles and pins since you left."

"Mario denied any wrongdoing, but I didn't buy his lies this time," he said, sobering far too much for her liking. "I served him the papers severing all contracts with Godolphin and walked out."

Could it be that final? Was she finally free of any threat from Mario?

"It's over then? I can go on with my life?"

He nodded and ran his palms up and down her back, his touch both soothing and erotic. "Is that what you want, *bella*?"

"Of course. It's what I've worked for," she said and smiled, only to sober when he didn't return the gesture. "The preparations for the opening of your therapy unit are completed as well. In fact they delivered the sign this afternoon."

"Excellent. Have you looked at it yet?" he asked, his beetled brow hinting he'd expected her to do just that.

She shook her head. "No. I told the workers to place the sign in the hall leading to the ski exit. I didn't think it would be in the way there." And it was less tempting.

"Let's take a look then."

He took her hand and led her to the hallway and the large covered sign that would hang over the glass doors of the pod. In seconds he ripped the heavy brown paper from the sign, then stepped back.

"Do you like it?" he asked.

She stared at it, stunned, not having expected or demanded her name be tied with his lodge. But it was here, large and bold. Another tie binding them.

"Caprice Tregore's Adaptive Ski Therapy and Sports Medicine," she read, her gaze flicking back to her larger-than-life initials in a casual script above the bold print to the smaller trio at the bottom of certificates and degrees she'd earned. "I didn't expect this."

"I commissioned two. One for my lodge and the other for yours," he said. "It is crucial we keep the continuity of the brand."

"Yes, consistency of my program is crucial," she said. "But why put such emphasis on my name?"

He slipped an arm around her shoulders, his laugh echoing free and clear and so welcome to her ears. "Your name is your brand. When people see this sign, they will know that this is the quality care and commitment they need."

She considered that compliment with a frown. "Like athletes with their endorsements?"

"Far more powerful and important than that." He kissed her forehead, her eyes, her cheeks, his splayed palm firm against her back, holding her flush against him—not that she needed that urging. "Athletes' accolades are the result of skill and luck. You are a trained professional who has earned the respect of physicians, therapists and athletes. You change lives for the better."

She buried her face against his chest, reveling in his spicy scent and strength. "You make me sound far more important than I am."

"Bella," he said, nudging her chin up. "That is your charm—you are adorably and honestly humble. I respect what you've accomplished. I admire you."

But he didn't love her. He would never love her.

How sad that he could freely give her what she'd worked tirelessly to achieve, respect and admiration for her work, yet the one thing her heart craved from him was never to be. That realization gave her the strength to gently pull away from him and manage a smile.

"Thank you," she said.

This time he returned her smile with one that melted her heart and stirred longing deep in her. "Come. Let's celebrate tomorrow's pre-opening."

"Sure," she said, letting him lead her back to his room.

Letting him strip off their clothes and adore her body with his hands and mouth. Letting him do anything he wished with her.

No matter the outcome of her time with Luciano, she refused to deny herself a moment apart from him. Their separation would come far too soon anyway.

CHAPTER NINE

LUC STOOD AT the back of the banquet room, gaze fixed on Caprice behind the podium, a glass of the local cabernet franc caught between two fingers. He'd arrived late and missed the start of the ten-minute video of her program in action from initial therapy session to a patient hitting the slopes, but it was obvious her speech had kept the packed audience riveted. Now that the lights had come back up and she was explaining in more detail the benefits of her program, he had the pleasure of appreciating her beautiful mind and open heart.

Had he ever met a woman more giving? More caring of others? No. He'd realized that the moment he'd caught her working with Julian.

"At Caprice Tregore's, we promise therapy to fit your needs so you can ski free again," she said and paused as the applause swelled again, only dying down when she raised a hand begging silence. "Regardless of your degree of disability or ski experience, there is a program you can benefit from, stimulating mind and body. We welcome all of you with open arms, today, tomorrow and into the future. Thank you for coming and please enjoy the luncheon."

She nodded and backed away from the podium as applause went up a final time, growing in volume as the audience stood in her honor. Her smile grew too large and trembled, and even across the room he noted the glint of moisture in her eyes.

Her rush of emotion wasn't a surprise to him. No, what stunned him was the wad of anticipation lodged in his throat accompanied by a flutter in his gut, sensations he hadn't experienced since the first time he'd stepped into skis and shot down a mountain.

His heightened interest in her remained steady, but he knew it wouldn't last. The excitement never did, waning in months, weeks or sometimes days from each challenging sport he'd topped, coveted business deal he'd secured and desirable, aloof woman that he'd seduced.

These sensations he felt for Caprice would die as well. But could the same be said for her?

No. Though she'd never said it, he knew she believed herself in love with him. Her every touch, every look, conveyed what was in her heart.

He dragged in a breath and heard the crinkling of the message in his pocket, the paper that had been handed to him moments before the program started. Selfish bastard that he was, he thought of tossing it so everything would proceed as planned. He could keep Caprice by his side and in his bed for another week or more.

But he wouldn't do that to her. He'd hurt her too much.

She must return to her life and he to his.

Her company would soar—he would make sure it did. She would find great success. One day she would find a good man, a thought he didn't like envisioning at this moment, maybe never would.

So be it. She would have a fine life and he would return to the one he'd chosen, one that didn't demand more of him than he was willing to give. It was the way it had to be.

He kept that thought in mind as the audience filed into the dining hall. No expenses had been spared for the selection of *antipasto misto*, *primo* of pastas, soup and risotto, *secondo* of meats and fish, *contorni* of vegetables and *insalata* and *dolce*, those being the first things some would select. Wines and mineral waters were in abundance as well.

Guests and prospective clients laughed and ate and drank and stole as much of Caprice's time as she'd allow. The new staff that she'd chosen remained busy booking appointments well into the next month, he suspected.

Everyone was happy, especially Caprice. She'd gotten the control she wanted, and he'd seen a new spark of life in his brother. That's why he'd hired her, and attaining his one goal should make him happy. So why wasn't he? Why was he gripped with the sensation that he was losing something he would never regain again?

"Congratulations, *bella*," he told Caprice a good hour later when she was finally free.

Excitement still danced in her eyes and kissed a rosy flush to her cheeks. Beautiful. She was absolutely beautiful.

She grasped his right hand and squeezed the fingers. "Never in my wildest dreams did I expect this wonderful response. You were so right about everything."

He saluted her with his *vino*. "Told you so."

Her grin shouted her happiness to the world as she accepted the champagne a waiter handed her. This was how he wished to remember her always.

Too soon she turned solemn. "What's wrong, Luciano? You look like you just lost your best friend."

He had, he admitted, taking a sip of the wine he favored and finding it bitter on his tongue, tainted by sour memories. "I'll tell you when this is over."

"Is it serious?" she asked, clear concern widening her eyes now.

He shook his head and managed the barest smile. "It

is good news for us. You're still much in demand. Smile," he told her as a young news reporter nabbed her attention.

It was the perfect cue for him to take his leave. In silence he retreated to his office. The amber silk tie went first with a shrug. Next he traded his cabernet for a generous glass of Bunnahabhain and slumped behind his desk, wanting to drown his irritation in Scotch.

Why couldn't he shake the feeling that he'd let the best thing in his life slip from his grasp forever?

The exhilarating high Caprice had floated on for the better part of two hours dropped her back to earth the second she stepped into Luciano's office. He sat at his desk, glass of amber liquid sitting before him either untouched or a refill. To the side was a clean glass beside the bottle of imported Scotch from the isle of Islay, a favored label of his.

"Forgive me but you don't look like a man who's received good news," she said.

One side of his mouth pulled up at the corner. "One man's good news is bad to another. Want a drink?"

"Am I going to need one?"

"Maybe." He upended the heavy glass, added two fingers of his imported Scotch and handed it to her.

She took the chair before his desk as well as the drink, struck with *déjà vu* of her very first meeting with him when she had just turned twenty and wanted desperately to be seen as a grown woman. That had been her first time drinking single-malt Scotch and dealing with an arrogant young champion. Both had been heady experiences she'd never forgotten.

"To you," he said, raising his glass.

She clinked her crystal to his, the clink clear and loud. "And you."

They each drank, hers a sip, his much more, then a spate of numbing silence.

A chill rippled through her, at odds with the whisky warming her tongue and throat. "Are you going to tell me this news?"

He nodded and cradled his glass between both palms, gaze lifting slowly to hers. "Mario is dead."

She blinked. "You're sure?"

He nodded. "Near dawn, a witness reported that Mario sped past their coupe on the A16, only to lose control. His Lamborghini shot over the stone wall of a viaduct and burst into flames on impact." He knocked back the remainder of his Scotch and grimaced, anyone's guess if the mouthful of liquor or distaste over the tragedy caused his expression. "It has taken an autopsy to determine Mario was behind the wheel."

"He's dead," she said. "He can't hurt me anymore."

"Correct." He pushed to his feet and paced the room. She massaged her temples, this day and everything that transpired happening far too fast for her to grasp. Or maybe the bit of alcohol had mixed unfavorably with the abundance of excitement.

He stood from his seat and walked to the view offered through the glass windows in his office. "With Mario dead, you can return to Colorado whenever you wish to. I will cover all expenses, as agreed to."

She caught the gasp that nearly burst free. He was setting her free. Giving her back the control over her life. She didn't have to remain in Italy under his protection a second longer. Not unless she wanted to.

And she did want to stay with Luciano. She didn't want this to end swiftly and so coldly. But every inch of him, from his body language to his words, made it clear he didn't share her view.

"Thank you for taking care of everything for me," she said in a surprisingly controlled tone that still made her tight throat ache. "I couldn't have done it without you."

She wouldn't cry. She wouldn't.

He frowned, tapping three fingers on the nearly floor-to-ceiling credenza. "I disagree. You are destined for greatness and would have achieved it with or without me. But I am glad, honored and grateful you agreed to work with me on the therapy pod."

"It was my pleasure," she said, painfully aware that was the only thing she could say because it was true. Being with him had been her pleasure and passion. Leaving was going to hurt for a long time.

He dropped in his chair and meted out another drink for them both, causing her to wonder when she'd drank all of hers. "To your continued success."

"And to yours," she said, retrieving her glass to join him in the toast.

Before all the past had tumbled out in a torrent of pain and confusion, she'd known that time would fly by in each other's arms. But to indulge in that now, even a kiss, would make their parting all the more heartbreaking. At least it would be that way for her.

She wanted to leave here the way she'd arrived. Chin up, determined to keep a careful distance from Luciano Duchelini.

"I'd better go now. There is so much I've left to do." She set her Scotch on the desk as she rose and started toward the door.

"Caprice," he said when she opened the door, and she steadied her nerves to look back at the most handsome man she'd ever met. "Would you join me for dinner tonight?"

She summoned up a polite smile. She'd been too nervous to eat much more than a few bites today, but all thought of food sickened her now in anticipation of their eventual parting. "I'd love to, but today is already packed. I have a meeting with the new staff now, and I want to find a flight out in the morning. Tonight I'll pack for the trip home."

His lips thinned, but he inclined his head once. "I'll arrange your transportation needs for you."

"Thank you." Did he have to sound too eager to see her off? She shook her head, refusing to show the pain this caused her, and told him the time.

She closed the door behind her and calmly strode through the outer office when every instinct in her begged her to run, to scream. If his PA noticed her state of distress, she held comment and continued sitting at her computer, diligently working.

Halfway down the hall Caprice gathered enough composure to return to the therapy pod. It took an hour to go over last-minute details with the staff. The pleasant surprise was seeing they'd received close to sixty applications for enrollment today and the phones were still ringing.

Success tasted sweet, but the sourness of heartbreak erased any pleasure. If she could just hold at bay the eventual breakdown of her emotions until she was away from her, until she was alone, she would be grateful.

Darkness had crept over the lodge by the time she found her suite. She'd no more than locked the door and kicked off her shoes when a knock came at the door.

She bit her lip, debating if she should ignore it. "Who is it?"

"Room service, Signorina Tregore."

A red flag waved before her eyes, but she fished several euros from her purse and opened the door. A smiling young man on the wait staff pushed a cart inside, the plate covered with a gleaming silver dome. Beside it sat one single yellow rose in a crystal vase.

"Shall I serve?" the waiter asked.

She shook her head and pressed the bills into his hands. "Thanks, but I'd rather wait awhile before I eat."

"Grazie!" he said with a bow and backed out the door.

A twist of the lock secured her privacy and a lift of the white drape over the table ensured there wasn't another surprise waiting for her there. The sealed white envelope on the cart stared back at her.

She knew before she broke the seal and pulled out the note that it was from Luciano, written in his bold, clearly read hand. "It is for the best this way. Luc."

Was it?

The note fell from her hands and her vision blurred. Pain knifed through her, drawing emotional blood. Yes, her mind agreed with him, but her heart wasn't buying it. Her heart wanted the man. Wanted his love.

Not to be.

She swiped at her eyes and took a long, hot shower, then packed everything but what she'd wear tomorrow. Exhausted, she fell into bed, the delivered dinner forgotten. If only she could just do the same with the imposing Italian she'd loved and clearly lost.

The wake-up call at seven gave Caprice the needed time to dress, secure her bags for the trip and leave her suite. One glance in the mirror confirmed that no amount of makeup could conceal the fact she'd had a fitful night's sleep.

She wrenched open the door and smothered a gasp. Luciano stood there, looking haggard as well.

His note flashed before her—*It is better this way.* So why was he here now?

She swallowed hard. "Is something wrong?"

He shook his head. "Not a thing that I'm aware of."

"Oh, good," she said, confused. "I trust everything is ready."

"To the minute." He glanced at his watch. "You are anxious to depart."

It was so tempting to refute that remark, but what was the point? She had to leave Italy and Luciano anyway. She had a ticket, lingering another hour or so threw that timetable off.

Even if she could easily leave at a later time, she still had to leave. Staying would only make it more difficult to walk away. And walk away she must.

"Allow me," he said, taking her bag from her.

"Thanks," she mumbled, closing the door behind her.

She trailed Luciano to the elevators and dreaded the ride down, secluded into close quarters with the man she would always love. And it was hell. More than anything she wanted to reach out to him. Touch him. Kiss him. But he stood like a Trojan, paying no attention to her at all.

After what seemed like forever, the elevator door whooshed open. He nodded for her to step out and she did, doing her best to pretend her nerves weren't scraped raw, that her insides weren't twisted into knots.

And then too quickly they were at the door with a private sedan waiting to whisk her to the airport, away from Italy. From the only man she would ever love.

This was what she'd wanted from the start. How could she complain if he didn't wish to accept her odd change of heart? He couldn't.

"Thank you," she said to Luc when they reached the door. "For everything."

And she meant it. His affection had given her back the confidence she hadn't realized she'd lacked. The incredible sex she'd been sure didn't exist. The faith he'd put in her as a businesswoman. The funds he'd given her to ensure she succeeded in her chosen field—not for a year but for decades, getting her over any foreseeable humps that may occur.

In short, he'd made sure she wouldn't need him ever again. Still, she was grateful. Everything he'd done for her was appreciated more than words could convey.

"It is I who should thank you for giving this opportunity to Julian." He smiled, though it was bittersweet to her eyes. "He seems excited."

"Julian will do fine. Tell him I'm just a phone call away if he needs to talk." And it took effort to not extend the same to Luc.

He nodded and crossed his strong arms over the muscled chest she'd loved to snuggle against. "I will. And please, if you discover you need anything more after you arrive at Tregore Lodge, just tell my assistant. She'll make sure you get it."

Not Luciano. No, he wouldn't want to hear from her once she stepped on that plane. When she left Italy and him.

"Goodbye," she said and slid into the backseat of the luxury sedan, not waiting for another clipped reply from him.

She wanted out of here, away from the temptation of going to him, of begging him to let her stay. That would never work. And if it did, it would be counterproductive to her forward progress.

By focusing on that thought, she endured the lengthy drive to the airport in silence. Once on the plane she asked the attendant for a sleeping aid and silently prayed that it would banish the insane desire to tell the pilot to turn the plane around and take her back to Luciano.

Her prayers were answered. When she awoke the next day, she was in Colorado. She was home, or an hour's drive from where she could watch the renovations of Tregore Lodge.

That alone made her deliriously happy. Or it should have. But she could barely manage a smile because she'd left something vital back in Italy. Her heart.

CHAPTER TEN

"You're an idiot," Julian said between breaks on the bench press Caprice had designed for upper-body strength and endurance.

For weeks, Luc had heard the same thing again and again, and he was tired of it. "Can't you think of anything else to say to me?"

Julian shrugged. "Nothing that makes me nearly as happy," he said, and resumed another set of reps, granting Luc a moment's peace.

Not that it would last long. Not that he was really complaining.

He'd gotten to where he enjoyed these early-morning workouts with Julian. It was like old times, save the fact his brother was using specialized equipment to suit his ability, and the unnerving fact that his brother was talking to him much more, though his favorite topic of late was to extol Caprice and her program at every opportunity.

Again, he couldn't complain or disagree. Julian had made remarkable recovery in such a short time, so much so that the old choking guilt that had held Luc responsible for the crippling accident had begun to wane. But it wouldn't totally go away, not when the ghosts from his past still hovered about, tossing kindling onto his guilt.

The memories of the accident continually scraped over

his emotional wounds, keeping them from healing. Being with Caprice and watching her personal struggle allowed him to realize that flaw in himself.

He'd seen firsthand the welcoming change in her once she'd unveiled the secrets that had emotionally chained her. It was time he came to grips with his past as well, accepting his guilt and moving beyond it.

"Next week Tregore Lodge hosts its grand opening," Julian said after finishing another impressive workout, his upper body gleaming with sweat, detailing muscles that hadn't been that well defined since the accident. "Do you plan to go?"

Luc stopped his tenth set of reps on the leg press and gaped at his brother. "I'm the last person she'd want to see there."

"Why would you think that? She loves you."

"Perhaps, but she deserves better than me."

"I was right the first time. You're an idiot." Julian shifted from the extra-wide bench he'd been on to his streamline wheelchair before an assistant could reach him, giving the wheel several hard pushes that jetted him across the room.

"Julian," Luc shouted and his brother stopped and stared at him, his heart in his mouth for what he was about to say. "I'm sorry. So damned sorry."

His brother wheeled to face him, frown deepening. "For what?"

Luc waved a hand in the air, the movement ponderous under the mountain of guilt he carried. "You wouldn't be bound to a wheelchair if I hadn't goaded you into that race. I know you looked back at me out of concern, and that's why you lost your edge and fell."

"You can't believe that."

"It's the truth," he said, the admission taking a long time to sort out. "I was out to prove I could be as reckless as you, but where your bravado was based on talent, mine was driven by guilt."

Julian sent the chair wheeling back to his brother. "Don't think that way. I wanted to best you in that race because you were the best in Alpine, winning medal after medal. And for the record, I didn't look back out of worry but relief. With you down, the win was in the bag. I took my mind and eyes off the game and that split-second error is why I'm resigned to a wheelchair for life. Got it?"

Luc let that sink in, feeling some of the weight lift from him in the process. "Got it."

"Good." Julian left again, but stopped at the opening to the massage pod, balancing his chair on its rear wheels and pivoting to face Luc. "It is not your fault that our family is dysfunctional. We are capable of making our own decisions. If they were bad ones, it is our own fault."

This time Luc cracked a smile. "You're pretty smart for a little brother."

"About time you realized that," Julian teased. "Have I told you lately you are a complete, utter ass for sending Caprice away?"

"That was your parting remark last night, brother," Luc said, resuming his reps with renewed vigor despite the pain of stretching the injured muscle in his leg. He was driven by anger at himself as he allowed that utilizing Caprice's program might help him improve physically.

Julian set his chair right and pushed through the opening. "Excellent," he shouted. "I don't want you to forget."

As if that were even possible.

Luc did two more reps, then stopped cold, realization slamming into him with the force of a lightning bolt. His brother was right.

He was an ass. A terrified one.

For years he'd carried the responsibility of all that had

gone wrong with those he'd loved on his broad shoulders, convinced that was his burden to bear for life. But Julian had just opened his eyes to the truth.

It had taken him years to see that closing his eyes to his wife's infidelity would have saved her life then, but it wouldn't guarantee the same wouldn't happen in the future. Chances were she would have left him at the first opportunity. Her death wasn't his fault.

Just as it wasn't totally his fault that Julian was disabled for life.

It was a hard admission to make, but it was the truth he'd avoided for years, preferring to use his failed attempts at therapy as his excuse to drop out of competition completely. He'd used guilt as the reason to hide from life. To avoid any emotional entanglement with a woman.

Yes, his recovery had been painful, but other skiers with far worse injuries had pushed themselves until they were back on the slopes. None of them had chosen the coward's way out.

But fear had consumed him, destroying the exhilarating challenge of mastering the mountain again. Not fear of losing, but of winning because he no longer believed he deserved it. Just like he'd convinced himself all women were after him for his money.

So he'd thrown himself into unbelievable challenges in the corporate world, but inside he was little more than a robot, a shell of a man, performing the role of ex-champion playboy without emotion. He hadn't realized how shallow and lonely his life had been until Caprice had come back into it, and even then he'd denied himself the true pleasure just being with her gave him.

Caprice. His chest tightened and his sex stirred at the mere thought of her. But it was the warmth in his chest—*his heart!*—that brought him to his knees.

Julian was right. He was an idiot.

Caprice was unlike any woman he'd ever met, challenging him on more levels than he'd believed possible, challenging him to look at the deeper part of himself that he'd hidden from.

But he'd resisted searching his soul until now and had totally refused to open his heart, so certain that doing so would cause him heartache instead of joy.

And oddly it did just that now.

He ached for Caprice. Wanted her. But by realizing that he wasn't the bad guy, that he did deserve happiness this late, he'd remained the taciturn machine and had driven her away. He'd let his guilt prevent him from opening his heart to her.

Now he was ready to do just that. But was she lost to him? Did he stand a chance?

He had no idea.

The only thing glaringly clear was the fact he couldn't let his relationship with Caprice end this way. He couldn't bear the thought of living without her, even though the prospect of giving his heart to her scared the hell out of him. It terrified him more to think of living like this— without her, without love.

Luc swung to his feet and stalked to his suite. He had one chance to make this right with her. This was the most challenging run of his life and for the first time in years he was ready to do whatever it took to win.

It took an entire month and one week before she could move back into the lodge.

She stood in the spacious foyer, turning a slow circle, in awe of the changes. Luciano had given her the plans to okay, but she'd never dreamed it would be so massive. So dominating a force perched on this ledge surrounded by denuded slopes where old pistes were being cleared while new alternative slopes for beginners were being formed. It was, in short, a miracle—a work of art, from the towering vaulted ceilings to a fireplace whose red stones took up a wall yet didn't overpower the massive room with heavy crossbeams.

All things she'd envisioned in the scant future. Luciano's largesse had made it all come true.

"Welcome home."

"Karla?" Caprice asked upon hearing that voice from her past, whirling to the friend she hadn't seen since high school to embrace her, ensuring she wasn't dreaming. "What? Why are you here?"

Her free-spirited friend laughed. "Luciano hired me the day I applied for the position of counselor."

"I had no idea."

About very little it seemed.

Throughout her stay in Italy, she'd been given updates on the progress in Colorado and asked for her signature regarding legal issues on the employment of "key staff," as he'd put it. She'd been too involved establishing the program at his lodge and dealing with her own conflicting emotions over him to pay close attention to what she signed.

Not good business sense at all and she wasn't proud of that admission.

Just how deeply had he dug into her past? Certainly enough to know that she'd been close friends with Karla. That her friend had been interviewed by Luciano—that he'd handpicked a women who'd befriended her when she'd needed it most. "You must be perfect for the position," she said and embraced Karla, "because Luciano is extremely particular about his employees and mine."

Karla laughed and gave her a friendly squeeze before

backing away. "Don't I know it! Hey, for what it's worth he raved about your fantastic program. If I didn't know better I would have sworn it was his baby."

His baby...

The thought of having Luciano's child fizzed through her blood like champagne, leaving her heady and wistful and yet sad. Her time had visited her on the flight back. There would be no baby in her near future.

Caprice shook off the odd melancholy with a smile. "Luciano has a vested interest in Tregore Lodge, so in a way it is his baby. And I don't mean to be rude," she added, "but I've had a long day finishing details on my therapy unit and need to get some rest."

"Say no more," Karla said. "We'll catch up later."

"Great!"

Caprice considered it good luck that she made the long walk from the front desk to fetch a key to her rooms without further delay. Sleep. She just wanted to bury her head under the blankets and let this hurt pass her by.

But when she awoke the next morning at 4:00 a.m., she knew quality rest wasn't in her future. Luciano had tormented her dreams, just as he'd managed to infiltrate those idle moments of her mind during the day while she was in Italy.

Would it ever stop?

It had to. She had to get a grip and move full speed on her lodge—the lodge that he'd poured more than a million dollars into for renovation. But even then, this program wasn't his baby, it was hers.

Now was the time to prove that.

Two weeks later she was settled and moving forward with establishing her program here, but nowhere close to feeling settled in her personal life. She missed Luciano. Far too often she'd caught herself reaching for him at night.

She had to snap out of it now. Somehow Luciano had moved heaven and earth to have the mountain and surrounding grounds well groomed before the first snow. Though that was months away yet, she would receive patients for the therapy unit before fall.

That gave her three weeks to have the interior finished and the staff totally ready to perform at top speed. Long, tiring hours were needed with her having a clear head focused on business. It would have been a snap to achieve eight weeks ago. Now?

She took a breath, held it and blew it out in a long, trembling rush. At this moment she struggled to find any peace of mind. Struggled harder to focus on anything besides the man she'd left in Italy, the same man who had made her dreams come true here only to break her heart.

It was maddening that she longed for him still and she hated herself for it. She'd known going in that it wasn't going to last. It couldn't last. She didn't want it. Didn't seek it. So why couldn't she let it go?

Her cell rang, or more precisely broke into song, a sound she hadn't heard in weeks while she was abroad. She checked the displayed number but didn't recognize it.

"Hello," she said after the sixth ring.

"Caprice, darling, how are you?" came a feminine voice she hadn't heard in decades.

She shook her head. Was she hallucinating? Her mother? Calling her now?

"Caprice?" her mother asked again.

Her stomach curdled. The last person she wished to engage in even the briefest of conversations was her mother.

Caprice dropped onto her bed. "I'm here."

"Oh, thank goodness," her mother said, not the least

deterred by her daughter's abruptness. "The baron and I just bumped into your Italian and discovered you'd been his guest in the Alps for a month. Is it true?"

She shook her head, always knowing her mother would call the moment she learned her daughter was involved with a billionaire. "Yes, Mother."

"Well, good. I was afraid to hope you were having an affair with a rich man."

"We're not involved," she said.

"Splendid. Darling, take my advice and choose a man with a title and not some sports medal. A woman never goes wrong attached to nobility."

"I'll bear that in mind." She bit her lower lip and gripped the phone, gathering strength to warn her mother about her upcoming announcement. "Mother, I'm giving a press conference tomorrow—"

"Oh, sorry to cut this short, darling, but the baron says it's time to leave. We're off to Brazil for Carnival. Do smile when you meet the press. Ta-ta."

"Right," Caprice said to a suddenly dead line that ended another typical out-of-the-blue call from her mother.

That was her mother, more concerned about how Caprice would look than what she planned to say. But then if her mother had known what she had prepared, she might have tried to change her mind.

That wasn't going to happen. It couldn't, she thought as she paced her office.

Where had her mother run into Luciano? And why was she letting him occupy her thoughts? Wasn't she nervous enough over the upcoming press conference? Stressed and terrified over what reaction she would receive from her friends and strangers?

As for forewarning her mother, she likely wouldn't have

believed Caprice was attacked, and she certainly wouldn't have wanted the world to know about it.

But Caprice knew she had to reveal the truth, the whole ugly mess, in hopes other woman would pay better heed to their own vulnerability.

In that regard, Luciano had been right. She realized it now. Knew she couldn't hide behind silence any longer, even though she no longer had to fear Mario's retribution.

God, she never should have feared that for years. That error in judgment had vindicated Mario and sentenced her into shamed silence.

That was the one thing she wanted to make sure never happened to another woman. Rape and abuse had to be reported or the victims were sentenced to suffer in silence.

Tomorrow was opening day at Tregore Lodge and she would stay up all night to ensure everything was ready. She desperately needed this premiere to go as smoothly as the one in Italy had. But at Luciano's lodge, she'd had his support and staff at her beck and call.

Her opening wasn't as grand or nearly as organized, despite the fact that his crew had done a remarkable job rebuilding the lodge. The timing was crucial. She had competition, and getting the word out that she was here and ready for both adaptive and standard skiers was vital. She had sent grand opening invitations to all the news stations covering the areas around Colorado Springs, Denver and Loveland, touting the merits of her program and mentioning that a sister facility resided in Italy under the direction of former champion Julian Duchelini.

She was smart enough to realize that name alone could draw skiers to her facility. Plus, having Julian make a surprise appearance tomorrow would make a massive difference. But what would he think of her announcement?

She couldn't fret about that now!

Tomorrow was enough to worry about. She had to wow the press and potential clients now or she stood a chance of failing. And she had to unburden her soul of the rape.

Her future as a whole person depended upon her nailing both points.

Luc slipped in the door of Tregore Lodge and took a position along the side of the great hall, pleased by the crowd gathering for Caprice's grand opening. He looked beyond the attendees to the beauty and integrity of the structure and furnishings and nodded, noting with pleasure the attention paid to detail, right down to the new mantel gracing the massive fireplace.

The entire lodge was impressively massive. Upbeat. Yet a touch of rustic appeal vibrated through it like a favored song, which was exactly what Caprice had wanted and he'd balked at, confident that a departure from original would look far better.

He'd been wrong, much to his surprise.

Now, as he scanned the people gathering for the grand opening, he was confident Tregore Lodge and her program would be a huge success. He threaded his fingers through his hair, fully aware she didn't need him or any man now.

But did she at least still want him?

He'd soon find out.

Luc slipped from the crowd and made his way to Caprice's office, wanting to catch her before she met with the press, wanting to see her, hold her, kiss her. He wanted her, and he knew exactly how he was going to win her over this time. Permanently.

"Mr. Duchelini!" Her secretary popped up from her chair, her frantic gaze flitting from him to the closed office door.

He pointed to Caprice's office. "Is she in there?"

The secretary wrung her hands. "Yes, but I don't think you should go— Wait! You can't do that!"

But he was already through the door and closing it behind him, or trying to with the secretary fast on his heels. He stopped, his hungry gaze arrested by the sight of Caprice digging through the mountain of papers on her desk, looking harried and desirable.

"Do you need something?" she asked, not looking up.

"Mr. Duchelini is here," the secretary said, shooting him a scolding look. "Luciano Duchelini."

Caprice jerked upright and stared at him, and the pain and worry in her eyes tore at something buried inside him he hadn't known existed. "Why are you here?"

"Julian asked me to come," he said. "He caught a head cold that quickly infected his lungs. His physician advised him not to attempt the trip. He sends his regrets along with me."

The lips he hungered for pursed. "Fine. Now if you'll excuse me—"

"I need to talk with you alone first."

She looked up again, and this time he saw a mounting sense of urgency spark in her eyes. "Sorry. We go live in five minutes."

And with that she ran out the door, leaving him standing there like a fool. A rejected fool. With good reason, he realized as he stalked to the door to take his leave.

He stopped dead in his tracks, hand on the brass knob. He'd accused her of running away from him and her feelings, but he'd been guilty of doing the same thing.

Luc shook his head, finding it ironic that it had taken losing Caprice for him to finally rip his blinders off. He wasn't backing down or away again.

He trailed her to the great room, followed her onto the dais and took up a stance at the side behind the curtain, but the sudden flash of cameras en route proved many in the audience recognized him. So be it if this moment was recorded forever. Whatever the outcome, it would certainly leave an indelible mark on his memory and his future.

"Thank you all for coming," Caprice began. "If I could direct your attention to the screen above the hearth, we'll run a short video depicting my program."

She moved to the opposite side of the dais, where a chair had been positioned for her behind a small curtain. Her gaze flitted once to his before the lights dimmed and the same video that had played at his grand opening began.

As soon as the ten-minute video ended, the lights came on and Caprice returned to the podium to give the same abbreviated speech. Lines of stress radiated from her eyes and mouth, and her stance was noticeably stiffer.

Luc frowned, alert to the rising sense of urgency Caprice projected.

"Any questions?" she asked.

"Is Luciano Duchelini involved in the day-to-day running of Tregore Lodge or is he just your backer?" a reporter asked.

She fidgeted with her notes. "My business association with la Duchi is not on the agenda for discussion. Next question," she said, pointing to another person.

The next twenty minutes she fielded random questions about the renovations and her program. "Any more?" she asked, allowing an overly long pause.

She took a deep breath and heaved it out, and Luc did the same, feeling the tension roiling through her, fearful what had upset her so. "There's one more thing I wish to touch on here. Take notes because I won't be answering questions at this time."

Luc was on the dais and by her side in an instant, hearing the strain in her voice and fearing she was close to losing control. "What's wrong?"

"You'll find out in a moment," she whispered with a faint smile before sobering and facing the audience again. Luc stepped back out of the limelight, giving her the stage.

"I wish to address this to all women in hopes it will keep another woman from living with the torment I have," she said, her voice surprisingly strong and clear now. "Seven years ago I was the victim of a rape. Out of fear, humiliation and worry I kept that dark secret."

She paused when the audience murmured among themselves, waiting for them to quiet. "I don't know if he attacked other women, and because he has since died I won't reveal his name. But I urge any woman who has been victimized to step forward immediately and seek help. Don't let one act of violence victimize you for life."

She stepped back, and he noted the barest tremble shake through her then and the audience stared at her in stark silence.

Luc stepped forward, faced Caprice and began clapping. Soon others joined in until the room exploded with applause.

"Thank you," she said once more as she stepped to the mic. Then with a bow, she reached for his hand and he escorted her back to the privacy of her office.

"That was extremely courageous of you," he said.

She shrugged. "It had to be said."

"I agree," he said, uncertain how to begin something so vital when his senses were on overload just being so near her again. "I'm very proud of you."

She glanced up at him and flushed a lovely pink, a nervous smile playing over the lips he longed to claim. "Thanks. Is there something you needed?"

Just the opening he needed. "Yes, you. Come back to Italy with me."

She stiffened. "I have a business to run."

"You could do that from Italy."

She slapped her palms flat on her desk. "I won't be your mistress, Luciano."

He nudged her chin up despite her attempt to pull away from him. "I wouldn't dream of asking that of you. My God, Caprice, I love you deeply. I want you with me. Is that so hard to understand?"

"What did you say?" Caprice sputtered.

"*Bella*, you are my world. My present. My future. I never realized what love was until you opened your heart to me." And as tears slipped from her eyes, he came around her desk and dropped onto one knee, his gaze riveted on the strong woman before him. "I love you, Caprice Tregore. You have stolen my heart, and I am nothing without you."

"I love you, too," she said, stepping closer to him, both trembling hands resting on his shoulders now.

In a blink her world narrowed to this moment. This man. This door opening to the future she'd dreamed of having and feared would never come about.

Luc smiled, his spirits lightening, realizing he was actually happy. The fear, the apprehension vanished. Absolutely nothing in his life had ever felt so right. So freeing. So perfect. Not the competitions that had challenged his mind and body on the slopes. Not the conquests he'd made in business or pleasure.

This was real and he wanted it. Wanted her, now and forever. "Marry me, Caprice. Make me a happy man."

"You're serious," she said, half sobbing, half laughing. "You really want a marriage with a house and children and a forever kind of love?"

"Yes, I want a real marriage with you as well as children

to start the next generations of Duchelini champions," he said with a grin. "Your answer?"

She choked out a sob, fingers pressed to her lips, and then slowly gifted him with a smile that made his heart swell with love he'd denied entrance to for years. "Yes," she said, tugging him up into her open arms. "Yes."

He raised one brow, holding her close. "How about to-morrow?"

"It's a date," she said.

They chose the closest spot, flying out that night for Vegas to become husband and wife the next morning, photos taken of the kiss sealing their commitment at Tregore Lodge splashed on all the gossip magazines and newspapers.

"No regrets?" she asked her new husband the second morning of their marriage.

"Only one," he said, pulling her luscious naked body against his, smiling to find her wet and ready for him again. "We waited too long."

"You'll get no argument from me," she said, kissing his chest, his chin before settling in for a long lusty kiss that left them breathless, prolonging the passion as long as they could.

"Let's keep it that way," he said, and surrendered to the sizzling passion they had found in each other's arms.

* * * * *

VISCONTI'S
FORGOTTEN HEIR

ELIZABETH POWER

To Alan – for always being there

Elizabeth Power wanted to be a writer from a very early age, but it wasn't until she was nearly thirty that she took to writing seriously. Writing is now her life. Travelling ranks very highly among her pleasures, and so many places she has visited have been recreated in her books. Living in England's West Country, Elizabeth likes nothing better than taking walks with her husband along the coast or in the adjoining woods, and enjoying all the wonders that nature has to offer.

CHAPTER ONE

As soon as she laid eyes on the broad-shouldered man who had just stepped through the door of the crowded wine bar Magenta knew that he was the father of her child.

She didn't suspect, or wonder, or even hope. She simply *knew*.

The stem of the glass she had been wiping suddenly snapped from the tension gripping her fingers, and as she put a steadying hand to her forehead she heard Thomas, her work colleague, enquire, 'Are you all right?'

The laid-back, long-haired college graduate who, like her, was helping out part-time behind the bar until something better came along, was frowning as he came away from the cash register.

She shook her head. Not in answer, but in an attempt to make some sense of the jumble of distant memories that were leaping chaotically through her brain.

Anger. Hostility. Passion. Over all a hungry, all-consuming passion...

Someone spoke to her, trying to give her an order, and she looked up at them with her velvety-brown eyes dazed and her fine features ashen against the darker sheen of her thick swept-up hair.

'Would you mind serving my customer for me?' she appealed croakily to her colleague and, dumping the two pieces of glass and the tea towel down behind the counter, made a hasty bid for the merciful seclusion of the Ladies'.

Grabbing the cracked and solitary basin, she struggled to regain her composure, her lungs dragging in air.

Andreas Visconti. Of *course*. How could she ever have let anyone persuade her into believing that her child might have been fathered by anyone else when she'd known in her heart that she wasn't the type of woman to sleep around, even during those lost and irretrievable months of her life?

She felt sick and stayed where she was, leaning over the basin, until the nausea subsided, trying to sort out the tangle of erratic thoughts and images in her mind.

The doctors had told her not to try and force things, and as the years had passed they had said that the memories she had lost might never come back. But they were going to. Even if they were appearing like the distorted shapes of a jigsaw puzzle she was going to have to piece together. Either way, right now, she thought, hearing the outer door open and one of the regular bar staff urgently calling to her, she had to go back out there and face the music. Even if she didn't know— or like—the tune that might be playing.

As the countless people in front of him were gradually served, and a spindly young man finally took his order, at first Andreas Visconti thought he was imagining things when his gaze drifted to the young woman who was filling glasses further along the bar.

She was slim, beautiful and flawlessly photogenic, with her magnificent hair pinned up to emphasise high cheekbones, stunning dark eyes and a lovely mouth above that long, elegant neck. The vision of her held Andreas in thrall. As if he was seeing a ghost. Or hallucinating. Both of which were pretty unlikely, he thought wryly, for a hardened cynic like himself.

Then someone called her name and he realised that he

wasn't imagining things. It really was her. Magenta James. The girl to whom he had once almost sacrificed his heart— and the whole of his life.

She was looking over her shoulder, listening to something a much older man, whom he guessed was the landlord, was saying, and cruel memory made a hard slash of Andreas's mouth as he caught her tight and rather strained-sounding little laugh.

The last time he had heard that sound was when she had ridiculed his lack of prospects, flaying him with accusations of trying to hold her back from the glittering career she intended to pursue. And now here was Miss High-and-Mighty James pouring drinks in a West Country wine bar! He was, he decided grimly, going to enjoy the next few minutes!

Abandoning the position he had virtually fought to secure, he allowed his curiosity to pull him through the sea of Friday-night revellers which, sensing an unspoken authority, parted effortlessly for him as he shouldered his way along the crowded bar to where she was working.

'Hello, Magenta.'

Beneath her simple black dress—her only concession to colour was the red and black choker she wore around her neck— Magenta's whole body stiffened.

It was inevitable, she thought, her heart racing uncontrollably, that he would notice her. Speak to her. She was unprepared, however, for what his deep, chocolate-rich voice would do to her—or for the impact of his masculinity at close quarters as she turned around from returning a bottle to its shelf at the back of the mirrored bar.

'Andreas…' She could hardly find her voice as she met his unflinching eyes. Sapphire-blue eyes that were a legacy of his mother's English heritage. How easily she had remembered that! she thought, amazed, when her mind was struggling to remember anything else. But those eyes were glittering with a chilling clarity, and though Magenta strove to recall exactly what it was that had transpired between them she was certain of nothing beyond the feeling that they had parted on bad terms. *Very* bad.

'Quite a surprise,' he commented dryly. 'For both of us, I would imagine.'

Now Magenta recognised a transatlantic lilt in his deep tones that she somehow knew hadn't been there six years ago, and with another kick from the darker corners of her mind she recognised that the healthy bronze of his skin owed as much to time spent living in the States as to his Anglo-Italian roots.

His well-layered hair was shining like polished jet beneath the lights, but he looked bigger, broader and tougher than the young man surfacing from her memory banks. This man was harder and more forceful. His maturity was reflected in the span of his wide shoulders, and in that commanding air that said he had done a lot of living, while his darkly shaded jaw and the dark hair that was curling above the open neckline of his casual yet beautifully tailored striped shirt seemed to scream of his virility.

'I have to admit,' he was saying, oblivious to the turmoil going on inside her, 'this isn't the sort of place I would have expected to find you.'

His thinly veiled cynicism stopped her from telling him that her job there two evenings a week was just one of her means of being gainfully employed. That she had a day job as a typist and would shortly be moving on to better things if the position she had been shortlisted for and was pinning every last hope on came good during the course of the coming week.

The need to recover those lost months of her life was more pressing than the need to maintain her self-esteem, so now, overcoming her fear of what the answer might be, she ventured to ask, 'Wh-where exactly had you expected to find me?'

His mouth jerked down at one side in a gesture of increasing cynicism. 'Is that meant to be some sort of joke?'

The hardness of his eyes made Magenta feel as though she was being touched by cold steel. But, whatever he had expected of her, he wasn't aware that she had lost her memory, was he?

She wanted to tell him but he seemed so hostile, and yet she was trying to make sense of the wildfire he'd ignited in her blood the second she had seen him walk into the bar.

Even the solid barrier of the counter between them couldn't protect her from the images which were bursting from her memory banks. Images of this man kissing her. Undressing her. Of his deep voice whispering sensual phrases that had driven her mindless for him as he'd pleasured and worshipped her body...

She might have forgotten but her body hadn't. This realisation hit her with frightening clarity. And yet the specifics of the bitter conflict that stood so obviously between them continued to elude her memory.

Trying again, she uttered almost involuntarily, 'I don't remember you,' and flinched as her flat little statement produced a sharp, incisive laugh from him.

'You mean you don't *want* to,' he amended with a humourless smile.

I mean I don't. I don't remember what happened.

She put her hand to her forehead, trying to smooth out the chaos of jumbled pieces that were floating up from that part of her brain that remained dormant. In denial.

'You were younger.' She brought her hand down slowly. 'Thinner.' And surely possessing only a fraction of the dynamism of the man who stood before her now?

'Most probably, as I was only twenty-three.'

And working like a slave in your father's restaurant.

Where had *that* come from? Magenta wondered as another recollection kicked in to bring her hand up to her head again.

'Are you all right?'

Through the buzz of conversation she caught an element of concern in the deep, masculine voice.

'Has seeing me again been too much for you? You look a little pale.'

'Well, anyone would compared to you,' she said snappily, realising that he still didn't understand or believe her. 'You look disgustingly healthy.'

'Yes, well…' His hard mouth quirked, tugging in a gesture that was all at once familiar, lazy and disturbingly sensual. 'Life's been good.'

He seemed to need to tell her that, she decided, sifting through the chaff and debris in her mind to try and discover what it was that had brought them from lovers to this hostile place where they now found themselves. But just at that moment her gaze fell to the two tumblers that Thomas had come to put down on the counter in front of them.

A Scotch and soda for Andreas and a bottle of orange juice for…

Trying not to be too obvious, Magenta made a quick survey of the crowded space behind him, catching his mocking expression before she was able to assess who he might have brought with him. She asked quickly, 'Do you come here often?'

Had she really asked him something so trite? So totally banal? she thought, cringing.

'Never.' He was reaching into the pocket of superbly cut grey trousers as Thomas flipped the cap off the orange juice bottle.

'So what brings you here tonight?' Magenta swallowed, wondering why she was dallying with such trivia when all she wanted to do was grab him by the pristine cloth of his shirt and demand that he tell her what had happened between them—except she was afraid of finding out.

Dragging her gaze from the glass that was being filled,

she lifted her velvety-brown eyes to his. A little frisson of awareness shivered through her when she noticed him assessing the slender lines of her body, saw his lips move in a calculated smile.

'Who knows?' he murmured, deeply aware. 'Fate?'

For a moment, from the way he was looking at her and from the husky note he had infused into that beautiful voice of his, the years seemed to fall away and she was nineteen again. Free-spirited. Giddy with hope. *Flighty.* That was what she remembered someone calling her in those days. Yet, whatever faults or failings she might have possessed, she knew now that she had been desperately, terrifyingly besotted with the man before her.

'So what is *this?*' On that rather derogatory note he jerked his chin towards where she stood on the service side of the bar. 'A bit of pin money between assignments? Or didn't the modelling world quite live up to everything you were hoping for?' He tossed a note down on the counter to cover the cost of the drinks.

Of course. Her modelling career. Or lack of it, she thought wryly. Because it had never really taken off.

'Not everything works out the way we plan,' she responded quietly, absently aware of her younger colleague picking up the note before moving away to the till. Thomas was used to customers chatting her up, even if this particular customer had more wow factor than all the others put together.

'Really? So what happened to Rushford? The miracle-maker?'

The deeply intoned words burned with something corrosive, and she wasn't sure whether it was that or the sound of the name that made her suddenly shiver.

'Didn't he live up to your expectations either? And there I was, under the impression you were really going places with that guy.'

With Marcus Rushford? Magenta wanted to laugh out loud.

Instead she was suddenly despairing at how her mind could have let her forget Andreas and yet retained a nightmarish memory of the slick-talking managing agent who had been promoting her for a while.

Confusion swirled around her and she had to take a deep breath to stem the almost physical pain that trying to remember produced.

'Well, as I said…' She gave a little shrug and felt a surge of panic when she realised she had completely forgotten what it was she had been going to say. It still happened sometimes. Times like now, when she felt hot and flummoxed and abnormally stressed. 'Not…' Mercifully the words flooded back, even though she stumbled over them in attempting to get them out. 'Not…everything goes to plan.'

'Evidently not.' He glanced towards where Thomas was waiting behind the middle-aged man who clearly paid their wages, who was sorting out some problem with the cash machine.

Magenta wished he would hurry up. It was purgatory standing there talking to a man who so clearly resented her when her screaming senses were taunting her with the knowledge of how his skin had felt beneath her fingers and how he had shown her pleasure such as her untutored body had never known. If it *had* been untutored, she thought. As far as she knew she could have been as free with her favours as her mother had led her to believe. She had no recollection of those lost months of her life, but her torpid brain had always rejected that thought as repugnant and totally alien to her.

'So what happened to the career? Did Rushford fail to deliver on his promises? Or is that just a rumour? Like the way he cut loose because he couldn't face the responsibility of fatherhood?'

The fact that this man knew she had been expecting a baby sent Magenta's thoughts spinning in a vortex of confusion.

Her hand went to her forehead. Noticing the way it trembled, she brought it quickly down again.

'I'm sorry,' he said, sounding anything but. 'Is that still a sore point?'

His sarcasm dug deep, but she was too busy trying to stay upright to ask him why he believed Theo was Marcus Rushford's child.

Gripping the edge of the bar with both hands for support, and dragging in lungfuls of much-needed air, she murmured, 'I'd prefer not to discuss my son, if it's…all the same to you.' Had he detected that awkwardness—that lack of fluency in her speech which it had taken her a long time to overcome? 'Not here. Not over a bar.'

Not anywhere, she resolved silently. *Not until I know what happened. What it was I did to make you despise me, as you clearly do.*

His black hair gleamed as he dipped his head in acknowledgement. 'I can't help admitting I'm surprised that the girl I knew would let a little thing like motherhood stand in the way of her plans.'

That didn't sound like her at all, Magenta thought, puzzled. She loved little Theo more than anything else in this world. He was the moon and the stars and the earth to her, she mused with a wistful little smile, and she loved him so much it hurt.

Tentatively, resting her arm on the counter and supporting her chin with her hand, she invited, 'So, tell me about the girl you knew.'

He laughed softly and leaned forward so that she caught the shiver of his breath against her hair, the subtle and yet disturbing sensuality of his personal masculine scent. 'I really don't think you'd welcome hearing it,' he murmured silkily.

The glittering blue of his eyes touched on her upturned mouth. A mouth more than one photographer had complimented, saying it had a natural pout.

Quickly Magenta drew back, standing tall again now that the swaying sensation of a few moments ago had passed.

'Maybe you're getting me mixed up with someone else,' she ventured, hoping against hope that it might be true, but knowing in her heart of hearts that it wasn't. The way her mind and her body had reacted the moment she'd seen him come through that door dispelled any doubt that they had been lovers. 'Or maybe you just didn't know me very well.'

'Oh, I think I did.'

His tone, though soft, held a wealth of derogatory meaning, and Magenta wished someone else would grab her attention—demand to be served. But no one did. He obviously commanded too much respect for anyone to challenge him over monopolising one of the bar staff, and secretly she wondered what he did for a living. What it was that gave him his unmistakable air of autonomy—that bred-in-the-bone confidence? Because he hadn't got that from working all hours in a backstreet Italian restaurant, and from the flashes of hazy memory that were puncturing her brain that was the situation in which she was putting him.

'Well, as I said, I don't remember.' She would hate to admit it to this man who was being so openly hostile, and yet she was on the verge of telling him why, in the hope that he would be able to break down some of the barriers in her brain, when he let out a sound of increasing impatience.

'You're still trying to deny we even *knew* each other?'

He sounded so hard and looked so forbidding that Magenta felt her confidence waning, felt herself shrinking back behind the curtain of self-protection she'd created in order to hide from life until she was ready to grit her teeth and allow herself to take on new challenges—challenges which at the start had seemed insurmountable. But, determined not to let this man's prejudice undo all the good that the past few years of hard work and perseverance had produced, she swallowed her fears and misgivings and plunged in.

'What did I do? Stop seeing you because of someone else? Or was it my career? Whatever it was, at least you can go away with the satisfaction of knowing that I probably got my just deserts and didn't realise all those dreams I was obviously stupid enough to throw you over for.'

His lips held a ruminative smile that did nothing to warm the icy blue of his eyes.

'Now, there you're wrong,' he murmured in a voice that was silkily soft. 'Our little…interlude wasn't significant enough for me to harbour any long-term desire for revenge, so there's no need to beat yourself up over it unnecessarily, Magenta.' His tone suggested that that was the last thing he expected her to be doing. 'We're all guilty at times—especially when we're young—of setting our sights beyond what we can realistically achieve.'

He'd said he wasn't harbouring any desire for revenge over whatever she was supposed to have done, but it was obvious to Magenta that he was getting satisfaction from seeing her now.

'You'd be surprised what I've *achieved* over the past five years or so.' Her pride forced her to utter the words before she could control the urge.

'Oh, really?' A quizzical eyebrow lifted. 'Like what?'

Like learning to walk again. Like holding a knife and fork! Like taking over responsibility for my own precious little baby. Like staying alive!

Unconsciously she fingered the red and black choker that lay strategically over one of her now fading scars. He didn't need to know any of that. Or about the Business Studies course she had taken, which had enabled her to apply for the new position she was hoping to get, which would lift her out of temping by day and working behind a bar a couple of nights a week and allow her to provide a better future for her and her son.

'It isn't important,' she dismissed on a defeated little note. Anyway, he was acknowledging lanky young Thomas, who had loped back with his change and was apologising for keeping him waiting.

Magenta's gaze fell to the lean, masculine hands now lifting the tumblers off the counter. Hands which she knew had once taken her to paradise and back and which were surprisingly devoid of any rings.

But there *were* two glasses. Two drinks…

His eyes caught her unconcealed interest and he shifted his position slightly—deliberately, Magenta guessed—creating a breach in the crowd and allowing her eyes to make their way to the smartly dressed, very attractive redhead sitting at one of the tables. She was looking at Andreas with a smile born of familiarity and undisguised appreciation.

Looking quickly back at Andreas, Magenta felt his eyes resting too intently on her face. Eyes that were penetratingly perceptive. Much too aware…

'As I said…' His mouth twisted with cruel satisfaction. 'Life's been good,' he reiterated, before moving away.

Magenta stood there for a moment, feeling as though she had just come through some invisible, indescribable battle. She felt sick, and her head was thumping, and all she wanted to do was run away and hide. But someone had started giving her an order and she knew she couldn't just run off without doing her job, even if it *was* under the smug gaze of a man who clearly despised her.

'Is that guy a boyfriend of yours?' Thomas asked over his shoulder as Magenta finished serving the woman.

Over the sounds of a live band setting up their instruments in the designated corner of the wine bar, she could only manage a negative murmur as she shook her head.

'No?' A mousy eyebrow disappeared beneath a tangled mass of equally mousy hair. 'Then why was he looking at you as though he was determined to rip that dress off?'

'Don't be silly.' Dazed though she was, her colleague's observation pumped up Magenta's skittering heart-rate, lend-ing a pink tinge to her otherwise colour-leeched face. 'He's with someone.'

'He was.'

'What?' She couldn't see past the wall of customers and the band doing its sound check against a babble of laughter and mixed conversation.

'I swear he downed that whisky in one and hustled his girlfriend out the door before she had time to draw breath.'

For some reason Magenta's stomach seemed to turn over. 'He did?' Another glimpse towards his table through a sudden gap in the human wall showed only an empty tumbler and a barely touched glass of orange juice that had clearly been hastily abandoned.

'So? They must have been in a hurry to get somewhere,' Magenta supplied, wondering why they had left in such a rush. Was it because of her? she speculated, her heart hammering against her ribcage and her head starting to swim. Couldn't he stand being under the same roof with her long enough for the woman he'd brought with him even to finish her drink?

'Hey! Are you all right?' she heard Thomas ask again as she staggered, dropping her head into her hands to try and stanch the rising nausea.

'No, I'm sorry. Could you call me a taxi?' she appealed to Thomas, before staggering to the Ladies' again, where she was violently sick.

He had behaved badly, Andreas thought as he was driving home alone, but it had been both shocking and unsettling—far more unsettling than he wanted to admit—seeing Magenta again.

He had been twenty-three to her nineteen, and just a dogsbody in his father's floundering business, and yet he should have known right away what kind of a girl she was. She had been living in a rundown terraced house with her man-crazy alcoholic mother, who hadn't even known who Magenta's father was!

He'd taken pity on her, Andreas told himself, as the beam of oncoming headlamps slashed cold light across his hardening features. Why else would he have got himself mixed up with her? But hot on the heels of that self-deluded question came the real answer—one that heated his veins and caused a heavy throbbing in his blood.

Because she'd been warm and exciting and more beautiful than any other girl he had ever met in his life—and he had known quite a few, even then. Although not enough to have learned that girls like Magenta James were only out for one thing. A good time—regardless of the cost to anyone else, particularly the poor sucker who happened to be providing her with that good time!

Tension locked his jaw as he turned the steering wheel to cross a junction.

She had known she was beautiful. That was the problem. A part-time receptionist who had been on every model agency's books, following every lead and promotion she could grasp in a bid to capitalise on her beauty. That was when she hadn't been at home, trying to shake her mother out of a drunken stupor!

They had become lovers almost at once, just a few days after they'd started dating, and only a week after he had seen her in his father's restaurant with a group of women during a lively hen party. Surprisingly, she had been a virgin the first time he had made love to her, and yet he had unleashed a fire in her that he'd been foolish enough to believe burned for him alone.

They had made love everywhere. In his van. In the flat above the restaurant when his father and grandmother were out. In her surprisingly immaculate, sparsely furnished little bedroom which had seemed like an oasis amidst the clutter and chaos of her mother's damp and crumbling, sadly neglected Edwardian house.

It hadn't mattered one iota that his family hadn't liked her—although he had wondered, with the gentle memory of his mother, how she might have viewed Magenta if she hadn't died while he was still very young. His grandmother, though, had been totally out of touch with people of his generation, and his father...

He slammed his mind shut as a well of excruciating pain and reproach threatened to invade it. Their disapproval, he remembered, had only intensified the excitement of being with her.

Of course they had known what she was like; they had been able to see through the thin veil of her bewitching beauty when he hadn't. He had been blinded and totally duped by her impassioned but hollow declarations of love.

He had been hardworking, loyal to his father, and yet ambitious. And he had at least been able to see and recognise the flaws in the way in which his father had run the restaurant. Giuseppe Visconti had been a far more proficient chef than he had been a businessman, and as proud an Italian as he'd been a dictator of a father, and he had refused to listen to his son's radical plans for saving and developing the business.

'Over my dead body.'

Andreas still flinched now from recalling his father's exact words.

'You will never have a foothold in this business. *Dio mio!* Never! Not while you are stupid enough to be mixed up with that girl.'

He had been a blind and naive fool to believe that love could conquer all, that with Magenta James beside him he could overcome his family's prejudices and his father's stubbornness. What he hadn't realised, he reflected coldly, was that the lovely Magenta had only been amusing herself in his bed—that even as he had been drowning in the heat of their mutual passion she had already been sexually entangled with someone else.

He hadn't wanted to believe his father's smug revelations—and wouldn't have if he hadn't gone round to her house unexpectedly and seen Rushford's car parked outside. A huge and expensive black saloon that had stood out like a sore thumb in her rather downmarket neighbourhood, and especially outside her mother's particularly rundown house.

He'd driven away on that occasion, still unable to believe his eyes—and indeed what his family had been telling him. But hadn't he had graphic proof of her infidelity himself?

'Do you really think I was ever serious about you? About *this?*' she had scoffed on an almost hysterical little bubble of laughter the last time he had seen her.

She'd shot a disparaging glance around the deserted and already failing restaurant. That was when she had informed him of all her precious Svengali was doing for her and all that she was intending to achieve.

He had had a row with Giuseppe Visconti that night. One of many, he reflected. But this one had been different. It had been the squaring up of two male animals intent only on victory over the other. Savage. Almost coming to blows. He'd blamed his father for the outcome of his relationship with Magenta. Giuseppe had called her names, foul names that Andreas had never been able to repeat, and he'd accused his father of being jealous of his youth and his prospects, of depriving him of his right to be his own man.

His father had died in his arms that night after the angry tirade that had been too much for his unexpectedly weak heart to take. Two months later his grandmother had put the restaurant on the market to pay off the loans the business had been unable to meet, determined to go back to her native Italy.

Some time afterwards, when Andreas had been in America, someone—he couldn't remember who—had told him that Magenta was living in the lap of luxury with a big-shot called Marcus Rushford and that she was expecting his baby.

Yes, he'd behaved badly tonight, Andreas reflected grimly as he swung his car through the electrically operated gates of his Surrey mansion. But at the end of it, looking back, he decided that he hadn't behaved badly *enough!*

CHAPTER TWO

ALL THE WAY home in the taxi Magenta's head was throbbing, pulsating with an invasion of jumbled images. When at last she had paid the driver, was staggering towards the privacy of her own bathroom, the kaleidoscope of confusing images started to take some form.

Meeting Andreas in that restaurant. Laughing with Andreas. Making love with him.... Where, it didn't matter. It hadn't mattered then. She pressed the heels of her hands against the wells of her eyes, her breath catching as a heated and desperate desire took hold in her mind. Why had it been desperate? She shook her head to try and jolt herself into remembering. She *had* to remember...

There was a big man. Sullen. Andreas's father! And Maria. Maria was his grandmother! Oh, but there had been such ill feeling! She recalled feeling the lowest of the low. There was shouting now. Andreas was shouting at *her*. Telling her she was shallow-minded and materialistic. Telling her she was no good—just like her mother.

In a crumpled heap beside the toilet she relieved herself of the nausea that remembering produced and wiped her mouth with the back of her hand. For the first time she was glad that Theo was spending part of his school holiday in the country with her great-aunt. It would have distressed her little boy to have seen her in such a state.

Winding her arms around herself, she ached for him, missing him as much as on the day when she had woken up from that coma to realise she'd lost not only two months of her life, but also the baby she'd remembered carrying. It was the only thing she *had* remembered. Except that she hadn't lost him…

She started sobbing with all the same poignancy with which she'd sobbed that day when her widowed aunt, Josie Ashton, had brought her healthy eight-week-old son into the hospital and laid him against her breast. Dear Great-Aunt Josie, with her abrupt manner and her outspokenness, whom Magenta hadn't seen for at least ten years. But the woman had had no qualms, she remembered, about answering her mother's cry for help when a sick daughter and the arrival of a new grandson had been too much for Jeanette James to cope with.

She was sobbing equally, though, for the way her mind had blanked out her child's father. How could she have forgotten him? she agonised, feeling the loss for her son, for the lack of a father figure in his life, rather than for herself. What had he done that had driven her subconscious into shut down so completely? What had *she* done? she wondered, suddenly seized by the frightening possibility that she might somehow *deserve* his condemnation.

For heaven's sake, *think!* she urged herself, desperate for answers.

But the floodgates that had started to open refused to budge any further, and by the time she arrived at her interview the following week, she felt worn out from the effort of trying to force them apart.

'I see from your CV that you only acquired your qualification in Business Studies over the last eighteen months, and that you didn't work anywhere on a permanent basis for the preceding four years,' said the older of the two women who were interviewing her.

There was a middle-aged man there too, who suddenly

chipped in with, 'May I ask what you were doing in the meantime?'

'I've been bringing up my son,' Magenta supplied, relieved to be able to say it without any hesitation in her speech, especially when she felt as though she were facing an inquisition.

The interview was for the post of PA to the marketing manager of a rapidly expanding hotel chain, and Magenta had gone for a totally sophisticated image. With her hair up, and wearing a tailored grey suit and maroon camisole, with the stripes in the silk scarf around her neck blending the two colours, she didn't think she could have looked smarter if she had tried.

She was desperate to get this job to help her pay off her mounting debts so that she could stay on in her flat and give her child all the security and comforts she herself had never had. For that reason she had chosen not to disclose everything about herself when she had applied for this position three weeks ago, certain that the reason she hadn't been offered any of the endless list of the other jobs she had applied for was because she had been too forthcoming with the truth.

But this job looked as if it was hers—particularly as the older woman on the other side of the desk was making no secret of the fact that she favoured Magenta over the only other candidate on the shortlist.

'And you won't find it a problem dividing your time between the demands of the office and those of a five-year-old?' The younger, fair-haired woman, by the name of Lana Barleythorne, was challenging her. 'He can't have been at school very long...'

'Well over a year,' Magenta supplied, proud of how bright and advanced for his age her little boy was. 'And I do have very satisfactory childcare.' She didn't tell them about Great-Aunt Josie, who had shown her and Theo such unconditional love when they had needed it most.

Her answer seemed to please her interviewers, because

the more matronly of the two women was now explaining that the marketing manager for whom she'd be working was attending a conference that day but had asked if Magenta would be prepared to come in and meet her later in the week.

Yes! Had she been on her own Magenta would have punched the air in triumph. 'Of course,' she answered calmly instead, hoping she didn't look too desperately relieved.

She was still trying to keep her concentration on what they were saying, and to stop herself grinning from ear to ear, when a knock had her gaze swivelling across the large modern office to the tall man in an immaculate dark suit who was striding in.

Andreas! Magenta tried to force his name past her lips but no sound came out.

What was he doing here? she wondered, aghast. And why had he barged in dressed like that, as though he had every right to?

'Mr Visconti...' The older woman, looking surprised, was getting to her feet, but a silent command from him had her subsiding back onto her chair. 'This is Miss James,' she explained. 'We were just about to wind up her interview.'

'I know.'

The deep voice was calm. Matter-of-fact. But he hadn't yet looked her way and Magenta guessed that he hadn't connected the name with her or realised that it was his ex the woman was referring to, now sitting there in a state of shock.

'That's why I came in.'

The impact of his sudden entrance had made her go weak all over, she realised, and then he suddenly glanced her way and his intensely blue eyes met the stunned velvety-brown of hers.

'Mr Visconti is our Chief Executive,' her principal interviewer was telling Magenta, through what seemed like a thick and muffling fog.

Chief Executive? How could he be? she wondered when she finally managed to grasp what the woman had said.

'He's the man we're all ultimately answerable to,' said Lana Barleythorne, who seemed to be having difficulty keeping her eyes off him. 'He has the last word on whatever changes might be taking place throughout the chain.'

'And I'm afraid this position has already been filled.'

He took his eyes off Magenta only briefly, to direct a glance towards the people she now realised, staggeringly, were his employees.

'But we thought—' piped up Lara, his clearly adoring fan.

'It's Miss Nicholls—the last candidate,' he stated tonelessly, and in a way that imparted to anyone who might dare to challenge him that his decision was final and no one else had the authority to question it. 'I've already spoken to…'

Numbly, Magenta only half heard him saying that he had spoken to his marketing manager and she was happy to take the other candidate on.

'I see.' The woman who was obviously the spokesperson for the three sounded surprised.

And all at once, through her shock and mounting dismay over losing a job that had not only been within her grasp but which she had been counting on to get her out of financial deep water, Magenta began to see things as they really were.

He had known she was in here. Probably from some list he had vetted before coming in. Which was why he hadn't shown any sign of surprise or shock when he had seen her. Because he had already decided—even before he had opened that door—to snatch the chance of that job right out of her hands!

'Miss James…'

The woman Magenta knew she had won over from the start made a futile little gesture with her hands.

'What can I say? Except that I think we owe you an apology.'

For what? Magenta thought, hurting, angry. For building

up her hopes? For making her think she could be out of the woods with her finances and her barely affordable flat? For throwing her back into the never-ending queue for far too few realistically paid jobs? Perhaps they didn't have bills to pay and debts to settle, but she did! And now, just because she'd walked into a company controlled by this man with an obvious score to settle, none of those bills were ever likely to be paid!

Not caring any more about what impression she created, she leaped up from her chair and, in response to the woman's suggestion about owing her an apology, uttered, 'Yes, I believe you do! I've had to take a whole morning off work—without pay—to enable me to come to this interview today, and I think that the least you could have done in return would have been to get your facts straight! It might not be any skin off *your* noses to drag people here under false pretences, but if this is the way your company operates then I hope your paying customers don't arrive at their hotels only to find the previous guests still occupying their beds!'

She felt sorry for her interviewers—particularly the woman who had shown such enthusiasm for her capabilities before their cold and calculating boss had walked in. Her venom was directed solely at Andreas. She hadn't wanted to show him up in front of his staff, but if she had, she thought fiercely, then after what he had just done it was no more than he deserved!

'That's all I have to say,' she concluded. And she had done so without embarrassing herself, or even tripping over her words, she realised, pivoting away from them—from *him*—as the ordeal and the thought of what it would mean for her and Theo brought shaming tears to her eyes.

'Miss James.'

The deep, masculine voice addressed her formally from across the room but she ignored it, tearing over the high-polished floor to the door through which she had come with such high hopes only half an hour earlier.

'Magenta!'

He didn't seem bothered by what the others might make of him calling her by her first name, and images of a young man swam before her eyes. A young man who was determined, high-spirited and unrestrained—a young Andreas who refused to be dominated by his father's will....

His softer command—and it *had* been a command, though infused with a persuasive familiarity—stopped her in her tracks.

Standing there, with her heart banging against her ribcage, she brought her head up, breathing deeply to control her humiliating emotion, squaring her back beneath the silver-grey jacket before she steeled herself to turn around.

'There is another vacancy,' Andreas said.

The distance she had put between them had given him a greater vantage point from which to study her, and he was doing just that, allowing his cool gaze to travel over the slender lines of her body in a way that made Magenta almost forget that there were other people in the room.

She looked at him questioningly but he was addressing the other three, who appeared to be silently querying his declaration.

'It's all right. I'll handle this,' Andreas told them, and one by one they filed out—the younger woman seeming to shoot daggers in Magenta's direction, the elder sending her a surprisingly knowing smile.

'So what is the vacancy?' Magenta's mouth felt dry as the door closed behind them. The air seemed charged with something sensual, stiflingly intimate even in the spacious modern office. 'Or is this all a clever ploy to try and keep me here?'

Andreas moved around the desk and leaned back against it, his hands clutching his elbows, one foot crossed over the other.

'I think we should talk first,' he said.

'What about? Why you just ruined my chances of getting a job I was counting on?' Tremblingly, because she was almost afraid of knowing the answer, she tagged on, 'What did I ever do to you that you should dislike me so much?'

He laughed very softly, but there was no humour in his eyes. 'Come and sit down,' he ordered with a jerk of his chin towards her vacated chair.

'I prefer to stand, if you don't mind.'

She did, however, move closer to him—close enough to bring her hands down on the back of the chair for some much-needed support.

'As you wish.' This was accompanied by a gesture of one long, lean hand.

'Tell me what I did. I told you—I'm having difficulty remembering.'

'That's convenient.'

'It's the truth.'

'And from experience we both know that you can be remarkably sparing with *that*.'

His tone flayed, bringing Magenta's lashes down like lustrous ebony against the pale translucency of her skin.

'We dated...' She came around the chair and like an automaton, despite what she had said, sat down upon it, starkly aware of the cynical sound her comment produced.

'Well, that's one up on what you claimed to know last Friday,' he remarked. 'But if *my* memory serves me correctly we did a whole lot more than that.'

Images invaded of ripping clothes and devouring kisses. Of tangled limbs and naked bodies. Of herself spread-eagled on a bed in glorious abandon to this man's driving passion.

She shook her head and realised that he had relinquished his position on the desk.

'You're crying,' he observed, coming towards her and noting the emotion still moistening her eyes after losing the job she'd struggled so long and hard for. 'It always heightened my pleasure to kiss you after you had been crying. It made your mouth so inviting. So unbelievably soft…'

His voice had grown quieter, Magenta realised, tormented again by sensual images of the two of them together, by the arousing sensations that were invading every erogenous zone in her body.

'I'm not crying,' she bluffed, in rejection of everything he was saying—and then caught a sudden, startling glimpse of herself from somewhere in her past, crying bitterly. She was sobbing because she had to leave him. She'd known she had to get away from him. But *why?* 'I'm annoyed—angry— humiliated. But I'm certainly not crying. If you want to hurt me then that's your problem—not mine. But, just for the record, was that rather uncalled-for remark a roundabout way of saying that *you* were always upsetting *me?*'

Within the hard framework of his features his devastating mouth turned uncompromisingly grim. 'I wasn't the one responsible for causing you pain in the past, and I certainly did nothing to make you weep. Except in bed.'

His continual references to the passion they had shared were unsettling her beyond belief. As he probably intended them to, she realised, catching a different sound now from the darkest corners of her mind. The sound of herself sobbing with desire at the enslaving, unparalleled pleasure he was giving her. But there were other things too. Things she didn't want to remember, which his disturbing presence alone was bringing back to her.

'Your family hated me.'

'That was my family.'

'Especially your father.'

His face took on the cast of an impregnable steel mask. 'And with good cause, I think. In the end.'

She wanted to ask him why. What it was she had done to make him despise her so much. But he was still too cold, too distant and far too unapproachable. And anyway she was afraid of what hearing the truth might do to her.

'How is he? Your father?' she enquired tentatively.

'My father's dead.'

From the way he said it he might easily be implying that *she* had had something to do with it. Oh, no! She couldn't have, surely? she thought, shuddering at the hard, cold emotion she saw in his eyes which seemed to be piercing her like shards of ice.

'He's dead,' he reiterated. 'As you would have known if you hadn't been so tied up with making a name for yourself.'

'Oh, I had a *name,* Andreas.' It rushed back at her, hurtful and destructive. 'And it wasn't very complimentary. But I suppose you think I deserved what your grandmother called me?'

Her voice was low and controlled. She was determined not to let him see her trembling. And it wasn't just the remembered pain of that time that was ripping through her memory banks and slashing at her now with such wounding cruelty, but the cold way she had just been informed that Giuseppe Visconti had died.

She wanted to ask Andreas what had happened but was even too cowardly to do that. Instead she dropped her head into her hands and groaned as a sudden vision flashed before her eyes.

It was of plate glass and fluorescent lighting where once there had been red and white chequered curtains and candlelit windows; an internet café where the little restaurant had been. She had found herself standing outside it once a couple of years ago, not even realising why, or what she was doing there. She only remembered that the experience had chilled her to the bone.

Watching her, Andreas frowned—and then reminded himself what a good actress she was.

'I'm afraid I'm not really taken in by this display of crocodile tears,' he said bluntly, but as she lifted her head and dragged her fingers down her face the dark smudges under her eyes and her pallor shocked him. 'Are you all right?' he asked, concerned.

'I'm fine.'

'No, you're not. I think you'd better come with me.' He was urging her up from her chair before she had time to think.

'Where are we going?' she asked weakly as he bundled her into a waiting lift in the lobby.

'As I said, we have to talk,' he said, setting the lift in motion.

Released now from the pressure of his hand at her elbow, but finding his whole persona too disturbing in such a confined space, Magenta stepped as far away from him as she could.

A faint smile touched the firm, masculine mouth, as though he knew exactly why she had done that.

'And, as *I* said, what about?' She could feel the blood returning to her face and was managing to gather her wits about her again. 'There isn't any other vacancy, is there? You just wanted me to stay behind so that you could taunt me with whatever it is you think I did to you in the past. So go ahead. Get it all out of your system!'

At least then she might know, once and for all, what it was all about.

Instead he merely laughed, and that soft, mirthless laugh seemed as controlled and calculated as everything else about him. Then, with a suddenness that had Magenta's instincts leaping onto red alert, he reached out and caught one end of her scarf. Winding it carefully around his finger, he drew her gently into his dominating sphere.

'Is this a fashion thing?' He tugged lightly at the silk. 'Or is its purpose merely to conceal the remnants of your current lover's carnal appetite?'

'How dare you?' She made to push him away, only to find

her hands trapped between his own and the warm hard wall of his chest.

'Yes, I dare,' he growled, and his head came down, stopping with his mouth just a breath from hers.

It was the unfathomable dark emotion she saw in his eyes as her trembling gaze wavered beneath his that seemed to rob the breath from her lungs—that and the thunderous hammering of his heart.

She wasn't sure who made the next move, but suddenly their mouths were fused in a hungry and antagonistic passion, and her arms were sliding up around his neck as his stronger ones tightened around her, welding her to him.

She was nineteen again and she was laughing with him, her heart on fire, wild with a new sense of freedom and excitement. But he wasn't laughing with her. She was laughing all by herself. And she was being weighed down with such a feeling of remorse and shame.

Fighting Andreas, she was surprised when he let her go— and so roughly that she almost stumbled back against the far wall of the lift.

Groaning, she put her hand to her mouth, stemming a new bout of nausea. She realised it wasn't that devastating kiss that was responsible for her crushing feeling of self-disgust.

'Forgive me for being under the impression that you wanted that as much as I did. Even when you were sleeping with another man you were never averse to my touch.'

Whether she deserved that or not, Magenta felt her hand itch to make contact with his dark, judgmental face.

'Don't even think about it,' he advised, breathing as erratically as she was.

She was grateful when the lift opened, and didn't need Andreas's prompting to step out.

'Where are we?' she demanded over her shoulder. Before he answered she realised that they were on the top floor of the building, where wide windows gave a breathtaking view of the bustling capital below.

'You aren't feeling well,' Andreas commented as he moved past her and used a security key to open the door to an executive suite. 'Whether from fatigue or simply—as your weight seems to suggest—because you aren't eating enough, I didn't welcome the thought of you passing out on me down there.'

'Thanks,' Magenta responded tartly, her breathing still irregular from the unexpected and disturbing scenario in the lift. Or *had* she expected it? The question raged through her consciousness with the disturbance of a ten-force gale. She only knew she had wanted it. Dear heaven, had she wanted it!

A low whistle passed through her lips as Andreas let her into a luxuriously decorated office. It was all there: the solid wood floor, an imposing mahogany desk that looked out over the city, the softest leather settees, luscious plants and huge windows to complete his commercial kingdom.

'What did you do? Win the lottery or something?' Vague as her memories were, Magenta couldn't equate how the son of a humble restaurateur could have gone from a virtual dogsbody in his father's restaurant to CEO of a chain of exclusive hotels.

'You know I never leave anything to chance.'

Fat chance. His declaration brought those two words to the forefront of her mind. It seemed to be something she had said once in connection with his telling her what he intended to do with his life.

'I think you should have a brandy,' he advised, already on his way over to a cabinet on the far side of the room.

'I never drink.' If there were still facts missing from her life then that was one fact she had never allowed herself to forget. 'I've seen what it can do to people.'

He nodded, knowing what had prompted her to say it. Her mother.

Magenta recalled how hard she had battled as a teenager

against her mother's addiction, which had been constantly fuelled by a string of broken relationships.

'In that case I'll send for some coffee.' Andreas picked up the phone and ordered some to be brought up in that deep, authoritative voice of his. 'Sit down,' he invited.

Magenta stood there, thinking of the young man whose hands she had been so drawn to when he'd set that first cup of coffee he had made down in front of her. She couldn't get over how this new present-day Andreas didn't even have to perform *that* simple task himself.

'So what happened, Andreas?' she asked, still standing her ground. 'I know you're dying to tell me, otherwise you wouldn't have brought me up here.' Unless, of course, he had it in his mind to take up where they had left off in the lift, she thought, her mind rejecting the idea as strongly as her body was responding to it, just to mock her.

'You're perfectly safe—if you're thinking what I think you are,' that masculine voice intoned, startling her into obeying his silent command to sink down onto one of the huge and plushly inviting settees. 'I don't intend to make overtures to a woman who showed such repugnance at my kisses. You put on a good show of displaying that out there—even if we both know that that's really all it was. A *show*,' he emphasised.

He was entirely miscalculating the reason for her shattering reaction in the lift—something she was certain he didn't do very often.

'I had a lucky break when an uncle I never knew died and left me three restaurants between Naples and Milan.'

'So you *do* believe in luck?' she uttered, reminding him of what he'd said a few moments ago about never leaving anything to chance.

'If one can expand on that luck and make things happen.'

'Which you did, of course.'

'It was a gruelling, round-the-clock enterprise, building up those restaurants and then opening more in the States, where

I was living until less than a year ago, then investing in and turning around the fortunes of a series of small hotels. That led on to bigger things that finally brought me here. Nothing is impossible if you're prepared to work hard enough.'

That judgmental note was back in his voice again, and unthinkingly she uttered, 'Instead of trading on one's physical attributes like you seem to want to accuse me of doing?'

He gave her a withering look but didn't actually comment as he crossed the room and came and stood in front of her. 'Tell me about your son,' he said without any preamble. 'It can't be any picnic, bringing up a child on your own.'

His words triggered something that was too elusive to grasp, yet what lingered in the forefront of her mind was a real and crushing fear. An intangible yet instinctive knowledge that if this man realised she'd had his child he wouldn't hesitate to try and take Theo away from her....

'What...what do you want to know?' she faltered, casting her eyes down briefly, her lashes dark wings of ebony against the wells of her eyes. Had he detected the tension in her? she wondered when she saw the deepening groove between his thick black brows. Guessed at the reasons for her reluctance to discuss her little boy?

'Did Rushford really dump you before you'd even reached the full term of your pregnancy?'

So he was still insisting that Marcus Rushford had been her lover. The thought of sleeping with her former exploitative agent made her stomach queasy, even though he was an attractive and very worldly man. That was preferable, though, to the possible consequences of explaining to Andreas that *he* was the father of her child, and crazily she uttered, 'If it makes you feel smug, believe it.'

His response to that was merely a slight twitching of his mouth. 'So...does Rushford even see his son?'

Magenta's mouth felt dry. She wished the coffee would

come as she struggled for composure under this very disturbing line of questioning.

'His name is Marcus. And, no, he doesn't ever see Theo.'

'What?' Hard lines of disbelief lined Andreas's face. 'Never?' He looked and sounded appalled.

'Never,' she uttered dismissively, deciding to end the conversation there and then. 'There never was another vacancy, was there?' she accused again, deciding he really *had* only brought her up here to satisfy some warped agenda of his own. 'So now you've shown me just how well you're doing…' quickly she got to her feet '…and clarified that all those rumours you heard about me were probably true, I'll be on my way.'

Trying to save face before she walked away from him, wondering how in the world she was ever going to pay her mounting bills, she forced back her concerns and told him, 'This wasn't the only job I was being interviewed for today.'

She hadn't even reached the door when she heard him say confidently, 'Liar.'

She swung round, speechless at his mocking arrogance.

'I haven't got where I am today without gaining some insight into human nature,' he disclosed, moving towards her with the self-possessed demeanour of a man who knew he was right. 'A woman doesn't normally go to pieces over losing the prospect of a job, as you nearly did down there, if she has another package tucked neatly up her sleeve and hasn't pinned her hopes on just one that she thinks might be a little way out of her league.'

Was that what he thought? That she wasn't suitable for the post? 'I didn't think any such thing! And I wasn't going to pieces, as you'd like to imagine I was.'

'Weren't you?' The trace of a smile played around his mouth. 'You seem to forget—I know you. Although you've done your level best since we met again last Friday to try and make me believe you're suffering from some sort of selective memory loss, I *do* know you, Magenta. Very well. I know how your eyes always glitter when you're inviting me to challenge you. How the excitement of some delightful reprisal serves to put colour in your cheeks.'

He was moving purposefully towards her, making her instincts scream in rejection. Her body, though, trembled with the excitement he had spoken of—even as she feared that he might just remind her of what other responses he could evoke in her, as he had done on the way up here.

'Apart from which,' he added, coming to a stop just centimetres in front of her, 'you were almost visibly shaking. Just like you're doing now.'

She wanted to protest and say that she wasn't shaking, and that the other responses he had mentioned were just a figment of his self-deluded ego. But if she did that then they'd both know that she was guilty of doing what he had accused her of doing a few moments ago. Telling lies.

He was playing with her just for his own warped sense of satisfaction, she guessed, feeling the burn of humiliating tears sting the backs of her eyes again, and she knew she had to get out of there before she showed herself up completely.

'Goodbye, Andreas.'

He was at the door, blocking her exit, even before she had time to reach for the handle.

'Do you really think I asked you up here just for my own amusement?' he drawled, startling her with how close he had come to reading her thoughts. But then—as he had said—he *knew* her, didn't he?

'You didn't *ask*.'

'All right, I brought you up here,' he amended casually, as though it was of no consequence. 'But at the time you didn't seem in a fit state to handle anything else.'

His eyes were raking over her face as though looking for signs of her earlier weakness, but his subtle reference to that kiss they had shared earlier was far too disconcerting and Magenta swallowed, taking a step back.

'Do you have a point?'

That smile touched his lips again as he moved around her, away from the door.

'Ah, the same old Magenta. Always cutting to the chase.'

'I'm in a hurry.'

'Of course. Your other interviews.' His tone mocked. 'However, despite all your accusations and suspicions regarding my ulterior motives, there *is* another position becoming vacant in this company.'

'There is?' Magenta's heart gave a little leap of hope, although she was still viewing him with suspicion.

'Another PA is taking an indefinite spell of leave,' he told her with a grimace. 'Rather sooner than we expected her to. We haven't yet found anyone suitable to fill the post.'

'And you're offering *me* the position?' Something like relief started to trickle through her veins. Could this mean that there was an end in sight to her endless and ever-increasing money worries? That she wouldn't be forced to impose on her great-aunt's generosity when Josie had given so much of herself already?

'Why so surprised, Magenta? Your CV looks promising, if a little lacking in experience, and it does say that you can start right away. The PA in question is taking time off to look after her mother during a period of scheduled surgical operations and she's expected to be away for four or five months. She's the one, incidentally, whom you were trying very hard not to let me catch you looking at in the bar the other night. I was trying to talk her out of going so soon, but circumstances dictate that I have to be a gentleman about it and comply with her wishes. In short, Magenta, you'll be working for *me*.'

A tremulous little laugh left her lips—something between amazement and utter disbelief. 'Tell me you're joking?' A crushing disappointment was replacing her premature relief.

'I never joke about business matters.'

'Why? *Why,* when you so obviously don't like me, would you want to employ me?'

'You know…I've asked myself that very question,' he said.

He moved closer to her—close enough to reach out and lift her chin between his thumb and forefinger. His warmth seared her skin, making her catch her breath.

'And?' It came out as a croak. She was trying not to let him affect her, trying not to breathe in the tantalising freshness of his cologne.

He shrugged. 'I need an assistant. You're looking for a position.'

'I had a position—or as good as,' she interjected. 'Until you came and snatched it from me.'

His hand fell away from her, although his eyes never left her face. 'Well, maybe I'm just nursing a masochistic need to have you working for me.'

'So you can remind me every day of how badly I treated you?' *If* she had treated him badly. *Think!* she urged herself, but nothing would come.

Andreas's laugh was infused with irony. 'I thought I made that clear when I saw you last Friday? Your actions in the past left no indelible marks.'

'Well, that's all right, then, isn't it?' she breathed, silently disturbed by his chilling declaration. 'And you'd still take me on after you've intimated that the job I was applying for was out of my league. This is obviously a far more responsible position, and you've already said I'm lacking in experience. What makes you imagine I'm up to meeting all your requirements?'

'Oh, you'll meet them, Magenta. Rest assured about that.'

He wasn't saying anything, but something in the dark penetration of his eyes made her shiver. Somehow he didn't seem to be just talking about his requirements of a PA.

'Well, thanks, but no thanks,' she said, turning away.

'You'll walk away knowing that the lease on your flat is hanging in the balance and that you don't even have the resources to renew it?'

She swung round to face him, the tears she had been fighting since the moment he'd strode in and ripped all her hopes apart now glistening unashamedly in her eyes. 'How did you know that?'

'You've just confirmed it,' he said. 'Apart from which one of my colleagues who attended your first interview mentioned the letter that you asked for.'

'The letter?' she murmured, and was suddenly mortifyingly aware of what he meant.

She'd made a fool of herself at that first interview by prematurely believing, from the way the conversation was going, that they were already offering her the job. She'd been so desperately relieved that she'd asked if she could have their offer in a formal letter, which she could pass on to her landlord's agents. It didn't take half a brain—let alone a keen mind like his—to work out the reason why.

'So you decided to capitalise on my misfortune?'

'I'm offering you a job.'

'Not the sort I'm willing to take.'

'On the contrary, Magenta. I think you'll take any job you can get. And may I point out that I'm not the one implying anything improper? You are.'

'You're not?'

'No. And I'm not sure what you're getting so falsely modest and indignant about,' he stated. 'It wouldn't be the first time you'd sold yourself to the highest bidder.'

It was obvious that he believed what he was saying, and that he would never cease to remind her of it or to exact retribution for it—which was the only reason, she was sure, that he was offering her the position now.

'I've never *sold* myself!' she emphasised, trying to ignore the goading little voice inside her head that was asking, *How do you know?* 'I haven't,' she reiterated, trying to convince herself in spite of it. 'And I'm not selling myself to you, Andreas,' she tagged on. But there was desolation in her eyes as she realised that for her own sake, and especially for Theo's welfare, she had very little choice but to accept his offer.

His mouth compressed with evident satisfaction as a knock on the door announced the arrival of the coffee.

'Well, we'll see, shall we?' he said, knowing as well as she did that she was beaten.

CHAPTER THREE

MAGENTA WOKE WITH a start, sweating and trembling. She had been dreaming that she was looking for something and didn't even know what it was, but as the trembling subsided and the fog lifted from her brain things started to become a little clearer.

She had been sobbing while she was asleep because of something she had lost and desperately wanted back, but it wasn't anything tangible that she had been looking for. She knew it had been something to do with Andreas....

She was lying on top of the bed, where she had slumped, drained and exhausted, after coming home from that interview today and after that unsettling time in his office. She'd remembered so much. The restaurant. His father and grandmother. Even snatches of their brief but tempestuous affair. But there were aspects of their relationship that still continued to elude her. Like what had happened to make him so hostile towards her? Had it been to do with her modelling career? And why was he so convinced that Marcus Rushford was Theo's father?

Think!

She lay there for a while, until her brain felt fit to burst, and then with a frustrated groan forced herself off the bed and into the bathroom.

Her body had changed very little since her teenage years,

she thought, catching a glimpse of the tall, slender figure in the mirror. And ever since she had grown up her unusual looks had attracted far more attention from the opposite sex than she'd wanted or encouraged—and because of it a name she hadn't even earned.

Stepping into the shower, Magenta thought reluctantly of how her mother's reputation hadn't helped. With no father, and no knowledge of any, she recalled that she'd had a string of 'uncles' who had drifted in and out of her young life. Her mother had been unable to maintain a steady relationship with any man. One disastrous affair after another had led to her seeking solace by drinking too much, and it had been her daughter who had always borne the brunt of it. Add the stigma of her birth poverty, because Jeanette James had never been able to work, and Magenta's schooldays had been hard—both at home and in the classroom. Somehow she had never quite fit in with her classmates, and consequently had never made friends easily. For that reason she had grown up wanting to rise above the situation she was in. And because of her face and figure—both accidents of birth—a modelling career had seemed the only way to do it.

Her physical attributes together with her background, however, had caused men to expect more from her, Magenta thought bitterly, than she'd been prepared to give. But she had resisted them all until...

By instinct alone she knew that there had only ever been one man who had set her body on fire, and that man was Andreas Visconti. But everything he had said to her today—and the other night in the wine bar—implied the contrary. For some reason he truly believed that she had had some sort of sexual liaison with Marcus Rushford....

As she lathered soap over her body a picture of a room and then a whole apartment rose before her mind's eyes. A coldly furnished, expensive apartment. Marcus's! she realised, shocked. She had been staying there. No, not staying. *Living* there, she thought, shaking her head to induce more of the same troubling recollections. But try as she did her memory refused to oblige. Whatever it was that still remained buried, she knew that it fell within a definite period. And that was the nine or ten months prior to the day just over five years ago when her mother had woken up unusually early and found her collapsed on the bathroom floor.

Her cell phone was ringing just as she was stepping out of the shower, and Magenta raced over and snatched it off the windowsill.

'Hello, darling.' Emotion welled up inside her until she thought her heart would burst just from hearing her little son's voice.

'Aunt Josie asked me to ask you if you got the job.'

Of course. She'd talked of nothing else for weeks, she reflected, shrugging into her robe and thinking of the better life she had told Theo she'd be able to give him if she was lucky enough to get through the interview—of the new football boots and the *Thomas the Tank Engine* duvet cover she had promised him.

She shuddered as she thought of how—almost—she had had no job at all, and wondered how she would have coped if Andreas had blocked her chances of working for his company altogether. If he hadn't gone on to offer her the temporary position she had finally agreed to take.

'Tell Aunt Josie I didn't take that one because I got an even better one.' She tried to sound excited, although she didn't know what could be *better* about securing a job that put her immediately under a man who had no reservations about showing how much he despised her. Except the money...

Selling herself to the highest bidder.

She shivered, wondering if by agreeing to work for him she wouldn't be playing right into Andreas's hands.

She had to take this job—she didn't have any choice. Even if she was still dangerously and unbelievably attracted to him, and even though he was displaying a ruthless desire to get even with her.

But was he going to use her vulnerability and her attraction to him to do it? she wondered, with a contrary mix of apprehension and excitement. Everything about him had suggested he intended to when she had been in his office today. If he was, she thought, she only hoped she would be strong enough emotionally to resist him. At least taking this job might help to restore her memory—even if she had a deep-rooted anxiety inside about what remembering might reveal....

Andreas had arranged to pick Magenta up the following Monday morning, and he noticed the curtains twitch in an upstairs window as he pulled up outside a characterless nineteen-seventies semi-detached house which, from the two doorbells beside the rather jaded-looking front door, had obviously been converted into two flats.

Magenta was locking the inner door to the ground-floor flat before he had even made it to the crookedly hung gate, and just the sight of her produced a swift sharp kick to his groin.

She was wearing her hair down this morning. Its rich, dark lustre reminded him of how it had felt to run his fingers through it, and he noticed how much it emphasised the porcelain-like texture of her skin. With that hair, those thick black lashes and those dark eyes she had a look that was almost as continental as his own ancestry. But it was that kissable pouting mouth that today she'd enhanced with a subtle pink lip cream that was doing untold things to his libido, and he had to force his gaze down. That didn't improve matters, because then all he could think about was the beautiful slim body underneath the black pencil skirt and tailored jacket of which he knew every delicious and delectable inch.

'Keen to make a good impression, Magenta?' His reluctant awareness of her forced him to say it, but he was irritated at the power she still had to affect him physically as he leaned against the long, low-slung silver Mercedes, watching her approach.

'No. I just don't like to keep anyone waiting.'

It was a cool, unflustered response. Remarkably unflustered, he noted, opening the passenger door for her.

'Thanks.'

She didn't meet his eyes as she said it—probably because she'd had to pass so close to him, he decided. Close enough for him to catch the subtle yet sensuous perfume she was wearing.

Not so unflustered, he thought smugly, noticing the quickened rise of her breasts beneath her pale grey camisole, as well as the nervous little movement of her throat. A silver-set ebony pendant lay against its pulsing hollow, attached to the silver torque she wore around her neck today.

He wondered at this fascination she had with scarves and chokers and accessories. She'd always worn things like that with reluctance when she'd been going somewhere special, or her outfit had demanded it, and she'd always ripped them off as soon as he'd taken her home, proclaiming that jewellery of any kind made her feel cluttered. It was with tantalising decorum, he remembered, that whenever they were alone she'd always waited for *him* to remove her clothes.

'I thought I would have the chance of meeting your son this morning,' he expressed after he had put the car in motion. His voice was slightly hoarse from the direction his thoughts had taken. She'd told him only that she had adequate childcare when he had challenged her about it the other day; when he had reminded her that they were only just at the start of the school summer holiday.

She was stealing covert little glances around the interior of his car, as though she couldn't quite believe how successful he had become.

'No. He's away for two weeks.'

'With your mother?' He couldn't think of a less suitable candidate to look after a five-year-old child, and thought it was probably for the best that the boy's father didn't know about it. Had *he* been in the man's shoes, he couldn't help thinking grimly, he would have taken immediate steps to do something about it. 'How is she, by the way?'

She spared him a glance that seemed to challenge why he was asking. There had been no love lost between Jeanette James and his family ever since the day the woman had come into the restaurant, the worse for drink, to accuse his grandmother of spreading gossip about Magenta. She had probably guessed he was only asking because protocol demanded it.

'She's fine—and she's living with her partner in Portugal,' she told him sketchily, deciding not to enlarge upon how much better her mother seemed since meeting a man who had kept her on the right road after coming round to paint her flat three years ago. 'Theo's gone away for a couple of weeks with my great-aunt to her stepdaughter's in Devon. They've got sons a similar age to Theo.'

'I didn't know you had a great-aunt.' He was slowing down to let another car out of a side turning, but he sent a questioning glance at her when he sensed her hesitation in answering.

'Just because I didn't mention her, it doesn't mean she didn't exist,' she said as he brought the car back up to speed again.

'Do I take it she's your mother's aunt?'

'That would be the most natural assumption, since I don't have the first idea who my father was.'

And that was something that had always chafed, he reflected, picking up on the familiar defensive note in her voice.

'So she's more like a grandmother?'

'Yes.'

'And naturally she's getting on in years?'

'Meaning...?'

Her dark eyes were challenging again, and he wished he

had been able to contain his criticism. But it was too late. All he could do was continue along the same track.

'Meaning is it really fair to expect someone of her age to take on the responsibility for your child? Especially one so young? Has she had children of her own? Any experience in looking after infants?'

'She should,' she returned tartly, 'she brought him up for the first—' She cut short whatever it was she had been about to say.

'For the first what, Magenta?' he asked, slicing a steel-hard glance across the air-conditioned space that separated them. 'Just how long did you stand by and allow someone else to bring up your child?'

She was sitting staring out of the windscreen, looking tense and rigid, with her pale pink nails almost digging into the soft leather bag she was clutching on her lap.

Had she really put her career before her baby? A muscle twitched in his clenched jaw as he gave his attention to the road again. If so, what was it that had finally made her stop? He wasn't even sure he wanted to know.

'Where are we going?'

For the first time since she had got into his car, bowled over again by how well he had done for himself and by that air of authority he wore as effortlessly as he wore those dark executive clothes, Magenta realised that he wasn't taking her to his office. Distractedly she'd noticed the sign for the only route they should have taken well over a couple of miles back, and now he'd crossed over into the lane that would take them to the motorway.

'I'm taking you back to the house because there are things in my diary I need to go over with you.'

'The house?' *His* house? Magenta swallowed, wondering exactly where he lived. Before she knew it she was blurting out, 'Over my dead body.'

'You're my PA. You do as I instruct. Or weren't you aware that that was one of the conditions of your employment?'

His sarcasm rankled, but Magenta bit her tongue to stop humiliating herself still further. Whatever they had been, she thought, he was now her boss and she was just his employee. There was no getting away from the fact.

'Aye aye, sir,' she snapped, still riled by how he had automatically assumed that she had let her mother—of all people!—raise Theo while she...what? Pursued a glamorous career? Or did he imagine she'd whiled away her time in some rich man's paradise?

She knew he already had a low opinion of her. What she couldn't take was him—or anyone—thinking that she was an uncaring mother as well.

Her pride kept her from telling him how wrong he was, and why she hadn't been able to look after her own baby—share in his upbringing—for the first few months of his life. If he wanted to think the worst about her, then let him, she decided resignedly. He didn't know anything about her—least of all that Theo was his. That same surfacing fear reinforced her decision not to take a chance on telling him. If he wanted to hurt her, for whatever reason he was harbouring in his mind, then that would give him all the ammunition he needed. And if his derogatory comments today about Theo's care were anything to go by, she had no doubt he would do everything in his power to take her son away from her.

The gates through which the car had swung revealed a mansion of breath-catching style. A modern white house in Georgian design, with clean lines and perfect symmetry, its wide arched doorway was centre-set within an abundance of long, multi-paned windows, and its drive gave on to manicured lawns and grounds that meandered away to the woods. Magenta even glimpsed a tennis court towards one side of the house.

'This is…yours?' She knew she sounded awestruck, but she couldn't help it. She had already realised he'd become rich. The company and the car had told her that much. But she hadn't fully realised until now just how rich he was.

'Not bad for a lad who was never going to amount to anything, mmm?'

Was that what she had said? Knowing herself as she did, she couldn't believe she ever could have, but from the way he had said it, and that self-satisfied look on his face as he came around the bonnet to where she stood, dumbfounded by his beautiful house, she obviously must have.

'And you're obviously enjoying rubbing it in.' If it was true, then it would be no more than she deserved, Magenta accepted, wondering just how long he intended to make her eat humble pie.

'Come on.'

His arm was fleeting across her shoulders, but surprisingly Magenta felt the loss of it with a keenness that made her almost ache as he brought her across the pale shingle of the drive. As she walked with him her senses were awakening to the familiarity of his stride, the way his body moved beside hers, the intonations of his voice, and she felt herself responding to them with an ease that was as stimulating as it was scary.

He opened the impressive front door and let her into his home. It was a house filled with light and space, exclusive furnishings and fine art. In the wide reception hall and in the sumptuously furnished drawing room into which he showed her fine silverware on polished surfaces threw back reflections of the sunny morning through the floor-to-ceiling windows. A display of old-fashioned amber roses graced a crystal vase in the centre of a Regency table, their scent so sweet it seemed to permeate every inch of air space in the luxurious room.

'They're my favourite flowers.'

Images rushed up in her, so vivid she had to grasp the tall back of one of the richly upholstered chairs to try and steady herself. Each deep breath she took was filling her lungs with the heady, evocative perfume… Andreas giving her roses… amber roses from his grandmother's flowerbed…

She glanced up and saw him watching her. His eyes were smouldering with a dark intensity that had her looking quickly away, her gaze skittering over a couple of original-looking oil paintings on the wall to the huge windows and the breathtaking view of the eternal grounds beyond.

'Feel free to look around.' Some deep and private emotion seemed to colour his voice. 'I know you're longing to. '

But not as much as he was enjoying being able to show her!

'Bastard!' She didn't know why the invective escaped her, except that it spilled from a well of pent-up frustration with his attitude, from remembering so much and then hitting a blank wall whenever she tried to push her thoughts too far.

'Why?' If his home had made her speechless, then his eyes were holding her spellbound as he moved with the stealth of a stalking cat across the pastel-tinted Turkish carpet that graced the pale oak floor. 'For refusing to stay in the lowly situation you clearly saw me in? For having the gall to claw my way to the top?'

'I can't image you clawing your way out of anywhere, Andreas. Fighting, maybe—metaphorically speaking. Or slaying anyone who stood in your way.'

He laughed that soft laugh that seemed to ring alarm bells in Magenta. But then he reached out and gently tilted her chin with his finger.

For a moment, with his penetrating eyes probing the wary depths of hers, silence seemed to wrap them in some sort of sensual bubble. She was aware of a clock ticking quietly on the white marble mantelpiece, the poignant scent of the roses, and Andreas's steady breathing that seemed to mock the rapidity of her own.

Her breath seemed to stand still as his fingers trailed lightly down her throat, but then his fingers curled around the open-backed torque and gently tugged at the clinging silver, bringing Magenta's hand slamming down over his.

'Take it off,' he ordered softly.

'No.'

'Six years ago I wouldn't have needed to ask.'

'Six years ago we were different people.' They must have been, otherwise how would she have found the nerve to take him on? she wondered. Let alone try and cross him— humiliate him? And if everything he had intimated was true then that was what she had done.

'Really?' An elevated eyebrow assured her that he didn't believe it. 'Do people really change that much?'

No longer trying to rid her of her necklace, his fingers were now playing along the sensitive skin beneath the heavy curtain of her hair, his touch so light that Magenta's lids came down against the exquisite yet dangerously stirring action. She could feel his eyes on her face—glacial eyes, reflecting a chilling satisfaction because he knew how he was affecting her.

Now, with her eyes flickering open, and in response to what he had just said about people changing, she was startled to hear herself utter a simple yet heartfelt, 'You have.'

'Yes, well…' he breathed, just as his cell phone started to ring.

He turned away, taking his phone out of his pocket and answering his caller with brisk efficiency, as though Magenta were the last thing on his mind.

However she remembered him being before, he was cold and cynical now, and she listened to him speak with growing amazement at the authority he wielded. He would command respect, she realised, from the office cleaner right up to his peers at top executive level. Yet she knew instinctively that he would offer them respect in turn.

And because of what had happened in that lift the other day he obviously had no respect for *her* whatsoever, believing she was easy. Believing she was still the same girl who had…what? Left him for some other man?

She was standing by the window when he finished speaking on the phone, re-energising her spirits with the peace and serenity of the sunny gardens. There were a couple of willows beyond the lawns, their graceful boughs overhanging what had to be a narrow body of water winding its way through his property. Closer to hand, the tennis court looked inviting enough to make her want to play. Across the terrace, which swept down and wrapped itself around the other side of the house, she glimpsed a pool area, half hidden by trees, its clear blue water sparkling beneath the glittering sky.

'Andreas…' she began, tensing at the soft sound of his approach over the luxurious carpet. 'Just because I—I was stupid enough to—to get carried away in that lift the other day, don't—' She was losing the fluency of her speech, just as she had in the early days during and after her spell in hospital, and she gritted her teeth, her fingers clenched like curled claws sinking painfully into her palms. *Dear Heaven! Don't let me fall apart now!*

'Don't what?' he enquired, his face a mask of questioning complexity.

'Don't think I'm easy.'

He uttered one of those low, sexy laughs, his brows drawing together as his gaze slid downwards.

Surprising her, he caught her hand and dragged it up, unfolding her tight, tense fingers. His hooded eyes took in the red half-moons her nails had left in the soft flesh and she caught her breath as he suddenly dipped his head and pressed his lips to the angry marks.

'I promise you I won't do anything you don't want me to do,' he murmured, his breath warm and recklessly exciting against her palm. 'Now, let's get to work.'

He was the CEO again, speaking to her as he would to any employee—as he had to that caller on the phone—confident in the knowledge that he only had to touch her to make her want him to do all sorts of things to her. Because she had shown him he could....

She somehow knew she had never been able to control the way her body responded to him, and simply prayed that she was mature enough now to be able to resist his devastating masculinity—just as he appeared to be able to resist her. Otherwise where would she and Theo be, if circumstances made it impossible for her to stay on and work for him and she found herself having to give up this job?

His study was at the other end of the huge house, and as well equipped as any modern office. A smaller room right next to it was fitted with filing cabinets and a desk where his PA could work. Both rooms enjoyed a fuller aspect of the poolside.

Magenta spent the morning going through his diary with him, rearranging and confirming meetings over the telephone, and generally tidying up files and correspondence.

'What made you so sure you were right in your assumption about my...circumstances?' she challenged, albeit hesitantly, as she was nibbling a biscuit with her coffee. It had been brought in by a middle-aged housekeeper who had smiled warmly at Magenta while maintaining an air of detachment that respected her employer's privacy. 'I could have asked for that letter simply because...well, because I had my eye on some luxurious and exciting new place to live.'

From behind his desk he gave her a look that suggested she wouldn't have been working as she had been if she'd had that much money to throw around. 'I always make it my business to learn as much as I can about anyone I'm intending to have working closely with me.'

'So you intended it? Even before I got to that final interview?'

Jacketless, his tie loosened beneath his opened collar, he was picking up his mug, his fingers long and tanned around the pale glaze. 'As I said, I never leave anything to chance.'

'Did you know on that Friday? When we bumped into each other in the wine bar?'

He made a rather cynical sound down his nostrils. 'I didn't have a clue. Not until I noticed your name on the shortlist on Monday morning.

'So how did you get the low-down on my situation? Through extra-sensory perception?'

He finished his coffee, looking composed and relaxed as he laid his mug aside. 'Even I can't claim to have *that* particular gift at my disposal.'

'How, then?' she demanded as she swallowed the last of her biscuit. Inside she was feeling exposed and vulnerable, and she was wishing that he wasn't doing funny things to her just by sitting there looking so disgustingly handsome.

'It isn't important.' He sat back on his chair. 'Only that you're here.'

'It is. That information was confidential.' She dumped her mug down on his desk. 'Whoever told you, they had absolutely no right!'

'Maybe not,' he drawled laconically. 'But I've found that in this world anyone will tell you anything if you make it worth their while. Your landlord's agents being no exception.'

'Bribe them, you mean?'

He chuckled low in his throat. 'You *do* have a low opinion of me,' he drawled.

Magenta surveyed him with narrowed eyes, her head tilting slightly. 'No lower than your opinion of me. So what did you do? Ring them and ask what the situation was on the flat that's got the "To Let" sign outside?'

He didn't answer as he stretched out his arms, flexing his fingers before cupping them behind his head.

'You're unscrupulous,' she breathed.

'And you aren't?'

For wanting a career? She didn't say it, although she knew instinctively that it was something to do with that, and it was a long moment after his rather scathing remark before she spoke again.

'Whatever I did that you think was so bad, I was nineteen,' she reminded him, thinking about asking him to spell it out for her, but deciding to bluff her way around it instead. 'And, despite what you said, people *do* change.'

'In that case I'm looking forward to a very enlightening few months,' he said.

There was definitely something different about Magenta, Andreas thought, watching from the window and waiting with growing impatience for his caller to ring off so that he could go out into the garden and join her.

She'd gone outside after finishing the tea and sandwiches his housekeeper had sent in, telling him she needed some fresh air. Now, as he watched her looking up at a kestrel that was gliding over the garden, he realised that she had the power to fascinate him as she was fascinated by that bird. She was drawing him in with her dangerous attraction even more strongly than she had in the past. But something had changed...

For a girl who was once very conscious of the way she looked, always retouching her make-up and absently playing with her thick, lustrous hair, she seemed remarkably oblivious to her femininity. She seemed more reserved too than the effervescent nineteen-year-old who had gone a long way to destroying his faith in her sex. Then there was that hesitancy he noticed when she was speaking sometimes, as though she wasn't too sure of herself—although he was certain that it wasn't through a lack of confidence.

Listening to her speaking to his colleagues and clients

over the phone this morning, he had been impressed with her charm and her efficiency. But there was something about her. Something he couldn't quite put his finger on...

His call took too long and she was already in the hall by the time he was able to join her.

'My grandmother,' he informed her, noticing her interest in the small oval framed oil painting hanging above one of the Georgian tables. 'As a young woman.'

'She was very beautiful.'

'Yes.'

'Is she still—?' She broke off, as though deciding it was too imprudent to ask.

'No,' he informed her. 'She died last year in Italy, without a day's illness, after a very long and active eighty-nine years.'

The eyes that met his were dark and guarded. 'I'm sorry— and about your father too.'

'Yes.' He exhaled deeply as he said it. 'So am I.'

'What happened?' she asked, sounding as tentative as her eyes were wary.

'A heart attack.'

'When?'

'Six years ago.'

'Six years...' He saw her velvety brows come together. 'When you were in America?'

'Before I left,' he told her succinctly.

What he didn't add was that it had been only hours after she'd been round to see him and they had parted for the final time. Or that they had been arguing because of *her*. The remorse and regret he carried because of it were constant companions deep within him, along with the scouring knowledge that if he had listened to his father the man would probably still be alive today.

Her frown was deepening and she started to say something else, but he cut across her. 'Let's have done with the reminiscing, shall we?' he said abruptly.

* * *

'I'm going to be working at home for the next week or so,' Andreas told her as he brought the Mercedes to a standstill outside her flat that evening. 'And as you don't have your own transport—' he had already learned that she didn't own a car '—I think it would be far more convenient if you stayed there too.'

About to get out of the car, Magenta viewed him with disbelief. 'You didn't say anything about staying under your roof when I agreed to take this job.'

Clicking on the handbrake, he turned off the engine before swivelling round on his seat to face her. 'Well, I'm saying it now. I've got several meetings, all based within a twenty-mile radius on the wrong side of the office, and I'm afraid I'm going to need you with me for at least two of them. Those are the terms.'

'Does your usual PA—or any of your other staff,' she tagged on, thinking of the obviously smitten Lana Barley-thorne, 'always bow to your command and move in with you whenever you snap your fingers?'

'I'm hardly snapping my fingers, so don't go convincing yourself you have no choice in the matter,' he advised, effectively taking her down a peg. 'And I think you need reminding that you aren't my regular PA—or any other loyal and long-standing member of my workforce.' His tone implied that she was never likely to be. 'So stop making a fuss, pack a bag, and I'll pick you up at eight tomorrow morning. After all, you told me your son's away, so it isn't as though there's anyone you have to get back for. Or is there?' he enquired, with curiosity suddenly underlying the cynicism in his voice.

'I don't really think that's any of your concern,' Magenta retaliated, and immediately wished she hadn't. If he hadn't offered her this extremely well-paid position then she and Theo would have been out on the street at the end of next month.

'Will there be anything else?' She almost added, *sir,* but decided that might be pushing things a little too far.

'Yes. It's promising to be a sizzling week ahead, so bring a swimsuit,' he instructed, causing Magenta's stomach to flip as she stepped out of the car.

Somehow, she thought, letting herself in through the rickety metal gate, she didn't think he was just talking about the weather.

CHAPTER FOUR

A CHAUFFEUR-DRIVEN car arrived for Magenta at eight o'clock sharp the following morning. A long, dark saloon with tinted windows. She knew it would start the neighbours speculating, even without the dark uniformed man who rang her bell.

'Mr Visconti has an early appointment and won't be around until later, but I'm to take you to the house and see that you're settled in before he gets in.'

'Thank you,' Magenta said, stepping through the back passenger door with a little pang of misgiving. This was certainly some way to travel. But she was beginning to feel more like some rich man's mistress than a temporary personal assistant, and with a little tingle of something she didn't want to question too fully she considered that that was probably exactly what Andreas was intending her to feel.

The privacy panel was up and, grateful for it, Magenta wasted no time in ringing her great-aunt's cell phone. It was Theo who answered, just as she'd hoped he would.

'Hello, darling.' She was missing him dreadfully and told him so, without revealing just how much. His childhood was to be enjoyed, not dogged by adult worries and problems as her own had been. 'You'll never believe the car Mummy's sitting in,' she enthused brightly and, knowing his passion for anything with wheels, went on to tell him all about it.

'Be careful, my girl,' Aunt Josie warned when she took

over the conversation and Magenta told her that she was going
to be working at her new boss's home for the next few days.
'I know you said you knew him years ago, but—well…he's
still a man…and a very good-looking and eligible one from
what you've told me about him.'

'You don't have to worry about me, Aunt Josie,' Magenta
assured her, in a way in which she couldn't reassure herself. She could visualise her mother's aunt, her iron-grey hair
slightly ruffled, wearing her 'Home is where the Hearth is'
apron, which Magenta had bought last Christmas and which
she was never without, even when she went to visit her stepdaughter. 'You've done enough of that over the past five years.
Besides, I'm perfectly able to take care of myself nowadays.'

'I still worry,' her great-aunt replied. 'Especially when my
favourite girl is involved with a man who's rich and no doubt
charming enough to get anything he wants.'

Warmed by her motherly concern, Magenta laughed—
although a crease was deepening between her eyes. She'd
told Aunt Josie about knowing Andreas before when she'd
informed her that she had got the job. She had been too fazed,
however, by those almost debilitating snatches of memory
and the equally weakening battle to try and make sense of
images and fragments of conversation that still continued to
elude her to tell her anything else. Nor was she prepared yet,
with one of his staff within earshot—even if he might not be
able to hear her through the transparent screen and above his
softly playing radio—to let anyone who didn't have to know
in on the fact that she and Andreas had been lovers. She didn't
want to risk anyone sharing in her humiliation when he cast
her off, as she knew he would sooner or later, whether he'd
settled the score he felt he had to settle or not.

The suite of rooms she was shown into when she arrived
at Andreas's mansion was, like the rest of the place, luxuriously furnished, with deep-piled Turkish rugs, designer

fabrics gracing the expansive bed and long, multi-paned windows. The bathroom, with its pale, exquisitely tiled floor and matching walls, displayed a huge, free-standing bathtub and a gleaming white suite in Italian marble that promised to pamper her with the highest level of indulgence.

The bedroom had three deep windowsills where she could sit and look out onto the grounds and acres of sprawling countryside beyond. The air coming in through the window where Magenta had paused to take in the view was heavy with the scent of a climbing red rose, overlaid with the occasional hint of wild honeysuckle.

She could have sat there all day, but she knew she couldn't linger long and went down to the study. Andreas wasn't back yet, so she went through to the smaller office and immersed herself in her work, tidying up files and handling any correspondence she could deal with in his absence.

She was just winding up a conversation with a local councillor who was clarifying a question about building regulations within the site of a new hotel when Andreas walked in.

'How long have you been here? Since three this morning?'

He looked genuinely impressed as he came over and flipped through the tray of letters and copy e-mails she had printed off for posting or filing, his gaze taking in the pile of orderly files that were ready to be put away. It gave her a ridiculously warm glow inside.

'Just doing my job,' she murmured, swivelling round on her chair and whipping another page of perfectly typed, perfectly worded text out of the printing tray, trying not to let her pleasure show.

'In that case I think you've done enough for one morning. It's twenty-seven degrees out there and it's nearly lunchtime. Time, I think, to fit in a pre-lunch swim.'

'If it's all the same to you, I'd rather finish this e-mail,' Magenta answered, trying to ignore her body's response to Andreas in his short-sleeved white shirt, tie and light grey hip-hugging trousers, even though she knew she was fighting a losing battle. His scent alone—a heady blend of pine coupled with warm, masculine skin—was working on her senses and making her far too aware of herself. And of him.

'The e-mail can wait,' he advised, in a tone that was quietly impatient. 'Go and change. Or didn't you do as I suggested yesterday and bring a swimsuit?'

'I did what I felt comfortable doing,' Magenta told him pointedly, letting him know from the outset that she wasn't going to be bullied or browbeaten into doing anything she wasn't happy with. That over with, she tagged on, 'Yes, I brought a swimsuit.'

'Then will you be my guest, Miss James...' his dark head tilting, he all but bowed '...and kindly consent to join me in the pool?'

'Don't overdo it.' His excessive attempt at courtesy lent her mouth a wry twist as she pushed herself to her feet and started towards the door.

'And Magenta?'

She glanced back over her shoulder, her hair a rich ebony curtain against her face.

'Get rid of the scarf.'

It was only a whisper of cream gossamer silk, which she had worn to complement her bronze collarless blouse and cream suit, but it was obviously irritating him immensely.

'Get rid of it,' he said softly. 'Otherwise I really will be obliged to remove it myself.'

The suggestion of his touching her, in any way whatsoever, sent a throb of tension pulsing along her veins. It had been second nature once to have him undress her. She remembered that much—and vividly. Now, though, the excitement generated by the thought of letting him was overlaid with an almost sickening fear. Fear of her vulnerability. Of knowing that if she did she would be playing right into his hands. Fear of his seeing the marks on her body that would give rise to a lot of questions, and fear that in a weak moment she might even tell him the truth about Theo.

And if she did that…

She had survived a lot, but she didn't think she would survive if he took her son away from her, and the only way to ensure that he didn't was to remain immune. He didn't like her, and therefore it was imperative that she resisted whatever plan of seduction he might be carefully mapping out for her, she thought, as she pulled on her swimsuit in front of the pearly wardrobes that filled a whole wall of the luxurious dressing area annexed to her bedroom. But as she caught a glimpse of herself in one of the floor-to-ceiling mirrors she could see the way her body was betraying her in the flush across her pale cheeks and in the pink burgeoning peaks of her small breasts.

Andreas was already in the pool when Magenta came down. Chest-deep in water, his face upturned to the sun, he was leaning with his bronzed arms outstretched on the warm marble tiles behind him. His eyes were closed and yet he sensed her presence as tangibly as the sun that was caressing his face and the warm breeze that brought with it the evocative scent of his favourite honeysuckle. Lazily, his eyelids drifted apart.

He had seen her naked before, so it wasn't as if there were any surprises in seeing her scantily dressed. But the years hadn't tempered his hot-blooded desire for her. He had realised that in the wine bar, and again in the lift, when he'd been unable to contain how she made him feel. But never had he wanted her more than he wanted her at this minute, when she was wearing the most demure and yet the sexiest swimsuit his fevered brain could ever have imagined.

Virginal white, it encased her throat in a collar of see-through mesh that extended down across the upper swell of her breasts and continued in a tantalising 'V' which finished just below their silken valley. The stretch fabric of the garment emphasised her still-small waist and slender hips, and the legs were high and cut away, revealing her beautiful lean thighs and shapely calves. Add to that the stark contrast of her hair, which she'd swept up in a loose twist of ebony, and the rather moody, come-hither pout of her lovely mouth, and he was glad that most of his body was under water, so that she wouldn't realise the effect her appearance was having on him.

'Well? Are you going to join me or not?' His voice sounded husky, even to his own ears, but she seemed as tense as he was and didn't seem to notice. Or she was pretending not to, he decided with a wry smile.

The ripple of the water as she slid down off the poolside caressed him in a way that was wholly sensual.

'I see you haven't lost your touch,' he remarked, watching the easy glide of her breaststroke and thinking how gracefully she moved through the water.

'Did you expect me to?' She didn't even turn her head to look at him as she glided effortlessly past.

'With you I learnt a long time ago never to expect anything,' he assured her.

'Anything?'

'Except disappointment and—'

'And what, Andreas?' She kept on swimming. 'Heartache?'

'Heartache?' His laugh seemed almost to taint the peace and beauty of the perfect day as he started swimming after her. 'Nothing so sentimental. I was going to say desire.'

'Desire?' She'd swum over to the side of the pool and now grabbed the tiled edge, using it to propel herself round to face him.

'Sex, if you want it in its most basic definition.'

'I don't.'

'Why not?' A faster, stronger swimmer than she was, he was level with her now. 'Are you going to try and deny that you weren't as hot for me as I was for you? Even more so, if that were possible, judging by your insatiable appetite when you were in my arms.'

The slap that she had itched to administer to that hard cheek the other day now found its target with stinging precision. She heard it and regretted it the instant she saw the water from her errant hand running down his face.

'So you prefer to play rough these days, do you?' he rasped, and the darkening of his eyes promised retribution, sending her front-crawling away from him like a hunted fish.

Andreas's laughter held no warmth as he sliced after her through the clear blue water, catching her easily and curbing her futile attempt to climb out.

'No!'

It was an anguished little sound, strung with panic and something else—something that called to his most primal instincts and sent his testosterone rocketing sky-high. Her eyes were wary yet bright with the same excitement that was driving him as he pulled her round to face him, but the depth of tortured emotion he saw in her face was his total undoing.

'Why did you pretend not to remember me when you saw me in that wine bar, Magenta? What was it you were hoping to gain?'

'Nothing. *Nothing*,' she emphasised, bluffing. 'I was just hoping you would go away.'

'Go away?' He made a derisory sound through his nostrils. 'Did it repel you to speak to me that much?'

Water ran into her eyes and distractedly she brushed it away. Then, standing on tiptoe, she reached up and gently pressed her lips to the spot where her hand had struck him. And that was a mistake, she realised, when he dipped his head and claimed her mouth with his, leaving her rejoicing in her folly as his arms tightened mercilessly around her.

She should stop this madness!

Magenta heard the warning bells clanging away inside her

but took no heed of them as Andreas's mouth became harder and more insistent.

She wanted this! She screamed it silently, in spite of herself, as her body moulded itself of its own accord to the hard planes and angles of his. That physical part of her *knew* him and was recognising its mate, acknowledging him as the other half of a whole that had formed the most fundamental bond, the half that had planted its fertile seed in her willing womb. And she could tell how much he wanted *her*.

His lips and hands were rediscovering her body and she welcomed them like a long lost-part of herself. She had been born to do this with this man, and to know his hands as completely as she knew her own. To carry on his DNA in the shape of her little boy and to be forever lost—her senses only half alive—without the stimulating possession of his kisses.

'How do you get this thing off?'

He was breathing raggedly as he tugged at the restraining fastener at the nape of her neck. One slip of the clasp and he would have her naked in his arms. His to do whatever he wanted with. And she wouldn't have the willpower to resist him. Only the thought of Theo and the resurfacing fear of losing him had her pulling out of those tormenting arms.

'*You* don't!'

With an immense effort of will she struck out for the side of the pool, only the thought of her son keeping her going, and she could already feel the sun-warmed tiles beneath her bare feet by the time Andreas had caught up with her.

'What is it with you, Magenta? Exactly what sort of game do you think you're playing?' The sun was reflecting off his wet, near-naked body like burnished gold.

'No...game.' It was a struggle suddenly even to say that much, and she put a shaky hand to her throbbing head.

'Do you get some warped kick out of turning men on and then switching off the instant you think you've got them hooked, like you did with me first time round? Is that what you did to Rushford? Is it? Is that why he couldn't take any more?'

She knew nothing was further from the truth. How could it be? she agonised. Suddenly she was flinging at Andreas, 'Oh, forget him, will you?'

One side of his mouth lifted in a less than friendly gesture. 'I wish I could. But I'm sorry, darling. Bad memories do tend to die hard.'

Then you should be like me! Magenta screamed silently. *With only half of them intact. See how much you'd like it!*

'And you haven't answered my question. Did you treat him the same way, even though you were pregnant with his child?'

The glare of the sun on the water seemed to be acting like a laser on her tortured head. She heard a deep groan and only realised it came from her own lips a moment before the vibrant pink and greens of the foliage around the poolside splintered into a thousand pieces and she saw indigo tiles rushing up to meet her.

When she opened her eyes she was lying on a bed.

Andreas's bed! she realised at once, from the collection of very masculine furnishings within her sight.

She sat up quickly. Too quickly, she decided, flopping down again when her head swam sickeningly in protest.

'Take it easy.' Andreas's voice above her right shoulder was deep and steadying. It was the only steady thing in the wavering room. 'You passed out and I thought it best to get you inside. How do you feel?'

'Lousy,' Magenta admitted with a grimace, too weak and unbalanced at that moment to try and prevaricate. She was still in her sodden swimsuit, but he had wrapped a towelling robe around her. *His* robe, she realised as things began to settle down. There was the recognisable scent of his cologne clinging to it, along with more elusive traces of his own personal scent. 'It must have been the sun.'

'Possibly, but not very likely.' His sensual mouth pulled

down at one corner. 'Staying up too late, maybe? Or perhaps you just haven't been taking care of yourself properly.'

'What—what do you mean?'

Damn! She wasn't going through a set-back after all these years, was she? she thought in despair, sitting up again, but much more carefully this time. It had taken her months of hard work and effort to perfect her speech in the long battle to reconstruct her life again.

'What are you saying?' She studied him fully now, and wished she hadn't when the sight of him sitting there on the bed in a grey striped silk robe that did little to hide his flagrant masculinity caused a different sort of throbbing in her. 'When her son's away, Magenta will play?' she misquoted. What did he imagine she was doing every night? Having a whale of a time, painting the town bright pink?

'What I meant was that from the way you felt when I carried you up here—like a wisp of nothing—I'd say that you haven't been eating properly.'

'Oh…' she uttered, feeling suitably chastised.

But she didn't tell Andreas that he was right. That lately she had had to be so frugal with her own diet in order to make sure her son had enough to eat that sometimes she'd wound up skipping meals altogether. She hadn't been sleeping properly either, ever since she'd met up with Andreas again, and when she did eventually manage to drop off she was plagued by troubling images that had her waking up trembling and perspiring, struggling to make sense of her disturbing dreams.

'You're just so hunky that any woman would seem light to you,' she parried, trying not to think of how devastating he had looked with his bronze and muscular body all wet and glistening when he'd chased after her out of the pool. 'Besides, I've been a model. I've never quite managed to adopt the desire to over-eat.'

'That's all going to change while you're working for me,' he remonstrated, his hand suddenly palming the curve of a rather too-slender shoulder, where the robe had slipped down, too voluminous for her slim frame.

'You're going to fatten me up?' Her voice sounded squeaky now, but for a different reason. She ached to lean in to his massaging hand. 'Is that another condition of my employment? To put *on* "all those unwanted pounds"?' She dropped her voice as she said it, as if she was advertising some new-fangled slimming product, trying to ignore his casual but very disturbing touch.

'Very necessary pounds,' he corrected. 'I'm not having you passing out on me again at the drop of a hat.'

'That's probably unlikely too, as neither of us wears one,' she quipped, trying to make light of the situation.

She needed to say something to distract her from those lusciously dark-lashed eyes that were using the subject of her weight to examine her with disconcerting thoroughness. His thick black hair was still damp from his swim and she had to stem the almost irresistible urge to run her fingers through it.

'I'm making your bed all wet.' Her voice was husky, and she sounded breathless. But the robe she was wearing was soaking up the water from her swimsuit and it couldn't be doing much for his duvet.

'It wouldn't be the first time,' he said wryly.

Colour touched her cheeks at the significance of what he meant.

'Could I have a shower?'

Thick black brows drew together. 'Are you sure you're up to it?'

She wasn't sure she was, but she needed to get away from him—and fast! 'I think so.'

'Go on, then,' he conceded, getting to his feet so that she could get up off the bed. But as she started towards the door he put a restraining hand on her shoulder. 'No,' he said firmly. 'You'll go in there.' He gestured towards the *en suite* bathroom on the other side of his room. 'That way I can keep an eye on you, just in case you feel inclined to faint on me again.'

Sitting on the bed while she showered and listening to the water cascading down over her lovely body was torture to Andreas, but he was too concerned about her to take himself off to shower in one of the guest bathrooms after what had happened.

But *why* had it happened? The question started up a train of thought that ran away with him as he considered her situation. His colleague had said she'd sounded quite desperate when she'd mistakenly thought she'd been given the job and had asked for that letter for her landlord. Why had things become so difficult for her?

If she'd been modelling since she'd had her son—as she'd implied when she'd accidentally let slip about the child being brought up by her mother's aunt—she would have been earning good money, so where had it all gone? Why was she in such dire straits now?

Her mother had been—and for all he knew still was— totally alcohol-dependent. Could Magenta have gone down the same road? Been swept up in a spiral of parties and social drinking as it was easy to do in the so-called glamorous circles she moved in? Was that why she had claimed not to drink when he had taken her up to his office? Not because of what she'd seen it do to her mother, but because she was in danger of getting hooked on the stuff herself?

Not liking the turn his thoughts were taking, Andreas got up and started pacing the room.

She had driven him nearly insane with her tender femininity in the past. But she had thrown his crazy feelings for her right back in his face. And since then—who knew? What sort of company or practices had she got herself involved with since? She was a woman men couldn't resist. Men and even women—the much older, motherly type—had sometimes stopped him in the street when he had been with her just to congratulate him or comment upon how lovely she was. He'd never experienced anything like it before or since. It had made him feel like a million dollars, knowing how much other men envied him, knowing how much they wanted her when she was his—all his. Except she hadn't been, he reflected, his jaw clenching almost painfully. She wasn't and never had been *his*.

With a sick possessiveness ripping through him he wondered how many men had held her—caressed her—lost themselves in that glorious femininity just as he had—since she had walked out of his life. How many had been made to feel like the only man left in the universe as she'd wrapped those long silky legs around him and fed his ego with her soft impassioned cries? He wondered if he wasn't inviting a whole heap of trouble down on himself by giving her this job, just because he hadn't been able to resist having her under his roof, when he was in danger of being drawn in by her dangerous femininity as hopelessly as he had been six years ago.

He had worked himself into a foul mood and, picking up the phone by the bed, he started dialling a number to try and immerse himself in his work, try and calm himself down.

She was a vamp, a witch, he thought, feeling his body hardening instantly. The sound of water running in the shower had ceased and he glanced towards the bathroom door, aware that she'd be stepping out now, that she'd be towelling herself dry. So what was stopping him from going in there? Dragging the admission from her—even without touching her—that she wanted him as much as he wanted her? He had always been able to arouse her with words in the past so why didn't he just do it? Give in to the promise of sublime ecstasy and instigate what they both wanted? To wind up in that bed together. The duvet was still damply creased with the imprint of her body, and Andreas had to take several deep breaths to engage all his powers of control.

He wouldn't do it because he was much too honourable to behave like that with a woman. Even a tease who lured men into her web of unbelievable ecstasy and then dumped them when it was time to move on to something more profitable.

He was deep in conversation with the manager of one of his American hotels when Magenta emerged from the bathroom. She'd slipped her arms inside the robe, belted it around her tiny waist, and with the collar pulled up to meet the damp loosened tendrils around her face she looked enveloped by it, so small and waif-like, and yet lovely and desirable.

He made a silent gesture for her to stay when she would have moved past him and then tried not to focus on her, because the thought of her warm nakedness beneath his robe was distracting him and his aching libido beyond belief.

Browsing along his bookshelves, while trying to ignore what the deep timbre of his voice was doing to her, Magenta was impressed by the diversity of his reading material.

There were beautiful gold-leafed, leatherbound volumes of an encyclopaedia, travel books—particularly ones about Italy—several biographies—mainly of business and political figures—and a whole host of general literature about looking after the planet, the world's wildlife, as well as the world's most prized hotels.

Had he read a lot six years ago? She wasn't sure.

'I didn't know you were partial to poetry,' she murmured when she heard the phone slip back onto its rest. Her head tilting, she noted Lord Byron's name on a comparatively small and dilapidated-looking little book. 'He's my favourite of all the romantic poets.'

'Really?' Andreas's voice sounded strange, and he was looking at her rather oddly. 'You could have fooled me.'

She couldn't fail to pick up on the sarcasm behind his remark. 'You think because I didn't have as good an upbringing as you that I can't appreciate good poetry when I read it?'

she uttered, wondering why he'd even say such a thing. 'We had to study him at school, which is where I developed my taste for romanticism, but this edition's beautiful and so...' *Old,* she was going to say. So old, in fact, that the spine was broken. She reached up to take it down. 'Why don't you have it rebound?'

'Leave it!'

His stern command split the air like the crack of gunshot, freezing her fingers against the dark green suede cover.

'I was only going to look at it,' she told him, defending her actions. 'I wasn't going to...damage it.' Not any more than it was already damaged, she thought, with a pained little crease between her eyes. The throbbing in her head that had been so debilitating earlier was threatening to return again. 'I was just curious to see if I could find my favourite poem.'

'And what is that?'

His tone was clipped and his eyes were coldly questioning— as hard and questioning as the lines that were now corrugating his high forehead.

'I don't know what it's called. It's the poem he wrote to the one woman people say he truly loved.' Funny that she could remember that, Magenta mused, when she had forgotten other, far more important things about her own life. 'I can't...' She put a hand to her head. 'I can't bring the first line of it to mind right now.'

'Try.'

Magenta looked at him quickly, wondering why his voice was so lethally low, and why the glimmer of concern he had shown her before her shower had vanished, to be replaced by what she could only describe as a hard and chilling detachment.

'I don't know...' It was a test she had to pass—for herself as well as Andreas. 'Something about destiny...'

Words and images seemed to be swimming around in a

fog so thick that she couldn't latch onto anything that made sense in her mind.

And then through it Andreas's voice came, like a guiding light through the haze. *"'Though the day of my destiny's over, And the star of my fate hath declined.'"*

That was it! Like someone hypnotised Magenta continued, without taking her eyes off his. *"'Thy soft heart refused to discover, The faults which so many could find...'"*

Her words tailed off, emotion clogging her throat. Had Andreas's heart ever been soft? Yet his eyes were darkening with such an intensity of emotion that it seemed to reach out and touch her. Because, of course, he *had* refused to see the faults in her personality, she remembered startlingly. Even when other people, his family in particular, had condemned her, he had still believed in her, trusted her. Though she knew without any uncertainty, and without even knowing why, that he had condemned her too—in the end.

The emotion was so acute in her chest that she thought she would cry out from the pain of it.

'I need to get dressed.' She struggled to speak in a small, strangled voice, and stumbled away from him before he could make some comment that she couldn't have borne.

He was on the phone, and seemed to wind up the call rather abruptly when he heard her coming into the study, Magenta thought later. He instantly started scribbling something down on a paper pad.

'Why don't you use your iPad?' she suggested rather lamely, feeling awkward and saying the first thing that came into her head because of that tense little episode upstairs earlier.

He didn't even glance up as she spoke, but carried on scribbling with his fine gold pen. 'That's why I'm paying you.'

Of course. He was her boss now, and he was pulling no punches in reminding her of that fact.

'I instructed Mrs Cox to prepare you a light but nutritious lunch,' he went on, with a more than studied glance in her direction now, as she gathered up various forms and other relevant papers she needed from his desk. 'Did she do that?'

Still tense, and smarting from his unnecessary comment a moment ago, she said stiffly, 'Would you rap her over the knuckles and send her packing if I said she didn't?'

In fact she had been given a poached salmon salad with some freshly baked wholemeal bread, a substantial slice of home-made apple pie and cream, and fresh fruit to follow— all which she had devoured with relish. Except the fresh fruit, which she had kept for later.

'Unlike you, my housekeeper doesn't seem to feel the need to oppose me at every given opportunity,' he remarked, his mouth tugging at one corner. 'I would have taken you out to lunch, or at the very least joined you, but in the circumstances I didn't think it would be a good idea.'

He meant because of that moment of weakness which had come over him—over them both—up there in his bedroom earlier. But now he had steeled himself against it—against her—and he couldn't have appeared more controlled and un-affected by her if he had tried.

'No it wouldn't have been,' she said woodenly, pretending to agree with him although she was hurting inside, tormented by the mental pictures that had been plaguing her ever since her shower. *After all, you wouldn't want to risk your reputation by getting too chummy with someone like me!*

He started to say something else, but then the phone on his desk began to ring and he snatched it up.

'Visconti,' he answered, with unusual impatience.

It sounded serious, she thought, closing a file and listening to the tone of his voice, his few clipped responses.

'I've got to go out,' he stated as soon as he had replaced the receiver. Getting up, he grabbed his jacket from the back of his chair. 'I don't know what time I'll be back, so have any calls you can't deal with personally redirected to my voice mail.'

And with that he was gone.

Left alone, Magenta waited for the sound of the Mercedes engine to die away. Then, with the stealth of a fugitive, glancing back every now and then over her shoulder, she crept swiftly and silently back upstairs to the master suite.

Going across to the bookshelf, she took down the little suede-covered volume of Byron's poems. Her hand was shaking so much she could hardly turn back the cover. But even before the inscription in that long, flowing hand leaped out at her she knew what it was going to say.

For my Magi—with all my love, Andreas

Her hand flew to her mouth to stifle a shuddering gasp. How could she have forgotten that he had given it to her? He had addressed it to Magi too, and she suddenly remembered him saying it, pronouncing the *g* like the softest *j,* with all the sensuality of his ancestors' native tongue. *My Magi...*

She didn't know why, but she found she was crying silently. And then all at once she knew the reason for it, and for that sense of loss in those dreams that had been troubling her over the past few nights. It was because of a lost love. Andreas's love.

CHAPTER FIVE

ANDREAS'S FACE WAS grim as he stepped out of his marketing manager's office—as grim as it had been when he'd ended that call from her assistant back at the house.

'She's had a late reference in for that girl you took on,' Lana Barleythorne had told him when she had telephoned. 'Magenta James, wasn't it? It seems she's been deliberately holding out on us, and Frances says that there's something about her you should know. She hasn't said what it is—has only intimated that it could be something that might make you want to reconsider your decision to have her working for you.'

He hadn't failed to detect that little note of triumph with which the young woman had said it. He knew Lana had an almost embarrassing crush on him, and he hadn't forgotten how miffed she had seemed when he'd pulled rank on her and the others at Magenta's interview the other day and taken matters right out of their hands.

'She probably hasn't rung you herself yet because she's been tied up in a meeting, but I know she wanted to see you as soon as you came in.'

He had driven like a demon up to the office afterwards, wondering what was so serious that his marketing manager couldn't even share it with her assistant. He'd been wondering about a lot of things. Like the way Magenta had changed. And the way she'd been behaving since their reunion. Like those bouts of selective amnesia she seemed to fake when their conversation turned a little bit uncomfortable. Like the way she'd casually pointed out that poetry book to him today. She'd acted as though she'd never seen it, let alone had any knowledge of the ugly scene it had caused between them. She'd even commented upon its condition, as though she didn't remember exactly how it had got into that state. As though she hadn't a clue!

He had planned to quiz her about it over lunch, but when he'd felt her weaving her dangerous spell around him after she'd come out of the shower he'd needed an hour or so's breathing space, had thrown himself into a working lunch instead. He'd planned to get the truth from her in his office that afternoon, but just as he'd been about to Lana's call had come through....

Now, as he drove back through the building rush-hour on the busy motorway, with the car's air-conditioning system on full to counteract the heat of the day, he sat grim-faced, going over all the things he'd wondered about and the things he now knew.

He'd begun to suspect that if Magenta's memory lapses weren't faked then she must have embarked on the same route to destructive self-indulgence as her mother after she'd walked out of his life. That the problem had to be alcohol-related...or something worse....

His foot hit the brake pedal, averting a near collision with the car in front, which had suddenly changed lanes without warning, nearly taking off his front bumper. With a hard decisiveness he threw on his indicator switch and pulled out round the offending vehicle, giving himself a clear run ahead.

He'd been certain he was right. In fact by the time he'd reached his London office he had been convinced of it, he remembered scathingly, as the big car gobbled up the miles, bringing him ever closer to her. But what his colleague had told him in the privacy of that office had made him sick to his gut, chilling him to the bone. Never in a thousand years could he have suspected what he now knew.

Magenta had stumbled upon the little wooden seat purely by accident. It was situated between the willows and a little stone footbridge spanning a brook, tucked out of sight of the house behind a trellis of wild honeysuckle.

A lovers' seat, she decided. And could no more resist sitting down than she could resist pulling her gypsy-style white blouse off her shoulders and tilting her face to the sun as she soaked up the scent of the flowers and the sound of the brook, the tangible warmth of the late-summer afternoon.

The tranquillity was like balm to the thoughts that had been troubling her ever since Andreas had left and she had crept upstairs to take a proper look at that book.

How could she have forgotten that he had given it to her? she wondered as she waved a rather inquisitive bee away from her hair. It was a special edition that he had bought for her, knowing how much she liked Byron's poetry, and he must have struggled to find the money for it on his meagre salary. But why had he not reminded her of it? Not said *something?* Because surely he must have thought it odd? And what was it doing on his bookshelf, and in such a broken state, when he had clearly meant *her* to have it?

Willing herself to fill in the gaps, she finally gave up and with a sigh of defeat decided to return to the house.

Her heart gave a wild leap as she came out from behind the trellis and almost collided with Andreas.

Tieless, as it had been when he had left the house earlier, his white short-sleeved shirt was half unbuttoned now. His light grey suit jacket was slung casually over one shoulder, and Magenta couldn't help but notice how the superb cut of his trousers emphasised his tight, lean waist and the flat stomach that was testimony to his punishing daily workouts in the pool.

'Magenta.'

She could detect an odd quality to his voice above the gurgling of the brook, even in the way he spoke her name.

'I saw Mrs Cox coming out of the house and she told me I'd probably find you here.'

There was a stark look about his face that released a little dart of unease in her. However, with a broad sweep of her arms, she uttered, 'Well, here I am!'

The movement brought that ice-blue gaze down over her bare, softly tanned shoulders and a crease appeared between the masculine eyebrows as his eyes came to rest on the little scar at the base of her throat.

Magenta wished she'd worn something to hide it. That she hadn't left it to chance to get back inside the house unseen in her overwhelming need to feel free of any jewellery or other encumbrances.

Her throat worked nervously as she asked, 'Did you have a successful meeting?' She had presumed it was a meeting. Why else would he have shot off the way he had if something urgent hadn't cropped up?

'*Very* successful,' he emphasised. 'And fruitful.'

So why didn't he look happier? she wondered. He looked hot and dishevelled, as though he had been battling with every juggernaut that had dared to use his stretch of the motorway, and from the creases in his trousers he had been sitting in his car for a long time. Nevertheless, that didn't stop him from looking utterly desirable. So desirable that she had to look away, so that he wouldn't guess at the sudden tightening of her breasts and the almost-painful throb beneath the stretchy material of her dusky-pink cropped leggings.

'Why didn't you tell me you had suffered a cerebral haemorrhage?'

Magenta looked at him, startled, swallowing to ease the sudden dryness in her throat. 'You didn't ask.'

'I'm asking you now.'

When she didn't answer at once, he said with mounting impatience, 'Weren't we close enough in the past? Did you think it didn't matter, not bothering to acquaint me with that fact?'

Magenta looked at him askance, wishing he didn't look quite so amazing. 'Perhaps I didn't want you thinking I was inviting any false sympathy from you.'

Incredulity leapt in his eyes, and now she could see how pale his skin looked despite being bathed by the early evening sun.

'You really put me down as being that indifferent?' He tossed his jacket down on the seat. 'And thought that I wouldn't feel as shocked and rebuffed by your omission as I feel after finding out, as I have now?'

'Why?' Why did it matter to him? she thought. 'Why would it even concern you? Unless you think it's likely to affect the way I do my job?'

'Don't put words in my mouth,' he advised.

His tone assured her he was in no mood for accusations or evasion tactics. Nevertheless she had to ask, 'Could I ask who told you?'

'One of the referees whose name you gave us. It seems he thought you were a remarkably efficient and pleasant-mannered receptionist at his legal practice, but he wondered if, because of the odd bout of things slipping your memory after what you'd suffered, you'd be capable of handling the position of a full-blown PA.'

'Well, of all the nerve...' Frustrated tears burned the backs of Magenta's eyes. 'The only thing I ever forgot was to jot down his dental appointment! And I misplaced a file once or twice. But everybody does that! And he *knew* my memory loss was only confined to things that happened for a spell immediately prior to...what happened to me,' she finished hesitantly, as though she didn't want to spell it out.

'So why didn't you mention it when you were interviewed by my colleagues?' Andreas enquired. 'Or at least tell me?'

'For that very reason,' Magenta admitted with a grimace. 'When people find out I've had a brain haemorrhage they tend to treat me as though I'm somehow inadequate. Less of a human being. They can't seem to help it. During the first couple of years after it happened I had to rely on total strangers to help me understand how to use a cash machine, or ask them to walk into the supermarket with me because I didn't have the confidence to try and find the entrance on my own. Some would help, but others would veer off as fast as they could—like I was an imbecile, or a danger to them or something. It was no use telling them that I'd once been as *normal* as they considered themselves to be, and that what happened to me could happen to anyone, regardless of age or nationality or intelligence.

'Some of that discrimination hasn't ended, even though I'm managing to raise a son, am back to jogging three miles round the block twice a week and have got myself a distinction in Business Studies. I found out that telling prospective employers about what had happened to me wasn't going to get me the sort of job that would pay the bills. In fact quite the reverse. You'd be surprised how many interviewers who seemed disposed to take me on suddenly turned off as soon as I explained why there was such a gap in my working life. By the time I got an interview with your company I'd already decided I wasn't going to mention it any more. It was easier just to say I'd taken a break because I was bringing up my son.

'But, yes, I had a cerebral haemorrhage. And, yes, it affected me drastically. I mean *all* my physical and some of my mental abilities for a while. But I was determined to recover. *Really* recover. I've been told I'm one of the lucky ones who do. So now you know the truth you can exercise the right I'm sure you must have as an employer and fire me for taking this job under false pretences.'

'What I'm going to do,' he said, in a lowered tone that

nevertheless revealed how shocked he still was, 'is sit down here...'

Pushing his jacket aside, his imperious hand was pulling her with him down onto the lovers' seat.

'And you're going to tell me everything. Everything you've omitted to tell me since I saw you in that wine bar. That is everything you can remember,' he appended, when they were sitting together beneath the creamy-pink flowers of the climbing honeysuckle. 'When did it happen. exactly?'

The colour was returning to the hard bronze of his skin, but he was still looking grim. Magenta wondered if it was anger at being kept in the dark over something so important or genuine concern for her that was responsible for the deepening lines around his eyes and mouth.

'Soon after we...' *After we broke up.* She couldn't say it. Even though she knew that that was when it had been.

'What?'

She flinched at Andreas's shocked incredulity as he guessed what it was she had been about to say.

'How soon after?'

One bared shoulder lifted almost imperceptibly. 'A matter of months.'

'Months?' He was looking increasingly shocked, the furrow between his thick black brows deepening. 'Then you didn't ever have a modelling career?'

'Not really.' She feigned a little laugh. 'I know. Ironic, isn't it?' she said, and thought, *Especially when you practically accused me of neglecting my son because of it.*

'Were you still with Rushford?' he pressed, choosing to ignore her last remark. 'Is that the real reason he left you?'

She shook her head. 'We weren't together.' *And we never had been. Not like that,* she thought. She was certain of it, but she didn't tell Andreas any of that, as that would make things too complicated.

'I was with Mum, but she couldn't handle it—especially

with the doctors having to deliver Theo while I was still in a coma.'

'You were in a *coma?*'

She nodded.

'While you were pregnant?'

Magenta could almost see his brain working overtime.

'He must have been very premature.'

'He was.'

But not by as much as he was probably thinking, she decided. She couldn't tell him that her baby had been delivered a mere three weeks early, because then he might put two and two together and guess the boy was his. And although she knew she should tell him she couldn't summon up the courage to do it. She was too fearful of what he might say—and, even worse, try to do. Besides, she thought, as a further means of justifying her actions in keeping the knowledge of Theo's paternity from Andreas, he had suffered quite enough shocks for one day without adding any more.

'Anyway, Mum sent an SOS to Great-Aunt Josie. She and Mum hadn't been talking for as long as I could remember. I think Josie had dared to voice her opinion about Mum's drinking when I was quite small and Mum had told her she wasn't welcome in our lives any more. I know I missed her. Despite my memory problem—' she pulled a self-deprecating face '—I hadn't forgotten that. She came like a shot, to take Theo off Mum's hands and look after him until I was able to start doing it for myself. And she took care of me as well, when I was able to come home from the hospital.'

'A very special lady,' Andreas commented.

'Yes, she is.' Just the thought of her great-aunt's kindness filled her dark eyes with tears.

'And you made it,' he remarked, smiling, his voice sounding oddly thickened.

'Yes, I made it.' *Even if* we *didn't,* she thought, with such an unexpected ache beneath her ribcage that she had to look away, breathing in the air that was heavily impregnated with the sweet scent of the honeysuckle until the moment passed.

'So you weren't kidding when you pretended...? Correction. When I thought you were pretending not to remember me, were you?' he asked unnecessarily. 'And today...when you went to pick up that book....'

She shook her head in confirmation.

'Do you really not remember what happened?'

She closed her eyes and shook her head. *Don't tell me, please,* she begged silently. She was becoming more and more convinced that she wouldn't like what the truth might reveal.

'Magenta.' He had slipped a hand under her hair, his touch so tender that involuntarily she turned her cheek into the stirring warmth of his palm. 'Magenta, look at me.' His voice was as gentle as his fingers.

Don't be kind, her mind pleaded with him. *I can't bear it if you're kind!*

He was only taking pity on her because of what he had just discovered, she realised, opening her eyes to a flash of scintillating colour as a kingfisher dived low over the brook. Its bright blue and orange plumage was almost fluorescent as it took off again with its glistening prize.

'However much your mind blanked me out, your body didn't, did it?' Andreas whispered, his mouth moving gently along the soft line of her jaw. 'You still remember this.' His lips were feather-light against the corner of her mouth. 'And this.' His mouth was but a hair's breadth above hers, teasing, toying with her, but not actually consummating the kiss.

She had forgotten Andreas's capacity for tenderness, but she remembered it now, feeling a surge of excruciating need building in her as his fingers played lightly along the smooth, yearning line of her throat.

A soft moan trembled on the air and she realised that it had come from her. She had no more defence against his particular brand of lovemaking than that little fish in the stream had had against its determined captor, she thought. But she didn't want to defend herself, or to resist him.

Knowing she was lost, she let her head drop back, her hair tumbling over his arm like a dark waterfall, while his thumb played over the small throbbing hollow at the base of her throat.

'Was this part of that time?' he breathed in a ragged whisper, bending his head again to press his lips against the jagged little white scar.

She nodded, reminded of the treatments and the surgery she had undergone to help her breathe—just to keep her alive—when the doctors had told her mother and her aunt that she probably wasn't going to make it. Against all the odds she had, and it had given her a different outlook—a totally new perspective—on life. But all that was a world away from this man, and this evening, and the scented warmth of these exquisite moments. She didn't want to dwell on anything that would spoil it for her.

When his mouth came down over hers she gave herself up to its demands, drowning beneath the kisses he had withheld. He was tugging her blouse down over her shoulders and she wriggled to get her arms free, bringing them up around his neck and clinging to him as though only his warm strength would sustain her.

As his hand closed over her breast and moulded her soft warmth to his palm, Andreas gave a deep groan of satisfaction.

Motherhood had made her breasts fuller, he noted appreciatively, letting his lips pursue the same path as his massaging hand. He heard her sharp gasp as his mouth closed over one dark-tipped nipple, and he smiled as he lifted his head to look at her.

She was lying across his arm with her eyes closed in total abandonment to her senses, the gentle curve of her forehead lined in rapturous agony, her long dark lashes splayed thickly against her cheeks. She was as enslaved by what he was doing to her as she had ever been, he realised gratifyingly, his hand measuring every soft curve and dip of the body that he knew so well and had long ago initiated as his.

He had mentally beaten himself up all the way back from his office because of what he had been thinking about her over the past few days. He had been ready to condemn her for a lifestyle of self-indulgence and self-seeking gratification when all the time she had undergone the worst physical, mental and emotional trauma it was possible for anyone to go through.

He had bellowed at his colleague when she'd asked if he thought Magenta was suitable to fill his PA's shoes, when really he had been bellowing at Magenta for not telling him— and at himself for the detrimental thoughts he had harboured about her.

He regretted them now with every shred of humanity he had in him, and although he had assured himself that he would never allow himself to get emotionally involved with her again, right at this moment he couldn't stop what was happening between them even if he wanted to.

'Let's go inside,' he whispered.

Those three little words broke through Magenta's sensual torpor, shocking her into realising what she was allowing to happen.

She was only here because he wanted to satisfy some warped sense of injustice. To get her to surrender to his mind-blowing ability to turn her on as no other man had ever turned her on. Really he had very little respect for her at all, and he would still despise her tomorrow.

'No...' It was a breathless protest as she struggled to sit up.

'What's wrong?' His face was a compilation of bewildered lines.

'I just don't want to do this...' Her own features were

pained, yet still flushed with the desire that had nearly allowed her to fling all her hard-won self-respect and dignity to the winds. But at least he allowed her her freedom.

'You could have fooled me.' He was looking at her as though she had just pulled a rug from under his feet. There were wings of colour across his cheeks and his eyelids were still heavy from the strength of his desire.

'I'm sorry. I got carried away. I thought I could, but I can't. We might have had something going six years ago,' she forced herself to say, with her agitated hands dealing with her blouse. 'But we both know it was purely sexual. At least it was for me.' It was taking all of her mental strength to reinforce what she had convinced him of—tried to convince herself of—all those years ago. 'And I don't go in for those kind of relationships any more.'

'How very commendable of you,' he said cynically.

'No, just realistic,' she corrected. 'A lot has happened since then. I have responsibilities now, and they have to come first.' Even though her body was still on fire from his love-play, and the thought of where that love-play could lead was driving her insane with wanting. 'I know it probably isn't the reason you gave me this job, but if you still want me working for you then we're going to have to keep things purely on a business level.'

A faintly mocking smile touched his mouth as he got up and stood looking down into her tense, rebellious features. 'You really think we can?'

The heaving muscles beneath his shirt assured her of just how much she affected him. His lids were heavy with the weight of his desire for her and there were slashes of deep colour infusing the taut skin across his cheeks.

He was right, Magenta thought. How was it ever going to be possible when their mutual chemistry was like two magnetic fields that splintered all reasoning and the most basic instincts of self-preservation, resisting anything in the way of their powerful and destructive collision?

But she had to resist whatever it was that made her so physically in tune with this man. Because if she allowed herself to get too close to him she would unequivocally wind up getting hurt. And, worse than that, on the way to her own self-imposed heartache she'd feel duty-bound to tell him the truth about her son. And if she did that, and he tried to hurt her by taking Theo away from her, she would never be able to bear it. No pain in the universe could ever be greater than that.

'I resisted death,' she reminded him, ignoring the way her body still ached for his touch. She had to drag herself away from him, and with her voice cracking from the effort as she started to move away she added hastily over her shoulder, 'It'll be a doddle resisting you.'

CHAPTER SIX

'IS THERE ANYTHING else you aren't telling me?' Andreas enquired from behind his desk the following morning.

'Like what?' Magenta responded, jolted out of her wild speculation as to what it might have been like if she'd wound up in bed with him yesterday to face his unexpected and startling question.

A broad shoulder lifted beneath an immaculate jacket. 'You tell me.'

The way Magenta's heart was racing was making her legs go weak. 'N-nothing you need to know,' she told him, slipping a folder back into its alphabetical place in the tall metal filing cabinet. Had he noticed the way her voice was shaking? She sincerely hoped he hadn't.

'Magenta, look at me,' he commanded softly.

He had said the same thing in the garden yesterday and it had nearly been her undoing. Nevertheless, after pushing the drawer closed on its runners, she did as he had asked.

'I think we should do something to help your memory,' he said, surprising her, because that wasn't what she had been expecting at all.

Her sidelong glance at him was wary. 'What do you have in mind?'

'Nothing specific.' He put down the pen with which he'd

been idly tapping his fingers. 'And certainly nothing like you're imagining.'

'You don't know what I'm imagining,' she countered, her mouth going dry.

'Don't I?'

He rose to his feet and came around the desk, starting warning bells clanging in Magenta's head.

He was going out this morning and was dressed to kill, and she couldn't keep her eyes off the superb lean lines of his physique, enhanced by the equally superb cut of a light beige suit.

'I told you last night,' she reminded him, thinking back to the conversation they had had over dinner, after that disconcerting episode in the garden. 'It's only specific things I don't seem to remember now, and even they are coming back...gradually.'

'Even so,' he maintained, 'I'd like my doctor to take a look at you. He's quite a specialist in the field of psychology.'

'You think my problem's psychological rather than physical?' she suggested, rather sceptically.

Andreas shrugged in a way that suggested he was keeping an open mind.

'I don't need a doctor,' Magenta argued. 'I've seen enough doctors to last me a lifetime and they've all said the same thing. That anything I haven't retrieved might not come back at all. If it's going to, then I have to be patient. That's all. As I said, things *have* started coming back....'

'That's good. But it isn't only your loss of memory that concerns me. You haven't been eating properly. You're passing out—'

'I passed out *once!*' she reminded him emphatically.

'Nevertheless, I think you've come close to it on more than one occasion, and it could happen again. Anywhere. Any time. On the underground. Walking downstairs. When you're crossing the street. And next time it could be when you're on your own.'

'No, it couldn't.'

'Oh?' He was frowning down at her from his superior height, an authoritative figure, in command of himself and everything around him. In fact everything she wasn't—or didn't feel as if she was just at that moment. 'What makes you so sure?'

Because it's only when I'm with you that I'm affected so drastically!

'Would you let me take you to see him?' he pressed, taking her last comment as a further obstruction to what he was suggesting. 'I've already checked and he has a free appointment late this afternoon.'

'If it makes you happy.' She conceded defeated. 'And only if it's a condition of my employment.'

The trace of a smile touched his lips. 'It is.'

So that was that, Magenta thought. Decision made.

'I told you it wasn't necessary,' she said, when they were walking down the tree-lined drive of the doctor's clinic much later that afternoon. Naturally it had been a private consultation, which had probably cost Andreas the earth.

'If you call being diagnosed with a clean bill of health— apart from a bit of expert advice on looking after yourself— unnecessary,' Andreas answered, his mouth pulling in a grimace as he handed her into the car, 'then I have to disagree with you.'

'Because now you know I'm fit enough to work for you, and you don't have to worry too much about curbing your need to have a go at me for my past misdemeanours whenever you feel like it. Is that it?'

'Right on both counts,' he agreed with a twitching of his mouth, before the passenger door clicked softly closed, securing her in his car's silent bubble of tasteful opulence.

Watching him moving around the gleaming bonnet, his commanding and superbly clad physique marking him as a man who was as rich and successful as the car he drove suggested, Magenta had the strongest suspicion that he wasn't talking about either of those things at all.

The next couple of days passed in a sort of fragile, unacknowledged truce.

Despite what he had said Andreas seemed to be going easy on her now that he had found out exactly what she had been through, and Magenta didn't feel the need to oppose or contradict him at the least opportunity.

On the other hand he wasn't actually doing anything to try and boost her memory either. Perhaps, she considered, he was doing as his doctor and all the other doctors she had seen since her collapse had advised, and allowing things to return naturally. Or perhaps he just wanted to dismiss that whole period of his life as too insignificant to waste any more time on, as he had been more than ready to assure her it was on more than one occasion.

She berated herself for the little twinge of pain she experienced just from thinking that might be the case, and forced herself to concentrate on her work.

Working alongside him, however, revealed just how dynamic a businessman he was as he plunged into his punishing work schedule with a driving energy that left Magenta breathless.

In turn she was kept busy herself—on the telephone, typing letters and conference notes, and generally being his right hand when he took her with him to his various meetings. It was harder and more challenging than any job she had done in her life, but she was delighted when she found herself rising to the challenge. She was even more delighted when he praised her ability.

She was convinced, though, that he was only going easy

on her because of what he had learned about her. For all her speculation about him wanting to forget the past she didn't doubt that her sexual capitulation was still on his mind, even if his need to verbally flay her had been tempered by what he now knew. He was still a healthy, virile man, who had made no qualms about wanting a woman who had once been unable to stop herself from showing just how much she wanted him. She only hoped that she could finish this assignment and leave with her pride intact before he called her bluff. Before he showed her that she *couldn't* resist his particular brand of persuasion, as she had so adamantly and stupidly dared to claim to be able to in the garden the other day, and she wound up exactly where he wanted her to be. Back in his bed.

And, because of the way her insides turned to mush every time he walked into a room where she happened to be, it wasn't just a case of *if* any more, but *when*.

'How are you getting on working in your rich man's mansion?' Aunt Josie asked matter-of-factly the following afternoon. 'Andreas, isn't it?'

Andreas had popped out for an hour, and Magenta had seen Mrs Cox leaving in her car for town with one of the maids at lunchtime. Consequently Magenta hadn't been able to resist telephoning her aunt to see how Theo was.

'He's rich, but he isn't mine,' she corrected, with an attempted little laugh.

'But you'd like him to be, wouldn't you?'

'What makes you say that?' Magenta asked, taken aback by the directness of the woman's question.

'I'm your great-aunt, yet you mean as much to me as if you were my own daughter. What is it, love? Something's bothering you, and it isn't just a hankering for a rich boss who sounds a bit too attractive for his own good.'

Steeling herself, Magenta said, 'I had a fling with him once. That's what's wrong. It was six years ago, and all mixed up in that period of my life that was wiped out after my brain haemorrhage. His doctor said I might have blanked it out subconsciously.'

'*His* doctor?' Josie Ashton noted. 'That sounds like this Andreas is a man with a mission.'

'Perhaps,' Magenta murmured, unable to explain to her aunt just what she thought Andreas Visconti's mission might be. 'But apparently his doctor's a bit of a specialist in the field. Anyway, things *are* coming back—although I still can't remember everything about what happened between Andreas and me. From things he's said, I don't think it ended very amicably, but one thing I do know...' Magenta hesitated, inhaling deeply before she went on to impart, 'Theo's *his,* Aunt Josie.'

There was a long pause at the end of the line before the disembodied voice replied, 'I guessed as much.'

'What do you mean?' Magenta asked. Her aunt was continuing to surprise her. 'How could you? Even Mum didn't know. I mean...she thought...she said...'

'She said that during the time you'd obviously conceived, which was just before that part of your life you've never been able to remember, you'd had several purely casual boyfriends.'

Magenta cringed at how she had ever allowed herself to be convinced of that, although her mother obviously believed it to be true.

'I know.' Josie Ashton let out a sigh. 'I've suspected that it was Andreas somebody-or-other for a long time—though your mother was under the impression he was no one special even when I raised the question with her as long ago as when you were in that hospital. But to me there's nothing casual about a man whose name is on a woman's lips when she's still drugged up, floating in and out of a coma.'

'Why didn't you ever say anything?' Magenta queried, amazed that she could even have spoken his name when, after regaining full consciousness, she hadn't remembered a thing about him until that night he'd walked into that bar.

'I did. Once or twice. After you came back to live with me when you came out of hospital. But you seemed to deny all knowledge of him, so I gave up asking after a while.'

And she probably didn't remember *that,* Magenta thought, because she'd been in a kind of daze, with her body still repairing itself, at the time.

'Have you told him?

Josie meant about Theo being Andrea's son.

'No.'

'But you're going to?'

It was more than a question coming down the line.

'I can't, Aunt Josie. Not yet.'

'Why ever not?' The woman's tone was incredulous. 'Doesn't the man have a right to know that he's fathered a child? Doesn't Theo have the right to know who his father is?'

'Of course he does. But I have to do it in my own time.' She could hear her son's eager little voice in the background, begging his aunt to let him have the phone. 'You won't say anything to him, will you?' Magenta begged, panicking. 'You won't tell him? Not until I can?' There was an almost desperate edge to her voice now. 'Promise you won't.'

'Of course I shan't tell him,' Aunt Josie placated her.

'What won't you tell me?' The little boy had obviously scrambled up on to the woman's lap, as he did with Magenta sometimes when she was on the phone, and was trying to reach the mouthpiece. 'What won't she tell me, Mummy?'

'Nothing, poppet.' Magenta's voice became gently protective. 'Now, more importantly, what have you been doing? Did you go riding this morning, as you said you were going to?'

It was with a suppressed sigh of relief that Magenta realised the little boy had forgotten all about his aunt's conversation with his mother, and was giving her a breathless account of how the little Shetland pony that the local farmer had said he could ride had been lame.

'Oh, darling, there'll be another time,' she consoled, hearing the disappointment in his voice. 'When you come home Mummy will see what she can do about sending you for lessons.'

A movement by the door brought her head whipping round. Andreas was leaning against the doorframe, listening to every word she was uttering!

'How—how long have you been standing there?' She sounded almost as breathless as the five-year-old she had forgotten about for a few seconds. 'Look, darling, I have to go. Mummy will call you later. Say bye-bye to Aunt Josie for me.'

She'd tossed down her phone before Andreas had had time to move.

'Why so jumpy?' He smiled as he moved away from the door. 'Do you think I'm the type of boss who's likely to extract payment for personal calls in office hours?'

When she didn't answer immediately, too disconcerted by just how much he might have heard, he came closer.

'Of course if that's what you were hoping…'

She didn't know how it happened, but suddenly he was leaning over her behind her chair, with one arm across her breasts, unleashing a riot of betraying sensations inside her as she felt his lips against the nape of her neck.

'Do you usually get your kicks out of listening in on other people's private conversations?' Her breath was coming raggedly and causing her breasts to rise with exquisite torture against his dark sleeve.

'Why? Were you saying something I wasn't supposed to hear?' He was lifting the collar of her white silky blouse away from her neck—devoid of any scarf today—and gently fanning the pale exposed skin with his breath.

Magenta visibly shuddered from the sensuous tingles that were running down her spine. 'Of course not.'

'Are you sure?'

Dear heaven! What was he saying? Doing to her?

She gave a soft moan as he dragged his hand across her burgeoning breasts.

'Have you ever wondered what it would be like to make love on a desk, Magenta? Or perhaps you've already tried it?'

'No, I haven't!' The fear of what he might have heard her saying was being replaced by another insidious fear, and that was being unable to resist giving in to this almost overwhelming and terrifying desire to succumb to him. 'Mrs Cox may come in.'

'Mrs Cox is off duty.' Long fingers deftly slipped the first button of her blouse.

'One of the maids, then.'

'Both off duty.' A smile laced his voice as he pushed the pale slippery fabric he'd loosened down over one silken shoulder. 'Isn't this making you remember? We almost made love on a table once, but unfortunately our…intentions were rather impeded.'

'*Your* intentions you probably mean.' It was a breathless accusation, and one threaded through with shuddering desire as his teeth grazed with arousing skill along her shoulder.

'Oh, no.' He laughed low in his throat. 'I never did anything without a willing accomplice. Don't you want to remember, Magenta, how sexy I said you looked draped in nothing but that tablecloth?'

The tablecloth! Slashes of colour rose before her eyes, but then the jumble of vivid images took very definite shape. It was red and white chequered linen, and its starched coarseness was an unbelievable turn-on against her painfully aroused breasts.

'You were afraid of being caught even then doing something you knew you shouldn't.'

She pressed her hands flat against her ears. 'I don't want to remember!' Her statement was one of negation and rising panic.

'Oh, I think you do.' He came around her chair, positioning

himself on the desk, so close that his bent knee was touching her arm. With a gentle firmness he pulled her hands down. 'A grabbed hour's privacy. We were desperate for each other. It was a Monday night and the restaurant was closed. We thought we were alone.'

But someone had come back... Magenta put her hand to her temple. 'Oh, dear heaven!' she groaned.

She could still hear the key in the lock—the door opening. Then voices—Giuseppe Visconti and a woman. Maria Visconti! It had been dark and they hadn't seen her! Had she really let Andreas undress her there at that discreet table at the back of the restaurant? How could she have let him?

She shook her head as other images raced in. Her panicking and Andreas whipping the cloth off the table and throwing it around her. He'd been still fully clothed. There had been a storeroom...no, a cupboard...which he'd hustled her into. She remembered standing there and keeping very quiet and still—trying not to move. And Andreas...Andreas having other ideas...

She closed her eyes, remembering the sensations that had fired through her when he had used that coarse cloth to arouse her. Moving it like a towel, slowly and calculatedly drawing it back and forth along her body in a deliberate and excruciatingly sensual attempt to see how long she could keep herself from breaking the silence with a moan of pleasure.

Had she really been a participant in that? Or was it all part of some hazy, sensuous dream? No wonder his family had thought her such a little tramp if they had guessed!

'You see,' she heard him say quietly above her. 'It's easy when you know how.'

Her eyes were troubled as they met his gaze and saw the faint light of awareness burning there. 'We didn't...do it there?' She had no memory of that.

'Not exactly.'

Because his determination to please her and drive her out

of her mind with wanting would have superseded even his own hot-blooded need for gratification. Because he was like that—and she had been his willing, subjugated toy!

'That wasn't me.' She groaned again, dropping her chin onto her bent hand and supporting it by her elbow on the desk. And, echoing her thoughts of a moment ago, 'No wonder they thought me so cheap. So easy.'

'I promise you no one ever found out.'

She sent a glance up at him. 'Didn't they miss that table-cloth?'

'I was responsible for setting up the tables for the following day's lunch. It was easy to let them think I'd simply overlooked it.'

'And you?' She leaned back, her arms dropping resignedly onto the padded arms of her chair. 'What did you think of me?'

'You drove me mad,' he admitted with a self-deprecating grimace.

'And because of the way I behaved with you, you imagine I behave in the same abandoned fashion with every man I meet, that I'd be just as willing to jump into bed with you again now?'

His eyebrow lifted, but he made no comment on that score. 'Stop feeling so bad about it,' he advised instead. 'We were young and hungry for each other.' Tilting her face to his with the crook of his finger, he leaned forward and lightly kissed her on the mouth. 'There were two of us in that cupboard that night,' he reminded her softly. 'But I'm more inclined to reserve the bedroom for making love these days, and I can certainly assure you that I would treat you with much more consideration now.'

But not respect.

He didn't even need to say it.

'Beautiful Magi…'

The caressing stroke of his hand along her throat brought

her eyelids down against his unbearable tenderness. His eyes, when she opened hers again, were two sapphire pools of unfathomable emotion as they raked mercilessly over her tortured face.

'I think that's enough recall therapy for one day, don't you?' he advocated, his hand falling away from her. And, getting up from the desk, he picked up some letters she had typed for him which were lying in her tray and casually took himself off to his own room.

Andreas had arranged to attend a business dinner that Friday, although it hadn't been marked in his diary and Magenta didn't find out about it until the actual day arrived.

'I'm sorry to spring this on you at such short notice,' Andreas expressed, coming into her office looking unusually rushed, his jacket hooked over his shoulder, only hours before the planned event. 'I don't suppose you brought anything dressier with you than suits and blouses?'

'Leggings and trainers?' she quipped. Guessing from the sudden frown knitting his dark brows that he wasn't in the mood for wisecracks, she went on, 'I didn't realise that my first week as your PA would call for dressing up for a night out at The Ritz.' She shrugged. 'Or wherever,' she added, not even certain yet where he was supposed to be going. 'I'm sorry. I imagined I'd be going home tonight.'

'Did you?' he breathed, in a way that made her wish that she hadn't. 'As you've already stated, you're my PA. That means you're on call twenty-four-seven. Is that clear?' When she nodded rather uncertainly, he said, with his keen eyes assessing her, 'Was there anything important you had planned?'

'No, but—'

'In that case we'd better get you something.'

We? Magenta darted a questioning glance up at him. He was already shrugging into his jacket.

'I'm sure I could probably find something in my wardrobe at home if you could spare me for a few hours.'

'I can't.'

Which was just as well, Magenta decided. She doubted that she had anything suitable for the type of venue to which he'd be taking her. She hadn't had much call to wear cocktail dresses since she'd had Theo—even if she'd been able to afford them.

'You're going to have to give me a sub on my salary,' she told him worriedly when they arrived at a busy village with upmarket little shops. She was already paying the maximum amount she could off her credit card, which she used to cover household essentials, and she had nowhere near sufficient funds in her bank account to cover her bills, let alone spend on dresses.

Andreas didn't respond as he pulled into a well-maintained car park.

'Come on. Let's get you kitted out,' he said a few minutes later, taking her hand.

The only dress shop in the village, Magenta realised, was an exclusive bow-windowed boutique. The type of place that looked as though it would stock just one of each luxuriously designed item displayed in its minimally dressed window.

'They must have known you were coming.' Andreas pulled a wry face. 'That dress was obviously made for you. Didn't blue used to be your favourite colour?'

It still was, Magenta thought distractedly, gazing up at the chic, exquisitely tailored dress in the window.

A sleeveless little number in royal blue silk, in a wraparound design that moulded itself beautifully to a slender figure, the dress had a plunging neckline that was low enough to be alluring without being immodest, and a hemline that was cut just above the knee. It was tied with a side-fastening sash that emphasised the waist and the bustline, and the long, loose ends of the sash fell freely against the flatteringly curved skirt.

'You have to be joking, don't you?' Magenta felt wounded anger welling up inside her. 'You *know* this sort of thing is way out of my league. I wouldn't have a thing to wear with it even if I could afford it—which I can't!'

A silver clutch bag and a silver and blue sequinned stole draped over a marble pedestal spoke of elegance in the extreme, while on another lower pedestal a pair of silver high-heeled sandals looked like something even Cinderella would have thought twice about losing. Pinpricks of small blue stones graced the sides of straps which were little more than silver strands across the ankles, so elegant they might have been real sapphires. They probably were, Magenta thought, if the fact that nothing in the window carried a price tag was anything to go by!

'I would have thought it wouldn't have taken much working out for you to realise that High Street is more within my budget.' Ridiculously, she was fighting back tears as she made to swing away.

What she didn't expect was to feel Andreas's firm hands upon her shoulders.

'Think of it as a business expense,' he drawled, and before she had time to argue he was hustling her into the shop. In response to the incredulous upward glance she shot him, he added, 'There *are* some perks to being at my beck and call.'

Evidently there were, Magenta agreed mentally as she tried on the dress in the scented changing room at the back of the shop. The shop owner had had to take it off the model, as the only similar one by the same designer had been too large. But this one, she realised with a lick of pleasure running through her, was a perfect fit.

'Do you think these shoes will look all right with this?' she asked Andreas when she came out of the changing room.

She was frowning down at the dainty low-heeled black sandals she wore every day.

He had been talking to the owner, a rather glamorous, middle-aged woman, who was smiling at Magenta from behind the counter. Now, as he turned and saw her standing there, he gave a low whistle under his breath.

He looked totally taken aback—unable to speak. But then he seemed to give himself a mental shake before glancing down at her very inappropriate footwear.

'Doesn't she look beautiful?' the shop owner enthused.

'Exquisite.'

Andreas couldn't seem to take his eyes off her, Magenta noticed with warm sensations infiltrating her blood, and for a few moments it felt as though there were only the two of them in the shop.

But he had totally forgotten what she had asked him! she realised, when he turned away towards the counter again and she saw him reaching into the top pocket of his jacket for his wallet.

'How much for the window?'

She couldn't believe what he had just asked, but the woman was jotting something down on a piece of paper, and after a nod from him started bustling around like a bee that had just scented a rare and beautiful pollen—which somehow indicated that Magenta *had* heard correctly.

'You can't,' she whispered behind his broad back, when the woman had moved into the window area to claim the shoes and bag and the matching stole.

'Go back to the changing room,' he said without looking at her as he took a credit card out of his wallet.

As she didn't feel like protesting in front of an audience, Magenta could only comply.

She didn't know if the shoes the woman brought her were the ones in the window, or if there had been another pair in her size, but the ones that had been handed round the heavy velvet curtain for her to try fitted her like hand-made gloves.

Or glass slippers, she thought wryly, remembering what she had been thinking outside.

Their purchases were being lovingly wrapped in tissue paper when Magenta emerged from the changing room in her suit and blouse. Andreas pulled a wry face at her transformation from virtual sex kitten to businesswoman as he slipped his credit card back into his wallet.

The clutch-bag was the last purchase to be wrapped, and Magenta spied a trio of minute sapphire stones winking up at her from the flap of soft silvery leather before they too disappeared within folds of rustling tissue paper.

'Your girlfriend's a very lucky lady.' The shop owner was silently admiring the tall man she had been addressing, although it was Magenta that her smile alighted on.

I'm not his girlfriend! she wanted to stress, but that would have made her sound as if she were something altogether more eyebrow-raising, so she just smiled and took the bunch of glossy carrier bags the woman handed her with good grace.

'I can't believe you just did that,' she remarked, flabbergasted, as soon as they were outside, walking away from the shop. 'You've just spent a fortune on something I may only ever wear once.'

His long strides were marking out their purposeful path to the car park. 'Is that all you have to say?'

'What do you expect me to say?' she uttered, still totally dumbfounded. She had to quicken her stride to keep up with him.

'A simple thank you would suffice.'

Of course. If his motive was merely to see her properly attired for a business dinner then she was behaving crassly and with total ingratitude. She was about to apologise and thank him, as he'd suggested, but the simple words he'd spoken were suddenly echoing back at her from out of the dark recesses of her mind.

A simple thank you would have sufficed.

She stopped at the end of the little row of shops, her hand going automatically to her forehead.

'What is it? What's wrong?'

Andreas's concern broke through the wild confusion of her thoughts.

'I thought…I just thought you'd said something like that to me before.' She shook her head as shapes started to form out of the mists of that lost time. 'It was that statue….'

A little porcelain statue of a mother and her child, a girl of about three or four, who was holding her hand and looking up trustingly at the woman. She'd seen it in a shop window and had wanted it for her mother, to try and cheer her up after another of her endless break-ups. To try and stop her drinking and let her know that she had so much else to live for. To let her know how much her daughter really loved her. Needed her…

'I went back to the shop and it was gone…' Her brow furrowed with the aching disappointment that seemed to have gripped her insides. 'What is it they say? The first time we remember something we actually relive it all over again? And the second time we think of it it's only a memory?'

'Discontinued,' the assistant had told her when she had asked if he had another, and it had felt like the end of the world. She couldn't believe how badly she had wanted that statue and how the anguish at losing it could have been so bad.

'You asked me why I was crying…' She looked up at Andreas. She remembered that when she had told him he had rung around shop after shop, trying to find another. And when he had he'd made an eighty-mile round trip in his father's van just to pick it up for her. 'You found one for me.'

She remembered showering him with kisses. Laughing and crying right there in the reception area of the pokey little solicitors' office where she'd worked. She could see him laughing. Looking amused. And, yes…he had said those words to her then: 'A simple thank you would have sufficed.'

His arm was around her now, warm and supportive, and without thinking Magenta leaned in to his steadying strength.

His shoulder felt like a rock beneath her trembling cheek, and for a few moments it didn't matter that they were in a village high street congested with local traffic. That there were Friday afternoon shoppers milling around the place and harassed mothers calling errant youngsters energised by the freedom of their summer holiday.

'Oh, Andreas! What happened to us?' she appealed to him.

'Not here. Not yet.' Determinedly he took her hand and guided her across the busy street. 'Perhaps not anywhere.' His voice had a strange quality to it as they reached the entrance to the car park on the other side of the road. 'Perhaps it's best forgotten,' he said.

CHAPTER SEVEN

THE DINNER THAT evening, attended by some of the biggest names in the UK hotel business, was held in the ballroom of an impressive nineteenth-century stately home, somewhere deep in the heart of the Surrey countryside.

Andreas had informed Magenta that he'd been in two minds about going, which explained why it hadn't been entered into his diary, but then he had heard that among those attending there would be two of his acquaintances from the States whom he was very keen to see. They were over here, he had explained, to sell their shares in some of the country house hotel properties they owned in the UK, and as it was a section of the market he was keen to move into he felt it would be beneficial for him to be there with his PA.

It was the first formal event Magenta could remember attending, although she knew from photographs she'd seen of herself that she'd attended one or two with Marcus Rushford during the early days of her short-lived modelling career. It was with a little shiver of nerves, therefore, that she viewed the long, beautifully laid tables, taking in with some trepidation the spectacle of sparkling crystal and gleaming silverware beneath the luminescence of two glittering chandeliers. Then she felt Andreas's supporting hand at her elbow, followed by a few, soft encouraging words, and she wondered if he'd guessed how she was feeling as he led her into the breathtaking room.

A few hours later, sipping her second cup of coffee, with the speeches and most of the business of the evening well out of the way, Magenta couldn't understand why she had been so nervous. The Ottermans were lovely, as it turned out.

PJ, as Andreas had introduced him, was a short, greying-haired man, with a ginger moustache and a warm, infectious laugh. His wife, Mary-Louise, was an elegant, quietly-spoken lady who, from her clear skin and slender figure, had clearly taken care of herself. She was, however, temporarily confined to a wheelchair, with her leg in plaster, as a result of a fall over an unattended suitcase at the airport on her arrival in the UK the previous week.

'That's such an unfortunate thing to happen,' Magenta sympathised when Mary-Louise made reference to her ill-timed accident. 'Especially with the weather being so beautiful here at the moment and you having to forgo all the organised walks you and your husband were planning for this trip.'

'Yes, I suppose it has been a bit careless of me,' the woman admitted with a self-effacing grimace. 'But secretly, my dear…' Her slim shoulders hunched, she leaned towards Magenta with a conspiratorial lowering of her voice '…I'm rather enjoying having PJ fussing over me in a way that he hasn't done in forty years.'

Magenta laughed, enjoying the American woman's company while Andreas was talking business to the woman's husband. Both men were on their feet, as they had been for some time now, and Magenta was very conscious of Andreas standing behind her chair.

If she leaned back she could touch him…

She was careful not to, however, because she had done so already, when she'd tilted her head back in response to something someone had been saying about the chandelier earlier and her hair had brushed the impeccable dark sleeve of his dnner jacket.

Mary-Louise was saying something about the London Eye, and shamefully Magenta found herself having to try and tune in to listen when really she wanted to hang on to every word that deep, masculine voice behind her was uttering. To breathe in the intoxicating scent of the cologne he was wearing and try and deal with the sensations that having him standing there so close and yet so oblivious to her produced.

'I haven't been on it,' Magenta confessed, reproaching herself for allowing her attention to stray from what her easy and genteel dinner companion was saying. 'I'm afraid I'm not the world's best contender when it comes to heights, but I'm—'

Her sentence was cut short when two over-animated young men in evening suits, beer mugs in hand, barged past Mary-Louise as though there was no one sitting there. At her small shocked gasp Magenta was appalled to notice that there were splashes of beer spilled down the sleeve of the woman's blouse.

'Here! Let me.' Magenta was on her feet and mopping up the liquid that was dripping off the chair with her napkin, while Mary-Louise dabbed at her blouse with her own.

'Are you all right?' Andreas and PJ spoke in unison, their business discussion discarded by their concern.

'Yes, yes—I'm fine,' the woman uttered quickly, clearly not wanting to draw more attention to herself than was absolutely necessary. But Magenta was quietly annoyed.

Having assured Mary-Louise that her blouse hadn't suffered too much, Magenta noticed that the two men who had bumped into the chair had not only stopped to share a loud joke with two other young men just a few metres away, but that one of them actually had the gall to be sizing her up.

'Just because she's in a wheelchair it doesn't mean that she's invisible.' The reprimand slipped out before she could stop it.

'I'm sorry.' One of the lads mouthed an apology and, looking shamefaced now, barged hastily through another group of people who were standing by a nearby table, with his three friends hot on his heels.

Andreas had been aware all evening of the growing rapport between Magenta and Mary-Louise. Now, observing them while conversing with PJ, he noticed the older woman close her weathered hand affectionately over Magenta's and heard her say, 'That was very sweet of you.'

With a sudden sharp kick of something in his loins he wished that *he* could be the one touching Magenta right then. The way she had stood up for his friend's wife had impressed him immeasurably. He guessed that it sprang from her own first-hand experience of other people's thoughtlessness at a time when she had been less than able-bodied herself.

He noticed, too, how easily the Ottermans, particularly Mary-Louise, had taken to her. People always had, he realised, despite her own claim to not forming many friendships. At nineteen she had had a warm and open spontaneity. He remembered how she had used it—effortlessly and unconsciously—to try and win over his grandmother. Maria Visconti, however, had refused to warm to her.

PJ and Mary-Louise were having no such reservations. With an unnecessary twinge of irritation Andreas caught their laughter at something Magenta had just said to them. She was sitting down again, and PJ had taken the seat he himself had been sitting in, his arm across the back of her chair.

She was wearing that glorious hair up, with soft tendrils fanning her face. He had a strong desire to delve his hands deeply into it, to hear the pleasured gasps from the dark burgundy of her tantalising mouth. The way that beautiful blue dress parted as she crossed her legs gave him an alluring glimpse of one silkily sheathed thigh. In fact the whole dress was driving him virtually insane with the need to feel her against him, and he knew he had to satisfy that need very soon or go mad.

'If you'll excuse us…?' He cut across something PJ was saying and caught her hand. 'Well?' he said to her, his body so rigid from battling to contain his arousal that it was an effort to smile. 'Are you going to show me what you can do?'

He sensed her recoil almost imperceptibly, as she had when she'd accidentally touched him earlier.

She smiled a little awkwardly. 'I think I'd rather sit this one out.'

Her glance towards Mary-Louise suggested that she might not want to dance because the other woman couldn't. He'd already heard Mary-Louise telling her when the music started how much she'd always loved to dance. Or maybe Magenta had another reason for refusing him, he thought. Maybe she just didn't trust herself to be that close to him…

'Nonsense, my dear.' The woman gave Magenta's hand a reassuring pat. 'Don't refuse on my account. You young people need a minute to yourselves.'

From the way she had been looking at himself and Magenta during the evening it was pretty obvious that she knew there was something more to their relationship than just business.

'And I can assure you that I'll be up there tripping the light fantastic before the next six months are up—although perhaps not to something with quite so much angst.'

Pretending to laugh with the others did nothing to relax Magenta as Andreas led her onto the dance floor.

'It looks like you were out-voted, doesn't it?' he mocked softly above the fluid notes of a first-rate female ballad singer.

He looked quite smug. As well he might, Magenta decided, having no choice but to follow him into the midst of the swaying bodies.

'I was just being considerate, that's all,' she bluffed as he turned her around and his arms came round her.

'Very commendable.' His smile was devastating. 'Now be considerate towards *me*.'

A shocked little gasp escaped her as his body made contact with hers. Never had she felt so naked dancing with a man in public. His hard warmth was penetrating the fine silk of her dress as if she were wearing nothing, and the sensuous cloth of his dinner jacket made her want to press herself against him.

'It feels good.'

He was referring to the dress, and Magenta felt his hand sliding down her spine before it stopped just short enough to observe the rules of decency, its heat searing through the blue fabric just above the gentle swell of her buttocks.

'Isn't that why you bought it?'

He gave a disapproving click of his tongue. 'Would you believe me if I say I didn't know there would be dancing here tonight? It wasn't mentioned.'

'But now that there is you'll take full advantage of the fact?'

'Can you blame me? Especially when I'm aware of how much you want me to.'

'That's not true.' She turned her head away so that she couldn't see the mockery in his face—and wished she hadn't when he took the opportunity to pull her even closer. She sucked in a breath, feeling *his* breath—warm and erotic—fan the sensitive skin at her hairline.

'You're a poor liar, Magenta. I can feel the way your body's responding to me now, and it isn't the response of a woman who wants me to leave her alone.'

'But you're going to.' It was a desperate little command rather than a question.

'Until you're begging me otherwise.'

She could tell he was smiling. A slow, sexy smile.

'Verbally, of course.'

His words mocked. But then he could tell from the tension in her body how much she wanted him physically. Her breasts were aching for his caresses and her thighs were tingling above the sheer Lycra of her stockings, sending vibes of raw wanting to the heart of her femininity every time they collided with the hard-muscled strength of his.

Tilting her head back so that she was looking directly up into his incredibly charismatic features, she said huskily, and in a voice that was unintentionally provocative, 'Did this kind of fascinating technique turn me on before?'

His smile was discerning. 'It's working now, isn't it?'

She uttered a shrill little laugh. 'Were you always this conceited?'

'I call it being one step ahead of the game.'

His gaze dropped to her mouth, sending little tremors of excitement through her.

'And I don't believe you've forgotten quite as much as you claim.'

'Well, that's your opinion,' she breathed, and didn't tell him that there were more and more pieces of her memory that she was beginning to link together. That it had begun to scare her, and that she was almost terrified of what those still-lost pieces might eventually reveal.

'What is it?' Andreas asked over the female singer's sobbing finale of a story about a woman tortured by love. 'Am I probing too close to the truth? Or are you having another of your recall moments?'

'No... I...' Why did he have to be so astute? So totally 'ahead of the game', as he had just claimed to be?

Someone jostled her elbow and Andreas's arm tightened around her. The steadying action brought her up against his hard, lean length, so achingly close to him that her head began to swim and primitive impulses sent a throbbing awareness trembling through her body.

'Why don't we go home?' His words were a sensual caress against the shining bounty of her hair.

When she didn't reply, too afraid of what she might say if she did, she found herself allowing him to lead her away from the dance floor.

She didn't know what he was going to say to his friends, but they were back at their table and he was offering the Ottermans his apologies, extending an invitation for them to come and stay at the house before they returned to the States. His manner was easy and charming, without any need for explanation and without any artifice or awkwardness in his deep tones.

As they were walking out through the luxuriously carpeted foyer, past a round central table containing a huge floral display, Magenta couldn't even remember saying her goodbyes. All she seemed able to focus on was Andreas's arm around her shoulders and the need that was escalating inside her with each collision of his hard hip with hers.

It was going to happen, she thought. Despite all she had said and all the objections she had raised she was going to bed with Andreas Visconti again. And she couldn't decide how she had managed to come this far in just a few short days.

She couldn't stop it now even if she wanted to, she realised, with her arm slipping automatically beneath his jacket and around his lean waist.

The heat of his body through the fine shirt was a turn-on in itself. Her fingers ached to pull at the expensive silk, just as her body was aching to be closer to him—close enough to feel his burning flesh pulsing against hers.

Weak with wanting, she was counting the seconds until they reached the warm, dark privacy of his car.

'Andreas! Andreas Visconti!'

A man who had been passing them had stopped and was walking towards them now. He had cropped, receding brown hair and looked a few years older than Andreas.

'What has it been now?' He was extending a hand to him. 'Five years? No, more than that. Six years?

Magenta felt the loss of Andreas's arm around her shoulders as he shook hands with the man who, from his formal clothes, was obviously also attending the function. Apparently he was called Gerard, Magenta learned when she was introduced to him, and he'd used to be an assistant chef in Giuseppe Visconti's restaurant. Now he had shares in a small hotel in Brighton.

'I was sorry about your father,' he was saying to Andreas. 'It all happened so suddenly. But I've heard *you're* doing all right.' With his rather too-generous midriff, and a waistband that looked uncomfortably tight, the man was regarding Andreas with unconcealed envy. As though he wanted a taste of all that wealth and success that seemed to ooze from the tall, immaculately attired man he couldn't even begin to emulate. He glanced at Magenta, adding, 'And in more ways than one.'

Feeling the stranger's eyes drifting over her body, Magenta drew the sequinned wrap more closely around her. She had a feeling she might have known him, but the vibes that she was getting, which were putting her on her guard, suggested that if she had then the experience hadn't been a pleasant one.

'I must say I'm pleased to see the two of you back together again.' Those wandering eyes were taking more notice of Magenta now than of Andreas. 'I always thought it was a tragedy, your letting this lovely girl go.' He used 'this' as an excuse to let a rather podgy finger brush her shoulder.

'I didn't realise you were aware that Magenta and I were ever an item.' Andreas's voice had turned decidedly cold.

'I think we all were.' The man gave Magenta a rather knowing wink. 'There wasn't a man working in that kitchen or out front when I was there who didn't envy you, old chap. In fact I was thinking of making a play for her myself when I heard you'd split up. But then your father died. The restaurant closed…' He made an expressive gesture with his arms, the action pulling at the fabric already straining across his middle. 'I was out of a job, and *this* beautiful creature had already grabbed the attention of someone far smarter and richer than the likes of you and me.'

She didn't even need to ask to know that he was talking about Marcus Rushford.

Beside her, Magenta sensed the hostility building in Andreas towards his late father's employee. Hostility and an anger so palpable it was unnerving—although outwardly he appeared rigidly in control.

'Well, it's been a pleasure seeing you again, Gerard.' Magenta could almost hear those strong white teeth grinding together. 'But, as you can see, we're in a hurry.' And with a 'goodnight' that sounded more like a growl he was urging her out into the darkness of the car park.

Soft lighting around the building showed off the gleaming metalwork of the Mercedes as they approached it. It also showed Andreas's face, slashed with shadows and looking like a grim mask, as he pointed the remote control at the car as though it were something living he wanted to kill.

'Did that guy ever make his intentions towards you known when we—?'

He broke off, and from his exasperated sigh she knew he thought it was pointless even asking her. But she was well aware of what he had been going to say.

'He made a pass at me.' She remembered aloud as soon as they were in the car.

'What?' He looked as though it was Gerard he wanted to kill now. 'When? Where?'

'I don't know!' She dropped her head back against the rest. 'I only know he did.'

'And did you welcome it?'

She looked at him aghast as he started the engine. 'You're joking, surely?'

The glance he shot her was insultingly sceptical.

'Yeah, sure. I *loved* it!' she breathed.

He pulled out of the car park with an unnecessary squeal

of brakes, his features hard and rigid. His shirt showed up starkly white in the darkness.

He was angry because Gerard had brought up her involvement with Marcus Rushford, unaware of the damage it would do. Or perhaps he had been aware, she thought. Andreas had already accused her of virtually selling herself to the wealthy tycoon. But *had* she? Her nails dug into her palms as she struggled to remember. She couldn't have. How could she when she hadn't even wanted him in that way?

'Gerard made a pass at me,' she reiterated, trying to make it sound as though it was trivial. Unimportant. But the images manifesting themselves now were ones of sick revulsion. 'Men did. *Do.* I can't help it.'

'Neither can they.' His censorious glance across the emotion-charged space between them had her pulling the skirt of her dress over a suddenly far too exposed thigh.

'So what are you going to do? Lock me up and throw away the key?' When he didn't answer, too involved with dimming his lights as another car passed on the other side of the country road, she breathed, 'That's possessiveness, Andreas.'

Was that what had broken them up? Had she felt stifled by a relationship that was too intense to cope with? Or was it simply, as she'd wondered all along, that he had resented the fact she had wanted a career?

'If it is, then I can hardly be blamed for it, can I?' he rasped, flooding the road with angry light again.

'Why? Because I look the way I do? *You* virtually dressed me today, remember? And you aren't exactly the type of man the opposite sex can ignore.'

'Is that your way of reminding me of where we were an hour ago?'

Was it?

'No,' she refuted quickly, because it would be far too easy to rekindle the mood that had propelled them out of that hotel ballroom, and she'd known it was crazy even *thinking* of allowing herself to become intimately involved with him even before they had bumped into Gerard.

'As you wish,' he accepted, with a long drawing out of his breath, and he didn't say another word to her for the rest of the journey home.

CHAPTER EIGHT

'Do you want a nightcap?'

Andreas had removed his jacket, and his bow-tie was hanging loosely below the winged collar he had unfastened.

'No.' Magenta was much too conscious of being with him, knowing that if it hadn't been for meeting that man Gerard in the foyer they would have been in bed, making unrestrained love to each other now. 'I think I'd like to go up and maybe read for a while. Would it be imprudent of me in any way to ask if you would lend me the Byron?'

He glanced up from the sideboard, where he was pouring himself a drink. 'Still the incurable romantic?' When she didn't answer, not sure whether he was being sarcastic or not, he said, 'I suspect that you've already guessed—or remembered—that it's yours anyway.'

She nodded, wanting to ask why, if that was the case, he had it in his possession. But the moment didn't seem right somehow.

'Go in and get it,' he acceded, turning away.

Bidding him goodnight, she walked upstairs on legs of lead, her stole and her bag clutched tensely in her hand. She wanted him and he despised her. And he probably despised himself for wanting *her* too. That was probably why he had reined in those ravaging desires of his after he had been reminded of the kind of woman he obviously believed she was.

But she couldn't have been that loose or free, with other lovers in her past, could she? Not Marcus. Not anyone! There had only ever been Andreas. She knew it in her heart as surely as she knew that day would follow night into eternity.

The book was where she had left it when she had crept up there alone the other day—back in its place between a tome of classic literature and a Winston Churchill biography.

Trying not to look at the enormous bed, she tripped lightly across the room with her mind anywhere but on poetry, fighting back the feelings that were stirring in her as she pictured herself lying naked with Andreas under the folds of that abstract-patterned king-size duvet.

Putting her bag and stole down on a Jacobean-style chest, she was quickly retrieving the book when the light she'd switched on suddenly faded almost to candlelight.

Pivoting round, she saw Andreas coming around the door. 'Still here?'

Standing there with her lips slightly parted in shock, and with reckless impulses suddenly leaping through her, Magenta wasn't sure whether he was surprised or not.

She made a careless gesture towards the book. 'So it would seem.' Her throat had contracted so much she could scarcely get the words out as she watched him, his smile distracted, advance across the luxurious carpet towards her.

Somewhere between the sitting room and the bedroom he had unfastened most of the buttons of his shirt, and Magenta was acutely aware of the hair-sprinkled chest it exposed. He was so close to her now that she could reach out and touch him. But she didn't. Instead she stayed exactly where she was, riveted by his nearness, his scent and that powerful magnetism that made her protest to herself go unheard and kept her eyes trained painfully on his.

With the briefest touch of a finger he lifted her face to his, and then with a tenderness that was excruciating brought his mouth down over hers.

Magenta's senses screamed from the lightness of his touch, the calculated skill with which he was arousing her. Or *was* it calculated? she wondered. Perhaps he was merely kissing her goodnight.

She wanted to strain against him. Put her arms around his neck and cling to him. But the not knowing kept her still, her fingers almost painfully stiff around the velvety cover of the book.

'So where do we go from here?' His eyes were half veiled by his long lashes so that she couldn't tell what he was thinking. She knew her own eyes would be dark pools of wanting, so why did he need to ask?

But he was leaving it to her.

Candidly then, her face racked with longing, she murmured softly, 'I don't want to be alone.'

Without a word he moved across to the door he'd left open and closed it. That penetrating gaze never left hers as he came back to where she stood, tense with anticipation. A hot and heightening excitement was licking through her blood. She was breathing shallowly. Her eyes were slumberous with desire, their pupils dilated, the dark chocolate irises showing him the depths of her need.

He glanced down at the book she was still clutching and, taking it from her trembling fingers, laid it aside on the chest. Then he lifted a hand to remove the pins from her hair while her greedy senses soaked up his warmth and his hard dark strength, the stirring musk of his skin beneath his cologne.

Her hair tumbled down about her shoulders like a cascade of dark silk and she sucked in a breath as he dealt with the twist of silver she wore around her throat.

He put it to one side with the pins and the book, those blue eyes scarcely leaving hers for a second before his dark head bowed in studied concentration as he returned to the task in hand. With sure and calculated fingers he tugged at the knot at her waist and the dress fell open in easy compliance with his bidding.

Magenta pressed her eyes closed, her trembling lashes and the irregularity of her breathing betraying the tumultuous sensations he was creating in her.

She heard a deep masculine sigh and knew a small thrill in the knowledge that he was pleased with what he was seeing. Colour seeped along her cheekbones as she considered what that was. A wispy bra and string in a marriage of midnight-blue lace; legs made sexy by the natural-toned lace of hold-up stockings and by the sandals he had bought her.

Then she remembered something else. The small scar across her tummy which hadn't been there when he had seen her like this before.

Suddenly, in a ragged little plea, she was appealing to him, 'Turn off the light. Please turn off the light.'

He didn't say a word as his long firm hands spanned her midriff. Their sensuous warmth on her bare flesh made her gasp and shudder with need. Those hands were sliding down her body, over her hips and buttocks, and his tongue was finding its own path along the valley of her breasts to her waist as he dropped to his knees in front of her and pressed his lips against the fine Caesarean scar.

'You're beautiful,' he whispered.

Even with her scars? Even though she wasn't as physically perfect as he remembered her?

'So are you,' she whispered, emotion clogging her throat and her hands doing what they had been longing to do for the past few days: luxuriating in the feel of his strong black hair.

She wanted more of him. *All* of him! she thought achingly, her breath catching in her lungs as he slid back along her body to press tantalising kisses over the upper swell of each straining breast.

'Be patient. Patience...' Though he sounded breathless,

his tone was softly teasing, while his hands were playing a mercilessly tormenting game of their own.

Slipping inside the wispy-laced cups at the outer edges of her breasts, they moved beneath each aching mound to cradle its blossoming softness without actually touching the hardening and torturously sensitive peak.

When he did, forcing the lace down to free them to his fervid and appreciative gaze, Magenta strained towards him with a shuddering cry.

'That's what I liked about you,' he murmured, and even his voice was arousing her, threatening to drive her crazy along with the warm breath fanning her ear. 'You were always so immensely grateful for the smallest things.'

It was all part of his technique—this withholding of pleasure and his feigned surprise at her frenzied response when he finally gave in and granted it. She knew it—and knew she had crossed the boundaries of ecstasy with this man before. That she had let him take her where no other man had ever taken her, or ever could.

Now, guided by the map of his experience and an inherent memory of the games they'd used to play, she strained towards him, gasping as he caught her to him. And with her lips but a hair's breadth from his, she murmured, 'So fill me with undying gratitude.'

He gave a low chuckle in his throat, a sensually inspired sound, before lifting her off her feet and carrying her over to the big bed.

Her body was soft, Andreas thought appreciatively, dropping down beside her. As silky as the dress that had already slid into a blue pool beside the bed. And whatever else she had forgotten, she remembered *this,* he thought, feeling his own body responding to the way she gasped and moaned from the pleasure of his hands and lips, the way her body rose to meet the burning demands of his mouth.

He made little work of removing her bra and its match-ing triangle of lace, then the delicate little shoes, but when it came to removing her stockings he took an almost shameful pleasure in stringing it out.

Lying there naked, with her arms in an abandoned arc above her head, she was waiting for him to join her.

Temptation mocking him, it took every gram of his self-control not to do so immediately, not to give in to his driving urges and take them where they both wanted to go. However, it was worth the agony of waiting to watch the way her lovely eyes darkened and closed as he moved to unsheathe her beau-tiful legs and, with a subtle sleight of hand, just managed to skim the warm apex of her femininity as he peeled back each lacy stocking top in turn.

'Andreas…'

She was wet with desire. He could feel her moist heat against his hand.

'What is it, darling?' His own arousal was so hot and in-tense he could scarcely speak as she writhed against him. He needed to be naked with her, to feel every part of her lovely body beneath his.

Now, with a swift shedding of his own clothes, and taking responsibility for her protection, he came back to join her, lowering himself onto her in a meeting of pulsing flesh that made her gasp and strain urgently towards him as he groaned his satisfaction deep in his throat.

Her hands on his heated flesh were a pleasure he had never forgotten, but he revelled in the mind-blowing experience now as if it was the very first time. He wanted her like he had never wanted any woman—before or since—but he couldn't just take what he wanted like some callow youth. Whatever this woman had done to him she needed to be treated with kid gloves, and with all the consideration and care his ma-turity demanded.

He'd once thought he had been put on this earth solely to

pleasure Magenta James, and he did so now with all the skill
of his acquired experience. Taking his time, he reacquainted
himself with every secret path and byway of her body, remembering her likes, what drove her craziest, as though the
last six years didn't exist. As though there hadn't been other
lovers—or at least one that he knew of—who had come after
him. For now he wanted to forget that—and he did.

A long time later, when she was sobbing for the one thing
he was withholding, he slid his hands under her buttocks and
lifted her body to accommodate his length. As soon as he
started to enter her he felt her recoil almost imperceptibly,
and he held himself there for a few seconds, finding her not
quite as he had anticipated.

Heavens! She was tight.

Magenta gave a shuddering gasp as he moved to sink further
into her softness—a sound of unbelievable pleasure after her
surprising initial discomfort.

'Am I hurting you?' Andreas asked, his breathing ragged,
as if he was on the brink of losing control.

She made a small murmured negation and through the
waves of sensation that were washing over her wondered
whether, if she had had a normal childbirth, he would even
have needed to ask. But she hadn't. And it had been so long
since she had done this…

Oh, but he felt so good!

As her body lifted to his he pushed more confidently inside
her, deeper and deeper, until he was filling her, completing
her, and then there was nothing between them and the earth-
shattering pleasure of their straining flesh and their bodies
locked together as one.

He started to move and she was moving with him, in a
rhythm that was as natural as breathing. Each breath-catching
thrust of his body was taking her with him, upwards and
outwards, to scale heights of rapture such as Magenta had

never conceived possible. She felt whole again for the first time since they had been together, and she clung to him as he took her to the outer edges of another universe until she was crying out from the shockwaves of pure pleasure ripping not just through her body but reaching down and opening up her mind and her soul as well.

She was his for eternity and knew she always had been, even when she had been young and foolish and fighting her attraction to him in a reckless, desperate desire to be free. As she acknowledged that fact, opening her heart to the realisation that she was and always had been hopelessly in love with him, the past rushed up on her like a tidal wave out of nowhere, bursting her defences wide open, and she saw the truth in all its shocking clarity.

At nineteen she'd believed the world was hers by right, that her face and figure were sure to get her the fame and fortune she craved. She remembered craving it to the exclusion of everything else. Her four-month affair with Andreas. His feelings for her. Even her self-respect.

She groaned inwardly as her brain reacquainted her with the selfish, mercenary creature she had been. She didn't want to remember, but the shattering experience of making love with him had severed the chains of her amnesia, and whether she was ready for it or not the last barriers of her resistance were finally caving in.

She'd been ambitious—ruthlessly so—and she hadn't planned on a man like Andreas Visconti coming into her life so soon.

'It isn't enough for me,' she had said, when he had asked her to marry him and told her about his future plans for his family's business.

But they could make a success of their lives together, he had insisted, before going on to show her just how persuasive he could be as, like always after one of their heated arguments, they both wound up in his bed.

Their rows had been tempestuous affairs, she remembered. And always over the same things. Her mother. His family. What Andreas had referred to as her 'hankering' after a career. She'd even accused him of trying to hold her back. Yet she hadn't been able to resist him, and they had both known it, but she had crushed her feelings for him by convincing herself that they were generated purely by sex and that she would probably respond in the same way to *any* attractive man she happened to fancy.

When Marcus Rushford had discovered her at the studio where she'd been getting some new photographs done for her portfolio she'd been flattered by his interest and attention. Older, worldly and debonair, with a lot of very important and influential contacts throughout the modelling profession, he had singled her out as the new face of contemporary chic— and she, like a fool, had been seduced by all his promises to make her famous.

Well, what girl wouldn't have been? she thought, striving for some justification for the way she had behaved. Living with poverty and her mother's drinking problems hadn't been easy. Neither had the stigma of those two words on her birth certificate: Father Unknown.

Just like on Theo's, she reflected, with a crushing feeling in her chest that made it almost difficult to breathe. Or at least a blank space where Andreas's name should have been. She tried reminding herself that Theo's had stayed blank for a totally different reason than hers, but that didn't help at all.

She had been taunted at school because of it, and because of her mother's reputation and the situation they had been living in. Was it any wonder she'd craved a better life? The big time? At the very least some kind of identity? she thought, harrowed.

At some point Andreas had rolled away from her and was now breathing deeply and regularly beside her. Pushing back the duvet, she slid quietly out of bed, so as not to wake him, and carried her anguishing burden of memories into the bathroom.

Finding his towelling robe hanging behind the door, she slipped it on and, huddled inside it, sank onto the luxurious mat beside the sunken Jacuzzi.

She had had her head turned by Marcus Rushford, she recalled, shamed by the memories that continued to rush back at her. Nothing else had counted but this new excitement in her life. For a girl who had had nothing, the older man's promises of having everything suddenly within her grasp had been too much to resist.

When she had been breaking up with Andreas and he had coldly challenged her to deny her feelings for him she had laughed in his face, fearful that he would use his irresistible and persuasive sexual powers to try and change her mind. 'You didn't really think I was serious about you? About *this?*' she had taunted, with regard to the restaurant and all that he had been offering. 'Did you *really* think I wanted to spend my life dishing up pizza in a cheap little café? And one I'd rather be seen dead than stuck in!'

She had been offensive and heartless. But she had been panicking inside because she had wanted to be free. Free to pursue her dreams of becoming a top model.

A few days later, guilty over how much Andreas must have spent on that special edition of Byron's poems, she'd gone to see him to return it, but done nothing to hide the evidence of another man's passion on her neck. She groaned at how sick it made her feel to remember how she had flaunted it like some prized trophy. Cruelly. Shamelessly. To the man who had wanted to marry her and whose bed she had left so recently she must have seemed contemptible. So cheap.

When she'd given him back that book he had hurled it across the room, telling her she was no good, just like her mother.

She hadn't cared. Nor had she given him any inkling that she had. Her one driving ambition had been to get on.

Selling herself to the highest bidder...

Inside the thick robe she shivered violently, fully aware of exactly what Andreas had meant. With her mother going into rehab and wanting to give up the house, Magenta had already been living in Marcus Rushford's smart, upmarket apartment.

Her big break had come only weeks after that shaming scene with Andreas, in a lucrative, high-profile contract with a hair products company. It was all she had been hoping for but she had had to turn it down, having just received the biggest shock of her life. She was pregnant—with what she knew was Andreas's child.

When Marcus had found out he had slapped her—hard. There was no way he was going to promote her, he had said, if she didn't take the necessary steps to do what she had to do.

She'd cried for a week, she remembered, reliving the anguish of that time. And at the end of it had told him there was no way that she would harm her baby. She'd taken a bus ride to the neighbourhood where she'd used to live, having decided that she would have to tell Andreas. She hadn't planned on asking him to take her back. She'd known she had behaved far too badly for that, and suspected that he probably wouldn't even believe that the child she was carrying was his, but she'd owed it to Andreas to at least give him the chance of making up his own mind.

When she had got within shouting distance of the restaurant, however, her nerve had failed her. She'd shrunk back into the doorway of a baker's shop, fear gripping her at something she'd remembered him saying.

'If you got pregnant with my baby and insisted on bringing it up alone—' as she'd threatened to do after one of their more impassioned scenarios '—then you'd better know now that I'd do all in my power to get custody of my child rather than see it brought up by a fame-crazed mother and a man-crazy, seasoned drunk of a grandmother!'

Fear such as she had never known had pressed down on her in that doorway. It was there she had realised that she wanted Andreas's baby more than she had wanted anything in her life.

She'd tried ringing him once after that, phoning the restaurant under the guise of making a booking in the hope that he would answer. Not to speak to him particularly, but simply to hear his voice. When someone else had answered she had put down the phone, too cowardly to say who she was. Later, someone whose name she couldn't even remember had told her he had gone to America.

Marcus had tried to put pressure on her when it had become clear to him that she wasn't going to give up her baby. She would blow her chances of ever becoming a model, he'd kept reminding her, pulling no punches in telling her what pregnancy would do to her figure. Either she did the sensible thing now, he'd reiterated, or she could kiss goodbye to her career *and* his apartment. It was as simple as that. Stardom or the streets.

She'd chosen the streets—or as good as. With her mother growing stronger, and renting a one-bedroom flat, Magenta had taken up her offer to let her stay on a temporary basis. Sleeping on the sofa at night, taking any job from cleaning to waitressing during the day, her only goal had been to try and save enough for a place for herself and the coming baby to live. That was until the day fate had taken a hand and she'd woken up two months later, paralysed, with a beautiful baby boy and the memory of its father and those terrible months following wiped clean from her mind.

Creeping back into the bedroom, making sure Andreas was still asleep, she gathered up her underwear and stockings and the few belongings in the bag he had bought her, and very quietly made her way back to her own room.

She had blanked it out because it had been too painful to

remember, and now it was agony coming to terms with the way she had behaved.

She recalled what Andreas had said to her in the lift that day, about her scarf hiding the marks of another man's lust, and she cringed, knowing now exactly why he had said it. But he didn't know the truth, and suddenly she was seized by the startling realisation that she couldn't tell him even now. That if she did then he'd realise that Theo was his. And she couldn't risk letting him know—not when he despised her so much. Even if it was with good reason, she accepted despairingly. That didn't alter the fact that he obviously thought she could still be bought, and that he had only made love to her now for his own satisfaction—to show her that he could. And like a fool she had fallen into his tender trap...

She was sobbing and she couldn't stop, the breath-catching pain after so much joy sending violent shudders through her entire body.

How could she have let it happen? she wondered despairingly. She'd known he despised her and now, having recalled how badly she had treated him, it wasn't any wonder that he thought her not only heartless, but promiscuous too. She had had his love and she had blown it—thrown it away as if it didn't matter. And with it whatever respect he had had for her.

Curled up in a tight ball on the bed, she thought how incredible making love with him had been. But all it had succeeded in doing was to make her fall more deeply and hopelessly in love with him. And he...

No matter how much it hurt, she thought, she had to face the truth. He had had his payback in her willing and unconditional surrender. He was too proud a man ever to allow himself to become emotionally involved with her again.

CHAPTER NINE

SHE HAD SLEPT fitfully on top of the duvet for what had remained of the night.

Rising late, she groped for her cell phone on the bedside cabinet, where she had dumped the contents of her bag, which she had then left with her dress in Andreas's bedroom. Eventually she found it in the deep pocket of the masculine robe that she was still wearing.

'Why didn't you tell me about Andreas?' she asked pointedly and without any preamble when her mother answered after the first few rings.

There was a long silence at the other end of the line.

'Why?' Magenta pressed, staring out across the grounds through one of the windows. A pheasant was wandering peacefully across the middle of the pristine lawn, its coppery plumage striking in the morning sun. 'Why didn't you tell me I'd had a relationship with him? And that my baby— my beautiful baby—was his son?'

'I thought it was for the best.' Jeanette's tone was defensive. 'I knew what that Visconti family thought of you—thought of both of us—and I wanted something better for you,' she said. 'I was relieved when you gave him up, but then afterwards, when you moved back in with me in that flat, I heard you crying every night. Sometimes when you were asleep you'd even call out his name. When you had that haemorrhage and you couldn't remember anything about him I hoped you'd forgotten him for good. I wanted you to make a fresh start. Not to have to rely on any man, or need one in your life as I always did. I didn't think it mattered if Theo didn't know who his real father was. After all, it didn't do you any harm, did it?'

No? Magenta thought with bitter self-derision, thinking of the vain and hedonistic glory-seeking creature she had been.

'You had no right to do that.' It was a small cry from the depths of her heart, stinging as it was from all she'd remembered about herself, all she had lost, and now the humiliation of winding up in bed with the man who despised her because of it.

'I was only thinking of you.' Her mother had put on her *don't be angry with me—you know I'm not strong enough to take it* voice. 'Why are you asking me all this anyway?'

'It doesn't matter now. I'll ring you later,' Magenta said wearily, unable to cope with explaining right then how she had met Andreas again, and how last night she'd remembered everything. Later, she thought, but not now. Not when she was hurting so much inside.

She was longing for a shower. She felt so groggy. And after what had happened last night between her and Andreas she didn't feel up to facing him just yet. Consequently, donning her white track top and matching joggers, and twisting her hair into a topknot, she decided that the best thing was to give herself some breathing space before she made up her mind what she was going to do.

The house appeared to be silent as she went down into the hall.

Spotting the fine gauze at the French windows through the dining room door stirring gently in the morning breeze, she decided to make a quick exit to avoid seeing anyone, and was halfway across the room when Mrs Cox's voice made her almost jump with fright.

'If you're looking for Mr Visconti he went out early,' the

housekeeper told her, from where she was arranging some bright blooms on a table behind the door. 'Would you like me to prepare your breakfast now or would you prefer to wait?'

'N-no, thanks,' Magenta stammered, her gaze on the colourful heads, utterly surprised that Andreas could just get up and go about his business as though nothing had happened. 'I mean I'll wait—thanks.' Somehow she managed a smile before slipping out onto the terrace, her lungs grasping greedily at the sweet scented air.

The morning was as refreshing as only an English morning at the height of summer could be, she thought distractedly—and, grateful for it, she instantly broke into a run.

Across the terrace, down across the lawn—she didn't ease back until she was over the little bridge that spanned the brook and well on her way through the woods.

The path was soft with leaf mould and her feet made a dull sound as they struck the ground. She thought of the first time she had done this, nearly two years after lying, paralysed, in that coma, and as she so often did, and in spite of how she was feeling, she offered up her silent thanks to everyone and everything that had pulled her through when she had thought she might never even walk again.

She wanted to keep running, but her breasts were too tender after the passion she had shared with Andreas, and with hot colour staining her cheeks at how willingly she had allowed him to use her, she slowed her pace to a brisk walk.

'Walking, Magenta?'

As though she had conjured him from her thoughts, Andreas was running up behind her. The contours of his chest and arms were emphasised by the white T-shirt he was wearing with black joggers, and with his hair slicked back he looked utterly superb.

'You're never going to stretch yourself, ambling along at this pace.' He bounced light-footedly past and turned to face her, his sparkling eyes alive with health and teasing.

'I'm stretched enough, thank you,' she responded succinctly, and then could have kicked herself for the unintended implication. She was glad when he chose to ignore it. 'I've already done my running,' she clarified. 'Besides, I'm not anatomically designed to be able to enjoy quite the same freedom as you.'

A swift glance over her anatomy beneath the zipped and clinging white top had comprehension dawning in those glinting eyes. 'Ah!' Like her, he had slowed to a walk, and was now falling into step beside her. 'Magenta, would you mind if I asked you a rather personal question?'

She sent a wary glance towards him and with a shrug said, 'Why not? You will anyway.'

His brows drew together as though he were questioning the chill in her voice. 'When did you last make love?'

His question was so unexpected that she didn't know how to respond immediately. 'You should know,' she parried, looking straight ahead.

'I'm serious, Magenta.'

He was too. A quick look at his face showed a keenly assessing absorption that she hadn't really seen in him before. But of course he had to be thinking how tight she had been last night when he had entered her—far tighter than he had probably been expecting.

'You're right.' She made a cynical little sound down her nostrils. 'It *is* a personal question.' How did you tell someone who thought the worst about you that there had only ever been one man in your life and that he was standing right in front of you? 'And all I have to say is that it shouldn't have happened.'

'Is that why you sneaked away before I was awake—and with *my* bathrobe?'

She could tell from his voice that he was trying to make light of it.

'Don't worry. You'll get it back,' she said tartly.

His hand on her arm was suddenly stopping her in her

tracks. 'The robe doesn't worry me. Your frame of mind to-wards me this morning does. What's wrong, Magenta?'

From the top of an ash tree near where they were standing the pure notes of a song thrush were rippling down through the dappled leaves like liquid gold.

'Are you saying you regret what happened between us?'

He was drawing her closer and Magenta's lungs seemed to lock—in contrast to Andreas's, which were still expanding deeply from where he had been running.

She wanted to speak but she couldn't, because his lips were suddenly brushing lightly across hers, sending traitorous impulses leaping along her veins.

'Don't…' she murmured tremulously, but her plea was lost beneath the shrill, lucid notes of the thrush.

'That doesn't sound like regret to me.'

There was warm satisfaction in the way he breathed against her throat, and then she felt the cool bark of a tree against her back, and his fingers dealing with the zipper of her top.

His hands were like some craved addiction, making her cry out with the satisfaction that they alone could supply.

As he took her mouth with his she moved involuntarily against him, stimulated by the warm contoured muscles straining beneath his T-shirt, aware of his arousal that was every bit as strong as hers through the light, silky material of his joggers.

When he cupped her aching femininity she could have let herself go and taken the release she was craving right there and then. But the shrieking of a blackbird as it flew up from somewhere close by in agitated alarm brought her to her senses.

'No—don't!'

In an instant she was pulling away from him, breathing deeply to restore the sanity she could so easily have lost as her trembling fingers struggled to reinstate her top.

'Magenta…' He sounded breathless, and his strong features revealed just how much he was fighting for control.

'No!' she said adamantly, to herself more than to Andreas, and she started to run from him, not stopping until she came back across the little bridge, wondering how she was ever going to say what she had to say when he only had to touch her to blow all her firm decisions to smithereens.

He was right beside her as she came across the lawn towards the back of the house and saw a beautiful bronze Mini parked there on the shingle by the terrace steps.

'You've got a visitor,' she observed, dismayed. All she had been hoping to do was take a shower and then somehow find the courage to tell Andreas that she couldn't possibly stay there in his home another minute. How could she ever reclaim her self-respect if she did?

'No,' he said unequivocally, pulling a key out of the pocket of his joggers. 'Take it. It's yours,' he informed her, handing it to her.

Magenta's immediate instinct was to recoil from his offer. 'What's this for?' she challenged. 'Services rendered?' She couldn't believe how much she was hurting inside.

He shot her a surprisingly censuring look. 'For services yet to be fulfilled,' he enlightened her. 'If you're going to be working for me—however long it's going to be—you're going to need some form of transport. I can't always put a car and Simon at your disposal.'

'Andreas.' She had stopped on the verge of the lawn where it met the shingle drive, refusing to take the key he was still holding out to her. 'I really don't think this is a good idea. Us working together.'

'Working together?' He was looking at her askance, his sapphire eyes too intense, too probing. 'Or do you mean sleeping together?'

'Yes. No. I mean both.'

A thick eyebrow lifted almost indiscernibly. 'You didn't seem to have too many qualms about it last night.'

'Last night I was…affected.'

'By what?' he challenged roughly. 'It certainly wasn't alcohol. You didn't even sip that champagne you were given for the toasts.'

'You know what I mean. Last night changes everything.'

'Why? Because you refuse to admit that there's something between us that even you can't fight?'

'It's only sex.' *Dear heaven! Listen to me!* she thought, despairing at herself, and wondered at the dark emotion that flitted across his face.

'Yes, I know,' he accepted phlegmatically. 'But we always knew that, didn't we? Or at least *you* did. Is it so bad, meeting me on the same level now? Surely it's preferable to come together on equal terms, knowing there's no commitment or strings attached on either side. Knowing that I'm not going to embarrass you by dropping to my knees and asking you to marry me this time. Knowing that no one's going to get hurt.'

Only me, Magenta thought. Because now Andreas Visconti had learned his lesson. There was no way he would ever open his heart or lay his emotions on the line for her again.

'I'm not staying here,' she told him firmly. 'And I'm not taking the car. Oh, I know you think I can be bought. And, all right, maybe I let myself be bought once. But like you I learnt the hard way that what we want isn't always right for us, and that all the things we think are important can be wiped out in just a minute. As for material things—well, they just don't count. So I'd rather not be made to feel indebted to you, if it's all the same to you.'

Her hands were stuffed inside the front-facing pockets of her track top as she started walking again, her eyes focussing straight ahead on the house while she strove to blink bright, betraying tears away, her trainers crunching over the shingle.

'Is that why you left the dress in my room? And the other

things I bought you? Because they made you feel indebted to me?'

'What do you think?' She didn't even look at him, just kept on walking.

'I told you they were a business expense,' he reminded her.

'Well, that's a fancy name for it, isn't it?' she decried bitterly. 'You wanted me in your bed just to satisfy a warped need for revenge. I knew it and I still went ahead and slept with you. But I've remembered, Andreas. I remember everything. I just hadn't realised until now how much you must have wanted to hurt me. And OK, perhaps it was with good cause—but can you have any idea of how I'm feeling now?'

'Magenta—'

'Yes, I'll bet you can!' She carried on across the drive, past the beautiful bronze car that would have made the young Magenta jump at the chance of owning it. She sent only a disparaging glance towards it. 'Well, you've paid me back, and you must be feeling *so* good—especially in view of the amazingly short time you had to wait! But I'm not going to—'

'Magenta!' Hard fingers caught her arm as she mounted the terrace steps, pulling her to a swift and determined stop. 'What happened…happened. There wasn't any intended sense of revenge or malice behind it.'

He'd moved just one step higher than she was, but appeared to tower disconcertingly above her.

'Ha!' She tried to move past him and found her efforts blocked by his superb masculine body. 'Let me pass.'

'No. Not until I've said what I have to say.'

She looked up into the hard severity of his tightly controlled features, her expression pained and wounded in the sunlight.

'I'll admit it started out that way, with me wanting to give you a taste of your own medicine. But revenge is a pretty cold bedfellow, and I don't want to dwell on the past any more than you do. I made love to you last night because there wasn't anything in the world I wanted to do more. And if you re-member I let *you* make the decision. I didn't force your hand.'

'But you knew that if you kissed me I wouldn't have any choice in the matter.'

'No, I didn't know that. I thought because of what you'd said when things got rather heated down there that evening in the garden you'd just tell me to go to hell.'

'I wish I had!'

'Why? Because then you'd still be hiding behind the safety of your lost memory? Is that how you would have preferred it?'

Guilt and shame propelled her forward, but as she tried to make her escape again his arms came up to stop her. His chest felt solid beneath her hands, making her gasp with the betraying sensations that even now were mocking her deci-sion to leave.

'Let's just accept that last night satisfied something in both of us—whatever it was that needed to be satisfied. But I'm not having you cutting off your nose to spite your face just because you're nursing a very strong case of hurt pride. You need this job, and I sure as hell don't want all the hassle of trying to find another temporary assistant when you've adapted to the position far more easily and effectively than someone who had been doing it for years.

'I don't want to be the result of you and your little boy winding up homeless—or dependent upon your great-aunt, if that's how you'd both end up. As for the car... Whatever feelings I might have been harbouring about you, life dealt you a pretty miserable hand all round—especially after we broke up. I was only trying to make things a little easier for you. It wasn't meant as a trinket with which to buy your fa-vours or more delightful interludes like last night.

'And don't pretend it wasn't delightful,' he chided softly, when she turned her head, her jaw clenching against the re-sponses his words were producing in her. 'For both of us.

Whatever you feel about it now. Go home, by all means,' he acceded, 'but take the car. It's a company vehicle. I had Simon take me up to the office to pick it up for you this morning,' he enlightened her—which at least went some way to explaining why he'd left without waking her or even leaving a message for her earlier. 'You can use it until… Well, until this assignment ends…or until you cease to work for my company—whichever is the longer.'

He had obviously made up his mind that she'd be in the office on Monday morning.

'It isn't—' It isn't going to work, she was about to say. But the shrill ring of his cell phone cut her dead.

'Magenta!'

She heard his urgent command but she was already running up the steps, away from him. She was relieved when, catching the sudden impatience with which she heard him speaking, she realised that he had stopped pursuing her to take the call instead.

She couldn't take the car because it would symbolise just another payment from him, she thought bitterly when she stepped under the jets of the shower a few minutes later. Like the dress and its accoutrements. Like this job. Which was why she couldn't possibly carry on working for him for another day. If she agreed to do so then she would be letting him manipulate her, as he had been doing from the beginning, she thought wretchedly. But that didn't stop her mourning the young man who had worshipped her, read her poetry and given her gifts he could scarcely afford, who had argued for her against his family's harsh judgement. In contrast to the mature Andreas, who could afford to give her everything now. Everything, that was, except his love…

A knock on her bedroom door as she was towelling herself dry had her quickly shrugging into a white cotton robe. Her stomach turned over when she saw Andreas standing there outside her door.

'I have to fly to Paris for an urgent meeting and I won't be back until late tomorrow evening,' he told her, sounding none too pleased about the prospect.

He'd obviously already showered, because his hair was curling damply against the clean white shirt he'd put on under his dark suit, and it was difficult to ignore what his cologne was doing to her. He was, Magenta thought achingly, with sensual shivers running through her, the epitome of every woman's fantasy.

'You can stay here if you wish, or if you prefer, and you're still being obstinate about taking the car, I'll get Simon to drive you home.'

She nodded, because if she argued she was afraid he'd try and talk her out of what she knew she had to do.

'If that's the case, then I'll see you in the office on Monday morning.'

She didn't answer this time, and when he tilted her chin to kiss her gently on the mouth she had to clench her hands at her sides to stop herself from throwing her arms around his neck and pulling him down to her.

Goodbye, Andreas.

Five minutes later she saw the Mercedes haring out of the drive as if the hounds of hell were after it. An hour later she was riding home in a cab, out of his life.

CHAPTER TEN

THE LITTLE BAY pony was being put through its paces, and from the wooden fence enclosing the beginners' arena Magenta waved to the little figure in riding hat and jodhpurs sitting astride the animal's back.

She had thought Theo might want her to accompany him, as this was his first time on a horse, but he had been happy to leave her standing on the sidelines and had gone off with only the riding instructor instead.

Independent. Like Andreas, she thought, praying the day would be a long time coming when his son wouldn't need her as she watched the boy and the pony walking away from her now, guided by the young woman out into the wider field.

She hadn't heard from Andreas since she had left his house two weeks ago, leaving her formal typed notice on his desk, terminating a contract she hadn't even signed.

He hadn't bothered to contact her. But then what reason would he have? she asked herself torturously. He had had his revenge when she had fallen into bed with him, just as he had predicted she would. The only contact she had had from him or his firm since had been in the form of a cheque that he had had paid into her bank account, representing what she could only calculate had to be three months' salary.

Not wanting to take anything from him other than that which was her due, she had almost sent back the unearned income—until a trip to sign on at the local Job Centre had again brought her to her senses. If he hadn't prevented her from taking the job she had actually applied for she wouldn't now be desperately trying to find another. And if compensating her for that was his way of easing his conscience, then it was a small price to pay on his part for having his revenge— and at her expense!

She waved to Theo again through a blur of tears as he completed his first few metres of a rising trot. He was preoccupied, though, and didn't look her way. Already leaving her, she thought with an absurd ache in her chest.

Her brain only half registered a car drawing to a halt in the stableyard just behind her. From one of the open stalls, another horse whinnied softly. Another child being brought to its lesson, she thought absently. The stables were probably very popular on Saturday mornings.

She was just wondering with crushing anguish how she was going to explain to Theo that this first of the riding lessons he had longed for was, for a while at least, going to have to be his last, when she felt a prickling sensation travel down her spine.

'Hello, Magenta.'

For a few beats her heart seemed to stand still, and then she was swinging round, her loose hair falling over the powder-blue T-shirt she wore with jeans and pumps like dark rippling silk.

'Wh-what are you doing here?' She knew her stammering had nothing to do with any problem with her speech and everything to do with the shock of seeing Andreas there.

'Looking for you.'

As usual he was dressed for business, and as usual he looked cool and calm and collected. Probably going to some important meeting—or just back from one, she decided with a stray glance at the Mercedes. The dark executive image of the man looming above her was doing chaotic things to her already strained and now tingling nerves.

'How did you find me?'

His mouth compressed, and against the backdrop of the rustic stableyard he cut an incongruous yet striking figure with his elegant designer clothes and his dark hair ruffled slightly by the cooling wind.

'Purely by chance. I called at your home first, and your neighbour from the flat above was just coming out. She said you'd told her you were bringing Theo for his first riding lesson today and suggested I try here first.'

Her fifty-something neighbour probably would have relished doing that, Magenta thought, deciding that it probably wasn't 'purely by chance' that the woman had come down just as Andreas was knocking at her door. Even here the luxurious car and its affluent owner were attracting the attention of two stable girls as they passed, one carrying a saddle, the other a bucket, before disappearing into one of the open stalls.

'Why?' Magenta enquired poignantly, looking up into his strong dark features.

'Because of the way you left. Without a word or any prior warning. Without even talking it over with me personally first.'

'I left my formal resignation. I didn't feel that any further explanations were necessary.'

She heard him take a breath before he came and rested his hand, like her, on the top bar of the fence, his body half turned towards her. He was so close that she could feel the pull of his dark chemistry evoking dangerous sensations in her, making her pulse quicken, her body yearn to lean closer to him.

'Is this Theo?' A jerk of his chin indicated the trotting pony and its little rider.

'Yes.' She couldn't even look at Andreas as she said it.

'He looks like he's been born to it.'

Magenta uttered a tight little laugh, clinging to the fence

with both hands now as if it was the only thing holding her upright. She remembered going riding sometimes with Andreas in the distant past, how she hadn't really taken to it, while *he* had ridden as proudly and confidently as his ancient forebears.

'Like you were born to drive men mad, Magenta.'

He had turned towards the field and was following the little boy's progress with studied absorption—as if he hadn't just landed a comment that had set her veins on fire.

'Then that's their misfortune,' she said swiftly, unable to keep the bitterness out of her voice. All her life, because of the way she looked, she had had more than her fair share of masculine attention.

'Yes.'

She didn't even need to ask to realise he was referring to himself. For a few moments they stood in silence, both gazing ahead at the pony, which was walking now, being led around in a figure of eight.

'I want you to come back,' Andreas said at length.

Magenta sent him a sidelong glance. 'As your PA?' When he didn't answer, she thought, *Of course. What else?* She'd probably caused him quite a bit of inconvenience, walking out as she had. 'Why?' Her eyes were wounded, wary. 'To save you all the bother of having to find someone else? I thought you would have replaced me—' she clicked her thumb and middle finger together '—just like that.'

The strong jaw tightened, as though he was restraining an element of impatience. 'I know you won't let me help in any way, no matter how much you might need it, but I'd like you at least to have the benefit of earning the salary you expected to be earning after I prevented you from getting the job you'd set your heart on.'

'Why? Because your conscience is probing you now and you suddenly feel responsible for me? I don't want your pity,' she breathed, with an excruciating ache deep in her chest.

'That's good,' he returned. 'Because I wasn't offering any. But as your employer…well, let's just say I acted more than a little unethically.'

'Unethically?' She gave a dry, brittle little laugh. 'And as my ex-lover?'

He didn't answer. After all, what could he say?

She saw him rest his elbows on the fence, his hands—those hands that had the power to do what no other man could ever do to her—clasped absently together in front of him.

'I convinced myself you owed me something, Magenta,' he admitted surprisingly, 'and as a consequence of that I find myself owing you.'

'If that's meant as an apology,' she uttered, 'forget it. I have.' That couldn't have been further from the truth. But her pride would never let her admit to him how much her folly in imagining she could work for him—for whatever reason she had convinced herself she needed to—had cost her emotionally. Far, far more even than financially.

'I'm afraid that doesn't fall within my rules of conduct as a human being. You said you found it difficult getting a good job because of the discrimination you encountered when you told prospective employers what had happened to you, and I robbed you of a chance without even knowing about it, or what you had been through. But if you hadn't had that setback which sent Rushford packing—I'm assuming that's what happened—then without a shadow of a doubt, with your single-minded ambition and determination, you would have been enjoying all the status and financial rewards of a top model now.'

Sucking in her breath, Magenta stared at the pony that was now trotting again with its animated little rider. Theo had only just spotted the tall man who was talking to her and he kept looking towards Andreas, completely distracted from whatever it was the instructor was saying to him.

Since her little boy had come home Magenta hadn't been

able to get over how much he looked like Andreas, and it struck her again forcefully now. The resemblance, though, had done nothing to jog her memory of Andreas *before* she'd met him again in that wine bar, and a little shudder ran through her at recalling the conversation she had had with her great-aunt when she had brought Theo home to Magenta last week.

'Have you told him?'

It had been one of the first things the woman had asked her as soon as she had stepped through the door, and Magenta hadn't even needed to ask who she meant.

'No, I haven't,' she'd admitted after she'd released Theo from her heart-swelling hug and he'd scampered off to play the DVD that Aunt Josie's stepdaughter had given him. With that she had broken down in those plump maternal arms and poured out the whole miserable story.

'I still think you'd better tell him, young lady,' the woman had advocated as they'd followed Theo into Magenta's clean and tidy yet shabby-looking sitting room. 'From what you've said about him he doesn't sound to me like a man who'd appreciate being deceived.'

Now, hurting and angry at the way he was continuing to judge her, and for allowing herself to be so deeply and hopelessly in love with him, she flung caution to the winds and tossed back a response to his remark about her single-minded determination. 'Well, that's where you're wrong. For a start Marcus Rushford was off the scene long before you're suggesting. And it *wasn't* my brain haemorrhage that put paid to my glorious career as a model. It was over long before that because I wouldn't give up *your* son!'

She wasn't even looking at him. Nevertheless she could feel his shock as tangibly as the cool wind that was penetrating her thin T-shirt.

'What are you saying?'

His sentence was little more than a rasped whisper. Perplexity clouded the eyes raking over her face, looking for some sign of clarification before they shifted to Theo, to Magenta, than back to the little boy again.

'Are you telling me he's *mine?*' His features as he turned back to her were contorted with disbelief.

'Look at him, Andreas, if you don't believe me.'

His doubting gaze returned to the child, and this time he couldn't take his eyes off him. His strong face was crisscrossed by a myriad of emotions. Bewilderment. Incredulity. And something else. Something that was beginning to look remarkably like acceptance.

'I don't understand. You were using protection.'

She shrugged. 'It happens.'

'And you were with Rushford...'

'Not in that way.'

Deep lines scored his face as he turned interrogating eyes in her direction. 'What are you saying?'

'I'm saying that—'

'Mummy—look!'

She broke off to see the pony being led back towards the stableyard. Theo was sitting proudly in the saddle, his arms outstretched on either side of him, the reins hanging loosely over the pony's back.

'Darling, be careful!' she called out.

At the same time Andreas was punching a number into his cell phone.

Of course. He probably had somewhere important to be, Magenta thought, realising with a stab of despair that he could only be attending to business at a time like this if he didn't believe her.

'Yes. Cancel my meeting,' he instructed abruptly. There was a wealth of determination in the eyes that clashed with hers.

The gentle clip-clop of hooves on tarmac, however, signified that Theo's lesson was over. Gratefully Magenta tore herself away from Andreas, glad of these few minutes when she could occupy herself with getting her son out of the saddle and so delay the moment when the ultimate interrogation came.

'Who's that, Mummy?' As the instructor handed her the pony's reins in order to go and attend to something in its stable Theo pointed towards Andreas who, to Magenta's dismay, had followed her across the yard. From his vantage point in the saddle, Theo was studying him seriously, his head tilted to one side. 'Are you Mummy's friend?'

Two pairs of identical blue eyes met and locked. 'Do you want me to be Mummy's friend?' Andreas asked.

The odd inflexion in his voice caused something inside Magenta to twist.

'Yeah! Yeah! *Yeah!*' Theo clapped his hands, so excited that it made the pony start.

Immediately Andreas's hand came up, at the same time as Magenta's, to steady the animal's head. Magenta quickly withdrew hers, feeling the havoc of his accidental touch like a collision of stars.

'Does that mean we can ride in your great big car?'

'Theo...' Magenta cautioned. Getting into Andreas's car was the last thing she wanted to do.

'You bet it does!' Andreas promised. While the child was looking excitedly towards the Mercedes he said to Magenta, 'May I?'

She nodded in response to his gesture to lift Theo off the pony, and yet he still enquired of his son, 'Would you like a hoist out of that saddle, little man?'

'Yeah! Yeah! *Yeah!*' Theo exclaimed again.

Watching the gentle way in which Andreas lifted their son down from the pony, and seeing the two of them together at last, Magenta felt as though her heart was being squeezed.

'It suits you,' she whispered, racked by emotion, but earned herself only a ravaged look from him before he set Theo safely down on his feet.

The stable girl had come back and was taking the reins from Magenta.

'You're both coming home with me,' Andreas told her as the girl led the pony back to its stall.

'I can't. Aunt Josie's cooking lunch for us,' she said, grabbing Theo by the hand as another, larger horse was being led into the yard.

It sounded a lame excuse after he had just cancelled what was doubtless an important meeting, having found out he was a father. She knew, though, that he would demand to know why she hadn't told him he had a son, and she didn't feel like explaining—especially when the fear that had kept her silent when she'd first found out she was pregnant, and again more recently, was still as rampant in her as it had ever been.

'What's wrong, Magenta? Afraid to be alone with me?' he suggested with an edge of steel in his voice, yet softly enough so that Theo couldn't hear.

Well, she was, wasn't she? she thought with a little shiver, but she said only, 'Of course not.'

'Then perhaps dear Aunt Josie won't mind stretching lunch four ways,' he proposed, the endearment mocked by his cynical tone. 'After all, I think it's time I met this paragon of virtue who had leave to look after my child when I wasn't even allowed to know I had one.'

'You were in America!' Magenta exhaled, knowing it was yet another black mark against her in his long list of grievances.

His jaw was set rigid as they came up to the car. 'Not two weeks ago!'

It didn't help Magenta telling herself that she deserved his anger as he held the car door open for the little boy to scramble onto the back seat.

'You've had him to yourself for five years,' he rasped as she stepped into the car beside her son. 'And if he really is mine then things are going to change. As of now!'

* * *

Josie Ashton was wearing her apron with a cheery fireside scene when she opened the front door of her modest home. A labourer's cottage, with just two rooms up and two down, and the addition of a small bathroom on the back, it was one of a terrace of twelve homes fronting onto a street that had been built for the workforce of a nineteenth-century printing factory, which had since been pulled down to accommodate a more lucrative and modern trading estate at the end of the road.

'Aunt Josie, this is Andreas Visconti,' Magenta told her uncomfortably, conscious that Theo was still standing there looking up at him with a kind of hero-worship instead of rushing in and down the passage as he usually did.

'Well, I didn't think he was the window-cleaner,' Josie expressed, with a grimace at the gleaming Mercedes that looked even more out of place parked outside her humble home than it had outside Magenta's flat a couple of streets away.

'Andreas, this is my great-aunt. Josie Ashton.'

'I'm pleased to meet you, Mrs Ashton,' Andreas said, shaking her hand and taking her a little off-guard, Magenta realised, with his effortless charm.

'And I suppose you're hungry too.'

Josie Ashton never did stand on ceremony, Magenta thought, but from the glow that lit the woman's face as she held the door open for them all Magenta could tell that her aunt had warmed instantly to Andreas Visconti.

The smell of roast chicken and parsnips met them as they stepped inside.

'That's very kind of you, Mrs Ashton, and I do regret having to turn down your offer, but I have some pressing business to discuss with Magenta. I hope it won't inconvenience you too much if I take her away for an hour or so?'

'Not at all,' Josie Ashton responded with obvious and increasing pleasure, unaware of the tension that was twisting

Magenta's stomach muscles into tight knots. 'Take all the time you need, Andreas. It won't be any trouble reheating her lunch.'

'I'll only be a little while,' she told Theo, stroking his dark hair.

As she stooped to kiss him, however, he scampered back along the passage towards Andreas, saying, 'I want to come too. I want to ride in Mr 'Conti's big car.'

'Not now, darling. You have to stay here and eat all the lovely lunch that Aunt Josie's cooked you,' Magenta explained gently, trying to pacify him.

But the little boy, usually so well-behaved, was having none of it.

'Why can't I come? I want another ride in Mr 'Conti's car.' He was practically in tears now.

'Hey! What's all this?' Andreas asked softly, dropping to his haunches so that his eyes were on the same level as the little boy's.

'I want to come with you,' Theo sobbed, and then, to everyone's amazement, he wound his arms tightly around Andreas's neck.

Magenta darted an anxious glance towards her aunt—who didn't notice, or was choosing not to.

'I'm flattered, Theo.' There was no mistaking the surprised emotion in the deep, masculine voice. 'But if just this time you'll stay here and look after your aunt, I'll be back for you later, I promise.'

Alarm bells started clanging ominously inside Magenta's head even as Andreas's statement went some way to pacifying the little boy.

'You shouldn't have said that,' she rebuked as soon as he had stepped into the car beside her. 'You should never make promises you can't keep.'

'Don't tell me what I should or shouldn't say, Magenta,' he warned, fastening his seat belt across his body with swift, economical movements. 'And, believe me, I *never* break promises. I'd appreciate it if you didn't say anything at all to me for a while,' he said as he pulled away, 'Because the way I feel towards you right at this moment, my dearest, I'm angry enough to bloody well crash this car!'

Andreas was sitting grim-mouthed as he steered the Mercedes through the heavy midday traffic, bringing it up onto the ring road and out of the hubbub of the crowded city.

When he had come back from Paris two weeks ago to find Magenta gone from the house he'd automatically assumed that she would turn up at the office the following day—until he had found the note she had left on his desk in the study.

He shouldn't have been surprised that she had walked out on him, but he had—and shockingly so. Especially as she hadn't said anything about leaving after their conversation in the woods or before he'd driven off for that meeting the previous day.

He had told himself it was for the best. That there was no way he would ever lay himself open to her fickle charms again. That he had suffered enough the first time. But there was something about this woman that he had never been able to prevent getting under his skin.

Even while he'd been telling himself that it was safer for his sanity's sake that she had gone from his life and—even more importantly—from his bed, some masochistic part of him had needed to see her again. A need to redress the wrong in the hardship he must have caused her had been a convenient excuse to delude himself over his main reason for wanting to see her. Because he darn well couldn't help himself! he realised, with tension gripping the hard sweep of his jaw. And all the time she had been able to simply walk away from him without even telling him he had a son!

As he followed the signs and took the slip road to a local beauty spot he realised that, despite all the possibilities that might have had him questioning her claim to paternity, there was no doubt in his mind at all that little Theo James was his. The boy had his colouring, his eyes and he looked just like he did in a photograph he had of himself playing cricket with his father at the same age. But why had Magenta denied him the right even to see his own son? Taken it on herself to keep his identity hidden?

Well, she had some explaining to do, he promised himself as he brought the car off the slip road to the roundabout. And she was going to have to make it good!

Magenta looked at him guardedly as he stopped the car in a deserted lay-by. They were high on a hill, among acres of grassland and managed forestry, and way down, through a bank of trees, she could see the glinting blue water of a reservoir or some sort of man-made lake.

'Why didn't you tell me?' he rasped. He was looking intently ahead, out of the windscreen, as though seeing something other than the white line along the quiet road. 'Why did you let me think he was Rushford's son?'

'I didn't. That was something you decided for yourself from the beginning.'

'But you didn't put me straight, Magenta. Why?'

She looked away, catching a glimpse through the trees of a white sail down there on the wind-ruffled lake. 'I don't know. I was afraid.'

'Of what?'

'Of losing him.'

'Losing him?' His tone was harsh and penetrating.

'To you and your family.'

'So you preferred to see him deprived of a father instead? Leading the disadvantaged existence he's leading now?'

'He isn't *disadvantaged!*' It was a ringing little cry, torn out of her guilt and anguish at being made to feel that she was somehow less than an adequate mother.

'Or were you intending that Marcus Rushford—or even some other man—would somehow be able to take my place and fill the breach?'

'No. I told you. Marcus was never anything other than my managing agent.'

'And you *really* expect me to believe that?'

'I don't care what you believe,' she tossed back, opening her door. 'It's the truth.'

She felt the tugging wind through her thin top as she jumped out, slamming the car door behind her. She heard him get out and close his door with far more respect than she had shown hers.

'Anyway, I did try to tell you,' she said defensively, stepping onto a grassy bank which sloped gently downhill before levelling off some distance away, offering a far better view over the lake.

'When?' Andreas pressed, following her.

'Not long after I found out I was pregnant. I knew you had the right to know.'

'That was very generous of you.' His sarcasm was flaying. 'So what changed your mind?'

'You did.'

'I did?' He gave a snort of disbelief as he drew level with her.

'I came all the way to the restaurant one day,' she explained, keeping her eyes trained on the little sailboat whose skipper was finding it hard to keep a straight course in the buffeting wind. 'But then I lost my nerve because I remembered what you'd said about if ever I got pregnant and wouldn't marry you. You said you'd fight me for custody. And that was how possessive you were simply over a hypothetical child!'

Crossing her arms, she moved down to a levelled-off viewing point.

Aware of him right behind her, she murmured, 'I was also worried that you might not believe that he was yours.'

She could almost see the derision lifting his eyebrow before he said, 'Whatever gave you *that* idea?' But she chose not to respond to his censuring remark.

While he was still so angry, and so obviously hardened towards her, she couldn't tell him the whole truth and put her heart on the line.

'I tried to ring you once, but you weren't there. Shortly afterwards I bumped into a girl we both knew one day when I was out shopping and she told me you'd gone to America. After I'd had the haemorrhage,' she added resignedly, 'I couldn't have let you know even if you'd been around— because I didn't even remember who you were.'

'Surely you must have told someone you knew—or at least your mother—who the father of your child was?' His tone was no less sceptical as he moved to stand beside her.

'Yes.'

'So what did you think whenever my name was mentioned? Didn't it even arouse your curiosity enough for you to try and find out who and where I was? Didn't you even care enough to want to find out?'

'I would have—if she'd mentioned you to me,' Magenta admitted, wondering how she could possibly explain her mother's silence without discrediting her character too much in his eyes. 'But she didn't. I think she thought there had been something going on between us that would upset me too much if I remembered it and she just wanted me to get well.'

He made a sound of angry disbelief, and she couldn't blame him. She couldn't forget how stunned and angry she had been herself when she had found out.

'So what did she tell you? That Rushford was the father? Or did she imagine you'd think your child had been produced out of thin air?'

'Andreas, don't...' It was bad enough that he was angry

with *her* without his turning his understandable venom on her mother. 'She didn't know what to tell me,' she uttered in the woman's defence, though she was still hurting unbearably because of it, and could see no reason for the way her mother had acted.

'I see.' From the grim cast of his mouth and the way his breath shivered through his nostrils he had clearly grasped the full extent of the situation. 'So she willingly put her grandson in the same situation as she put her daughter. With no father. No security. No—'

'Stop it!' She couldn't go on listening to him slating her mother, no matter how much he believed the woman deserved it, but above everything else she couldn't stand his pain.

'And what about *you,* Magenta?' he asked. 'Or is it an inherited trait of the James women to keep their children's fathers in the dark about their paternity?'

'No!'

'Then why didn't you tell me two weeks ago? Three?' His eyes scoured hers as he pulled her to face him. 'Just when was it exactly that you remembered who I am?'

The torment in his face was palpable, shredding her heart into what felt like a thousand pieces. 'That first night in the wine bar,' she admitted guiltily. 'It was an instinctive feeling rather than anything real, but over the next few hours—days—things started coming back.'

'And you didn't *tell* me?' Hard incredulity burned in his eyes as he let her go. 'All the time we were together at the house? Not even that night we made love?'

'I told you—I was afraid. You're rich now, and I don't have two cents to rub together.'

'What's that got to do with anything?' he demanded impatiently.

'I didn't want you using your money and your newfound power to hurt me. I was frightened sick you'd try and take him away from me.'

'And you didn't think it was any less of a crime trying to keep his existence from *me?*'

She did, but she didn't know what else to say to try and exonerate herself, when really there was no excuse for what she had done.

'At first I was just afraid,' she told him. 'But I didn't know what I was frightened of. There was this threat hanging over me—over Theo—and I knew it had to be because of something you'd once said or done. You already seemed to disapprove of him being left with Aunt Josie and you didn't even know he was yours! Anyway, things kept coming back in dribs and drabs. Then that night we made love I remembered everything. Until then a lot of pieces of my memory were still missing and my mind was a jumbled mess.'

'If you *have* remembered everything,' he said.

'What do you mean?' she queried, the face upturned to his etched with anxious lines.

A cold gust blew up from the lake, sweeping through the trees and penetrating her T-shirt. She wrapped her arms around herself to try and stop her shivering.

Without a word Andreas was removing his jacket.

'What do you mean?' she asked again, tortured by his sudden nearness, by his warmth and the fragrance of his cologne that was clinging to the jacket he was now placing carefully around her shoulders.

'I mean that you're still stating that Marcus Rushford wasn't your lover. Unless it's only me you're trying to convince, but your insistence does make me wonder.'

'I do remember. *Everything.* And he wasn't,' she reiterated adamantly.

'It was him you left me for. Him you wanted to be with,' he reminded her—as though she needed reminding.

'I thought I did,' she admitted. 'But it didn't take much more than a week for me to realise I didn't. OK, he was exciting, and he was offering so much, and I was young and naive enough to believe that any man could make me feel the way you did. That what we had wasn't important and I could just walk away. I didn't want to be stifled by commitment, to relinquish all my hopes and dreams. You were expecting too much and I wasn't ready, even though I really, really didn't want to break up with you.'

Emotion was threatening to overwhelm her.

'I couldn't stay at the bottom of the pile with—as you said just now—no security and no prospects, no clue as to where I'd even come from,' she said, managing to contain the sob that just for a moment had started to make her voice wobble. 'The girl with no father and most of the time no mother. With no money and no respect from anyone. Always the one who people pointed a finger at. The one who didn't quite measure up. I was determined to break free from all that, and when Marcus offered me the chance I jumped up and grabbed it.

'I truly believed he'd make me rich and famous and everyone would look at me and say, "Hasn't she done well? Jeanette James's bastard daughter. Who would have thought it, with her background and the type of upbringing she had?" I wanted respect and admiration, but above all else I wanted acceptance. To be able to show everyone who'd doubted me or shunned me—like your father and your grandmother, and all the kids I'd gone to school with—that I was every bit as good as they were. Yes, I wanted fame, and I wanted self-sufficiency. And somewhere among all those crazy mixed-up ideas of grandeur I wanted to help Mum.'

'So you didn't love him?' It was a cool, emotionless question. 'Is that what you're saying?'

'Yes.'

'Yet you still went ahead and slept with him? Moved in with him?'

Suddenly Andreas's voice seemed to be thickened by something. What was it? Magenta wondered. Disgust?

'No!' she denied fiercely, determined to put him straight.

'He offered me the use of his apartment because he'd just bought another one nearer his company and he didn't want to let it out. He wanted someone to look after it for him for a while. He said it would be better for my image to be living there rather than in "the hovel", as he called it, I'd been living in with Mum. He *wanted* us to be lovers, but I wasn't ready for that. I'm not saying we didn't kiss, because I did have a mild flirtation with him, and he did everything in his power to try and get me into bed. But it didn't take him long to guess that I still hadn't got you out of my system.

'When he knew I was coming to see you that day with that book I think he realised that you'd only have to touch me to send all his plans for my future awry. He said he'd only promote me if you were well and truly out of my life. That's when he… Well, you remember that…bruise…for want of a better word…on my neck? It was a deliberate act of brutality to stamp his mark on me before I saw you, even though he didn't stand a cat in hell's chance of getting me into bed. I think what mattered to him most was losing a marketable commodity—which was all I really was to him. He already had a long-suffering woman-friend in tow. But I was living in his flat for just a fraction of the rent, and he was already negotiating a big contract for me. I didn't want to give it all up and go back to my old life and the situation I'd been living in, so I did exactly as he told me to do that day. I knew that if you thought he had become my lover you'd never want to see me again, and I wanted to make you hate me so that you wouldn't try.'

'Why are you telling me this now?' His voice sounded almost hoarse. 'Because you're worried that I might take Theo away from you?'

Because I love you!

His face was such a hard, inscrutable mask that she couldn't say it. If she did then he could go away, satisfied that he had the ultimate triumph: Magenta James as crazy over him as he had been over her six years ago. And even if she deserved it, she couldn't take the humiliation of that.

'I don't want you to go on thinking the worst about me,' she answered steadily at length, but it was an effort when she was trembling so much inside. 'I know what I did wasn't very nice, but I just wanted you to know that I'm not entirely as bad as you would have me painted.'

'So what happened when the wonderful Marcus found out you were pregnant and had ruined all his plans?' he asked scathingly.

Flinching still from the resurrected memory, Magenta refrained from telling Andreas about the other man's brutal response. 'I was asked to leave the apartment when it become clear to him that I wasn't going to do "the sensible thing",' she informed him with bitter cynicism. 'I was planning to leave anyway. He just accelerated my departure, that's all.'

'And you went where?'

'To the new flat the council had given Mum when she left rehab.'

His features hardened but he didn't say anything.

'Then, three weeks before Theo was due... Well, you know the rest. I woke up from my coma thinking I'd lost him, but he was alive and well and almost two months old to the day. When they brought him in to see me I didn't have any strength in my arms to hold him. I was frightened that I was never going to be able to. He became my reason to recover. To get well.'

'And I wasn't there.'

Those four simple words conveyed an intensity of emotion before he looked away towards the lake, though Magenta knew he wasn't actually seeing a thing. His teeth were gritted and his face appeared slashed by some inner conflict.

'My son was brought into this world with his mother unconscious and a father who didn't even know of his existence!'

His self-condemnation was paramount, but Magenta could sense a multitude of other emotions in him too.

'Don't be too angry with me, Andreas,' she begged, wishing she could wave a magic wand and change the past. 'I can't ever make up for the way I behaved, but please believe me when I say I'm truly, truly sorry.'

He didn't say anything, just nodded his head as though he didn't trust himself to speak any more.

'Come on,' he said surprisingly softly, and though he put his arm around her shoulders, she knew it was only to guide her back to the car.

CHAPTER ELEVEN

'My son and I have a lot of catching up to do.'

That was what Andreas had said when they had been driving back from that beauty spot the day he had found out about Theo, and true to his word he had immediately seen to it that they made a start.

Rearranging his work schedule, he had taken a week's emergency leave from his office so that he could be with Theo, and he had certainly gone out of his way over the past week to spend as much time with the little boy as he could.

Theo had been thrilled when Magenta had broken it to him gently that Andreas Visconti was his father—although Andreas had insisted on being there too. As was his right, Magenta had accepted, and she had even been relieved that he had—just as she was pleased that he was so determined to be a hands-on father whenever he could.

What she still couldn't get used to, or help feeling uneasy about, however, was the way he was suddenly wanting a say in all her decisions about Theo—particularly as the little boy was treating him with such adulation, looking up to this new and exciting Daddy as though the man had always been in her life.

'I know you want to be self-sufficient and not dependent upon me in any way, Magenta,' he'd said, the day he had turned up at her flat with the Mini, 'and I'm sorry, but that

isn't the way I function. I have a responsibility to you now—
if only for my son's sake—so you're going to have to accept
this with the good grace with which it's being given.'

There was nothing she could say to that, so she didn't—
although she did stand by her guns over the issue of not working for him. It was torture enough having to see him regularly
now because of Theo, without subjecting herself to the aching
need for him on a daily and more formal basis, when it was
all too clear to her that he was never likely to return her love.

She had all but poured her heart out to him that afternoon
when she had told him the truth about Theo, and yet he hadn't
pursued the subject of her feelings for him any further.

He obviously didn't want to do anything to make his son
think that his parents were an item, she realised wretchedly,
which could only mean that he had decided they never would
be. After all, securing her capitulation when he had only himself to consider was one thing. Finding out that the child of
the woman he'd been hell-bent on humiliating was actually
his, and not some other man's, must have put a totally different complexion on things altogether.

Consequently on those days when he called round to take
her and Theo out she was careful not to give him any indication of the way she felt. She avoided his eyes whenever she
felt him looking at her, did her best to hide how the smallest
degree of physical contact with him affected her and managed
to maintain a cool, emotional distance, although it was agony.

'Relax,' he advised one day, when she was handing over
her debit card to pay for something for Theo. He had misunderstood the reason for the way she'd gasped when his strong
fingers over hers had stopped her from doing so. 'I know it's
an experience you didn't want, having your child's father in
the boy's life, but you're going to have to get used to it,' he
said quietly, for her alone to hear, and he handed his own
card to the cashier.

Taking further control, that week he had secured the riding

lessons for Theo that Magenta had been worried she would have to cancel, ignored her protests and renewed the lease on her flat and, to top it all, charmed her indomitable aunt into giving him one of her home-made blueberry pies.

'How does it feel to suddenly be everybody's favourite person?' Magenta snapped at the end of the week, when they were driving back to her flat after that gesture from her aunt, with Theo asleep in the back of the car.

Andreas laughed deeply under his breath. 'Do I detect some resentment there, Magenta?'

'Of course not,' she answered, adding as casually as she could, 'It's nice that you've been an instant hit with my family.'

But not with her, Andreas thought, conscious of the fact that she didn't really want him in her life. Although that was hardly surprising when she knew as well as he did that his sole intention in employing her had, from the start, been to humiliate her and teach her the lesson he'd felt she deserved. During that week of their working together, however, something else had taken over. Something that ever since had had him waking up feeling that he would go crazy if he couldn't kiss her lovely mouth again and feel her warm, responsive body beneath his.

Noticing the way she was looking over her shoulder at the little boy, with her lips curved in a gentle smile, as he pulled up outside her flat he had to fight the urge to drag her across the car—even with his son in the back—and plunder that luscious mouth until she smiled at *him* like that. Nevertheless, the way she had referred to Theo and Josie a moment ago as *her* family grated, and he had to restrain himself from making any comment and fuelling an already-difficult situation as he carried his sleeping son into the flat.

'As you know, I won't be here for most of next week,' he said, after they had tucked him up in bed, reminding her of the phone conversation he'd had with his colleague earlier in the day. 'I'm doing a tour of the properties in the Lake District and the north-east that I'm going to be taking over from PJ. It *was* scheduled for this week, but in view of more pressing developments…' He didn't need to explain how essential it had been for him to postpone as much as he had been able to in favour of getting to know his boy. 'I'll be gone until Thursday. That's if Lana's managed to book us an afternoon flight—'

'Lana?' she was querying, before he could finish.

'Yes, Lana Barleythorne. You met her at your interview,' he said unnecessarily. 'She'll be coming with me.'

He was about to tell her why, but decided not to, leaving her to speculate as he tried to gauge her reaction. In truth he was wishing that he could leave the adoring Miss Barleythorne securely grounded in the office, but she was becoming a darned good project manager and he was going to need her skills on this country house hotels enterprise—which was why he'd deemed it necessary to have her with him.

Now, though, as Magenta said only, 'Right,' with a dismissive little shrug, he wondered with some annoyance whether he shouldn't take the time to enjoy some of the pleasures that Lana would be more than willing to offer him. At least then, he thought, as he did the sensible thing and left the shabby little flat for the sake of his sanity, he might be able to appreciate a woman as he'd always done—on a purely casual basis—and drive this insane craving for Magenta out of his mind.

Over the next week, although she willed herself not to, Magenta missed Andreas terribly. She didn't know which was worse: hearing from him when he rang sometimes to speak to Theo and make casual conversation with her, or not hearing from him at all. She was getting through each day, she realised, just living for his phone calls, and she berated herself for loving him and for even thinking about him so much when she should have been doing what she had always done until Andreas had come into her life again—and that was channelling all her energies towards her son.

Having agreed to Andreas's request not to pursue the idea of getting another job, at least until after Theo started back to school, Magenta took the little boy out every day—either with her aunt or on her own.

Making the most of the continuing sunshine she took him to the park, or to their local nature reserve, or just to his favourite café, where she bought him an extra thick milkshake as a special treat. She started using the Mini too, which she'd accepted for Theo's benefit. Everything Andreas was doing for them was for Theo's benefit, she reflected painfully, since he'd found out that the boy was his.

At night she read to Theo, as she had done from when he was very small, encouraging him to read to her in turn, keen to develop his interest in books from an early age—which was probably why he was showing such an aptitude for learning now. Some nights they would watch a cartoon, or one of his favourite wildlife DVDs together while he was eating his supper, and then she would tuck him up in bed and tell him a story until his eyelids started to droop and he fell asleep.

Alone then, she would find her thoughts wandering too readily to Andreas—although the idea of him being away for nearly a week with a woman whose interest in him had been patently obvious at that interview was more than her bruised and aching heart could take.

She was glad when the torment was over and the Thursday of that week brought him back.

He had told her that Simon would be picking her and Theo up in the limousine that afternoon, to drive them over to Surrey. He was inviting them both to stay for a long weekend. 'We're going to need to discuss his future,' he'd said, in a way that had made her stomach muscles clench painfully. 'We can't go on without any set course, and it's best that we each know where we stand from the start.'

It was with increasing anxiety, therefore, that late that afternoon Magenta sat browsing through a magazine under the shade of a sun umbrella at the poolside, while Theo paddled in the little inflatable pool that Simon had filled with water. It had been another purchase by Andreas last week, for his son to use at the house in case his parents couldn't be with him in the main pool.

Later, when his flight had been delayed and he'd called to say he wasn't sure whether he was going to be able to make it back by that evening, Magenta showered and changed from her jeans and T-shirt into a simple white sundress as the day was still so warm. After letting Theo watch one of his early evening kiddies' programmes, she decided to put him to bed.

'I want to stay up and wait for Daddy,' the little boy protested sleepily as she was helping him into his pyjamas in the room that the housekeeper had prepared for him next to Magenta's. He was already rubbing his eyes to try and keep them open, but Magenta smiled understandingly.

'I'll send Daddy up to see you as soon as he comes in,' she promised, and was startled to realise how much she sounded like a normal wife and mother, in a normal loving partnership, waiting for her devoted husband to come home.

She knew, though, that Theo would be asleep in seconds after all his excitement that day—riding in the limousine, splashing about in his pool and hitting balls about on the tennis court with her until they had nearly laughed themselves hysterical.

'I don't even know if he'll be coming home tonight,' she whispered, kissing the little boy who looked so much like Andreas with her throat contracting. But already she was saying it to herself.

The sun was throwing its colours over the evening countryside when she stepped out onto the terrace, with dazzling gold already turning to pink by the time she'd crossed the lawn and reached the honeysuckle hedge.

The resident thrush was singing from the uppermost branch of an ancient larch tree, and the air was mellifluous with humming insects and the gentle gurgling of the brook.

She deliberately avoided looking at the lovers' seat. She didn't want to remember what had happened the last time she had sat down on that seat. Nor did she wish to remember what had happened in the house behind her when she had been here last—the torrid passion she had shared with Andreas that had finally shocked her into remembering.

The thrush had stopped singing and the sun was a big red ball through the trees by the time she made up her mind that he wasn't coming home tonight. With an agonised sigh she decided to go back inside—but she'd only made it to the end of the honeysuckle hedge before being brought up fast in her tracks.

'Andreas!' It was more of a gasp than anything else as every cell in her body went into meltdown from his devastating and achingly familiar presence.

English in all but looks and name, he was still wearing the short-sleeved white shirt and sleek grey trousers he'd worn for business that day—although he was tieless now, and his shirt was partially unbuttoned as usual. The perfect tailoring seemed to have moulded itself to every contour of his superb masculinity, and Magenta could only stand and gaze up at him, her lips parted in the sensual paralysis that seemed to have invaded her body.

'I didn't think you'd be out here…'

He too seemed unable to speak fluidly, or like her, to move. He took one stride forward—and Magenta didn't know how it happened but the next second she was in his arms and their hungry mouths were fusing, tasting, devouring each other, while their breathing came hard and impassioned and their faces were illuminated by the crimson glow of the setting sun.

Andreas's lips moved to her neck, her throat, her shoulders, and she was glorying in their ravaging possession, giving herself up to their mutual hunger, to everything she had been wanting, craving, needing, over the past lonely weeks. She didn't care about the past—about yesterday—nor even tomorrow. All she cared about was that they were both here—now—tonight—and nothing in the world could prevent what was going to happen next.

When he drew her urgently down onto the grass beside the lovers' seat she was more than ready for him, helping him as he tugged at her briefs and taking him into her with a cry of pleasure that came from the depths of her soul.

Her climax was swift and sweet, coming with his in a burst of pulsating sensation that was as glorious and spectacular as the sunset. It had all happened so fast that when she turned her head and looked at the red ball again through the trees it was still hanging on the edge of the horizon, like a silent witness to their reckless and unrestrained passion.

'I'm sorry,' Andreas said, breathless. 'I shouldn't have done that.' Already he was getting to his feet. 'I just couldn't stop myself.'

Magenta was breathing as rapidly as he was as she struggled to find her voice. 'Neither could I.'

'Then there's no harm done?' he suggested.

She couldn't look at him as she brushed down the fabric of her crushed dress.

'No.' Why was he saying that? 'Why should there be?' she managed to say casually, though she was hurting inside after having dared for a few moments to imagine that everything might have changed.

'Why, indeed?' He gave her a sort of ruminative half-smile, his eyes appearing dark and reflective, but then he seemed to gather control of himself as he finished adjusting his shirt and trousers. 'So it really doesn't matter?'

How could she tell him that it did? That it mattered very much?

'No.'

'Why?' he asked, in a slightly more abrasive tone. 'Because it's only sex?'

Magenta could scarcely speak now. 'Yes.'

How hard it was to lie!

'In that case you won't be too upset,' he said, plucking one of the honeysuckle flowers, 'if I tell you that…' He hesitated, tossing the delicate creamy flower aside. 'I'm thinking of getting married.'

The earth seemed to freeze on its axis, and with it every stirring leaf and insect.

'No, of course not.' How could she say that and not reveal how much her voice was trembling?

'Honestly?' Was that relief in his eyes? Surprise?

She wanted to say, *No, I'm happy for you.* After all she had had her chance with him a long time ago and she had thrown it right back in his face.

Instead she uttered, 'Wh-who is it? Lana?'

'Lana?' He laughed out loud. 'I'm sure she's very pretty, and has hidden depths that will make some man a very good wife one day,' he remarked, coming away from the flowers, 'but not for me, I'm afraid. No…' He spoke with that hesitation again, as though he was finding it difficult telling her. 'She's a woman I met some time ago.'

'You never mentioned her.'

'No…' He slipped his hands into his trouser pockets, glancing at the dipping sun that was only half visible now above the western horizon. 'The time hasn't been right.'

Involuntarily Magenta nodded, lifting a shaky hand to her dishevelled hair. Somehow, it seemed, since his startling revelation she'd forgotten how to breathe, and after a deep inhalation, she said, 'Wouldn't she be rather upset to think that you…that we've just…?' Unable to say it, she caught the quizzical sidelong glance he sent her way. 'Are you going to tell her?'

She gave a half-shake of her head and felt the throb of an

incipient headache at her temples. Suddenly the last bursts of flame from the fast disappearing sun seemed too glaring, much too painful for her to look at.

'Have you made love with her?' *Dear heaven! Why was she asking him this?* 'I mean recently? Since we…?'

'Yes.'

His answer really did almost take her breath away. Well, what had she expected? she thought, wondering how he could make such amazing love to her when there was an-other woman—a woman he loved more—in his life. But why was it so surprising that he should have so little respect for her that he could bed her as if it didn't matter and then go off with someone else? He probably still believed that she had done the very same thing to him.

'It does mean,' he said, 'that there will be someone here all the time to help me with Theo when he's here, and you must agree that that will make for a far better situation all round.'

Oh, God! She couldn't bear it! Suddenly her eyes were welling with scalding tears.

'Gosh! This sun's unbearable! It's making my eyes water!' And her voice was thickening with so much emotion that she had to get away.

As she brushed hastily past him, intent only on putting as much distance between them as she could, he was spring-ing after her.

'Magenta!'

'Let me go!'

His hand was like a vice around her wrist. She was cry-ing now, and it was too late for her to run from him, although she kept her face averted to try and delay the moment when he would eventually see.

'Magenta, look at me?'

'Why? Isn't it enough that you had my humiliation once without putting the knife in and twisting it round for one final time?'

'You're crying?' His hand was cupping her face, fingers touching her tears. His brow was furrowing in the gathering dusk.

'So I am!' Her tone was wounded; indignant. 'Are you going to make an issue of that too?'

'I thought you said it was the sun.' Something like amusement coloured his deep voice. 'But lo and behold! *"Tears fall in my heart like the rain..."!*'

Was he mocking her? Ridiculing her with some quotation or other? How could he?

'It isn't funny!'

'No, it damn well isn't!' His tone had changed in an instant, and with it his expression. 'But you'll do anything rather than admit it, won't you?' His chest was puffed out in anger now as he forced her to face him. *'Won't you?'* he rasped, almost shaking her.

'Admit what?' It was a hopeless attempt to maintain her dignity.

'How you feel?'

'How I feel?' She tried to wriggle free but he wouldn't let her. 'You don't *know* how I feel!'

'Don't I?'

'No!'

'Then why are you crying? And why are you shaking so much just from the thought that I might be getting married?'

'I'm not!'

'And why can you never stop yourself when we do this?'

His mouth came down over hers in a kiss that demanded, was almost brutal.

'You've said yourself. It's just sex,' she parried desperately when he released her mouth.

'No, it isn't! Not for me. Not for you. Not for either of us,' he said hoarsely, confounding her, because she couldn't grasp or understand what he was saying. 'But that's beside the point—because you're going to tell me, Magenta!'

'Tell you what?'

'Why you're crying.'

'So you can have your last pound of flesh? Is that it? Is that why you're forcing me to say it? All right, then! I love you!' Her head dropped back and she sagged against him in defeat. 'I love you. So, so much...'

'Then why didn't you tell me before this?'

'You know why.'

She couldn't understand why he was looking and sounding as though all the demons from hell had suddenly been let loose to torment him. The night was drawing in, but even in the encompassing darkness she could make out the anguished lines scoring his face. Why? Magenta wondered. When he should be looking triumphant? When he'd just taken great pains to disclose his intention to marry someone else?

'Because you thought I'd use it against you? To hurt you?'

Wasn't he going to? She couldn't understand the incredulity she heard in his voice.

'Oh, I'll admit I wanted to,' he was saying. 'When you threw away everything I thought we had six years ago. And when you turned up for that interview after pretending—as I thought—not to remember me in that wine bar... Well... To get you in my bed and make you pay through your submission suddenly became the only thing that mattered. My father died the night you left, while we were arguing over you, and I wanted to hold you solely responsible for it.'

She uttered a small groan at this further revelation, and yet there had been a note of self-deprecating futility in his voice.

'It was my fault entirely, but I needed to blame someone else so I blamed you—for everything: what happened to him, what you'd done to me. And I let it fester away inside me for years. When I kissed you in that lift it was to see if you'd respond to me. But as soon as I'd got you here I realised that I'd already bitten off more than I could possibly chew. I wanted to stay immune, to be the one in control this time, but even before that night we made love I'd already discovered I was no more immune to you than I'd been when we were just kids. When I'd found out you'd had that brain haemorrhage…'

His voice trembled as he cupped her face lovingly with both hands. 'Any desire to hurt you went well and truly out of the window. And not because I felt sorry for you…' He shook his head, as though unable to put it into words. 'After we'd made love I wanted you to stay here, because I couldn't imagine letting you out of my life again, but you seemed so determined to go. I knew it was because you believed my only intention was to hurt and humiliate you, and I couldn't seem to convince you that it wasn't. I don't think I really knew myself at the time why I wanted you to stay.' He grimaced. 'Or I wasn't ready to admit it. But then I spent the fortnight after you'd gone wondering why it was driving me so crazy not to have you around. And that day you told me about Theo and all that you had been through after we broke up—I knew.'

It still pole-axed him to think of the terrible struggles and the odds she had faced from which she had come through fighting. Alone. With his baby. And without him.

'I love you, Magenta. I've wanted to tell you so often over the past couple of weeks but you've seemed so distant. So cool.'

'Only because *you* were!' she exclaimed, trying to take in all that he was telling her. 'But why did you let me think you were marrying someone else?' Pain etched her face as her eyes scoured the shadowy structured lines of his. 'You aren't, are you?' She was still not able to believe that it wasn't true.

'Are you crazy?' He laughed, and now all the earlier anguish in his voice was giving way to pure and simple joy. 'I wasn't absolutely certain that I wasn't kidding myself in believing you might possibly be in love with me. And, forgive me, my darling, for being so devious—and too proud to face rejection if I really had been kidding myself—but it was the only way I could think of finding out.'

'You…!' She thumped him playfully, her eyes brimming with happiness, and through a blur of tears she saw the first sliver of a crescent moon rising in the night sky.

'Surely you must have realised that I was referring to you?'

Magenta shook her head, but then started to see how she might have if she'd dared to let herself believe it.

'Marry me.'

It was a request he had made of her a long time ago, but now she responded to his husky demand with a heart that was almost too full to contain.

'You try and stop me,' she warned him, the second before his face blanked out the moon.

An owl hooted somewhere in the woods across the brook, but the night breezes did nothing to cool their rising passion, and a small thrill ran through Magenta when Andreas lifted his head, just before things got too far out of hand again, to murmur excitingly, 'No. In bed this time.'

EPILOGUE

THEIR WEDDING IN the little register office yesterday had gone well, Magenta reflected, lounging in the big bed overlooking the softly illuminated Bermudian beach, waiting for her husband to join her. She had worn a short white Sixties-style smock dress that had complemented the small flowers in her hair while still keeping from everyone but the few people closest to her the wonderful secret of her three-month pregnancy.

Theo had been a page, standing proudly and with amazing solemnity behind his parents in a little dark suit and bowtie, while Aunt Josie had dabbed at her eyes from under a large brown hat through most of the service, proclaiming afterwards that something—dust or an eyelash—must have got in.

Jeanette James had flown over from Portugal, looking prettier and happier than Magenta had seen her look in years, and she knew it was all to do with the gentle silver-haired man at her side. Things had been awkward between her mother and Andreas when her mother had first arrived two days ago, and she had declined their offer of hospitality in favour of staying in a hotel. But standing there yesterday outside the register office, in a stylish green suit, with her brown hair beautifully cut and highlighted, the woman had genuinely wished them well, and had even reached up to kiss Andreas before being drawn into Aunt Josie's welcoming arms.

Now, as her husband came through from the *en suite* bathroom wearing nothing but a striped silk robe, Magenta's heart gave a little leap, as it always did when she saw him.

'Are you sure you didn't mind leaving Theo behind?' Andreas asked, as he slid in next to her under the light coverlet. 'I know he's ultra-independent, but are you sure he's not likely to fret?'

'With Aunt Josie moving in this week and a new pony to keep him occupied? Hardly!' Magenta laughed, knowing that she was the one more likely to do any fretting while they were parted from their exuberant five-year old. 'And anyway it's only for six days, until they fly over to meet us in Disneyland.'

Satisfied that she was happy, Andreas ran a tender hand down her cheek before reaching round for something under his pillow.

'My Byron!' she exclaimed as he handed her the familiar little book with its velvety green suede cover. 'You've had it repaired!'

And so expertly that no one would ever guess that it had once been damaged.

'We've rebuilt so much. Put everything right between us,' Andreas said. 'It would have been remiss of me not to have included this as well.'

Reclining there in a sheath of white lace and satin, Magenta ran treasuring fingers over the book's soft cover. He could have thrown it away six years ago, she thought. She remembered him telling her once that he almost had. But his grandmother had found it and put it away for him for when he returned from America, so she guessed she had Maria Visconti to thank for that.

'There are some lines from that favourite poem of mine,' she told him softly as they drifted to the forefront of her mind. 'And somehow I couldn't say anything better to you tonight to express exactly how I feel. "From the wreck of the past, which hath perish'd",' she quoted, '"Thus much I at least may recall…"'

A silencing thumb brushed gently over her lips as he finished the verse for her. '"It hath taught me that what I most cherish'd, Deserved to be dearest of all."'

Her eyes filled with tears, because he was so very dear and he had done so much. For her and for Theo. For her great-aunt. But most of all because he had given her back his love when she might so easily have lost it for ever.

'My Magi…'

Her heart missed a beat as he breathed the name only he'd ever used against the thick shining tumble of her hair.

'I always was,' she whispered. 'Even when you thought I'd left you, I hadn't.' She put a hand to her chest. 'Not here inside.'

As he took the book from her and laid it on the bedside cabinet she slid down and looked up at the fan circulating on the ceiling in wild anticipation of yet another glorious night ahead. It was just one in a long line of glorious nights they had spent already, since he had proposed to her by the lovers' seat three months ago, and Magenta knew it was only the beginning of a lifetime of glorious nights and days ahead that they would share together.

At some stage in the future, she thought absently, she might put her business skills to use again, but for the foreseeable future she was looking forward simply to being a wife and mother.

'You know, from what I've heard Lord Byron was really quite irresistible to women,' she murmured as Andreas switched off the bedside lamp. 'I suppose it comes from knowing the female sex inside out.' Then, with definite teasing in her voice, she added, 'A pity a girl can't stumble upon that type of man today, really…'

And then she let out a shriek as Andreas pulled her under him and proceeded to show her that she could.

* * * * *